Tanith Lee was born i̶... writer since 1975. She ha̶... short-story collections, i̶... books for children. She h̶... BBC, and two television ... Tanith Lee has twice wo̶n̶ ... ...Fantasy Award, and the August Derleth Award. She lives on the south coast of England.

CW00938403

TANITH LEE
VIVIA

WARNER BOOKS

A *Warner* Book

First published in Great Britain in 1995
by Little, Brown and Company
This edition published in 1997 by Warner Books

Copyright © Tanith Lee 1995

The moral right of the author has been asserted.

A CIP catalogue record for this book
is available from the British Library.

ISBN 0 7515 1550 7

Typeset by Hewer Text Composition Services, Edinburgh
Printed and bound in Great Britain by
Mackays of Chatham plc, Chatham, Kent

Warner Books
A Division of
Little, Brown and Company (UK)
Brettenham House
Lancaster Place
London WC2E 7EN

BOOK ONE

Death and the Maiden

ONE

Chapter One

Her father brought death into the castle. He carried it up the stairs. The pale horse.

The servants shrank back against the walls in terror. The armour of the man, the armour and hoofs of the horse, scraped against the stonework. On the narrow upper stairways of the House Tower, for a moment it seemed they would be wedged fast, this incredible composite nightmare figure. The gigantic man clad in steel, and in his arms the dead stallion with its horned headpiece still on it, its eyes fixed like black balls. Vaddix was strong but the horse, his war charger, was huge. Yet he held it across his breast as he might have held his young bride.

The bride herself, Lillot, huddled staring in the hall below. She was frightened, foolish in her wedding regalia with its embroidery and ribbons, now made so unsuitable.

And it was to the bridal chamber that Vaddix climbed, staggering under the horse's weight. He kicked open the carved doors with a crash.

The room was large, filled by the great bed. Mounds of pillows and coverlets of yellowish lace, all strewn with the late wild summer roses, every one scaled of its thorns. On to this couch of love, Vaddix heaved off the stallion. It fell with a shock and the great bed groaned.

Then Vaddix roared his grief. He howled, and the horse lay there, darker and whiter than the lace, among the crushed red roses, and the chamber began to reek with the smell of flowers and sweat and blood.

Below, Lillot started to cry, and her women, trembling, tried to console her. 'There, there, little lily. He's won his battle. He's won you. It will be all right.'

On the wider stair, the first one Lord Vaddix had traversed, his black-haired daughter stood watching. She wore a gown of dark red, heavy golden earrings, bracelets, and a girdle of gold in the shape of daisies. Fluidly slender, not yet sixteen, she clasped her hands loosely together, frowning slightly. Her face was a white triangle, but unlike Lillot, Vivia seldom had any colour, except, as now, when she had reddened her mouth.

All her life she had known her father, not as anything intimate, but as a storm-like being coming and going, periodically overthrowing her life. This, now, was no exception. Massive, powerful, loud and selfish to the bone, he dominated the castle in his rage of dismay, just as he had always done in everything.

Lillot, the little fool, was not used to him, so she snivelled. Vivia's frown was one of contempt. Lillot was three years older than Vivia, fatter, sleeker, with a mass of blonde curls. A doll-like, trivial child of eighteen.

Vivia herself was a woman. Not only physically, as of course was Lillot, but psychosomatically.

Lillot did not raise her eyes to the black, pale and red hill of Vivia, in hope of any help. ('There, there,' twittered on the stupid women.)

Lifting the gold-figured skirt of her gown, Vivia went up the wide stairs and into the gallery, as the raucous ranting howls of her father continued. She passed into the corridor that led to her apartment. She could hear too her own woman scurrying after her. Vivia closed the door in her face.

Ursabet beat on the door.

'Let me in, Vivia.'

Vivia put down the bar across the door, as if besieged. So she had been instructed to do if her father's battle had not been a success, and the enemy army, Lillot's kindred, had poured into the castle. But Vivia had not thought that this would happen.

Vaddix had stolen Lillot, after wooing her for about a month over an orchard wall, like a young man. Lillot, flattered and thoughtless, had not even resisted. Presently there was a feud, and Vaddix rode out and fought Lillot's kin, the Darejens, in the valley above the river.

The Darejens were levelled and sued for peace, but in the last instants of the fray, a cross-bow bolt had been fired directly at Vaddix, had missed him, and entered instead the brain of the white battle stallion, killing it immediately. After this Vaddix had massacred the last of the Darejens, and picking up the horse, alternately carried and dragged it up the rocky slope to the looming castle above.

Vivia crossed to her mirror, an oblong of impure glass mounted on a brazen lion. She looked in curiously. Like Vaddix, she was – or had had to become – self-absorbed. Each new event intrigued her, by its effect upon herself. Now she saw, apparently untouched, her stem-like form with its female breasts, her shining ebony hair, her beautiful cat's face that had narrowed its two dark, perhaps green, eyes.

Outside, the howls had stopped, and Ursabet had gone away. The castle hummed like a beehive, agitated.

From high windows, in the three grim towers of the castle, it would be possible to look out and glimpse the valley of the battle, where Vaddix, in his usual way, had crucified his foes in lines. The Darejens had been unwise.

Vivia wondered what Lillot saw in her father. Perhaps she was only scared of him. Obviously, she was weak-willed. If one of her tears was for her family, no one would know, perhaps not even Lillot herself . . . Something of an idiot.

The wedding now would probably be delayed. If he had truly flung the dead horse on the bridal bed, as the servants were whispering, doubtless they would not be sleeping there. Vaddix had already had the girl anyway, as he always had everything he wanted, at once.

*   *   *

The castle of Vaddix was like a fungus or vegetable, and its three towers stuck from its accumulations of stone like bony roots or stalks. Purple banners floated from the peaks. In a few windows, stained glass of raw rich colour showed pictures of the Christ, or heroic mythical scenes, giants and dragons and so forth.

The mountain flank which supported the castle was, in the last of summer, black, with a sparse fringing of pine and larch, and the land around rose up in enormous crags, or dropped into valleys of the river. This area of the river was, in spring, a carpet of greenness, bursting with flowers, but the summer water was lazy and brown with peat. The mountains themselves looked blank, merciless and obdurate, the farthest dipped in flat silver lines of snow.

Behind the castle of Vaddix was a walled garden, with walnut and cherry trees, wild pear, the old statue of a pagan god with beard and the horns of a sheep.

The villages crouched below the height, property of the lord, about a thousand persons, who lived their days and nights in the shadow of the stone vegetable, gave it their service, were recruited for its fights and festivals.

To these places now the peasant army of Vaddix was returning.

Some were brought in dead, carried as the horse had been up to the castle. Some were hurt, maimed or only scratched. Vaddix's men from the castle, the knights of his household, had allowed wholesale pillage of what was left of the Darejen army, and in a handful of days, normally, bands would have set off across the valley pass to sack the Darejen castle in turn. This outcome was now unsure, for Lord Vaddix was in mourning for his stallion. And besides, he was a bridegroom.

The men and boys, as young as nine or ten, as old as fifty and bent nearly double, carrying rough swords, hoes, hammers, the bits and pieces habitually gathered for a war, came down the village streets. The women pressed out, looking for their particular men. News of the battle and the horse death went about. The women sun-circled or crossed themselves.

The priests, who had absolved them before their going,

now came and welcomed them back, glancing at the wounded, seeing who might be saved and who was beyond saving. They packed down the eyes of the dead, the nearly dead. Life was cheap, souls emptied quickly like refuse on to the dump.

Dobromel the priest bent over the young man in the house door, who was refusing to go in or to recognize his wife, sister and sons.

'Where is he hurt?'

'No wound, father. Look, he's perfect.'

'I saw an eagle,' cried the young man, 'and it bore me up. But it tore me. Stop the pain, father.'

'Now, do you know me after all?'

'Yes,' said the young man. 'You're the dung-carrier.' He laughed wildly. Then gave a hoarse shriek. Blood oozed from beneath his left arm.

'You see, there is a wound. Take him inside. Bathe the cut with herbs and water.'

The women, used to obeying their priests, nodded. But one of the sons said, 'I saw him hacking at those Darejens. He said he had a pain there then. He had it all night since we waited for the enemy. It was in the meadow he got it. Perhaps something stung him.'

'Take him in,' said the priest. 'Look and see.'

Sunset. The sky red now as the blood of the Darejens, even the snow line red, and clouds banked like other mountains, equally obdurate and cruel.

Vivia had kept on her red dress, and as the sunset lit her white face, she crimsoned her mouth once more, at the lion mirror.

Her room was virginal and austere. A picture of Marius Christ painted on wood, his face hidden, as was usual, behind a mask of the sun. Roses in a pewter vase, slim as Vivia herself. The lean bed had curtains, and a lamp hung from the rafter. It was seldom lighted, thick with webs.

Ursabet, who had been allowed in at last, crouched over the chest.

'Wear this necklace.'

'No. It's too heavy.'

'He'll expect it. It's his wedding feast.'

'Perhaps he won't come to the wedding feast, and that fool will have to sit there on her own.'

'Nasty sharp tongue,' said Ursabet. But secretly she liked Vivia's spiteful ways, she herself had inspired them. She had had charge of Vivia since Vivia's sixth year.

Vivia in any case did not deign to reply. Rather than put on fresh jewels, she had removed the bracelets, girdle, earrings and rings. Now only her dress was festive.

With Ursabet shuffling behind her, an elderly grey woman of forty-six, Vivia climbed the stairs of the castle to the upper hall, the banquet chamber, where the marriage and victory feast was to have been.

It was laid out even as the men fought in the valley – to have failed in this would have been unlucky. Now the room was filled by the lord's hungry knights, his ten warriors, who, starved, had not scrupled to begin. This was their right.

They stood about, in their armour still, plates and planks of metal, shirts of mail, in portions repaired, or hung over by trophies taken in other battles, the gewgaws of men they had killed. They stuffed their mouths with bread, while the servants ran to bring them bowls of mutton hash, dishes of spicy rice, skewers of roast goat meat.

The chamber was red in colour, dressed with shields and weapons, and with painted rafters. Curtains of scarlet brocade hung down in places, and a tapestry so faded it was like a dead leaf picked out randomly in silver.

At the high table, draped with an embroidered whitish cloth, the bride, Lillot, was sitting in her finery, her eyes puffy and her round face pale.

Vivia in turn took her own place, at the upper table's end. A servant filled her pewter goblet with the rough mountain wine, and Vivia raised it, and poured out a drop on the floor, the old custom that even her father followed. She did not drink the wine herself, she did not like it, preferred water. She took a piece of bread, and crumbled some, putting a little in her mouth. Eating usually bored her, and she was not often hungry.

Besides, she knew – as surely the rest of them did, or

they were all fools – that soon her father would erupt into the banquet hall.

He came with a clanging note, like a warning bell. He filled the doorway, and the lighted lamps shone on him.

The tallest man in the room, the villages, perhaps the world, his head, from which the helmet had now been removed, just missed the lintel of the door. He was broad, massive with muscle and hard big bone. For a moment he looked like a suit of armour that had come alive of itself, for like his men he had not stripped his battle gear. Only the head was human, and that not very. Ugly, and scarred across forehead, cheeks and chin, the nose broken, pitted by some childhood pox, swarthy, with two beetle black eyes. Vaddix.

The thin gash of two lips opened to reveal strong teeth, broken only by war. He grinned at them, and one by one, his knights stopped chewing. They were afraid of him too. Only that had kept them, maybe, from banding together one night and hurling their lord off one of the three lurid towers. They hated and respected him, boasted of him, cursed him, challenged and cowered. Now, they bowed, and broke into a tardy shout. *'Lord Vaddix!'*

'Yes,' he said, 'your lord. And here you are stuffing your filthy mouths with my food. You verminous dogs. Fuck the pack of you, you scum.'

One of the knights, Javul, said quickly, 'Didn't we earn our bones, my lord?'

'Yes, you fucking muck. You earned them. But what of me? What of my loss?'

The room was silent. In the lamps the wicks hissed on the oil, and on the dark beeswax candles, the flames flickered, steadied, as not a nerve twitched. Then Lillot the idiot began again to weep.

Vaddix bellowed at her: 'Shut your row, you bitch, you useless cunt. Shut your noise. It's your fault, you cunt, I lost him. My horse. The best horse on earth. For *you* I lost him. *You*. Are you worth it? I think not.'

Then he walked to the table and slammed into his position beside her, the sobbing, snuffling bride. The candles dipped and dived. Vaddix crashed his fist on the table. Things spilled.

'What one of you, you rabble, is worth my horse? This slut of the Darejens – no. Or that thing there,' he pointed at Vivia, remembering her as he occasionally did. 'What use is she? Worth only to be married to some enemy, and my enemies I slaughter.'

Vivia did nothing. She looked before her, unblinking, down at the floor of her father's hall. She was used to his tirades. He had never struck her, for she was always docile, and failing that, swift, running away from him if need be. He soon lost interest.

Vaddix roared for wine and the servant filled his cup, over-filled it, and Vaddix struck the servant instead, sending the man sprawling. Then, absently, Vaddix dropped a little wine to the ground, the pagan courtesy to ancient gods. He drank. Turning to Lillot he roared, 'Stop crying, you little bitch, before I make you.'

Lillot had stopped crying. She lay in a half faint in her chair, her women afraid to attend to her.

Vaddix's knights were seated. They had eaten their fill, and now they drank. The hall drank, the people of the castle who sat down there. The vague relations, bastard lines engendered by Vaddix's own sire, or grandsire, their women. The fat priest Dobromel, who had arrived to celebrate the wedding and not been required to do so, who had hastily uttered a grace as Vaddix began to eat.

Vaddix had dined on copious amounts of meat, rice and pastry. He devoured these without words. The musicians who had come from the valleys to play lutar and harp and drum were redundant, sent out. No music tonight.

When he had eaten, Vaddix drank on, like the knights. He began to address the hall again. He was maudlin. Speaking of his horse, how it had carried him in fifty fights. How it had trampled and gored his foes with its metal horn.

Tears ran down Vaddix's scarred cheeks.

The silly girl did not attempt, not so silly after all, to comfort him.

'He'll lie there,' said Lord Vaddix, 'in that chamber. On my own bed. Where I was to have fucked *her*. He'll have that room until he rots. That's his.'

The heat pressed in at the narrow windows, one, its casement opened, showing in glass a winged hero who slew a bull.

The moon was not up, the night outside was black, but thick with the candles of blazing stars.

Tomorrow, left in the bridal room of the House Tower, the carcass would begin to stink. They would have to endure it. The whim of Vaddix was their law.

Vivia did not look at her father, or at anyone. She watched reflections of the candles, the falling heads of dying festal flowers. She had eaten a little rice and part of a tartlet with cherries, drunk water. She sat dreaming in her chair, thinking about incoherent glamorous things, stories Ursabet had told, still told her, which filled her sleep. This was how she kept tedium, the endless dangerous boredom of the castle, in check.

The coloured casement swung to a sudden night breeze. Red and emerald glinted on the hero's wings. What must it be to fly?

'Vivia,' said Vaddix.

She was alert at once. She said, not looking, mildly, brightly, 'Yes, father?'

'Did they tell you my horse was killed?'

'Yes, father.'

Vaddix said, 'Rather ten daughters dead than to lose him.'

Ursabet whispered behind Vivia's chair. It was a remedy for ill luck. Vaddix, fortunately, did not hear. He was deaf from his own shouting.

Some minutes later, Vaddix rose to his feet. 'Find a bed for that slut,' he said, of his unwed wife. 'I am going up the Spike Tower.'

His knights got up, in ramshackle unison, drunk and unready. He thrust them back with a gesture.

'What do I need you for, vermin? Who's left to harm me? I want to look out across the valleys. I want to see what's left of them, those Darejens.'

As he passed Vivia's chair, the hand of Vaddix caught a skein of her black tresses, squeezed it, let it go, showing how worthless was such stuff.

Black as her hair, the night out beyond the illuminated beacon of the castle. On the starry sky those towers, one with its eccentric quills, and a hole of light at its top.

Beyond the castle, down the slopes, the rocks, the sluggish gurgling summer river, with frogs in its water thickets and long fish under the stones.

The valley of the battle spread like a furrow, medallioned with boulders and bladed by pines, bent cedars and coarse chestnuts. To many of these trees were now affixed the fruited dead bodies of men. Vaddix crucified almost to a vertical, arms stretched up. Life did not often linger long, or if it did, in modified form. Limbs and blood, excrement and broken swords dangled off the trees, or lay in the pasture. In a stand of wild wheat other horses than that of Vaddix had perished.

The corpses lay, or hung, for about a mile, and with the vivid sunset ravens had circled from the mountains. Now they stood and perched upon the dead, picking and pulling busily.

Ravens, like bits of the night itself, feeding, sometimes uttering hoarse cries of appetite.

A feast for a feast . . .

Nothing to disturb the carnal scene, only the soft erratic passage of the night wind. And the white unlidded eye of the moon coming up from the east, between two crags.

From one of the villages a dog barked, starting off two or three more. Then silence. Only the rustle of the ravens, tugging and stepping, fluttering their night wings.

The young Darejen, fourteen years old, was breathing his last, with impossible difficulty, on the scarp of a chestnut tree. Above him the canopy closed out the sky, but one star had pierced through, vicious as a knife.

He had been thinking of the knife – the star – wondering if the knight who held it would come and finish him. He did not want to end, but yet he did. It was so desolate, this. And everything was over.

There had been terrible pain at first. Stunned, they had hauled him up, the two men, and then Vaddix's blacksmith had hammered in the iron nails, one at each wrist. The Darejen's hands were almost above his head, holding the complete weight of his body. He panted and choked, was constricted, and soon everything drew away from him, even the wish for life.

He had been fearful at first. For Vaddix would go now to the Darejen stronghold, and there he would work his violence again. Never before had Vaddix fought a battle so close to his own hold. Generally he laid siege. When once taken, the enemy house was destroyed. Vaddix had been known to crucify entire families, even children four or five years old.

The Darejen was afraid for his mother, but this fear finally also drew far away. Then he only hung there, not really breathing, waiting for nothingness, or for the Christ. Or for punishment, for he had often sinned – the girls of his castle, the prayers missed.

There had been sickness in the Darejen force – was this the anger of God? Had God brought them to destruction? Then what hope – ?

Dimly he tried now to remember Marius, the form of the Christ with blessing hands and his head of golden sun-mask and rays. Instead, the boy saw the dark valley before him, columns of trees hung with men, below, a fallen horse, everywhere, the ravens.

And then, the boy saw Death come walking down the valley.

It was – unmistakable.

The wind feathered over the grasses, murmured, eddied away. But this. This came straight and hard, pushing against the air itself. There was no shape to be seen, nothing but the passage of the thing. How the grasses *bent* away from it. And on the trees the scraps of armour tinkled, rattled and sang.

The ravens answered too. They flew straight up and out of its path. All but one. The creature – which was Death

– came by the fallen horse, and the mane of the horse
was ruffled – as if long fingers stroked it subtly. But the
raven, feeding on the horse's belly, too greedy to fly away,
sprang suddenly upwards. It spread its wings and its beak
opened wide. Then it dropped back. It lay as if it had been
crucified, wings wildly extended, beak gaping. Dead.

The boy on the tree hung and waited, and Death glided
between the chestnut trees. And there, floating up in the
darkness, two lamps were kindled, better than the star.
The eyes of Death burned softly through, red as blood,
yet cool, sombrous, and still.

The boy felt Death come to him, and fill him, his flesh
and sinews and bones. Pass through him. He died almost
instantly, like the raven.

Above the valley the moon drew clouds across her,
hiding her face, not wanting to see.

Chapter Two

VIVIA LIFTED HER LIDS. HER eyes were definitely blue now, darker than the sky outside the window. She looked about her slowly, carefully. The room was unchanged, but for two things. The roses had died in their vase, brown shrivelled heads, heavy, dismembered. And faintly, a rotten meat smell had entered. It was the stench of the decaying white horse above.

Prepared for both, Vivia sat up and threw off the thin summer cloth which had covered her nakedness.

She was white as a marble nymph, smooth as untouched cream. Beneath her arms and at the core of her, was long black fur, silky and cat-like. The rest nude as a pearl. The tiny pink nipples were like peony buds.

She shook back her hair. She stepped out of the bed. And from the corner where she slept, old Ursabet, like a grey rose-head, got to her feet.

'There's your wine and honey, my love. Drink it up.'

Vivia rinsed her mouth with the sweet drink, swallowed a sip or two, and set the cup (dull iron) aside.

'The lily girl slept all alone,' muttered Ursabet. 'And *he* was in the Tower of Spikes.'

'What do I care?' said Vivia.

She did *not* care. The fool, Lillot, was nothing to her, her father less than nothing, unless he came awkwardly into view.

Ursabet poured water, and Vivia laved her body. Water pooled on the stone floor. The woman dressed her girl, perhaps marvelling over the loveliness of her youth. (Or perhaps not, for Ursabet had grown used to this, as she had to what time had done to her own body.) A shift and stockings gartered by ribbons, the outer gown of plain blue today, a blue not worthy of those eyes.

'What will she have to eat?'

'Bring me some fruit.'

Vivia pulled on her cloth shoes and raised the wooden comb to attend to her hair. She did not like Ursabet's combings.

Ursabet went out, and returned from the ante-chamber where food had been left, in the regular way. Brown bread, and peaches from the garden.

Vivia cut and ate half a peach.

She smelled the smell of the dead thing in the bridal chamber above.

'Tell me about my mother,' Vivia said abruptly.

'Oh, Vivia. Well. She was a pretty girl. She would have been sixteen when you were born. She used to play with you.'

'And what happened?'

'She displeased him.'

'And he struck her.'

'Yes.'

Vivia put the uneaten half of the peach back on to the platter, and set the iron cup beside the rest.

'You shouldn't go there,' said Ursabet.

Vivia said, scornfully, 'You told me about it. Took me.'

'That was then. If he knew – '

'How will he know? He's drunk in the Spike Tower.'

'He'd kill me.'

Vivia said, 'Are you afraid to die?'

'Yes. I've been a bad woman.'

'Oh, you're afraid of *that*,' said Vivia, pointing absently, as if at a younger child, at the holy picture on wood of Marius Christ.

Ursabet crossed herself. 'He's without sin. He judges us accordingly.'

Vivia laughed. 'Am I sinful?'

'Very. But death is far off from you.'

Vivia shrugged. She raised the platter of fruit, bread and

wine. 'The castle stinks from his horse. I'm going down now. Down where he can't reach me.'

Ursabet shook her head.

Vivia paid no heed.

Down . . .

Through the stone castle, along its branching corridors, some narrow as a drain, others wide and hung with banners of the house of Vaddix, threadbare tapestry, old rusty axes, shields.

Down.

Past the warren where the servants of Lord Vaddix lived, the steaming kitchen with its hole of a hearth, and dead geese and onions hanging from the rafters. Down through the underchambers where stuff was stored and lost.

Past too the stench of open pipes, where the castle's bowel and bladder waste was extruded from the pile. Past ancient guard posts and secret funnels where rats chirruped.

Vivia was not afraid. She had come this way for almost ten years. Ursabet had brought her – *You'll be safe here*.

The under-part of the castle went into the rock of the mountain slope. Caves opened, natural pillars upheld half-made staircases. Then the way stopped at a terrible darkness, all the eyelets in the stone, which let in light, ended and over. No torch. No promise.

Here, in the black, cranky Ursabet had nursed the trembling child, Vivia. And later, Vivia, alone, seeking, had gone past the place, and found the other place. The *inside* of the rock, the *underneath* of the castle.

The caves were great and, unlike the dark just above, they shone. Phosphorescence lit them up.

Here natural steps descended. Waters trickled and in parts fell thick as plaits of white hair. Frogs trilled from the stony pools, frogs also white, as milk. And dark lizards, no larger than the palm of Vivia's then childish hand, fled over the rocky floor.

There were spiders with garnet eyes who floated in crystal webs dewed by moisture.

Other items had confused and intrigued the child.

For in the walls were coiled things, shells and ribs, and bones conceivably of the great dragons that once heroes had fought, so Ursabet said, on the land above.

The shells were especially beautiful. Caught in the rock walls, thin as lace. And from the roof of the underplace, long fangs of stone dripped down.

Vivia did not, six years of age, fear this region. No, it was a hidden spot, that might, as Ursabet had stipulated, protect her.

Later she heard a frightened Ursabet calling, from the outer environs, and Vivia went back to Ursabet. 'Where have you been?' demanded the woman. Vivia told her, and Ursabet then had circled herself, and made another sign, older and more recondite.

Vivia had not been warned by this, nor by Ursabet's subsequent admonitions. The area under the castle was her safe place. No one else had dared it or would dare.

When she found there the carved snakes, coiled round and round, each with a smooth beaked head and adamant eyes, Vivia was about nine or ten. Then Ursabet admitted that the underplace was a grotto, an antique source of power and pagan virtue. To such gods as had inhabited or visited there, the lord of the castle and his people spilled their pre-feasting wine. To these, clandestinely, they made little superstitious signs.

The carved snakes had been offerings to the fount of the power that abided in the grotto.

At twelve years, Vivia began to carry to the grotto beneath the castle scraps of food and fruit, cups of liquor. It had been, nearly, a prissy moral act. The Christ she did not trust. The Christ was only a painting of a man without a face. But the formless thing – that might safeguard her, for once it had done so.

She was not religious, nor conscientious in her duties to this new shrine.

Sometimes strange dreams would commit her to it. Or the uncertain straits of adolescence. Or only pique at the boredoms of the castle.

Now it was the smell of death. The reek of the dead stallion.

Vivia passed into the cloaca of the rock.

It was always necessary to draw a breath before walking into the wall of darkness that seemed to have no exit. But this air was clean, smelling of damp medicinal fungus, water, and curiously dry stone.

Vivia took the breath.

This was the magic. Now she had absorbed the darkness, and might go on.

She glided, fluent and graceful, her hair blackly raying out, as exact a priestess as that lower region might desire.

She felt her own flawlessness, it was true. Had often done so. It helped, her physical arrogance, to drive out fear, for otherwise she might have been constantly afraid and so rendered impotent.

She went into the maw of the dark and was received, and journeyed about twenty steps. And then the rock curved and the glow of phosphorescence began.

It was wonderful, the way in which you could all at once see.

The enormous caverns and the bones trapped in their walls, if such they were, the grey-green mosses. Pools glimmering. The constant chorus of the frogs which did not falter at her approach.

Vivia, with her tray of offerings, walked straight forward.

By waters; fountains fell from above like needles. She crossed the paved stones.

She reached the curtain of white-speckled (leprous) ivy, and slid by.

She was in the central sanctum, better than the chapel of Marius in the castle, that smoky smelly hut in the courtyard.

Beyond the curtain the rock rose sheer, and in it bones had gathered like bees and serpents. They knitted together, elements of limbs and arms and wings that Vivia had never properly deciphered – consciously. And at their apex, maybe only some freak of form, meaning nothing, a masked, helmed face.

It was a face, of course, of bones. Itself like a vizor. The eyes were open portals, two ovals of dark. Nothing looked out of them. And the lips too, were closed.

Vivia dropped her offering, the peaches and bread, and poured the wine, at the foot of this sculpture.

Here she had laid thousands of such tokens, near where the snake stones had been set. The food and drink had rotted. Formed new material, a primeval slime, a fungus itself, that vegetated and so achieved fresh life. There was no scent of decay. Rather a clear homeopathic smell.

She bent towards it, then lifted her head to study the creature locked into the wall.

It was like a huge bat. A bat with the face of a man. Or even, of a woman.

But then too, it was like nothing at all.

Vivia sat back on her heels. She considered.

She had been six, and playing with her playful mother. She could recall nothing of this woman, not even the shade of her hair. Perhaps a hint of some warm perfume.

The door opened, and the storm and thunder of Vaddix were there.

Vivia sank away, but the woman only laughed to him, inviting him to understand.

Then Vaddix had shouted something at her, to get rid of the child, to get up, something.

And Vivia's mother had, winsomely, held out her hand.

It was then he came into the room and hit her very hard. So hard that, presumably, he had smashed her skull.

She fell back mute on the bed of hair whose colour Vivia did not remember, and Vaddix turned his black mad eyes to the child.

She *did* recollect the smell of drink, sweat, and unwashed angry male body, a dark smell, that reminded her now of nothing so much as the pall of the dead stallion.

Ursabet had seized Vivia, pushed her down.

'Say a prayer for the good Lord Vaddix,' Ursabet had squealed.

So Vivia joined her hands and prayed to Marius Christ, as every night until then Ursabet had made her do, for the health and joy of her father.

And he, he had folded away, gone out of the door. And

then Ursabet took her, and running, bore her down under the castle.

Vivia glanced, sidelong, at the shape in the wall.

She did not ask for anything. (Her eyes – black now.)

She rose slowly, and going back through the ivy, she sat on the lip of a pool to watch the lizards and frogs darting in the water.

Chapter Three

UNDER THE WALL, THE GARDEN had pushed through. The arms of a walnut tree with hard woody blobs on them. Bushes sprang out of crannies. The other opposing wall, of the Short Tower, made the place into a passageway.

Javul stood above a bush, pissing heavily into it.

As he did so, he heard a woman's voice in the garden above. Lillot. He knew how she sounded. Very young, and ripe.

He leaned into the walnut. There was the crack there in the stone which the tree had made, and through it he could see the greenery of the garden, and a piece of the old pagan statue, the sheep-horned man.

Lillot was wandering aimlessly about, pulling at flower heads from nerves.

Javul eyed her. She was nicely fat, big breasts and fleshy hips and a pulled-in waist, set off by a silver girdle Lord Vaddix had given her before the battle.

Noon sunlight smeared Lillot's fleece of gilded hair.

Javul's stream had ended. He ran his glance over Lillot and fingered himself, rubbing across the head of his cock. But then he packed himself back and laced up. After all, the way things tended now, he might get to have her.

He inspected quickly the wet earth under the bush. Here he had come by night and buried the golden Marius token he had ripped off the neck of a dead Darejen. A ruby had been set in where the sacred wound was, in Marius' side. The item was worth a bit. Now he came here and urinated

regularly, checking that none of the others had found the
treasure; scent-marking.

Lillot's woman said something banal and cheering,
something useless.

Javul grinned, and walked up between the walls and
round to the garden door. He went in.

Lillot was startled. She clasped her plump white hands.
The waiting woman, sensibly, drew back, going in under
a cherry tree, pretending to look for fruit or something.

Javul went straight up to Lillot, tall and bulky in his
leather clothes and broad belt knobbed by iron. He put
out one big paw and took a handful of Lillot's large right
breast. She stared at him with her mouth open. Javul felt
her, then let her go.

'He's not treating you right, is he,' said Javul, kindly.
Lillot made a small noise. 'Oh, you can speak up to me.
I'm his man. His for life. But it isn't good, the way he's
not married you and all. It should have been done.'

Lillot said, in a soft vague whine, 'He vowed it to me.'

'No doubt he meant it, too. Then. But he's quick to turn.
The horse now. He won't get over it in a hurry. His father
was the same. Killed a man for sneezing in the chapel.'

Lillot crossed herself. Her breast seemed to bulge and
glow. She wriggled around it and he could hardly keep
his eyes off it.

'He told me,' she said accusingly, 'the garden was mine.
No one else would come in here.'

'Well, I came in to tell you, lady. I'm your man. I'll take
care you don't come to harm. You need someone, now.'

He could see her thinking. She would have a little brain,
not much room for thought, only the roots of her hair.
Would she perceive the sense of what he said, or be
too frightened? Vaddix *was* frightening. It was all very
chancy.

'I expect,' she said, 'to be Lord Vaddix's wife.'

'Let's hope so.'

She looked at the ground. Her breast beamed at him,
friendly.

The woman under the tree was scuttling about, rummaging, intent on not seeing a thing. The woman would

probably advise Lillot that Javul was a lucky bet, if Vaddix failed.

Javul bowed, for they liked that, the girls. He said, 'Give me that flower. I'll keep it. It'll remind me of you.'

She handed him the torn bloom and he put it into his shirt.

As he swung off back through the garden, he could still feel her breast in his hand, and the flower tickled him lasciviously. He would perhaps only have to wait.

When the knight had gone, the woman came out of the tent of tree and began to arrange Lillot's garments, as if she had been seriously disarrayed. The smell of the man was all over Lillot, she might have been sprayed by a dog.

'I want to go home,' said Lillot suddenly. She was childish and the woman held her in scorn, not like Vivia the lord's daughter, of whom the servants were generally wary.

'You can't do that. He's killed your father and brothers. You belong to Vaddix.'

'I must see the priest,' said Lillot. She had a religious inclination, hoping to persuade God, or the Christ, who were, after all, men.

They went out of the garden, and through walkways of the castle, down towards the chapel court. The sun cut in leaden gold between the deep shadows of high walls and louring towers. The Spike Tower reared like a porcupine, bizarre and intimidating. Up there he had spent his bridal night.

The rotting rancid smell of the dead horse hung in the air, adding an unseen brown colour.

There were always stinks, especially in Summer, but this was a terrible thing.

The chapel lurked under the walls, four stone partitions and a roof of slates. There was one window of rose, yellow and white glass, showing Marius the Sun standing on the back of an ascending dove. This glowed at them strangely as they approached.

Lillot went into the chapel alone.

The aroma here was better, bitter herbs and rose-heads

crushed on the floor, and incense in the golden censer hung from the beam.

Dobromel was sitting on his chair by the altar. He had been asleep, but, quick as a weasel, he heard the steps disturbing rushes on the floor. He feigned deep contemplation, and raised his skull slowly up, got to his feet.

'Do you wish to pray, lady?'

Lillot nodded.

She knelt down before the altar and put her hands innocently together.

What a baggage she was. In his youth, long ago, Dobromel had had one or two of her type, though none so opulent. It had been a sin, of course, but no one had ever found out, and even the girl who fell in the family way blamed it on the summer festival.

Now Dobromel had no leaning to sex. He found the idea of it remote and tiring, and so was able to be chaste.

Even so, there would be trouble with this hussy. If Vaddix did take her to wife, would she stay content? That round big bottom tightening her pastel gown, that crown of hair, were inflammatory material.

The castle was not safe, not reliable.

Dobromel would go back to his flock, the first village down the slope. After all, he was not needed for the wedding. And Vaddix was currently at his most insane.

Best to be away.

He watched the fat girl praying. She took a time over it, not he supposed from piety, but from trying to put sentences together.

Did God listen to her, or to anyone? Dobromel believed not. God existed but was unreachable. It did not matter what you did. You must only be careful of men.

Lillot rose. She looked sulky.

She put a silver bead on the altar, and Dobromel evaluated it in silence.

'Will you speak a prayer for my dead kindred, father?'

'I will, of course, if you wish me to. Although, alas, they were our enemies, and yours too, once you joined yourself to the lord.'

Lillot looked unhappy. The ramifications of such honour did not make any sense to her.

She went away.

Dobromel moved into the chapel door, and observed the bright sunlight, and snuffed at the stink of death.

The girl had smelled of lust; even over the candles and the incense he had picked it up.

But here only the odour of the stallion persisted.

High in the blue sky a hawk was circling, or perhaps a raven, noting carrion.

Dobromel went back behind the altar and the screen, and took up his small bag of priestly things, adding the silver bead absently. There had been plenty of spoil from the fight, but Vaddix and the knights had given him nothing. He would do better with his villagers, who reckoned he intervened between them and the Christ.

He wondered, as he went over the courtyard and down between the bulks of the rocky, flinty, lumbering walls, if the young man with the blood coming from under his arm had recovered. If he had not, they might gift the priest with something fine, out of fright.

The shadow of the hawk went over Dobromel's face like a blade turning black.

They should have gone and buried or burned the bodies of the dead in the valley. (It was late in the year and already the red wolves might be stirring on the mountain flanks. It was not wise to tempt them down.) This too he must egg the men on to, in the village.

As he drew away from the castle, the stench faded. The heat then brought out the tinders and smokes of summer flowers, and next the normal reek of goats and sheep blown in from the pastures.

And then – then, even as the roofs of the village came in sight below, swimming in a haze of temperature, the vile smell began *again*.

Christ. What was this? Yes, the villages stank – of animals and humanity, of their middens. But not – this smell. This smell like Vaddix's dead horse.

Did he imagine it? Was it so thick still in his nostrils . . .

The priest stopped. He shot a look back at the castle, black on the burning sky.

He looked down again, at his village.

It seethed there, trembling in the haze, as if it were slowly cooking over some hellish underlying fire.

The usual sounds did not rise. Grindstone and lathe, forge, dogs, women chattering, men arguing. Instead a sort of murmur. Restive – like the crickets, feverishly rubbing in the bushes.

So, they were slothful, were they? That was not Godly, and Dobromel knew his duty, for if they did not value God, Dobromel himself had no importance.

He must set them going again.

Was it five days he had been gone? Only that. Long enough, it seemed.

He strode towards the village, his robe and his fat swinging on his bones. His knotted girdle swung like a whip. He frowned.

And over the wooded meadows, he glimpsed the second village too, lying it seemed somnolent, like this one.

The bad smell got worse as he descended. It must be they had not attended properly to their chores. Perhaps some dogs had died, or sheep been slaughtered, and not correctly dealt with. Or, worse, men perished after the fight and not buried. No one had come to the castle to request Dobromel for any rite. He had assumed that, if there had been a death, they had called another priest from the adjacent villages.

Dobromel came into the main street.

The forge, he saw at once, was idle, no fire going, no one there.

Beyond, the door of the first house was fast shut.

He marched to it, and struck it.

A woman was screaming inside. He became aware of the sound as if it had been muffled and all at once the cloth was drawn away.

He knew the note. Not pain or a beating. They were fornicating in there.

A man grunted.

Dobromel glared, and smote the door open.

He said, loudly, into the gloom, 'This isn't the work for the day. Night things. What are you at?'

There was a sort of upheaval, and in the windowless murk he made them out, there on their straw bed by the wall.

They had performed it sinfully too, the dog or wolf position, the man taking the woman from behind. She was his wife at least, that much Dobromel beheld.

The stink was horrible. Death and sex all muddled, kneaded together, making something new.

But they were drunk, for there the beerskin was, lying by the hearth.

The woman laughed throatily. The man said, 'It's how we are, father. Since the battle. We earned it, didn't we?'

'No,' said Dobromel. 'You will come to me at my house tonight. I shall impose a penance.'

The woman collapsed under the man and he fell down on top of her. They were like some monster, changed abruptly into a legless snake.

Dobromel went out of the house.

A tiny child was sitting in the dust, playing with itself, with its genitals.

He shouted at it. The child slobbered and crawled away.

The air was so awful, stenchful, and thudding, like blood in the ears after a long run.

From another house came a woman's shrill cry, 'Get up on me! Wolf me! Wolf me!'

Dobromel walked straight down the street, ignoring the houses, until he came to the house of the man who had had the blood coming from him.

Dobromel rapped on the door. No one answered, and so he pushed it wide.

The house was empty. No one was there. There had been the man, his wife and sister, his old granny, and the two sons. None remained.

The interior looked as if something had gone on. Chairs overturned and broken pots, bedding across the floor, very stained. The smell was paramount here.

Dobromel backed out.

A man had appeared at another door. He beckoned. He said, 'My wife is sick, father. Will you come?'

'Sick in what way?'

'She vomits blood, father. And — there's something black, like a wart, under her arm and behind her knee.'

Dobromel said, 'Don't touch those places. Give her cool water to drink.'

'Where are you going?' said the man, bemusedly.

'I must return to the castle. Lord Vaddix demands it.'

A line from scripture came to him. *And man shall fall upon woman, like unto beasts.*

Dobromel hurried up the village street. He touched nothing that lay in the track, avoiding even the small shoe of a baby, and a cracked bone.

Within half an hour he had returned inside the castle. On a lower walk he met the strutting knight Javul.

'Plague?' said Javul, 'what are you saying?'

'What you've heard me say.'

Dobromel shivered. He was scalding hot with fear.

'But who's got it?'

'All of them, no doubt. Ill or sickening. The castle must be shut tight and nothing taken in from there. The other villages may be in the same condition.'

'Christ,' said Javul, 'may He fuck.'

He went away, and Dobromel sat down on the wall, shaking like an old man.

Thank God he had learned in time.

Even mad Vaddix was preferable — to that.

When the evening began to spread its blue wings, Vivia stirred.

She had been lying, dreaming, on her narrow bed for hours.

Earlier, she and Ursabet had played chess, but Ursabet was not a worthy opponent. Though cunning, she always let Vivia win.

Earlier too, Vivia had thought of going into the castle garden where, as a child, she had rambled about. But Lillot was there, and later a knight came into the garden also. Vivia hated the smell of men. Though she glimpsed, from an upper walk, the knight talking to Lillot, nothing of the conversation had struck her – she was too allergic to both participants to take in any detail.

The heat was awful in the afternoon, and the stink of death gathered, so Vivia laid across her face a wet scarf soaked in herbs.

The scarf had been her mother's, a floating amber thing sewn with golden swans.

Vivia felt no nostalgia at it. It was as if she were a child born from nothing, or from some odd combustion of heat and earth, water and air. She had no parents.

She had dreamed of flying, on blue wings, and seeing the dusk across the sky, its mottled petals, pierced her with a curious sweet hurt.

There was no one to tell of this. Ursabet was not there, and in any event inadequate.

Around her, the castle would be preparing for its nightly dinner.

Sometimes Vivia absented herself. This did not matter, she had no significance.

Tonight, unusually, she was hungry.

She wanted bread and wine.

She smoothed her dress and combed out her hair. One long black filament, a single hair, came loose, and she wound it round and round her finger. Now it was a black ring, a thing of powers –

From beyond the windows came a thin drear noise, one associated with the winter: wrong.

It was the howling of the red wolves.

She stole back to the window and peered out, as if to see their shapes gathering on the mountain sides.

Like threads of bronze, the voices coiled into the evening vault, where two or three stars had already been lighted.

Another star shone below. It was a murky reddish shade. In the village, they had lit a bonfire. Some celebration or calamity – those sounds, they did not come from *above* –

Ursabet crept in at the door.

'Oh, Vivia, Vivia.'

'What is it?' Vivia spoke icily. She was alarmed, for

Ursabet, infallible sundial of the dreadful, had her croaking voice.

'There's plague in the villages.'

In all Vivia's fifteen years, she had never known such a thing, but she had been told of it. Within her frame, a bell of steel seemed to sink, chiming dully, into her womb.

'They've closed the castle up. We must pray.'

Vivia said, with pure logic, 'Why?'

'It's God's punishment. We must entreat Him.'

Black winged, ravens flew across the blue wings of the darkening sky. Below, the weird fire, that must be of madness or cremation, deepened. Vivia did not contest Ursabet's statement. Vivia knew *she* would not pray.

Chapter Four

THE DAWN WAS LUMINOUSLY SCARLET.

Against a sky like a church window, flecked by golden notes of cloud, Vaddix's castle bulked like another, lesser, mountain. An ugly thing. And through its many-windowed towers, light ran straight by, like the shafts of spears and bolts.

The castle bled light.

Not a sound. Then the burnt cawing of ravens.

Vivia opened her eyes, and the blood light filled them, painted her face, the walls.

This was not a day like other days. Everything was changed.

A sudden terrible image – what was it? When her mother had been struck, and fell, a flying jewel, like a strange fly, astonishingly red – and it had touched Vivia's face. But Ursabet had wiped Vivia's cheek with her sleeve, before pushing her down to kneel.

'Ursabet,' Vivia said, sitting up.

Ursabet was on her pallet in the corner, looking old, and crumpled by the night.

'What is it?' Ursabet said, stupidly.

'Where's my wine?'

'Your wine? Yes, yes, I'll fetch it.'

Ursabet moved like an unwieldy piece of machinery. She had slept in her dress, which was rumpled, and patched darkly beneath the arms and between the breasts with sweat.

'You smell,' said Vivia.

'Do I? It's my age.' Ursabet cackled. 'Not young and sweet like Vivia.' In her eyes was a gleam of something equally cruel. Had Vivia ever seen it before – like a lean stoat looking from a hole.

Vivia drank all the wine. Last night the dinner had been rowdy and haphazard, the food scorched or half uncooked. The knights were extra loud, as if to stave off their fear. They had waited to hear the priest speak the full grace before they ate, and each tipped his cup, making the ancient offering, to which the priest turned a blind eye.

Vaddix sat at the central table, and by now Lillot had removed herself from his side. He said nothing, only ate and downed cup after cup. His mad face was unreadable. What was he thinking? What would he do? He did nothing.

They said he slept now in the bridal room, at the foot of the bed with the dead horse on it.

The awful bloody colour of the sky was reluctantly fading, and Vivia went to her window. There was no sign this morning from the stricken village. But the ravens wheeled overhead, perhaps a hundred of them, very black.

The castle was safe. Of course it was. Nothing could get in. No enemy. No sickness.

And she – Vivia – she stretched her white arms and felt her silken hair slide on her back. She was invulnerable with her youth, her *sweetness*, as she had always been. How else had she escaped her father? How else had she lived her life of boredom and alarms and arrogance.

It seemed to her the stink of the dead horse was not so appalling or so strong. Gradually it would evaporate leaving a clean heap of bones. The summer heat would pass and snow creep down the mountains. The cold would cauterize the plague. Everything would be all right.

Javul had woken bulging, but not masturbated. Self-abuse was a sin worse than fornication. But it was not this which stopped him, more the anticipation of what he would soon have instead. He could imagine squeezing that big white velvet bum, like a peach, and pushing in and in. He rose and pulled on his garments, drank the beer that had been left him, and went to seek his breakfast in the dining hall.

She was there, with the two waiting women, and they, noting him, moved off.

Javul sat down beside Lillot.

'I dreamed about you all night, girlie.' Lillot meekly ate her pastry. 'We were in the forest. I got down and lifted you down. We lay on some flowers.'

Lillot made no response. Neither did she flush or pale or draw away.

Vaddix was not in the room, and here and there the knights sat eating. There was not much noise. This talk of plague had scared them all out of their wits. Not Javul. Javul knew what should be done. There was the choice of riding away besides. But not alone.

Onic, the chestnut-headed knight, was heaping his platter with cakes.

Javul pointed at him.

'Do you see him? Look, that golden sun pinned on his shoulder. That's Darejen, from your kinfolk. A woman's token. Was it your mother's?' Lillot glanced at Javul. Her soft mouth drooped. She was apparently thinking whether to say the jewel was hers. She decided against this, presumably. Javul said, masterfully, 'I'll get it back for you.' Javul banged on the table. 'Hey, Onic. That piece of gold. Give it here.'

'Go fuck a goat,' said Onic.

'No. I mean it.'

'So do I.'

The other knights laughed, and looked on. The women who were present drew back against the walls and curtains.

Javul got up, and lugged out his sword. 'Come on.'

Onic stuffed cake into his mouth, swallowed it with wine, and stood up as well. 'Not here, bone-head.'

'Afraid of the lord? He's cuddling his stallion.'

The knights said things under their breath. No one spoke out against Vaddix so openly. Javul was pleased. Now was as good a time as any to show them, partly to assume control.

'Vaddix does as he wants,' said Onic.

'He's frightened of the plague. He's an old woman.'

'Quiet,' said the fat knight, Kul.

'Does he hear, does he come charging? No. I want Onic's gold sun. I want to give it to someone. Onic stole it off the Darejens.'

Onic scraped out from around the table.

'You took your share, Javul.'

Onic's big sword, like a cleaver, was in his hand. Both men were clad in leather, with plates of iron and buckles of silver. They made a metallic, creaking noise, but above that there was a sort of singing in the air.

In the middle of the floor they rasped together, once, twice, and the sword blades screeched over. Then Javul kicked Onic in the balls under the groin-guard of thin iron. Onic doubled and went to his knees, and Javul clouted him across the back.

Three or four of the knights, Javul's cronies, cheered and smote the table tops.

Onic grabbed Javul's leg, and hauled him sidelong, and Javul crashed against a table.

'Fucking bastard,' growled Onic.

Javul bashed Onic with the hilt of his heavy sword, and then banged a flagon from the board on to Onic's reddish matted head.

Onic subsided and Javul stepped free. He had not intended to cut or wound in any vital way. It was simply a brawl. He hooked his hand into the leather strap on Onic's shoulder, as Onic shook himself and spat up cake, and ripped off the gold sun.

Javul went back to Lillot, who was sitting very still. She looked impressed, as he had meant her to.

Javul put the sun into her hand.

Then he glanced back at the knights.

'It was her mother's,' said Javul. 'She's had enough to put up with. I've got it for her. Right?'

'You're in the right,' said Kul. 'Cheer up, lady. Javul's your champion, like in the songs.'

Javul, not usually moved by such notions, felt a surge of pride.

He took the sun from Lillot's hand, and himself pinned it to her bosom. He did not, now, attempt to feel at her. He was decorous. He said, in a whisper, 'Meet me in the garden. Don't make me wait.'

Her eyes became enormous. They were a clear, watery blue, like an uncertain spring sky. He liked them. They were ordinary, willing eyes.

Down in the garden, the sun was gradually pushing up towards its ghastly noon paroxysm of heat.

The green trees looked shrivelled, and in them only the corpses of old black unwanted fruit clung like clusters of flies. Wasps buzzed between the leaves.

There was a curious sound. Javul could not make it out, what it was, where it came from. He forgot it.

He walked to the part of the wall on the outside of which, where the extruded bushes were, he had buried his golden Marius. Climbing the stones, he looked. The spot was undisturbed.

Over the walls and blocks of the castle, Javul took in the Short Tower and the House Tower, in which the bridal chamber lay, and the upthrust quills of the Spike Tower. Ravens were passing slowly to and fro above the House Tower, for the obvious reason.

On a terrace below, a girl was standing in a bluish gown, Vaddix's peculiar daughter.

Javul did not find in Vivia any attraction. Her beauty was like an insult, and to his eyes her slender curves were thin. He thought her mad besides, not realizing that a madness now began to fix upon him.

What was she doing there? Was she there to spy? She should have been wed long since, big with a baby, in her place.

Watching the ravens, was it? They were black like her hair.

Javul thought of the antique custom of throwing captured enemies from the wide windows of the Tower of Spikes down on to the quills below, leaving the victims there for hours or days to die, howling and weeping. Vaddix had never done that, preferring instant murder on the field of battle.

The girl Vivia had moved away.

Javul got down from the wall and went to examine the statue of the sheep-horned god. Things seemed unique to him all at once, as if he had never noticed them before. His sight was very sharp. And that odd noise – what was it – a kind of ringing sibilance above the crickets and wasps.

He looked round, and Lillot was in the garden.

She was biting her lip and holding her hands up to her breast like a signal.

Javul hurried to her and drew her in under the cherry trees. Flakes of green light burned on their skins.

'You know what I want,' said Javul.

Lillot lowered her eyes.

Javul crushed her to him.

He investigated her, pulling out of the dress the round white globes of her breasts and nuzzling them. He grew huge and pushed her back on a tree, pulled up her skirt and felt for her mound. Crisp hot hair, like golden wires, lush centre. He crammed himself into her carefully, and although she gave a little squeak, she did not deny him.

'Lovely, lovely,' panted Javul.

He closed his eyes, and smelled her hair and the dry hot leaves. Lillot gripped his back in a frightened manner, as if afraid of being shaken away.

Every heave at her succulent inside brought him closer to explosion, but he tried to hold off too, he wanted it to last. Perhaps he could make her come? Her breath hit against his ear in small gasps.

Javul opened his eyes and stared straight through the green of the leaves, and beheld a demon on the wall, above where his treasure lay.

For a moment, in physical delirium, he thrust on, and then he stopped dead, locked inside Lillot, his eyes wide as an owl's.

What in Christ's name was he seeing?

It perched there, a brown and tattered thing, leering at him – fiendish and unexplained.

With a grunt of distress, Javul pushed Lillot off his pole and stepped back. He clapped one hand over his loins and with the other whipped out the penis of his knife.

He stepped through the trees, by the statue, saw – *saw.*

It was a man on the wall. Only that. But not only that.

Somehow the creature had climbed up the rough stones of the castle, had dared to. Obviously, it was not in its right mind. A man from the village. A plague-ridden thing.

'Off!' Javul shouted, but the man took no notice, grinning his bad teeth, crazy. And Javul threw his knife any way. It thunked into the man's chest with a meaty yet hollow thud, and at once he rolled off and over and away.

The knife went with him. As well, Javul would not touch it again.

He turned and saw Lillot poised there with her skirt still up and her tits hanging out. He did not want her now.

'Go in!' shouted Javul. 'Don't come out here again.'

Used to taking the orders of all men, she pulled her clothes over herself, and ran unevenly up through the garden, moaning.

Some of them had rambled away, out into the fields, where they had tried to harvest what had already been taken, or was not yet ready. Among the tall stalks and stubble they fell down, could not get up again.

Some went back to the valley of the battle, wandered among the dead and the crucified Darejens. The ravens did not fly off at their coming and going. Waited for them, until they too lay down.

And some were at the river, fishing.

Some lay in their hovel-houses, already putrescent. When death finally came, occasionally the body was so full of poisonous matter, it burst. A few like this. Discoloured empty sacks.

But some were dancing in the street, courtly measures glimpsed at some castle rejoicing long ago, or rumbunctious peasant gallops, throwing their women up to get a look under their skirts.

They were drinking all their store of beer. They had no need now to squirrel up provisions for the winter. They seemed to understand this, and not mind.

They fucked continually, thoroughly, violently.

They were mad in many ways.

And as the sun became a white hole in the noon sky, where the black ravens circled round and round, and from where the ravens frequently came down and strutted now along the roofs and over the midden and in and out of doorways, then some of the villagers straggled up towards the slope, towards the castle of their lord.

They carried things, sick children, healthy squealing pigs, chairs fashioned by their grandfathers, heirlooms and rubbish.

When they were under the castle walls, they looked at them, as if they had never seen the castle, which had loomed over every second of their lives.

Then they called. In shrill but cajoling voices. They wanted to come in. They wanted to put their hands upon the lord and his people, on their furnishings and food and wine and clothing. They wanted to walk along the terraces and climb the stairs. To stroke the purple banners hanging deadly straight in the foul stinking air that had, for them, only the aroma of honey.

There were flies, he had heard them buzzing, all the time, and now, obviously, as he climbed up to that room, the noise was louder.

Dobromel had been in his chapel, burning the incense thick and fragrant, when the big shadow filled the door.

The whole place seemed to shake at the coming of Vaddix.

'I want you up there,' Vaddix said, 'I want prayers spoken, over my stallion.'

Dobromel said, 'Yes, my lord. If you wish. It's – unusual.'

'He was better than any of them. Better than a priest.'

'Yes, my lord.'

It did not really seem so bizarre. It was as if he had been expecting it, Dobromel, expecting Vaddix to come in and say just this. A mass for the horse.

They climbed the narrow upper stairs of the House Tower, Vaddix first, the priest with his bag of implements, the censer in his hand (thank God for its odour) and the white stole draped around his neck.

Dobromel, arrived, braced himself for what he would encounter when the door was thrown open.

Bracing himself was not enough.

The room was full of flies, *clotted* in them, black and shining, glittering, crawling and buzzing and darting about. They were the demons of the stink.

Oh the smell. It was like drowning.

On the bed, among the melted roses and the ruined linen and lace, the cadaver was already falling in, sinking.

It looked like – putrid bread. The eyes were gone, but in their gaps, the flies dazzled, busied themselves. They worked in and out of the nostrils, which were still pale pink, like delicate pearl.

The mouth had collapsed. The jaw bone was visible, and the blunt large teeth which had bitten at Vaddix's foes.

Dobromel wanted only to turn and run away.

'Do your work,' said Vaddix, standing impervious in the midst of it all, beside the bed, while the flies roiled round him, crawled on his sweat, face and hands, and he did not even brush them away.

Truly, Vaddix was now entirely mad.

Dobromel went into the room. It caught him like a physical blow in the abdomen. He lurched into a corner and puked.

Vaddix took no notice. He only said, 'Start.'

Dobromel straightened, wiped his lips.

He edged forward and swung the censer.

The flies clouded up, and it seemed to him they were like a shining rain.

'Oh, Marius, Christ and lord, behold this, one of your children, who lies before you in the hand of death.'

Vaddix nodded.

Dobromel uttered the correct, inappropriate words. He called the dead horse the son, and the brother. He opined that God would receive the horse in Paradise, among the faithful, and that any sin would be forgiven it. Through the immolation of Marius, all might be saved.

As he had had the urge to vomit, Dobromel had abruptly an urge to laugh. It was terribly hard to suppress this.

He tried instead to listen to the flies. Were they singing?

Yes, singing and talking, praying to their own god, the Lord of the Flies, who was the Devil.

The tickle of laughter left Dobromel. He sprinkled holy water on the horse.

The ravens were like great flies, too, shiny and black, going round and round the tower, and round the village sky, where the smoke had stopped rising.

But Dobromel had seen that morning smoke rising in two other areas, the regions of the other two villages.

This was better than that.

'Get out now,' said Vaddix.

Dobromel took himself through the door, closed it, leaned there.

There were outcast flies also crawling in the lobby. They would have to get back into the room through cracks in the door.

What were they saying?

Dobromel strained his ears. It was a thin high note above the buzzing which was their speech. He had heard it in the village too.

Dobromel, said the flies.

Dobromel attended in amazement. They knew and used his name.

Dobromel, why is it you fail to worship me?

'But –' said Dobromel.

And then he realized that he was hearing, not the flies, but the voice of God.

'I do, Lord,' lied Dobromel.

He obeised himself awkwardly on the floor, and sun-circled himself. Then made too the mark of the cross. Marius had hung on the cross three days, and had not died, and so one came and in pity stuck a sword into his side. Was it the voice of Marius, or of the Father Himself?

Now Dobromel, said the voice, *surely you know me?*

And the revelation came to Dobromel, who was God and whom he heard.

The priest bowed his head, raised it, and saw the white sun in the window. The sun was God. The sun had brought the flies. The flies were the voice of God. But God, God was not as they said.

Dobromel had been foolishly thinking he knew the answers. He must relearn everything swiftly.

The red wolves were all around the castle. Vivia could hear them. But they were not wolves at all.

The villagers were there, howling and calling. Sometimes too they sang out sweetly.

Vivia supposed suddenly that one of the servants might open the castle gates, and then these people would race in. They would rush from room to room.

But that would never happen.

Vivia had walked through the castle. She had seen the knights, the women, the servants and relations of Vaddix. They had acted merrily, jollily. And then Vivia saw something falling through the air, down from the Spike Tower, something which caught and writhed on a spike. It was a banner, only that, somehow detached.

This filled her with fear.

She walked quickly, too prudent to run, back to her apartment.

It was as though she were invisible. None of those she passed, who passed her, appeared to see her. That had often been so, of course.

Nevertheless she sped to her mirror on the lion. There she was. Her eyes were wild and huge, a pale seared greenish colour.

It was no use. She was not safe, had known she was not. Unsafe, that was, in a new way. For from her father she would spring elsewhere. But to plague no one could say No.

Plague slunk up on the castle, like a rising tide, like the eldritch sea which once, Ursabet had told her, had covered everything, and so left behind it, in the mountains, crystal shells and branches of white coral.

Vivia began to cry. At once she struck her own face, hard enough that the mark emerged dully on her skin.

Tears were no use. And there was no one to entreat for help. No God. Nothing.

Only Ursabet, who had rescued her in the past, could assist her now.

And where was Ursabet?

Vivia glanced at Ursabet's pallet. The blanket had not been tidied, and on the floor lay some of her things, her tiny pewter sun, her dirty nasty comb.

Going to the door of her room, Vivia shouted angrily, 'Ursabet! Ursabet!' Anger a mask for fear.

When no one came, Vivia paced to her bed and lay down there. Like a cat, she could generally sleep at will, but now she did not relax. She twisted her hands, and remembered the black hair that had formed a ring around her finger. Was that unlucky? For in a world where no supreme goodly power exercised any sway, evil things abounded.

It was not, for example, that the smell of death was less. Only that she had grown accustomed to it.

Above her, as if in the tower-head of her own brain, Vivia pictured the rotting horse.

The plague had been with the Darejens. The horse, killed by the bolt of a Darejen crossbow, was ripe with plague.

Plague, shut out below, drifted down on them from on high, just like the banner dislodged from the tower.

How long did she have left to her?

Vivia did not weep. She knotted herself into a ball and howled with terror, as the mad human wolves howled below.

Chapter Five

IN THE NIGHT, SOMETHING MOVED in the austere maiden room. Only half waking under her sheet, Vivia lay still, listening. A bear? A nightmare caught her, and the bear lurched towards the bed. But, in very darkness, it dissolved. Nothing was there. A silence like a high thin noise filled Vivia's ears, and again she slept. She had exhausted herself with terror, did not want to be awake and aware.

Later, sunrise filled the windows, tinctured the gold-leaf of the painted Marius Christ. Not a hectic dawn today, nor luminous.

Vivia woke again, and fear came instantly and took hold of her. Her belly gurned, her skin prickled. She sat up at once and got out of the bed which was hot and clinging, like a coffin.

'Ursabet,' Vivia said, 'there you are. Wake up.'

Ursabet lay on her pallet, stretched straight out, her arms wrapped over her slack big stomach. She was frowning slightly.

Vivia walked to her and stood looking down. Ursabet was very deeply asleep, and she had been eating fruit, for from the corner of her mouth had dribbled out a dark red stain.

Vivia shivered. She went away, not bothering to call Ursabet again or shake her roughly. No wine and no honey waited for Vivia's thirsty mouth. In the lobby beyond the door, no food had been brought for her.

Instead she drank some of the tepid washing water. She

washed her body over, reassured momentarily (falsely) by its clean new smell.

She put on her other dress, which was grey and had been darned under one arm. She did not know why she chose this lesser garment.

Ursabet had not woken even now.

Vivia turned again, and stared at her.

She had been accustomed to Ursabet. For all her life that she could recall, Ursabet had been with her. And, in extremity, surely Ursabet would have had some solution. At the very least, some charm to be spoken, or some herb eaten as a protection . . . a story of a young girl who was saved from danger, possibly by a prince with wings and hair like gold.

Vivia opened her door once more, and listened to the castle. There was a sound going on, some sort of celebratory rumbling that was not reasonable. She could not hear the howls of the human wolves on the slope below, but these had, anyway, died out sometime after sunset.

The castle was in the grip of a madness. A different madness, for she had never thought it sane.

Vivia went back to Ursabet and crouched down. Cautiously, she patted Ursabet's cheek. The face was swollen and congested, and cold and flaccid as stale dough. Ursabet did not breathe and was dead. The stuff that had run from her mouth was blood and pus.

Vivia stuck her nails into her palms to stop herself from whimpering.

She got up and combed her hair.

Someone must come, the priest must come, and say the rites over Ursabet. Not because they were of any worth, but because Ursabet would be afraid without them. And then they must lug the corpse out of the room.

A single fly hung in the air like a winged bead of jet.

Vivia ran out, checked herself, began to walk stiffly along the gallery, towards the wide stairs.

There were people in the hall below, two knights and some of the women, an uncle of Vaddix's, half senile. *He* was clambering about on chairs, laughing. And the women laughed. Suddenly one of the knights, the red-haired man,. seized a woman. He clapped his mouth to hers and next instant had pulled up her skirt. They fell back together on to a table draped by a carpet, and rolled there.

Vivia halted and went aside from the stair, down other corridors, until she reached the stone steps leading to the chapel courtyard.

Servants were running about from room to room, passing her blindly, but at the turn of this stair, a man abruptly rose up from the gloom, and balanced in front of her.

'Pretty girl,' said the man, whom she recognized as some steward of the castle. 'Did you come to see me?'

'Get out of my way,' said Vivia.

'No, you come to me.'

'Don't you know who I am? The lord's daughter.'

'Come and feel me,' said the man. 'I'm big.'

Vivia felt panic and rage, equal, rising from her very vagina into her brain.

'He will have you crucified.'

The man looked puzzled. Then he fell back, straight over, like a board of wood. He crashed on to the lower stairs.

His eyes had already glazed. He was quite dead.

Vivia picked across him, which was hard, trying not to let any part of her touch him.

The door came open and she got out into the yard and sprang over it.

Geese and chickens were there, somehow let out of their houses, pulling at the dry weeds that poked between the stones. The glue of incense wended thickly from the chapel door, and inside, the darkness stayed her.

'Father – Father Dobromel?'

He was not present.

On the altar the censer smoked, and one candle burned in a slush of wax. One other thing was there, a dead rat with a distended belly.

Vivia removed herself from the chapel and stood in the courtyard. Overhead the sky was choked and dull, and on it wheeled the black embroideries of ravens.

From somewhere came a peal of savage laughter, followed by a shriek.

A man sat against the wall. She had not seen him. His shirt was bloody, but he had pulled out his member and was massaging it urgently, smiling all the while at Vivia.

She returned into the castle by another door. She went slowly now. At turnings where there were sounds, she hesitated. Usually they eddied away. Or else the couples were too engrossed to notice her.

She did not think to go towards the gates. The kennels of the big dogs were there, and the stable. Besides, the gates were shut fast. Outside too were plague demons.

Should she attempt to find her father? Perhaps, as his property, he would protect her. Vivia went up on to the terrace below the Spike Tower.

Was Vaddix up there? Ursabet had said he spent much time there, or in the chamber with its bloating horse. She could not, could not bring herself to attempt that room. And anyway, would he know her? That had always been a problem and an oblique safety, that he seldom remembered her.

The banner that had dropped away still hung on the spike. It did not move, there was no wind. Heat pressed on Vivia like a suffocating hand.

Terror threatened her again. She would not give up her own reason. She would not become like *them*.

She gazed down across the mounds of the castle.

In the garden, very small, on the wild pear tree, she saw a bony child, apparently grown like an improbable fruit. The child, like the banner, did not move.

Vivia crossed over the walks and reached the narrow door of the Tower of Spikes. The door was ajar. Was Vaddix above?

Then, in the funnel of the tower, she heard shouting, the drunk roars of men.

She turned her back on the tower.

The scenes came to her, all the women she had beheld, coupling, half naked, like some painting of the damned. Never before today had she witnessed this, though Ursabet had often described to her the sexual act. Ursabet, in her youth, had been fond of it.

And Ursabet lay dead in Vivia's room.

No one would help Vivia now. No one was to be trusted. The servants ran in all directions, carrying objects – sheets, pans, bottles – ants whose nest had been disturbed.

Vivia would have to see to Ursabet herself.

The summit of the Tower of Spikes was a wide platform, roughly circular, with, in every side, east, west, north and south, a huge opening in the stone. From these doors prisoners had been cast down on to the waiting, rusted, jagged primal steel below. Every spike was once three feet in length, though some were now a little less; weather and use had snapped them. A few had turned over the wrong way, pointing down. In a well far beneath, the broken bones of what had finally been sloughed and splintered off the spikes had long since become dry and nearly featureless.

In the time of Vaddix's sire, a kitchen urchin had toppled into this well. He was left to perish. His had been the last wails, the last body which had ornamented the foot of the Spike Tower.

'He'll come,' said Javul. 'He comes here every day. He looks around. You can see the valley from here. Where we did for the Darejens.'

They stared, across the castle, the fields, the hump where the village was – not noting its appearance – away towards the valley.

The ravens flew low, beside the windows. One man had brought his bow, and tried now and then to pot them. But his eye was out. They had all been vastly drinking.

'I've had his woman,' said Javul. 'I'm his match. And you're with me, aren't you, you fine fellows, eh?'

'We're one,' said Kul.

Red-headed Onic sat in the eastern window space. Now and then he would lean over like an infant seeing how far it can go before it falls. Sometimes he teetered. Always got himself back.

They were all there. The ten knights of Vaddix. But they were done with Vaddix now.

'You should marry the daughter,' said Kul, ever practical. 'That makes it legal.'

'That skinny nit? Well. Maybe I will. Give the girl some happiness. I'll do it the old way, wed both of them.'

They sat, contemplating. Onic tottered over the edge of the window, righted himself. 'The bastard is coming.'

They got ponderously to a sort of attention, and each man drew his sword. These at least had been beautifully sharpened and burnished. A flash like lightning filled the tower's head.

Vaddix's feet beat, slithered on the crooked stair.

The men were like stones.

And he, a heavy granite stone which had motion, slouched in at the entry.

He wore his armour still, had not taken it off for all the days and nights since the battle. His huge hands were empty.

He stood there, a swaying colossus, and the pocked, scarred, ugly sculpture of his face turned round to look at them, one by one.

'What's this.'

They could not find words, confronted by him.

Then Javul said, 'Your time's come, Vaddix.'

Surprising them, he said, 'I knew it when I lost the horse.'

Then Onic, with a guttural choking roar, tore straight at Vaddix, sword swung high.

And Vaddix stepped, daintily as a girl, from Onic's path.

Onic soared out through the eastern window space, descended a moment screaming, and then they heard the antique noise, flesh impaled upon a spike. Onic's scream stopped. And then he began to scream in another way, like a baby with the lungs of a man.

'Get him,' said Javul.

He, Kul, three others, dashed forward, and stuck their blades into the body of their lord, between rivets and into weak parts of the armour.

Vaddix seemed to burst around them like a vast black gout of blood. And then he was pulling them, dragging them forward.

Javul wrenched away and danced on to all fours. His own sword sliced off a finger but he did not feel it.

He saw Vaddix folding over, like a bolt of cloth, and in the folds of him, Kul and the others, kicking and scrabbling – to no avail. And out of the west window now they slowly span, upending as they went, so that five pairs of boots, ludicrous, were the last thing that went from sight.

Javul crawled to the west window, and the rest, the last four knights, went after him.

Vaddix was arched over two spikes, a thing of leather and iron and gold. His chin jutted up, and already he was dead.

Kul spasmed, impaled through the belly under his guard. He made a retching mewling noise.

The other three had fared similarly, and were giving up the ghost with curses and screeches and groans. Only Onic had been caught by the leg. He was the loudest, as they craned to see him, in a special agony, since he was still likely to live.

'Go to the west window – can we get to him?' said the man with the bow.

'Not one chance. It would be a kindness to shoot him now. They hung there for days, those that were taken that way. And the birds picked at them.'

Not one of the men in the tower, however, moved.

It was, oddly, Onic who did that.

His frenzy had ripped his leg, on which all his weight was hanging, and it gave way, releasing him. He dived straight down until another spike went through his throat.

'The castle's ours,' said the bowman knight.

'Fuck the castle. Let's get away from the plague. Those scum that came up to the gate are dead, I went down and took a look. Nothing to hold us. We can come back in a month, when it's safe.'

They gawped at him.

Javul said, 'But I'll take the girl with me. The lily. She's mine. Don't forget. No tricks.'

*   *   *

So weighty. Unyielding. No longer a friend.

Vivia tugged on the body of Ursabet.

She had not wanted to touch. But she had had no choice.

Ursabet, unknowing, struggled off her pallet. Her pathetic grey hair spooled along the floor, and Vivia stopped, looking at this hair. She could recollect, could she not, a time when the hair had been brown and rich. When Ursabet was slim and vivacious. Or was that Ursabet's own fantasy, projected through her tales?

Vivia lifted her own body a fraction, and pulled hard upon the corpse of her woman. Her second, unregarded mother.

Something snapped. In Ursabet's shoulders. The horrible unfluent arms were suddenly loose.

Vivia dropped them with a cry.

Outside, the ravens cawed and circled.

There were more flies in the room. They buzzed softly, sitting upon things, even on the mirror, where they were doubled. *Ten* flies.

Soon the chamber of the maiden would be like the bridal room, the tomb of Vaddix's horse.

Vivia stood away and watched Ursabet lying dead and unhelpful on the floor.

Vivia ran to the door and opened it.

The castle was murmuring and calling and crying. Laughter came and went like breath.

Then Vivia saw Dobromel the priest. He poised like an icon at the end of the gallery, looking right at her.

'Father,' said Vivia, in a cold formal voice, 'I must ask your assistance.'

'You shall have it,' Dobromel said. He spoke quietly, secretively, and swam towards her. Shadows had filled the gallery. He ebbed in and out of them, and now he was before her.

His fat face was puffed up like a bladder.

Out of his cleverly unclever eyes shot rays of strength and purpose. He had a clammy odour. She stepped back and he said, 'I know the truth.'

'Do you?' said Vivia.

What on earth could he think the truth was?

Dobromel said, 'I'll tell you. We prayed wrongly. To God. But God isn't what we said. Oh no, not at all.'

Vivia listened. If he tried to put his hand on her she would recoil, smite him. Like the rest, he had the plague, and his breath was very vile.

'God is the Devil. Yes. The Devil made the world. We're his subjects. We've done him wrong. These lies . . . But I saw a vision. Was granted it. And the Devil is the sun, and the Lord of the Flies, and the bringer of the plague. I'll tell you,' he leaned closer and she further away, 'how to recognize him. He's dark like darkness, and winged. He flies by night. Horns sprout from his head. Like a horned bat. His eyes are red.'

'Thank you, father,' said Vivia.

She made the sign of the cross.

The priest shook his head.

'Not that sign. Not the sun sign either. He hasn't told me yet what it is. But when I know, I'll come and tell you.'

Vivia closed the door and heard him shuffle away.

She was alone now, with the dead thing on the floor.

Chapter Six

THE STORM BELLOWED THROUGH THE mountains, across the cauldron of the sky. Grey rain coursed down. The world was slick and black as prehistoric things, the castle a cumulus of stone. Lightning lit like a window, and every atom of glass flashed back blue and crimson, white and deathly green.

It did not refresh. Did not renew. It was like a deluge of hot mercury. The ground steamed. The river thrashed, and frogs flopped to safety in the reeds. Through the fields, whose stems were flattened, the masterless goats and sheep trotted bleating, with mad rain eyes.

On the slope before the castle gate, the dead villagers were spread in attitudes of repose, like statues which slept, gleaming in the rain, which had washed away the blood and matter, and their souls.

Carts had overturned. A chair was set up as if for some judge.

Pigs walked through the rain, snuffling. They had already eaten a little of those who, in the normal way of things, would have eaten them.

The ravens, wet as black rags, sat along the rims of the castle, cawing occasionally, black daggers of beaks and eyes like mirrors.

Some way off, on the mountain side, a wolf howled, and then two or three others.

The ravens bustled, fluffed themselves up. Old adversary, greedy partner at the feast.

But there was something the wolves would not have.

Up on the spikes of the tower where the lightning flashed in vanilla splashes. Six dark things hung there.

A blank sun parted the clouds.

Up in the Spike Tower there was activity.

Figures whirled and flapped like ravens.

With a long shriek, one plummeted out. A spike seemed to reach, catch it. Squalling, it knotted and unknotted, the darkness on the silvery spike in the silver rain. And then another one down, not crying, run home like a hunk of bread on to a toasting fork. And another, with flying hair.

Up in the Spike Tower, four of Vaddix's relatives, his three cousins and the bastard brother, rested from their labours.

The brother said, 'This is the way. Vaddix, with his household round him.'

They looked. The last consignment was a child already dead. They tossed it free and it curled over a spike, not pierced, perfectly balanced.

Some ravens flew through the rain, to inspect the fresh gift.

'There are more below,' said the oldest cousin. 'Do we get the men to haul them up?'

'I like the work,' said the bastard. 'Out with them, the plague-infested garbage.'

The living plague victims howled on the spikes, and the ravens circled, and tore first at the child who did not fuss.

The men glanced through the rain, towards the valley, where they had crucified Darejens.

'Something moving there?'

'The villagers went back to eat them. Steal their valour.'

'No. Only the birds.'

'Or wolves. The wolves love this. No more corpses for those wolves.'

They put out their hands into the rain, to cleanse them.

The youngest cousin eased his left arm. He hurt under there. He wanted a woman.

Hot as blood, the rain shot by, and the ravens circled through the rain.

*   *   *

From the porter's room Javul stepped back.

'He's dead.'

It was true, the man sat smiling, perhaps with pain. He had a beard of blood.

Javul and his four knights had taken their horses. The dogs whined, padding up and down in their enclosure. They had already partly chewed through it, and soon would be at liberty to run up into the castle. They were hungry, the dogs. There would be food.

Javul looked at his lily, standing behind him in her cloak, the rain large as diamonds on her yellow hair. He too smiled, to reassure her, but she was expressionless, almost featureless, with fear.

Well, things would be better soon.

They mounted, the horses jibbing and jerking in the rain, and at the smell of fruity death so close.

Javul put the girl in front of him. He felt her firm round flesh. 'Cheer up, lily. Trust me.'

They did not use the gate, but the spy door under the stable. They got out easily.

The dead were all over the road, and bits of furniture, and ambling happy pigs with bones in their mouths.

'Bloody hogs. Creatures of the Devil.'

They rode down the slope with propriety, skirting everything. The woman with the baby at her breast and the hole in her and the pig, eating. The man who seemed to have ended eating a loaf, his teeth clamped in it. There were enormous piles of vomit the rain was sluicing away . . .

Beyond the downslope they turned towards the river, kicked in spurs, slashed the horses' necks. The animals ran at once, frothing and grunting, headlong for the valleys, the way out of this place.

'We'll go towards the west, Lillot. I know people in a town there. It's warmer in winter and there are great trees. You'll have a house like a lady.'

He felt too hot, sore in his own skin. His stub of finger still bled and ached like a tooth. He was not sure after all he wanted Lillot. But he had got her.

* * *

In the dining hall, a naked woman had wrapped herself in a scarlet curtain. She taunted and flaunted, until seven men took her, one after the other. She was dead before they were done.

Dobromel saw this from the threshold. He nodded. This was correct.

He walked into the middle of the hall, and exhorted them.

'Fornicate – drink – commit obscene acts. Yes. This is how you must worship him.'

Flies buzzed and the air sang with the red-brown effluvia.

Someone had killed Vaddix. The first offering. And now they threw the dying off the tower, when they could get to them.

All this was very good.

Dobromel sank down.

'Praise him,' he said, 'Lord of the Flies. The white sun.'

Thunder rocked the castle, and bald lightning slashed.

A man pushed Dobromel over, and the priest lay on the floor.

He must worship too.

He looked at the other woman, the one whose breasts were bare. She was eating bread, stuffing herself. Then she would pause and throw up. Presently she would eat again.

Dobromel twitched up his skirt and tried to finger life into his staff. But his penis was sluggish and reluctant. He could not make it work.

He got up slowly. He would go up to the chamber of the horse and pray there. Where the flies gathered in a congregation.

There was that girl, that Vivia. She should go too. If Vaddix had lived, Dobromel would have urged him to take his own daughter. Incest was excellent.

Dobromel went out and down the castle, thinking of how Vivia had stood in her doorway and looked at him. And from his useless rod came a quiver. Perhaps there was a chance of life after all.

                    *   *   *

Vivia sat on the island of her bed, her knees drawn up.

All around her she could hear and smell the castle, and outside even the rain was like a busy terrible engine, a threat and a decree.

Ursabet was turning sodden now. Vivia did not look at her, for leaves of flesh might begin to fall.

Vivia waited. She did not know for what.

When something rapped on her door, she thought for a moment some person had come, someone sane, to help her.

But then, almost in the same instant, she knew this could not be.

Dobromel the priest called through the panels.

'Lady Vivia – you must come with me now.'

She did not speak, but then, when he went on calling, she cried, 'Go away!'

'No,' said Dobromel. 'Come, there's a way. We must only show him.'

The priest had told her of a god who was a bat, horned, winged, flying by night.

Vivia held her body rigid.

The rain gushed, and Dobromel beat feebly.

She could not bear these noises.

Abruptly the priest threw himself against her door with colossal force. That was no use. She had let down the bar.

'Your father is dead,' shouted Dobromel, breathless, 'they threw him on the spikes. Come with me now.'

He did it again, throwing his full fat weight on the timbers. Which shuddered.

Was it possible he could get in?

Vivia put her hand out and touched the little knife she kept for cutting her fruit. It was not sharp; however, it was all she had.

She took the knife, loosened her body, and stepped off the bed. She went to the door and froze as again he rammed against it and again it quaked. The bar racked in the socket. The socket slewed.

'Dobromel,' said Vivia. 'Go away.'

'Let me in,' said Dobromel. 'I want you.'

'Let me in,' said Dobromel. 'I want you.'

'What do you mean?' She knew.

'Let me lie on you, Vivia. Then we can be safe. I can, with you. Only with you.'

She had a vision of his gross carcass pinning hers, her gown stripped off and her white legs bare and spread.

Vivia lifted the bar off the door, and opened it, and there he was, heaving and sweating, his face innocent as that of someone witless. He was.

She wanted to kill him, to kill them all. Her terror was transformed into a burning itch of malevolence. She cut him across the innocent face, screaming at him.

Dobromel staggered back.

He clutched at his eyes, and the blood, and went careering off along the gallery. She wanted to run after him, but instead she closed herself in again and again let down the bar.

He had told her, her father was dead. On the spikes.

Vivia did not want to die. She was not yet sixteen. She clutched her body and wailed, waving the bloodied knife in the air, cutting at the air, hating it.

Gradually the rain eased, dripped and trickled. Vivia's passion ran down.

The girl stole to the window. The sky was like a heap of ruined stone, and the castle too seemed ruinous.

The sugary meaty smell of Ursabet assailed her. And at the same ill-assorted moment, Vivia's stomach growled with hunger. She would die in this room. The plague would find her here.

Rain *dripped*.

Vivia went all about the room. She made a bundle of her mother's scarf with swans, and into this she set her comb, the red salve for her mouth, her iron cup, some stockings and a shift.

Then she took off the dull dress. She put on the red gown with gold, and over her narrow hands went the bracelets, into her ears the earrings, for her fingers the rings of gold.

It was sombrous. Had the sun set? Vivia had lost all track of time. Or, rather, time had ceased to exist.

Vivia knotted her bundle. She spared a look for Ursabet.
'I'm sorry . . . He wouldn't say the rites.'

Vivia undid the door and went out on to the gallery.

All around now the castle thrummed and moaned. It
was like, although she had never heard one, a sinking ship.

Through the dusk she walked glowing red in the shadows, white in the last traces of the light.

No one stopped her, impeded her.

She saw – no one.

But, at the turn of the stair, she saw through a window,
whose shutters had been thrown back, the Spike Tower.

Its shape had altered. It was massy and uneven. Dark
lumps protruded from it, and at the top, the dead sneer
of the dying day passed through its upper eyelets. A
monstrous needle, threaded with dead. And round the
shape the ravens buzzed, now and then alighting.

Vivia ran. She ran through the stone vegetable.

Downwards, down, to the only hope she had.

Chapter Seven

As they rode through the night, illness began to come over Javul's knights.

Above was that late summer star, the Iron Peg, dull but large, often visible through the swag of cloud. The rain had ended leaving the world to drip and smoke in darkness.

'Stop,' yelled out Blord. 'I can hear my mother – she's calling me.' And frenziedly he wheeled his horse about, sat staring up at the mountains, while the animal cavorted under him.

'Wolves,' said Javul, 'red wolves howling.'

They had come through the valley of death, passed above it among the trees, where only one man had been crucified. His corpse shone pale as they went by, half bone. Things flapped about the lower areas. The river rumbled after the rain.

Riding up, westward, they went through pine woods. They first heard the wolves there, their cries, moving distantly, saw nothing. The horses kept running.

Beyond the tree line, the mountains strode with them, crags and crests, where lightning still sometimes flickered like a fairy light, pretty; noiseless.

The wolves sounded on, but they remained some way off. They would want the valley of death, the castle too. Not strong men on fleet mounts.

The strong men began to see things in the flashing by of the trees. As they descended through a wooden fence of larches, Blord saw Vaddix on a bough, laughing at them. Another man saw this too.

Only Javul knew Vaddix was not there.

Javul began to grasp plague was.

Then he swore, swore filthy things into the fair girl's hair, which was an acid colour in the dark.

When Blord stopped on the track, another man copied him. Their horses rolled about, wanting to fly.

'Leave it,' said the knight known as Ullip, 'come on, you bloody fools.'

'Let them be,' said Javul. He spurred his horse again and sent it blundering down the incline between the sinewy trees. It would go faster without the damned girl.

Rocks tumbled, pebbles spun away, and here a slip of the river slid below. Ilexes bowed like glossy crones to the water.

The horse leaped the course and pelted on.

Javul heard two others at his back. Only two. Blord was lost. Good riddance. Ullip's horse he could hear, and the sharper race of a thinner man's mount.

The star stood clear and hideous, almost lightless, yet visible. The eye of God.

They tore through the valleys, up into the valley pass where the mountain sides crowded close, edged like knives.

'They're coming,' called Ullip. 'I can hear them behind us.'

The red wolves had ceased their gruesome song. Feeding no doubt in the valley. The night seemed huge, hollow, like a bell. Javul's head rang. He had the wish to have the girl, there, as they rode. But there would be time for that. He had never completed his lust in her. She owed him.

Skittering, and regular soft falls of feet not like the hoofs of the horses. Unnaturally, Javul now heard this. What was it? Was it Blord and the other one, catching up?

Ullip glanced over his shoulder.

He yelped.

'Javul – it's wolves!'

By the glow of the phosphorus, Vivia gazed at the grotto under the castle. At first it seemed the same to her.

The falls of water, thin and thick, the gemmy pools,

some suddenly ringed by the diving of an albino frog. The stalactites stabbed down, and in the walls of stone, the fossils were stacked: fans of shells and curled ammonites, the skeletons, slender as hairs, of fishes, lizards, birds. It was quiet, but for the harping of liquid, the intermediary slight ventures of indigenous things.

Then, she noticed that some of the water which fell was black. It siphoned through slowly, as if wanting to be sure of, or to tease, the region it entered.

And next, Vivia saw that the walls in some parts *moved*.

Bats crawled down the stone. Hundreds of them. Portable darkness. They felt their way with agile delicate hooked wings, and the fur of their bodies sparkled with cold dew. Their eyes sparked in a different way, more glutinous yet half opaque. They winked at her. Tiny teeth showed, flawless white. And then the grey tongues, licking and licking at the black fluid which dropped so hesitantly from above.

Blood. It was blood. Somehow seeping through from the doomed castle overhead. Through curious channels, unknown tubes of stone.

It spangled down and the quiet calm bats lapped. Their tongues turned black.

Vivia stood as if petrified.

Her sanctum had been polluted. What would this mean?

She glanced, towards the curtain of leper ivy. Did blood fall there, too?

Vivia did not go to see. She sat down on the lip of a pool. She bowed her head and scrutinized her bundle of pathetic possessions. She was defeated. Death breathed on her, cold as snow, dank and ripe as the falling blood.

'No,' said Vivia aloud.

How could she die? She was everything to herself, the centre of the world.

But perhaps already the sigil of plague had been raised in her body.

Vivia screamed.

Then she was still.

From nowhere and from everywhere a low deep throbbing had answered her. It was as if the cave temple spoke in words too arcane to be understood. And then something beat towards her, something she did not behold, from behind her – a giant bat flying low, brushing over her scalp so every hair stood on end.

She flung up her head to see. A shadow drifted on the wall, shimmered over the forms of all the bats. Was gone.

Nothing had cast the shadow.

Even in the dead light of the star, they were red.

They leapt from the night, and their coats streamed with old red rusty rain. The wolves –

Ullip yowled and smote at them with his sword, which seemed to make no impression. Behind him the other man tried only to outrun them.

Awash in speed, there seemed ten of them, or more. But there were only four, five, perhaps. They raced about each other, proving no mutual obstacle.

One was very big, taller than a hunting dog, almost the height of a horse. They could be this big, larger, the red wolves. Their eyes flamed like slices of bad fire. From their lips the curving sabre teeth overhung upper and lower jaw, wet with saliva.

Javul kept ahead of them. He ignored the shouts and yells of the men, and the faint whimpering of the girl. He *rode*.

With a guttural growling, its voice doused in spit and foam, the nearest wolf, the giant, reared up and took hold of Ullip. One moment the man was on the horse. Next second he had been torn from it.

He went down screaming, in a crash of metal and night.

The big wolf climbed on him and Ullip thrust at it with his sword. Another wolf was there and closed its teeth in his arm. The sword glanced away, useless, on the track, and other wolves bounded over it. The horse reared off from them and flung aside.

The big wolf leaned down and tore out Ullip's throat.

Three of them pulled at Ullip, instantly feeding, shaking the broad human body, opening it like a cushion.

The others hurtled on – one, two – and the first danced up and took the leg of the last man in its long sickles of fangs.

'Javul – help me!'

Javul heard the sound as his final knight went slithering and bouncing, clanking and shrieking, down on to the road.

Free, two riderless horses plunged past Javul and were gone.

Javul rode.

Falling back, nothing to him now, the feeding noises. No more screams.

'That'll hold them,' said Javul, to Lillot. 'We've got a good chance.' He nuzzled her hair, loathing her. 'Just me and you now, girlie.'

The road was all at once open, the mountains pressed sidelong. Trees made pillars and arches. Up ahead, the way through into some higher angle of the pass, rock and shale, harder going. But more difficult for the wolves to catch them there, climbing up the vertical incline.

He could, of course, go faster without the girl. But the horse was nearly done.

Something came up, devoid of warning, from Javul's belly, and he leaned aside and vomited quickly, without trouble.

He was sick. He wanted to screw the girl. He was afraid the wolves would come and get him.

Javul pushed the horse, which was faltering, juddering, up into the runnels of the shale, and there a wreck of a pine tree rose, gaunt and awful as some totem of chaos.

Javul reined in, and the horse stumbled to a halt, solid and dripping wet, its flanks heaving. The other pair were long gone, down into the lower valleys probably, nicer running.

There was no sound now, above the horse's blowing lungs, but the old rain, uncoiling from the rocks, the tree. The star shone mindlessly on.

'Get down,' said Javul, as he moved himself off the

horse. The girl stupidly obeyed, without his assistance nearly falling.

Javul looked back. The wolves had let them go. For now. But if they should come up again, something must be here to delay them.

He observed Lillot, Vaddix's whore, and laughed. So, he had the plague. Javul was strong. He would survive. Men did survive. Find some bolt-hole, sweat it out.

But the bitch; there was no use but one for her. And after all he would not bother. No, it was better to attend to himself.

It was all her fault, anyway. Bitch, fucking Darejen.

He went to her and took her arm, not even roughly, and led her up to the tree where it faced on to the track.

'Put up your hands,' he said, mildly. 'No, higher. Now, over your head. That's it. And one on the other. Yes.'

Lillot stood against the pine, white as the moon which was invisible, soft white meat. It was not the pose quite of crucifixion, but then, he had no nails. This would have to do.

Javul took out his new knife, and hammered it home, through both her soft upturned palms, into the trunk of the tree.

Lillot squeaked. Then she cried out, a long, desolate note that had nothing in it, no pleading, no question. She knew, she had always known.

'There,' said Javul. He took her in. She would be a lovely treat for the wolves, if they came. And she had served her function, as a Darejen. A sacrifice to the ancient gods of the trees.

Up in the rock, where the roots of the mountains began, Javul found a small cave. He had been looking for such a thing. Instinct, primitive and necessary, had taken up where reason had left off.

He climbed into the cave, quite leisurely now, feeling drunk and almost happy. He was sure of life. It would not let him down.

Near the cave entry was a boulder. Drawing on vast strength, wanting to shout with a sort of glee, he dragged the boulder up after him and closed the mouth of the cave.

Like Marius in his tomb. And like Marius, Javul would cause the stone to roll away at the proper time.

There was water, he could hear it, running along the cave floor. Javul took out his tinder and struck it.

The cave was not exactly as he had guessed. Though small, it opened, further in, on to a greater space, all shadow.

Javul was looking at this, when two fires spurted up on the darkness, reflections of his own. For a moment he did not know what they were.

And then the enormous wolf stepped forward into the light.

It was old, the wolf, tangled. Briars grew in its auburn coat, which streamed down it nearly to the ground. Scars showed, hairless parts, like cuts into the mountain itself. Its head was almost level with his own.

'Marius,' said Javul softly, 'save me now.'

He drew his sword gently, switching the burning tinder to his other hand.

The wolf's eyes seemed to float like lamps.

It was so old. Behind it, bones of things, but others had brought it food. It did not hunt for itself. It was no match for him.

The wolf rose slowly up, on to its hind legs, and its head touched the ceiling of the cave. It was much taller than Javul. Its belly was a mass of pocks and healed wounds, muscle and matted fur.

Vaddix . . . it was like Vaddix.

Javul ran forward to sink his blade into the wolf's gut, and the huge paws came down on his neck.

He felt himself crushed into the stream that bubbled over the cave floor. His face was in the water.

The wolf dropped massively upon his back, and Javul felt its teeth go into him.

Even so, he did not believe. He thrashed and coughed in the water as his own blood furled around him. As he heard the wolf eating him and roared at the agony of its teeth – even so, he thought he would live.

*   *   *

Her mother had loved her. She had. Oh, the memory.

Lillot remembered.

New born, she had been held, fondled, and that beautiful warmth and kindness. She remembered that.

There were days under the apricot trees. The mother walking with the child.

Lillot too had loved her mother. Nothing was so true. The magic instant when the mother bent over her. Eyes blue as skies.

Lillot thought of her mother now, her pain mostly forgotten. All of it, mostly, forgotten.

For since she had grown, what had there been but dire drab frightful things. Her constriction to womanhood. Her trammelled life in the Darejen castle.

A man wooed her, over a wall.

How she had feared him. He was so big. Like a wolf. Scarred. Terrible.

She gave way. She went with him.

Lillot hung from her bleeding hands, pierced by the knife. She hung and she dreamed, half dead.

She thought of how her mother had put on her a necklace of gold, and later how her mother had given her the golden sun of Marius. But these things she had left in fear, to go with the man. The man who was death.

She was a maiden, before he had her.

So cruel. Her mother had advised her. Men were not temperate.

It *hurt*.

And then, in the alien castle, where was she to turn? No one to tell her now.

Her mother . . . long dead.

It seemed to Lillot that her mother spoke to her from the bristles of the wicked pine.

'Don't be afraid.'

The nurses had washed her. Warm water and delicious herbs. Their sleek soft hands, sinless as fish along her sides.

And now. Such a thing. Warm and firm and good, the washing of the nurses.

Lillot smiled. Her uplifted face was full of trust.

The wolves licked her, ate her, devoured her. She felt only the marvellous washing of their tongues.

Growling, spitting, fighting, they rent out chunks of her flesh.

Lillot lay and knew only the beauty of truth, the washing, there and there.

Good girl, so the wolves sang to her. Their snouts in her vitals.

She felt only their love. Whose, otherwise, had she recently known?

She died, soft as a seed. And silent.

Vivia was dreaming of the Tower of Spikes. There were more bodies on it now. Half the inhabitants of the castle, it seemed, had been flung there. They hung, in humps and knots, some writhing slowly, some immobile. Some called and cried. But the sound was all one sound, amalgamated, and musical in a fearsome way.

The impression of the tower was of darkness, rippling a little here and there, making its melody. And through the tower's head light streamered.

The sky behind was white and faintly scrolled with cloud. Had snow fallen early? It appeared so, for the ground too, and the other hillocks of the castle, were white on black.

The ravens swarmed about the tower, feeding ceaselessly. It was also possible to hear the whirr of their wings, and sometimes one of them would caw.

Vivia saw the ravens fly back to their nests among the trees, carrying titbits of death.

The nests were made of wood and bone, and occasionally stolen jewels showed, glittering bright. The eggs of the ravens were a smouldering red, and from them the chicks had started to hatch out.

The raven chicks were not like their parents.

They were scaled not feathered, though black as ink. Red eyes gemmed their narrow heads. Their beaks were very long, and when they opened them, there were teeth inside.

The chicks took the titbits and next their parents off

the edges of the nests, hauled them inside and ripped them apart.

The children of the ravens ate them.

Black feathers gushed from all the trees like a black snow. Discarded claws lay on the white earth, one with a ruby stuck to it.

Vivia, in her dream, was walking under and among the trees, in the black and white snow. She was not afraid. She knew now death had passed her by.

Above her, the tower blotted on the sky. She did not look at it any more.

The death of others, maybe, had enabled her to survive. Could she say she was sorry?

A low wind blew among the trunks, fingering her skirt.

After all, she did turn, and look the way she had come.

Something flew, lower than the wind, among the stands of pines and larches. It was not to be seen. A vague shadow ran and swirled away, like dye in water. She heard the beat of its wings, massive, like a mechanism, not resembling the wings of the ravens which had been eaten in the nests.

Vivia ran, but she could not run quickly. In fact, she was running on the spot.

Dobromel sat some days with his back to the chamber wall, where a mural was of flowers in garlands. He gazed steadfastly at the bed.

The bride horse was no longer pale. It was a black horse now, raven black with flies.

Dobromel listened carefully to the flies.

Now and then a crowd of them would lift up and come to him, and he let them alight on his face and hands with great pleasure.

It was a pity the girl had not joined him here, but he had thought of her, and given his seed to God. He was glad and proud of this action, and drank wine.

He did not feel sick any more, not nauseous or hot or in any pain. He felt cool and reasonable.

The flies told him many things. How the world had

been made from a globe of dung, and how animals and
and men and women had sprung out on it, automatically,
like maggots.

They spoke of Heaven too, which was a glory of things
to feed on, honeycomb and rotting meat.

Sometimes they sang, and their voices were holy.

Never in his life had Dobromel the priest been so happy
as he was in the chamber of the flies.

At last a unique miracle was granted him.

A fly slipped into his mouth and, at its prompting, he
swallowed it.

Then it spoke within him, from his stomach.

'Dobromel,' said the fly, 'you are blessed among men.
You will see the kingdom of God, and sit among the
favoured at the right hand of the Lord.'

Dobromel wept for joy.

He slipped down the wall and lay now on his back, and
the fly went on talking to him softly, from his inside, until
the ceiling lifted up, and he beheld Paradise.

It was so beautiful. He could not begin to describe it,
even to himself. But he had earned it, and it would
be his.

He rose slowly into the sky, and when his body (poisoned and blown up to a prodigious size) burst like a
bloated grape, he was far away, he was in Heaven, where
the angels of the flies had taken him.

The castle was now only a rock. A tomb mounted on a
mountain side.

Nothing lived there any more, but for the wandering
dogs which ate the dead, the chickens and geese in the
yards. The horses had kicked down their stable sides, and
dashed away into the surrounding landscape, through the
handy spy door Javul's men had left open. The dogs and
other creatures would also eventually take this exit.

The land about was rife and empty of men. Soon the
crops would lean over and fall down in the autumn winds.
The river, densifying with storm rains, would sweep away
corpses that had dropped into it, and leave only their
skulls, like balls of glass, among the stones.

Through the dumbness of the villages the goats and sheep paraded, pulling at vines and flowers with their vegetarian teeth.

It was not yet time for snow, or for the red wolves to come this far, directed by the odour of carrion and winter hunger.

A strange country this, without human things.

Birds perched on the chimney holes and roofs, screeching derision, pigs padded through little chapels, knocking down the candlesticks, mouthing the incense.

Gales fled across the tall corn. Purple cloud crowded the sky. Apples and other fruit turned to coarse jammy wine in the grass.

A deserted place.

Like the end of the world.

Chapter Eight

HOW LONG HAD SHE BEEN here, in this darkness? She did not know. She should have kept a reckoning. Put by some small stones for each day – but then, how could she have told the days, the nights?

Vivia drank from the clear chain of water which fell from above into the pool.

She had been hungry, but that had gone away. She was seldom hungry. The lack of food did not bother her, except that now she felt a weakness. She was frightened of this, for it might mean that she was ill . . . She watched for signs in herself, but there were none. Her skin, in the subterranean light, did not have the look of *their* skins – bulbous, swarthy, shiny skins, swelling with inner bane –

Vivia walked round areas of the grotto, round, and in and out. Her only mirror now, the water.

She could not have been here so long. It was like endless time, an hour that began on her arrival and did not conclude.

Eventually, she would have to go back, up into the castle of her father, who was dead. Those who still lived would help her. Someone would help her.

Vivia paused, frowning. She acknowledged that terror was coursing through her, trying to reach her brain. She forced it down.

The words came unbidden: 'Don't let me die – '

But to whom did she address them? Not to the Christ, who was useless, not to God in whom she did not believe.

To the god Dobromel had spoken of? To that? Horned and winged. Yes, he did exist. She had heard him flying in the cavern, and in her sleep he had pursued her. She woke before –

She knew where he was, behind the curtain of the ivy, where she had always taken her offerings.

She walked, not quite steadily, between the broad pocks of water, through the interlocked ovals of the caverns. Ursabet had told her this place would safeguard her. And Dobromel, who was a fool, even he had come to know of the ancient thing that was here.

Why should she fear this god? Had she not always been polite and generous to him?

She delayed a few instants at the ivy. Then she drew it back and passed through.

There, in the wall of rock, it was. The beast of bones. Its vizored skull, remote and undeniable.

'Here I am,' she said.

She sat down before it, near to the fungus growth that she had created from her fruit and wine. A pink fragment of peach still curled there, fresh as if new. Her mouth watered. But when she put her finger on the peach, it went to liquid.

Vivia began to cry. She was not yet sixteen, and had held off her tears with slaps and pinches, all this while. Now it seemed wise to let him see, the creature in the wall.

'They died,' she said, 'don't let me die. You'll keep me safe – I always gave things to you. I knew you were here.'

But her tears stopped. She was so unused to weeping.

An eerie memory (Ursabet's tales) fluttered in her mind. She had nothing to give now except this one thing, which the old gods loved: blood. How to do this? She did not want to cut herself.

She opened her bundle, and took out the lip paint which, when once a festival had been celebrated, and travelling hawkers were in the castle yard, she had bought for a copper coin.

'Will this do?'

She coloured her mouth blindly. Then put the salve

at the foot of the bat god, just beyond the debris of the fruit.

She was being naive, or attempting to be, trying to pretend to a childishness which was not real. Trying to deceive.

But anyway, it had had blood. The blood that dripped through the roof of the caverns. Or had she imagined or dreamed this – those moving walls of bats, sipping and drinking? When she woke they were not there.

In the phosphorous glow, red looked black. Even her dress was the wrong colour. The lip paint was only muddy. It would not want that. *He* would not. But she had done her best.

She stood up, and as she turned, she heard again that ominous beating engine of wings.

It was some noise of the caverns. It was not the winged god coming. Vivia was cold as ice.

What was he? The Devil? Or was he, after all, Death himself?

She pulled aside the ivy, and as she did so, saw out into the cavernous area beyond.

Her heart stopped. For a moment there was no life in it, and then it began again with enormous thundering blows.

Something – something was there.

Across the floor of paved stones. Its reflection lay like a black pillar on the mirror of the pools. It was only that, an upright column of pure darkness.

Vivia stared. Her terror now was so vast it was no longer terror, but some other thing, essential, motivating.

The column of darkness moved.

It came gliding through the rocky bays of the grotto, through the teeth of the stalactites. It was not a shadow. Solid as black umber.

To her, it came to her, and she could only stand there, waiting. She had no voice. She had no means to run or even to throw herself down. She had turned to stone, and in the stone of her, her heart crashed on.

Then, in the approaching blackness, two scarlet candles

lit, high up. She knew that they were eyes. The eyes of the god.

It was near to her, it was only a foot away, and there it halted. She gazed up the height of it, into the scarlet flames of eyes. She heard it *breathe*.

And then it spoke. Not aloud. Not in any tone or timbre. The words were in her ears. That was all.

Who am I, Vivia?

Then she too could utter, if not with her voice, with her mind.

The god.

She listened to it breathing. It was like the sound of blood in the head, moving like a sea.

It said to her, *I'm death, Vivia. But not the death you fear.*

Then it came forward again and it enveloped her.

She was lost, she was adrift, in the air, weightless. She had shut her eyes. She felt an exquisite warmth, pressing at her, drawing on her, her throat and wrists, her ankles. Waves of sensation winnowed through her as if she were transparent, insubstantial, like lights and shades.

Now she lay on her back. In the blackness a silver thread seemed to be pulled out of her.

Ursabet said sternly, 'I've told you these sinful things I did. But it's not for you. You mustn't do anything like that.'

Was it this? Was the being making love to her?

It seemed so. And yet –

She was floating now on a lake of night. And then she was static, and the rocks hard under her.

Vivia glimpsed for a second the face of a man. But not of a man. The face of the god. Pale as death, with eyes that were at once burning red and black as nothingness, and which had in them stars. His pale mouth was stained darkly (like hers?). He had been eating plums. Drinking wine. She must have brought them, after all.

TWO

Chapter One

THROUGH A GOLDEN VEIL, THE light . . . a veil like the wings of bees. The window was high and arched, and a dusk sky rested in it like a pale blue egg.

She could smell the trees of the garden, the evening ripeness of the fruits, and the late flowers, the roses bathed all day by the sun. And other perfumes.

A young woman with a pretty face drew back an edge of the golden veil. Behind her, in the window, a pale mote.

Vivia acquiesced. Moonrise, of course. Once she had risen at sunrise, or so it seemed. She could just remember it.

A golden cup with a slender stem in the figure of an angel was offered her.

The wine was aromatic and delicious. Vivia drained the cup, and the girl filled it again from a ewer of white alabaster, inside which the drink was like a moving blush. Long ago, Vivia had seen alabaster in the hands of a priest. But now. These things were hers.

The room smelled beautiful, and as Vivia walked through it, naked, she saw her reflection pass three times in long polished mirrors. Another girl, pretty as the first, held back a curtain of green velvet. Beyond, the bathing chamber, with its marble tub filled by warm water, scented with herbs and essences. The girl coiled up Vivia's hair with silver pins.

Vivia washed herself. She was happy, excited. So that her stomach fluttered, yet pleasantly.

When she had bathed, they wrapped her in soft sheets that dried her with a caress.

The table was also marble, and here the fruit lay on dishes of enamel the colour of the dusk, which had deepened.

Vivia ate only a few morsels, counting the stars, which had begun to appear.

She noticed, as she did so, things in the room. For a moment they would seem quite new to her. Then, she would recognize them.

The bed was of mahogany under its bees-wing draperies. The footstool was a tortoise of gold with a shell of dark green velvet.

When the attendant drew the sheet away from Vivia, she was not concerned, as she had not been concerned to walk by them naked. They were her women. She did not know their names. But this did not matter. She had never known.

They brought a dress of golden tissue. It was like a priest's robe. Embroideries of pearl had made it stiff, and yet, on her body, it grew pliant.

They combed out her hair and wove into it little golden rings.

She was being prepared for a great occasion. What was it? She knew – yet did not know. She wished for it very much. Nothing worried her.

Lastly, before a mirror held in a frame like a snake of gold, one of the pretty girls powdered Vivia's face with a white silken powder, of which it seemed – for a second – she had only heard before, and then drew dark lines along her eyelids. Her mouth was coloured like the rose they put into her hands.

Descending through the castle.

Had she never before truly appreciated the elegance and finery of this house? Large windows set with panes of coloured glass in the shape of flowers. Statues of marble and bronze that had been garlanded. The stairs were wide, and presently she moved on one that had a carpet at its centre of crimson stuff. Signs of the Zodiac were woven in gold into the carpet. Vivia beheld Virgo, fire and ice, and the Scorpion – a sting.

People crowded the hall below, and they stood there smiling in a sort of golden mist from the gentle brilliance of the candles. Jewels flashed and silk rippled.

They were marvellous people, clean and couth, all clothed like lords. None was unshapely or slovenly. Some held musical instruments, some roses, as she did. Large dogs with shining hair and silver collars sat quietly. And here and there, on gemmed leashes, were other animals, great yellow spotted cats, such as someone had once told her of, and there a bird with a tail of emerald and sapphire.

Blooms burst up from golden urns, and from silver ones the smoke of incenses and gums lifted.

The light in the windows was almost gone, the clear panes showing blue as the richest indigo-coloured glass.

They had made a path for her. Now she remembered. It was her wedding day.

With a start of amazement, Vivia stopped still, and in that moment music played, and had she ever heard music like this? Surely she had.

Through the parting of the golden crowd, she began to see the man who was there before her, under the golden arch. There were two priests in white, and he was like the night between them.

She had seen him before. She had known him all her life. And that this hour would come. And she had longed for this hour.

His clothes were black, silken materials, with flakes of silver caught on them like rain. His black hair fell back from his face, clothing him again. It hung to his waist, long as her own.

His face had been in all her dreams. She had waited since childhood.

Like a painting on ivory. The eyes and brows long and black. The mouth long, formed as if by a brush. A face like a wonderful mask, a vizor of handsomeness, and of some strange motionless turbulence, enormous power held as if in a drop of crystal.

Vivia trembled. And he, he came down to her between the priests, between his court of men and women. He took her hand.

His touch – cool, vital. So charged with *life*.

He led her to the priests, who turned to them their thin saintly countenances – unlike his own.

Her wedding –

Not day but night.

Wedded to night.

Who was he? She did not know his name. Yes, she had waited so long, and yet never before – never had she seen him save in dreams, asleep or awake.

Would the priests speak his name? They did not. They sang ancient words that meant everything and nothing to her. She could not follow, yet she understood. And when they motioned to her, she said one word only, which was an assent. She said, Yes.

They crowned her with a golden crown, and him they crowned with another.

King and Queen. Husband and wife.

They sat in tall black chairs and the golden people were dancing in mellifluous groups on the mosaic floor, which showed pictures of some heavenly garden, perhaps as lovely as the gardens of this castle.

A leopard came to them, and he fed it from a silver dish. Vivia gave the leopard grapes, and it licked her fingers. The sensation of its tongue –

Was this a dream, after all?

Who was it had told her of leopards? An old woman who had been her servant. It occurred to her, she had had a father. Where had he gone?

Vivia could not remember him.

She turned to her husband, who had spoken to her quietly now and then, ordinary things, would she drink this wine? Would she eat this peach?

Vivia said, softly, 'I don't know your name.'

'But I told you.'

Abashed, she glanced away. The dancers flowed together and parted. In the ceiling above, some white birds were flying about.

Vivia felt a pulse of exaltation.

'You are the god.'

He looked at her, and his eyes were so full of darkness, she was spun away from them.

'King Death,' he said. She was not afraid. She did not believe him. 'Dance with me,' he said.

He drew her down, and the glowing people made them the centre of a ring. Here they stepped, and she did not falter, in the gestures of a dance she had never danced, or learned, or been told of.

But as they danced, he moved her away, and then a door was opened for them and a stair ran up between tall lamps of malachite – of which, maybe, she had heard.

King Death lifted Vivia in his arms as if she weighed less than the flower which she had dropped.

He carried her up and up, and as they went, it seemed to her the lamps depended now in starry space. Above was only a colossal night, jewelled with the planets. The constellations wheeled in silvery fire, Virgo the maiden dancing with the Scorpion in his crown of gold.

There was a bed. A bed in space. Its canopy was the whole sky of the world. Black, and stemmed with fires.

He had trodden through pools of stars.

He laid her there, on that bed; they were adrift, far up. Above the earth.

She saw his face hover over her. White as a moon. Carven like a skull or shell.

And suddenly she recalled the couplings in that other castle. The copulations of the damned. *Then*, she did fear.

'Don't – ' she said.

'Ah,' he said, 'do you think I could be like men?'

His face, the sum of all faces, came to hers. His smooth, firm, fashioned lips fastened upon her mouth.

Dry, warm kiss. And then a melting kiss. She opened to him like the rose.

He filled her.

Serpent, serpent within blossom.

Deeper and deeper he probed her. Like silk. Like a bee. Like her own soul.

Was this eating? He ate at her mouth. No tooth, no sharpness. All silk, velvet, fire, water, air.

Vivia raised her arms and caught at him.

But he was in the atmosphere. He lay *above* her. And now – *now* – she heard the fan of the vast wings. They beat. An engine. The power of him, beyond the power of his being. He rested over her, borne on by the vast black membranous sails which held him up.

His mouth clasped hers.

He fed from her lips.

Sweetness.

And then, she felt again, simultaneously with his kiss, his lips upon her breasts, as the tissue gown slid away, her skin . . . upon the diadems of her breasts, two tongues, firm and smooth, warm and insistent.

And upon her arms and torso, the tracery now of a hundred tongues, leisurely, savouring. *Tasting* her.

She was dissolved and consumed.

She felt his lips upon every inch of her. Her arms and belly, her fingers and her toes. Inside her spine and pelvis.

Last, his mouth upon her core. Upon her other lips. Upon the middle of her. Vulva, vagina. Limpid fire that stroked. Flame that lingered, dived, entered. But not as she had seen. A tongue like a snake.

She did not break. Virgo. Virgin. Too limber to pierce and tear the sheath. Rose within rose.

Vivia, writhing beneath the cloak of darkness, hung in space from the lamp of a single burning star.

He was all one *mouth*. A multitude of mouths. That licked and sampled, tenderly devoured, feeding on her honey.

For an instant, crucified by velvet in her every orifice, pore, secret part, the girl strained in ecstasy.

But then she was boneless and voiceless. Hung like the bed and the lamps from the star of joy.

She heard *his* voice, though all his mouth was on her, her mouth, her second mouth. *Vivia*.

He knew her.

She was his.

And then, against her throat, the first and only pain.
Two silver barbs entering. After all, a *penetration*.
Not only the juices of her willing body.
Her blood.
He drank her blood. As he had done before.
Her husband. Who was Death.

And now he raised her. Pulled her up by the grip of his arms.

She too flew in space among the lagoons of stars. Held fast.

She heard the silent cry of him.

Death, her husband: fulfilled.

Chapter Two

❦ THIS BED WAS OF BLACK velvet. Its draperies were black. She lay as if inside a womb of panther fur, lulled by the breathing of the beast.

But it was he who breathed. Her lover.

And – she lay upon him, on his body, her limbs stretched out over his, her belly on his groin, her breasts against his torso. Her head rested on his hair.

The scent of him surrounded her.

She had never smelled a man who had this tincture. Clean and sombre, panther pelt and cool skin.

She touched him. Under a robe of black, the white hardness of his body. His loins were hidden. She had never seen them. Perhaps . . . being a god, he was not like a man.

Vivia lay mesmerized, thinking that, but not afraid. Men were frightful. Even Ursabet's merry descriptions had perturbed her. And what she had seen –

She turned her face into his body. She wanted to know only him. She was safe, for he had rescued her. And she was his.

'For a little while,' he said. His voice was like a murmur of the air. Did the wings stretch behind him? She gazed and could not tell. Instead, his face looked down at her.

Could she be sure of his features? His beauty was all that was possible. The two nights of his eyes from which, endlessly, she slipped away, dazzled.

'But I'm yours,' she said.

'Yes.'

'Is this,' she said, childishly, 'your magic castle?'

'In a way.'

'Did you bring me here?'

'You were here already.'

She puzzled. She said, 'But we were in the underground caverns.'

'Look,' he said.

She turned and saw that from the ceiling an icicle of diamond hung straight down. And in it was a spider with red eyes. The web had been spun, and every filament pleated, salty with ice.

Vivia said, 'What is that?'

'We are in,' he said, 'a web of illusion. Which I made to please you.'

She felt a twinge of delight, that *he* had done something solely for her sake. At the same instant her heart shied with a start of dread.

'It isn't real?'

'None of it.'

Vivia sat up. She stared back at him. He lay behind her, black and white, his face like a silver mask of bones. Of course, he was the lord of the underworld. He was Death. He could transform all things.

'Do you want,' he said, almost playfully, she thought, 'to see the truth?'

'No, but show me.'

He lifted his strong slender hand, indicated everything.

Vivia beheld the caverns all about her. Black as night's source, yet lit by their eternal phosphorus. The funguses which gleamed and bulged. The waterfalls. It seemed to her the stalactites had been tinted red. Perhaps the blood, which had dripped in here, had coloured them and now she could make it out. They were, these fangs of stone, like teeth. The caves therefore were parts of a great mouth.

'And there,' he said. She saw a white frog sitting at the edge of a pool. 'Your pretty attendant by the marble tub.'

Vivia frowned. Even if for her pleasure, she had been made a fool of. Did he despise her then? He had said, *For a little while*.

'What am I to you?' she said.

'My need.'

'Am I your wife?'

'If you wish.'

'The priests were frogs too, or lizards. There wasn't a marriage. But – my blood.'

'I craved it,' he said. His face shifted almost imperceptibly, and there, she did see it, exactly, the face of bones which had been set into the wall.

She groped for fear. Fear did not come.

'What have you done to me?'

'Ruined you,' he said, 'and reformed you. Didn't the old nurse tell you stories?'

'Of demons who sucked blood,' said Vivia.

'Then she told you of me.'

'But – you are the god.'

'A god of darkness and vast hungers. Now you are a goddess. My wants will come to be yours.'

'I shall hunger for blood,' said Vivia. It was absurd.

She wrapped her arms about her body. She wore the red dress she had put on and her golden ornaments, which in the phosphorescent light seemed tarnished.

They had lain on a bed of luxuriant wet moss.

A pale snake coiled away under the glacial ferns.

It was cold.

'You came to me,' he said. 'This happens. I took what you gave. Now, as you willed, you'll always be young, and beautiful, and you need never be afraid of death. You sought me for these gifts. In your new life you will taste fruit and sip wine and crumble a little bread into your mouth. But for your sustenance, it will be blood.'

'And I must lie in the grave,' said Vivia, still frantically searching for her fear. 'The sun will scorch me up.'

'The sun,' he said, 'will depress you. You won't like the sun. But it can't turn you to stone or dust. You'll like to live by night. You'll see the stars in heaven that others have no eyes for, and the moon will burn brightly.'

'You've amused yourself with me,' she said.

'And you have called me King Death.'

She looked back at him, and in his hand was a crimson

rose. It was huge and flawless, every petal shaped as if by some master artisan.

'More illusions,' she said.

'Take the illusion.'

Vivia obeyed him. She took the rose, and lifted it. It had a strange hot smell in the cold of the caves. It brushed her mouth and broke. She felt the burning blood go over her lips and down her chin.

Not repelled, only curious, she licked out her tongue.

What was it? It had no taste, and yet – She raised her hand, in the cup of which all the blood had gathered, and drank it down. No more than water. Yet water in thirst. It was not water, but fruit. It was wine. She must have more –

'There will be more,' he said.

She said, 'Must I go up and prey on those creatures in his castle?'

'Time has passed in the castle,' said the vampire who was a god and Death. 'Did you want to see?'

Struggling with the thirst, which now was fading, reluctant to let it go, she flung round to struggle also with him.

'I don't want – '

'The world,' he said, 'you must have the world.'

And then he sprang right off the couch or rock, and she noted the awful magnificence of the feathers and pinions unfolded. She was carried as the girls were in Ursabet's tales, by her prince with wings.

Illusion or reality?

The ceiling of the cavern parted like a thunder cloud –

The doggess was feeding, slowly, upon the marrow of a bone. It had been human once.

She had known many things, this brindle bitch dog. She had been a favourite, a hunter, dragging down the wild pig of the woods, courageous. They had petted her and made her gifts, the bowels of hunted things, a silver collar.

Then came the time when she grew older. Not loved then.

They did not cast her out. Let her feed upon the scraps.

Sometimes the younger males would bring her some titbit. They did not mount her. She was done.

Her self-esteem dropped in the castle of Vaddix, whose name and wars she was too elderly to know.

Then came the plague.

She saw, the doggess, her masters fall. The young dogs fed on them when they were dead, and all day, all night, the castle rang with howling. And in the open valleys beyond, wolves howled too.

She waited. And in the end she crept to take her share.

An old human doggess lay in a fine room where a mirror was upon a crouching lion. The bitch doggess did not notice this.

She dragged the rotted stuff and pulled it out, and ate it, piece by piece.

Poor things.

Last of all were the bones. They were good. Enough youth left in them to be toothsome.

She fed slowly.

And presently in the awful cold a warmth came that reminded her sullenly, suspiciously, of spring. And she wagged her moth-eaten tail.

But something came up and was there. Something not dead, nor human.

The doggess growled, and with her bone, she ran away.

Vivia stood and saw the room which had been her apartment.

They had dragged out Ursabet after all. And Ursabet was eaten. Even the bones had fang marks.

Vivia went into the room.

How cruel, unkind of him, to bring her here, to this.

The snow had come and covered the earth. And into the castle also, the snow had passed, through wide windows.

Now, upon the floor, white drifts, dirtied slightly by the passage of paws and dusts. Not melted.

Frost on a mirror.

She cleared it with one finger.

Vivia saw her face and gasped. *Gasped* at her own loveliness. She lived. She was alive.

She turned, and looked – for him. And in an incoherent shadow, thought she saw him.

'Nothing left,' she said.

He did not – no one did – answer.

Vivia walked to the window. Over the snow-hulled humps of the castle, an ice-world. Sky like wadding. No sun.

But, he had said, she would not like the sun.

She came from her room, the room which had been hers, feeling nothing. Or perhaps feeling the accustomed boredom. The menace of mundane death was everywhere, but did not matter to her.

Through the castle she went. In her red dress like blood.

In corridors where the white snow heaped. Through chambers of bones, not so white, gnawed and scattered.

The other dogs had gone away. It was empty here. A dismal venue.

It occurred to her, *he* was no longer with her. She stopped and called. Not his name – he had given her no name. *'Where are you?'*

An echo slewed madly through the castle. From everywhere at once. But it did not reply.

Alone, she went on. She entered the chapel. So many rats, all bones now. And the halls of the castle all bones, and red cloths pulled askew, and one dead dog, frozen. Had the others killed it?

She saw, from the terrace. the Spike Tower.

It was white now with snow, and underlined in dark by what jumbled beneath.

'Where are you?'

She wandered. She was alone. Had she dreamed it all, and survived merely by her flight into the grotto – where nothing was but fossil things?

Bones by the gates, thick in snow. A skull on a mound, winking at her with one snow-closed eye.

The ravens had flown away.

Yet a distant howling lifted. The red wolves, in the valleys.

'You need never fear an animal,' he said.

He was beside her, there on that battlement in the cold-blasted nothing of the winter day.

'How long did you have me?' she asked.

'Days and months. Enough.'

'I don't feel the cold.'

'You do. But it can't harm you.'

Vivia shivered, contrasuggestively.

They walked together, down through the castle of her dead father, and moved out by that narrow spy door. The horses had vanished from the yard, like the dogs.

The world was white.

White upon stalks of black, the trees. And black runnels, fine drawn on the lost fields.

She thought he did walk, as she did. A prince in a cloak of heavy fur (the wings?) and black boots. They came down into the valley where the river was.

He showed her. Blue opal fish caught in the slick of the ice.

Vivia gazed, and thought, was she such a fish, caught in time, saved and exquisite, so lovely and so strange?

She said, 'What will become of me?'

He said, 'What will become.'

And then she looked up, and a pack of the red wolves was bounding to them, fast as a red wind, over the plain of snow.

He had said, there need be no fear. But would he give her to such beasts, let them feed on her? Himself laugh, or sigh.

She clutched at his arm, and it seemed real, flesh and muscle, bone and blood, all that had been destroyed in the castle.

He let her hold on to him.

The wolves raced up.

The wolves were all about them, a tide of dull russet hair. The snouts were long, and at their edges the terrible sabre teeth had sprouted. Their eyes were yellow, appallingly intelligent, uncaring and insane.

She had seen such eyes in the faces of men.

But he. He merely stood and let them come, and the

wolves, even the massive ones among them, tall at the shoulder almost as a horse, did not try any attack.

They were silent, too. Yet a kind of sound seethed over them, like a high thin whistling. Their yellow eyes were on him.

She thought, would he feed her to them?

He said, and now it came to her that he had no voice, it had remained a music in her head: 'No. Not you. But they're hungry.'

The god – the vampire – raised his arms. Sleeves like black rain washed back.

The ice of the river cracked, and splintered.

There came a noise like the rushing of water.

From the depths of the river, the fish leapt. They vaulted out in arcs like aquamarine fire, and snowed upon the banks.

The red wolves reared, their snouts snapping.

Fish glanced like swords into the mouths of the wolves, and were trampled by their teeth.

Vivia watched in amazement.

The storm of fish –

She thought of the scriptural text, how Marius had fed the multitude beside the sea, with loaves and fishes, but some, the wicked, received serpents.

The wolves guzzled on the snow, which was rosy now, stained by the pallid blood of the fishes.

Then *he* called.

One wolf, a huge animal, like a rusty nightmare, turned and padded to him.

It thrust its head into his hand.

She recalled the leopard. 'Touch him,' he said. She recoiled. 'Their kind,' he said, 'are now your slaves.'

Still she could not extend her hand, and the wolf looked up suddenly, right at her, with eyes of brimstone and honey.

'*Touch him.*'

Vivia put out her hand and let the wolf mouth it. Her legs gave way, and as she sagged into the snow, the wolf caught her against itself, supported her.

Its breath was fishy, like a house cat's.

It licked her neck.

Vivia turned, and took the wolf's ruffed throat. She bit into it under the jaw, tasted its raw feral smouldering juices.

The wolf fell over in the snow, offering her all its throat and belly, and Vivia stood up. She spun about and sped away.

Up on the tower, Vaddix lay over backward, arched, his head dangling. He no longer had eyes. But, through the weave of snow, he looked at her.

'Where's my wife?' said Vaddix.

Vivia said, 'I don't know, father.'

'I wed her, she's mine. I killed them all, the shit.'

Vivia wilted. She thought of the horse of bone in the House Tower.

'This is death then,' he said, 'is it?' He was conversational, as he had never been in life.

'Please,' she said, foolishly.

But he did not respond. Had she offended him – or hallucinated?

Vivia returned into the castle, and sat down at the hearth of the lower hall.

What must she do?

She did not feel the cold. She had drunk blood from the throat of a wolf – the blood of men . . . would not be like this.

She thought of her mother. Of Ursabet. But there was not enough of them to get hold of.

Something traversed the hall.

Vivia looked. It was an old and mangy dog. A female, limping.

Was it dangerous? No. The wolf had been her subject.

'Come here,' Vivia said, and the doggess limped towards her and waited there, with the slow tail flickering, while at the same moment she growled.

Vivia tapped her. 'Quiet.'

The doggess lowered her tail and her noise, and sank down at Vivia's feet.

He was not with her, again. Since she had left him

would he discard her? She had heard the dead speaking, perhaps.

He was only a dream? A demon.

None of it was true.

Chapter Three

✤ But that night he flew with her up into the sky. Or, it seemed so.

He appeared before her now out of a low dark mist which had crept in along the floor. She was aware of it, half thinking it was natural. But the doggess growled again.

Vivia rose. And so did the mist. Up into a column, like smoke, which hardened. And there he was. Her prince.

'Why did you leave me?' she said.

'You ran away.'

'Did I,' she faltered, 'did I drink the blood of the wolf?'

'Yes. It let you. Animals will always feed you. But they won't be enough.'

'Am I already changed?' she asked.

'You know that you are.'

'But you – what are *you*?'

'Not what you see.' He was languid, more like a hero in a tale than ever before. The fading white daylight did not show through him, was only in his eyes, in two luminous slim crescents.

'A ghost,' she said.

'Energy,' he answered, carelessly. She had never really heard his voice.

To what then could she compare him? The storm, lightning, fire? Yet he was so still.

'Why did you come?' she said.

'You called me, Vivia. And all that welter of blood.'

'Before that?'

'Nothing. A sleep. Or, what you would take for sleep.'

The doggess had skulked away, going almost on her belly, sideways, and tail down, back across the hall to another doorway.

'You frightened my dog away.'

'She isn't yours.'

'No. I didn't like the dogs. But –' Vivia fell silent.

Then he came to her and was before her, this prince who had no form or substance, was light and shadow and air.

She tried again to look into his eyes. Again, failed.

'In my sleep hereafter,' he said, 'your memory.'

Yet she might imagine all he said, putting the words into his unheard voice, from fragments of Ursabet's stories – what she wanted or dreaded to hear.

'You'll leave me,' she whispered. It struck her how commonplace she was, to sound so sulky. In the midst of *this*.

And he only put his hands on her waist and turned her about. And they walked up from the hall, up through the castle of snow and bones.

The dull day was quenched as they stood on the high terrace. She saw it go from the snow-capped trees of the garden, from the towers.

Nothing moved but the day, slinking off. After it had sunk down behind the horizon, the snowy world became slatey blue and the sky the same shade.

How bleak and vast it was, that lonely region. Never before had Vivia acknowledged the desolation of the spot, and the heartless crags of the mountains rising, only another deadlier blue, behind everything.

She would like to go away from here.

As night expunged the blueness, transparent streaks of new snow started to fall.

The vampire prince stretched out his hand, and in the palm he caught one of these parings. He showed it, unmelted, to Vivia.

And for the first time, with a wild alien vision, she saw its shape, intricate as embroidery on a festive gown.

'Each one,' he said, 'is like that. Yet not the same.

They touch the earth and vanish. Others replace them and vanish also.'

Vivia thought of the bones in the castle. They were so alike. She knew none of them – not even Ursabet.

'You,' he said, 'will never come to that. Your fall is eternal. No arrival. No vanishment.'

For a second she glimpsed it – eternal life. And she laughed out loud in a malice of greed and power.

But the snowflake had melted in his hand at last.

The moon blew up on ruffled wings of wind. The moon was blue as the sky had been before the night.

'I'll show you,' he said, 'kingdoms of the earth.'

'Like the Devil.'

Pleased to have given him back a concrete title, she rested in his arms as he raised her.

They flew upwards.

And she wondered, though she heard the beat of his wings, though she felt the muscles close and expand in his chest against her back, she wondered at this latest illusion, for surely it was nothing else.

A golden meteor flashed across the black sky behind the snow. Vivia exclaimed.

Then they were miles up, and the land had opened under them.

The castle, tiny, a mere outcrop of the mountains. The mountains themselves like citadels, framed and drawn in by snow. Then a frozen river that hung in a curtain like glass between two peaks.

And higher still they climbed, effortless, on his black pinions.

The mountains flattened now, folded like monsters changed to granite. Forests spread in black waves. The land descended in a hundred white pure steps towards a waste of darkness.

At its edge, a glittering mirror, on the rim of which lay opaque shoals of ice. They swooped, but lifted.

'Is it the sea?'

'One sea,' he said.

'Take me nearer,' she said.

'Not yet,' he said.

They flew across savage winter, and she saw the glints of miniature lights, which were here a village, and there a town or city, fuming in a mauve haze amid the snow.

She saw a wide road that was like a thread, but a thread which had been sequined. Lamps stood along the way for a great distance.

'Go down, let me see.'

'Not yet,' he said again.

Dizzy and elated with the freezing flight, she thought and hoped that perhaps he meant she would herself seek these things – the lighted road, the cities, the sea. Without him, of course.

She saw an open place. There were humps in the earth. Stone things stood there. It was gone.

They were gliding back, downward.

The castle was there once more, looming and ugly and unwelcoming.

She saw the Tower of Spikes in its conglomerate of corpses and snow.

They alighted on the terrace.

Vivia said angrily, 'Why won't you stay with me?'

'In a way, I shall.'

Far off, or near – for the world deceived – a wolf howled like an instrument of iron. Others chimed behind it.

She did not need to fear the wolves.

'But men,' said Vivia, 'people will try to destroy me.' She had the stories firmly in her mind. 'They'll hack off my head – burn me –' terror enveloped her.

'No,' he said.

'But how can I escape?'

'By living.'

'But if – fire can kill me after all.'

'Nothing can kill you, Vivia. Nothing. Can fire kill fire?'

'I don't understand.'

She looked at him, and he was only like a column of darkness again, a pillar of night.

If she herself invented these words for him to say, then she must know –

He was enigmatic. He did not answer her questions properly. A tiresome adult with an inquisitive child.

But he had said she would not die.

'Make love to me,' she said. She flinched, and turned away. 'My lord.'

He said, 'All your blood's gone, Vivia. You have something else now. I've had all I want.'

She remembered her ecstasy in his embrace. The mouths and lips and tongues, the pain of his vampire kiss, which, it seemed, had drained her at once.

Her father had drained the silly girl Lillot and cast her aside. Now she –

'You must,' she said.

Could she force him to her will? If her own will had called him, created him . . .

He was a man, who took her hand, and led her again into the castle.

Nothing moved there now. In the darkness she could see very well, as if the phosphorus of the caves was burning there.

And where the moon shone in, a thousand candles seemed to sparkle, blue candles with magenta shadows.

To her own bedchamber they went, and he drew her to the narrow bed.

'This is the last time,' he said.

'No. You're mine,' she said.

'No one's. But also yours.'

She was naked in the snow-covered room and felt no cold. She was warm from his touch. Under the lapis lazuli candles of the moon.

Serpents traced down her sides, the hollows of her arms and knees. The flames flowered on her breasts. Inside her lower gates, twice over, the honeyed lapping.

Orgasm swept her up in a rush and she plummeted through space. But now there were no wings. She missed the hurt of his teeth in the vein of her throat. She wanted the bite of the demon.

Floating back, she lay beneath him, and stroked his body which, possibly, had no organ, no penis. She stroked him, and felt the smooth long muscles, the area in his back from which the huge wings emerged, but there was nothing there, nothing at all. He seemed human.

And then, she was caressing only the warm air, which gradually, spitefully, went chill. Empty.

He was gone. Again, he had abandoned her.

The last time, he had said.

Vivia wandered the castle.

She was not searching for him.

She called for the dog, not by name, for the dog had no name for her, as he had none. And the dog did not come.

In the dining hall Vivia paused.

She closed her eyes against the moon and willed an illusion.

When she looked, it was there. The moon was yellow now, and lit everything like a noonday sun. The draperies were all in place, gorgeously red. White cloths covered the tables, and a plate of fruit lay out, green apples and pink peaches, pears, cherries. And there was a silver cup on a tall stem, and in the cup a deep red liquid which was not wine.

Entranced Vivia gazed about. Golden spiders wove silver tassels in the ceiling. Music was playing, lutar and drum.

Rage came in its turn and Vivia clapped her hands.

Everything flew up in a cloud like bats. Rags of scarlet and gold. Vanishing like snowflakes.

The silver chalice was a skull. The plate of fruit a bone.

The winter night was settling in as if for a hundred years.

Things cracked and the beams groaned. Snow slid in at the windows over the blue moonlight.

The girl walked back to her apartment and sat down before the lion mirror, on which the ice was now thick, a glass before a glass.

She saw herself as if inside a frozen lake, trapped as the fish had been before the vampire drew them up to death.

She was not cold or hungry. She was not afraid. Not even really angry, bitter or ill-used.

What did she want? Was it only to sleep? That might be

best. Sleep away the frigid night, and in the dawn, when
and if the sun came, then she could see if she hated it
or not.

Where had he gone to? Back into the earth. It would
be pointless to go down into the grotto, the region of
his being. All that was over. It was as if she had been
removed in time, by many years, from the moment of his
manifestation and of his departure.

Vivia stole about her bed, lay down on it. She pulled the
coverlet casually up to her knees. She did not need a covering, and in any case, strips of ice had gathered on it.

Her hair plumed over the pillow.

She heard her father, dimly, from up on the spikes.
But it was as if he spoke in another language, the language of death which, now, she could no longer, ever,
understand.

In the morning she might go down to the nearest village.
Maybe some of them had lived. They would know her, the
lord's daughter.

And the sun – would not smite her.

But the moon – was beautiful.

Chapter Four

✺ HAVING ELUDED THE CASTLE, THE doggess limped down the slope and away into the winter country.

She could smell the wolves on the night wind, but they were males, and probably would not be offended by her. Besides, they had fed, and fed very well. The fishy reek was lush in their breath, which blew around her head like the wind.

But, when she had gone some way, and was among the valleys, under the slanted shadows of the snow-deformed trees, the red wolves came and gathered round her.

She waited, trembling, her impoverished tail wagging placatingly.

The wolves grumbled, panted.

Then five of them came up to her, and this would be death. But death nudged her and licked her, they were making peace. After which, they pushed her on, the way she had been going.

So she passed, unaware, the bone heaps of Javul's knights down deep in snow, and finally reached a pine tree like a spine of snow. And on this hung the upper bits of a skeleton, its palms crossed under the knife which impaled them to the tree. Lillot's blonde hair coiled still from her skull. Not till the spring would birds come to gather it.

Just beyond this place, an old, old creature, a gigantic wolf, came out of a rock, one of a series of caves in the mountain side, and he, limping as the doggess had, approached her.

The doggess ran back a little and snatched a bone (one of Lillot's) out of the snow. Then she crept to the giant wolf on her belly, and presented this prize.

The wolf was scarred, but the escort of five young wolves who had brought the doggess there bowed to him, avoiding his eyes in a token of respect.

The old wolf licked at the doggess' spontaneous present. Then he went off and dug up out of the snow the large leg bone of a man. And this he brought to *her*.

As she wondered over it, the old wolf went round to the back of her, wetted her genitals courteously with his tongue, then mounted her.

The doggess bore his weight and the pain of his attention. The male dogs had never wanted her. Now, before his subjects, the old wolf made her his queen.

He finished quickly, with a little whine, swung off and went to urinate against the pine tree.

Gravely the doggess gnawed at the leg bone he had given her. It gave easily, for her teeth were still good, and the rich marrow ran into her mouth.

BOOK TWO

The Queen of Night

ONE

Chapter One

THE SKY WAS ROSE-RED WITH a long sunset that had begun at noon. The smokes of the fires had caused this phenomenon, and the mists rising from the blood-soaked mud of spring.

West, the range of mountains was at its most surly and dominant. North, south, east, they lay or seemed to lie flatter and farther off. The plain was wide, and spread now with the panoply of the battle. The air blistered with sounds.

Through the red mists, the whirling devils were coming down from the advantage of the hill.

As their wheeled sleds rolled them forwards, the poles, six feet in height, rotated the conical plates of their heads. Rods of iron and steel, chains and barbs, spun out and round, rending and whipping and ripping and severing. They passed among the ranks of the enemy, some of whom fled screaming. Others were felled and the devils trundled across them, a quantity bumping and overturning. Clockwork, they were unguided, of limited use, but quite effective.

The porcupines had gone before, each a barrel bristled by steel, between two runners. These, as they somersaulted, bringing down horses and men, became quickly glutted with trophies of blood and flesh, and finally, too clogged to move, squealed to a standstill. They were everywhere to be seen along the ground, with here and there groups of their victims beside them, mutilated and mostly dead.

For their part, the foe had been at the usual practice, crucifying those they could get hold of, hammering them up on pine and fir trees, or on stakes planted in the wet soil beforehand.

The prince had ordered already two volleys of crossbow shots to put such poor unfortunates (his own men) out of their misery.

Now Zulgaris rode along the incline. Fifteen knights, his Companions, kept up with him.

From the ridge above, a quartet of cannon spoke. The balls roared over in an arch of darkness and struck bright somewhere among the enemy ranks.

Zulgaris reached the emplacement of the ballistas.

He reined in, and the war-trained horse stood steady under him. It was a golden horse, the colour of some saffron wood. These horses were bred especially for the prince, to match him. For he too was golden. His long hair, thick as gilt fringe on a priest's robe, hung below his shoulder blades.

He looked about, stilly, waiting as the men scrambled up and down to him.

Zulgaris' face was very handsome, yet quirkish, the nose crooked from an accident in childhood or adolescence, the mouth also out of true, like a clown's mouth, but a handsome clown. Beneath gilt brows, two large tawny eyes, nearly the yellow of his hair.

The men kneeled in the mud. On every shoulder, the flash of the prince's heraldic colour.

'Time for it, I think.'

'*She's* been calling for it,' said one of the ballista crew, with a grin. He pointed off to the high platform, a kind of tower, on which a small figure waved its arms and railed against the prince's opponents, voice like a rat's squeak.

'Yes, she's bloodthirsty, our Witch. I'd have spared them, but they refuse to give in. These savages never know when they're beaten.'

Zulgaris scanned the field.

Under, somehow caught *in*, the rose sky, it boiled with turbulence, smoulder, fighting and dying.

Already the perfumed bolts had been loosed on them. Zulgaris considered this a preliminary, a sort of fore-play, and sometimes it had worked. It was frighten-ing. As each bolt went home in man or animal, the tiny phial exploded, and attars burst into the atmos-phere.

Perishing, live things went down, scented like the gardens of God. The pefume mingled with the stench of broken intestines and abdominal blood, with shit and excrement of all types, and formed a miasma worse than anywhere, any pit or sewer ever dreamed of.

This would dismay.

But it was often not enough.

And today these arrogant barbarians, this evil wretch of a lordling, that Zulgaris had come here to destroy, would not give in.

They had sent cannon balls, fusillades of shards and missiles. Thick smokes. And now, as the Witch upon her tower – and even the Witch alone had sometimes won Zulgaris' battles – as she had demanded, now they must send against their adversaries (beasts uncivilized, who crucified fallen men) the globes of poison.

Zulgaris spoke a few religious words, and crossed himself. He had begged God's pardon.

But God knew, the mountains were thick with these terrible, ignorant men, cruel and rapacious as the red wolves that also laired here.

Zulgaris had, this season, set himself to root the tyrants out. Out of their castle fastnesses which bulged with loot – Zulgaris took this. Where they surrendered, he led them away in chains. But few had done so. Only a month it had taken him, to come so far. Success on success.

The knights in their yellow velvets and polished steel had already trotted their horses back, and Zulgaris went with them. He signalled to the captain of the ballista crew.

The long arms of the ten gaunt machines were cranked back by their ropes.

Down the plain, Zulgaris' own men saw, and began

to run home towards them, away from the spot where
retribution was due to descend.

The ropes were released.

With a skriking groan, the ten arms flew head-foremost,
and crashed into their buffers.

A glittering rain – like great bubbles, weightless – went
sailing away across the rosy field.

She had no name, they called her for what she was: the
Witch.

She pranced now about her platform, craning to see.

Sometimes her imprecations were enough. She cursed
an enemy and the men fell vomiting and swooning on the
ground, and would not fight.

She was an awful sight. Her black hair like serpents,
standing up in writhings, quivering and seeming to hiss.
She was in her latter years, thin as a stick. Her skin was
smooth on her bony face and arms. But for the deep
grooves beside her mouth and in her neck, she might
have been some hideous elderly girl.

Her face was all points. Her nose like an owl's beak. Her
long teeth, which had decayed, had been dug out by steel
and set with small emeralds, topazes and rubies. Through
her right ear passed a snake of silver that dripped to her
shoulder.

Her eyes were thin and long, pale in colour, perhaps
grey, or only *white*.

She shrieked at the bubbles of death and raised her arms
so her bracelets and talismans chattered.

Then she ran against her parapet and poised there
motionless, coiled up tight, to watch.

The first globe came down.

It smashed against the side of a hill, where men, engaged
in fighting, did not all at once see. Some did turn at the
impact, and gaped. Others roiled over it, struggling.

A new smoke began to come up, the alchemical gases
in the globe mixed now with open air. Such globes might
be carried, harmless as flower buds, days and months
and miles. One crack, and a score of men could die.
It had happened – Zulgaris' own troops – a wagon

rolling over. The horses had been led to safety. Men in the way –

It was happening now.

Across the distance, the Witch watched avidly. She put the lens of her spy glass to her stronger eye.

The combatants in the lens – a man of Zulgaris' army, who clearly had not realized, and the enemy, some ruffian in bear furs.

Their tussling interrupted. The furred man coughing and blood coming from his mouth. The other one turned in horror, noted, and tried to run away.

The Witch saw him so perfectly.

His face was a white slab that broke suddenly into blotches. He cupped his throat and fell face down on the blotched white face.

Other globes had fallen by now.

The smokes were various.

Some attacked the lungs, some the stomach. Others the skin.

The Witch watched as men abandoned the battle to tear chunks off their bodies, shrieking. She saw their eyes boil, and smiled her green, red and yellow teeth.

Zulgaris from the slope took in the scene.

'A pity,' said Zulgaris. 'I could have taken more.'

Earlier he had ridden about the field, guarded by his knights, but generally quite careless. A wild man had rushed at him, drawn maybe by the golden colours of horse and rider, to know *this* was the prince. Zulgaris had slipped the sword from his side and clipped off the fool's head, even as he tried to run up the side of the golden gelding.

As he went about, Zulgaris had pointed out certain men, wounded a little, incapacitated, but likely to survive.

'That one, there. And him. He's strong.'

The servants who ran behind the horses, under cover of the knights' attention, dragged up the selected persons on to whippy stretchers of spring boughs.

These rescued were taken away, up among the tents of Zulgaris' army, safe behind the battle lines. Later . . .

Later Zulgaris would go among the men and see what use they might be to him.

Science was his passion. The spiritual science of alchemy. He knew very much.

His army cleaved to him, knowing he was supreme, clever, perhaps unassailable and blessed of God.

Some, it was a fact, were dying now, through their faith. They should have been more wary. They had known the gas globes would be loosed, most probably.

The further heights, up against the shadow of the western mountains, were wreathed now in fantastic colours. A fog of brass and mauve and green and amber-red.

Men staggered from this place, and fell.

'Soon be over,' said Zulgaris' First Knight.

'Yes, Demed. After all, it's never long.'

'Savages,' said another.

Zulgaris said softly, 'But we've killed them. Now only that other one to confront.'

Already, while men choked and died, planning the next fight.

'We haven't used our leopards.'

'They'll be jealous. Fretful.'

Zulgaris said, 'When the smokes fade, once it's safe, perhaps, let them go. They can tidy up the field.'

And half an hour after, by the careful hourglass, when the gases of the globes had gone to nothing, Demed and three others rode laughing along the line of cages, and let out the favourite leopards.

Yellow as Zulgaris' livery, spotted with night, they padded up and down the stretch before the tents, the catapults and cannon, preen-sheened and casual in light armour, breast, belly and forehead, and the lower stalks of their swift legs.

Glaucous stones glimmered in their head-pieces.

They scented the blood, as they had done since midday, but also the acrid after-taste of the deadly smokes.

Zulgaris laughed too. He strode among the leopards, roughly fondling their hound-like heads.

'Go, my damsels. Take what you want. The battle was beneath you and everything is safe.'

The sleekest, Talia, bounded from the slope and away.

One by one the other beasts followed her. They were all females.

They sprang among the finish of that small war, finding men who could not move to fasten on with razorous white teeth.

Talia herself, most brave, ran up into the dead halo of the gas.

She walked there about the dead she did not fancy. They were a gruesome sight. A terrible sight. But they did not interest her very much.

Among the rocks below, she found however a boy of thirteen who was not dead and who tried to beat her off. Talia killed him, breaking his neck, and fed, for form's sake. But she preferred, by now, the delicacies of Zulgaris' table.

The sunset, by contrast, was inky, the sun a single rent of virulent orange.

By then the last prisoners had been taken and killed, beheaded by an axe which, gradually blunting, took two or three blows to accomplish its task.

Zulgaris heard of this and reprimanded the axeman. The axe was sharpened and did better.

They would ride to the tyrant's house at sunrise and see what might be had there.

They fed, the army of Zulgaris, very well, and barrels of wine were opened. There was no brawling, only a steady procession to and from the tents of the whores. Zulgaris, although he risked and disciplined his men, believed in treating them otherwise indulgently.

In the large yellow tent, with its straps of gold and black, Zulgaris dined among his captains and his knights, the fifteen Companions, the fifty-odd lesser warriors.

Roast kid came on silver skewers, white bread, purple wine that had a scent of flowers, not the rough vinegar served outside.

Zulgaris fed Talia from his dish. She had on her evening wear, a collar of green stones set in chains of gold, and on her right foreleg, a golden anklet with a bell.

The Witch did not enter the tent. She was up on her platform, divining with dead men's bones.

'It will be a rotten place tomorrow,' Demed said. His tunic was patterned with golden roses and his shirt was silk. The campaigns of Zulgaris had made Demed rich.

'Yes, no doubt hardly worth a visit. But we must finish what's begun.' This from Kazun, one of the four knights of the second rank of Companions.

Zulgaris let them argue it over.

They would be going, anyway, to the stone house in the valley where this latest tyrant, whose name Zulgaris had even forgotten, had had his stronghold. The house would be razed or at least gutted, and the servants and children taken. The lesser women his men might have. They did not always seem, he thought, to mind it, and often ended as the army's resident prostitutes.

The better women Zulgaris made a practice of giving to female religious houses. Here they became the drudges of the nuns. He also made gifts to nunneries and priest-houses, large showy items, gold suns and painted icons which he himself found vulgar.

After the sack of the tyrant's castle, they would march on, towards the last monster Zulgaris' campaign had planned to overthrow.

This man's name Zulgaris did recall.

There had been another nest, but they had seemed likely to give in, the Darejens. The worst and most feared lord of the area was the other one. Vaddix.

Zulgaris had heard many dire things of Vaddix, which had whetted Zulgaris' appetite.

They were perhaps four days' march away from that castle. The mountainous terrain might slow them down.

Then again, there was a story that Vaddix had destroyed the Darejens, and thereafter some curse had befallen him and his people. Some bane the Darejens had cast, just as the Witch was supposed to be able to do.

Curses were sometimes effective, Zulgaris understood. Not through any intrinsic power, but because of the occasional credence of those against whom they had been directed.

Zulgaris mused, thinking of Vaddix. Zulgaris would like to capture this man. He was reportedly hugely strong and tall. A debased, almost subhuman prize.

The name-forgotten tyrant of today lay aside from the other heap of corpses, which already fastidiously they were burning.

Headless (but with the head an accessory in a sort of cage) the tyrant's body would be paraded before his household. So Zulgaris had seen to them all.

It was only Vaddix he would like to keep. To make one with his other exhibits, perhaps, or for more complex uses . . .

Near midnight, Zulgaris walked about his camp. Demed and Kazun moved behind him. It was almost a ritual, this. Drunk men stood up and cheered. A boy ran to kiss Zulgaris' rings. Those with any grievance were too lessoned to offer it.

Away against the dark sky and the line of mountains, the big piles of dead burned redly, with the faint tasty smell they always had.

Nearer, the Witch had her brazen cauldron full of fire that now and then flushed green.

She leaned down to Zulgaris.

'King among men!'

She always flattered. He had given her status, and in her dry locked loins, she lusted for his beauty.

He saluted her and went on, to the black tent that lay behind the yellow.

The two knights stepped aside.

Five men, who guarded the black tent, let down their lances, and Zulgaris walked by and in.

A makeshift, this, for the march. But he had done, and witnessed, even so, interesting things in this pavilion.

Bronze lights burned on stands, and there the physician stood ready, his bowls and knives to hand.

One of the prisoners had died, and they had pulled a sheet over him.

Another was sitting up. He looked promising, fair-haired and eager, hopeful maybe.

'Good evening,' Zulgaris said to him.

The man smiled. He had been wounded in the shoulder, might lose the left arm. This the physician had bandaged up.

'Do you know who I am?' Zulgaris asked.

'Yes, my lord. Their prince.'

'That's right. You fought well and bravely. Will you take some wine with me?'

The man nodded, anxious to display his good will. 'Yes, sir.'

The physician brought the black jug and the glass goblet.

Zulgaris poured the wine. It too was very dark. He handed the cup to the prisoner, who looked for a moment surprised – after all, the prince was not drinking.

'To comrades lost,' Zulgaris said.

The man's eyes clouded. 'Yes – '

Psychologically motivated, he raised the goblet and took down half of it.

'Do you like the wine?'

'Yes, my lord.'

'Do finish it then.'

A hint at that. Usually they took this hint. Alarm speeded up, invariably, their responses.

'Was it – was it wine?'

'Wine with a little of something mixed in it.'

'What something – ?'

'Now I shall see.'

The man looked frightened.

Zulgaris observed him calmly, reassuringly.

The man tried to get up, but his hurt shoulder hampered him. And then he said, slowly, 'My feet are cold.'

'Are they?'

'My feet and my belly – what did you give me?'

'A new potion that I required to try. Have you any pain?'

'No – no pain – '

'That's good. I'm searching for something that doesn't cause undue distress. That's quick – you're having difficulty in breathing?'

The man was trying to catch his breath. His eyes blazed with terror and sweat glistened on his face. His mouth opened in an abrupt rictus and he fell back making harsh glottal sounds.

When he was dead Zulgaris shrugged.

'Not pleasant. I'd hoped this would be more subtle.'

'Do you want to try the other tincture on that one there? He's asleep and is weak.'

'No. I'll leave that for now. Let's employ the skin with him, and see how he does.'

They walked to an older man who lay in a stupor on his pallet. He had lost blood from a sword cut in the thigh. The physician pulled away the dressing, and Zulgaris observed the parted flesh.

Then, from a greenish tank of fluid, Zulgaris lifted out a length of thin webby stuff. Almost like fish skin it looked, in the dull bronze light.

Beyond the black tent, from the yellow one, Zulgaris' clock struck the hour.

'And the best time for it,' Zulgaris murmured. 'The crossing over of day and night.'

He laid the opalescent skin upon the torn thigh of the unconscious man.

'Sew it into place.'

The physician bent low with his golden needle.

Zulgaris had never known this experiment to work, but men varied. In his palace, a fellow had lived for two whole months with the paw of a panther attached at his wrist.

The part-flayed skin of the dead horse might be less inimical.

Zulgaris touched things on the tables. In a crystal tube, a tiny near-human specimen floated. It was only a vegetable, and yet it looked so like a man.

Such mysteries God had presented to his creatures. But he had given them brains whereby to seek out the truth.

'It's done, my lord.'

'That's very good.'

The man stirred in delirium. Would he dream now, the horsehide gold-stitched on his limb, of racing through the battle, of the ball which struck him?

Zulgaris stretched. He was fatigued. He left the black tent and the bowing physician, and crossed back to the yellow pavilion, where his bed waited. It was a soldier's couch, hard and narrow, and by it a great book for companionship.

His servant undressed the prince, who lay down and was swiftly and silently asleep.

Chapter Two

THERE WERE BONES IN THE trees. How had they got there? It was simple, perhaps. The winter boughs weighed down by snow, swinging back in the thaw, taking up the load of clean death with them.

A skull peered from a wild pear.

The first village, when they reached it, was empty of everything – except bones. Sheep and goats, picked white, and human remains, also fastidiously scoured. These bones were scattered everywhere. About the vacant floors of houses, on the wooden tables, and in the cold hearths. Other debris had frozen, solidified, lost its pungency and form.

A bone hand with a silver ring lay by the well. The red wolves, who had come in the snow, had not set much store by metal.

They paddled, the army of Zulgaris, through ladles and dolls cast aside on the tracks. Some stole aside to filch. The word came, and this was stopped. Their prince did not often prevent them. What had gone on here? The new word came, and now they kept close. They tied rags and scarves over their noses and mouths.

The castle came visible above the woods near sunset. They camped below in the night.

Owls called like witches over the valleys. And up on her platform, their own Witch made spells, her fire glowing like jade, to safeguard Zulgaris and what was his.

In the dawn, the castle stood on a ruby sky. It was black

and forbidding, no sign of life, a petrified excrescence of stone. Black birds, ravens, went about it.

Zulgaris rode up through the second village, which was like the first. (The hoofs of the golden horse scuffed toys and clavicles on the path.)

Demed pointed, as they got clear of the hovels.

'Do you see, my lord?'

'I see. Barbarians. We knew. Such things are common, here.'

It was a tower of spikes. Even from this distance and below, it was possible to note the wreathes of whitish twinings caught there. In places a darker rubble of flesh remained, and the birds were visiting these spots.

Kazun spat.

Zulgaris drew rein, and they waited.

He said, softly, 'They're dead, all of them, I would say. Plague. No curse, something more thorough. The Darejens died of that too, the ones that were left in their bolt-hole.'

'What shall we do, my lord?'

'We can take precautions. The men may draw lots to see who'll go into the castle. We'll need no more than thirty. I want to be sure none of these rats are left.'

'I'll see to it, sir,' said Kazun, and wheeled his horse.

'And a gold piece,' said Zulgaris, the generous leader, 'to every man who dares it.' As Kazun rode off, he added, idly, 'There isn't much danger. The cold's burnt the sickness out.'

'Yes, sir.'

'And besides, my knights will have protection.'

'I'll be beside you, sir.'

'Good. I expected no less.'

The sky had paled to an unworldly blue, holy and cloudless. They looked up at the castle and the spiked tower of bones and feeding birds. The spring wind brought them their cries, but only the scent of leaves and water.

They entered the castle in the afternoon.

There were thirty soldiers, armed with swords and pikes. And ten knights of the lesser ranks. Demed and

Kazun of the Companions. Zulgaris led them, riding the golden horse up the track of broken bones and the strewn bits of what might have been carts, wheels.

They appeared like an assembly of demons, the knights and horses of Zulgaris.

Where the soldiery had bound its face with cloths steeped in medicines, the knights wore each a beak stuffed by herbs and unguents. They had become, in their glittering armour, strange birdmen. The horses were also birds, each with its yellow beak.

Prepared to an alchemical recipe, these herbals were a failsafe against plague.

There was a small door open, rusted wide by the seasons, in the castle's side. But, disdaining this, the soldiers bashed in the main doors with a ram of wood and metal.

The barrier collapsed with a clash and clang. Beyond, the empty yard, with the bulks of the castle rising from it.

Zulgaris rode up the stairway into the main hall, and his men rode and ran after him.

No challenge. No defender.

If Zulgaris expected anything, it was some weakling – for often it was the weak who survived a plague – crawling to them from a passageway or annexe. These he would kill without thought, unless it were a young woman. She might be of use to his troops.

But no one crawled to them for death. Death had already had them all.

Above the hall, they rode through stony galleries. They entered chambers, and where the stairs were too narrow for the horses, they went on foot.

There were riches, and the men who had had to follow the knights became more cheerful. Even so, they lifted their wraps and spat on objects, wiping them over, before putting them into bags and sacks.

Later, the rest of the men would be permitted in to pillage. First Zulgaris would select. But there was not much he liked. That gold jug for some priestly house, yes, that carved icon for another. But he found these upland curios distasteful, blatant.

His knights were not so choosy. Demed took up a wristlet of silver that lay on a stairway. He counted aloud three garnets and a topaz, and put the thing in his pouch.

Zulgaris smiled inwardly. Most men were like children.

'My lord!' A soldier ran up to him along a corridor.

'What is it?' His own voice in the beak was muffled.

The soldier knew he must understand. 'There's a door locked, or stuck, my lord.'

'Some treasure trove,' said Kazun hungrily – he had missed grabbing the wristlet.

'Well, break it in.'

The soldier scurried to obey. They did not need the ram. Three of them put their shoulders to the door, and presently tumbled into the room beyond.

Then came a silence.

'They've found something,' said Kazun. He was barely audible.

'Go and see.'

Kazun, no longer mounted, strode along the corridor-gallery and straight into the room.

Zulgaris could hear Kazun curse.

Then Kazun came out again. He was grinning around his herbal beak.

'Treasure of one sort, my lord.'

Zulgaris felt impatient. He frowned.

Kazun said quickly, half shifting the beak, 'It's a woman, sir. A girl.'

The soldiers in the vicinity stirred. A girl – but was she tainted by plague? Would it be safe to fornicate with her? A fuck was not worth death.

Zulgaris slid agile from his horse, which stayed rock still after he had left it. He walked to the room and went in at the doorway, a tall golden man with the beak of a bird.

The chamber was damp and full of cobwebs. Spiders had spun everywhere, but not across the strip of bed with its dim curtains . . . An impure mirror mounted on an outlandish brazen beast, perhaps a lion, reflected him, and this he saw first, the eagle Zulgaris.

Then it occurred to him that the girl was not crouching

anywhere, but stretched out upon that slender bed. Her feet in little spangled shoes shone up at him, and the red and black were not some coverlet, but her gown and hair. There was gold on both.

A lady of this barbarous castle after all. Not for the soldiery. *Asleep.*

Zulgaris went nearer, up to the bed.

Marius Christ.

No, not for the soldiery. Never in his life –

Never in his life had Zulgaris, who prized the special and the rare, beheld a human thing that was so beautiful. Apart, of course, from himself.

He studied her, smiling a little outwardly now. Not Kazun's uncouth grin. The pleasure of appreciation.

She was over sixteen. Very slim, yet firm soft breasts rose in the gown. Her hair was a stream, a river of blackness, dotted by tiny glints of gold. The face was exquisite. What colour were those sleeping eyes?

She was not dead, he saw the smooth rise and fall of those tantalizing breasts. But – how had she slept through all this disturbance, the fall of the castle gates, their entry, the shouting of the men, and horses' hoofs on the stone floors?

She was untouched by illness, wholesome as new fruit.

But was this not sleep?

Could she be woken?

Zulgaris turned to Kazun. 'Go out and close the door.'

Kazun obeyed at once, his comradely male leer shut off.

Outside, the men shuffled, but Zulgaris ignored them. He removed, without hesitation, the beak of herbs. Was now, also, a man.

He leant forward and set his forefinger gently on the pale and perfect lips of the girl.

For a moment, nothing, and then, maybe at the scent of his skin, clean and perfumed yet tainted by the metal of his sword, she caught her breath. Her eyes did not open, but her mouth did. She took his finger in, and he felt against it her tongue, rough as a cat's. His skin bristled, every hair, and his manhood filled like a bladder.

Then her teeth came, cat sharp. She bit him and he knew she had drawn blood.

He snatched away and slapped her heavily with the back of his hand, across the face.

Her beautiful head lolled.

Then her eyes did come open.

They were green as the eyes of his leopards by night. And then they darkened, and were more like royal purple.

She raised her own hand slowly to her face, where he had hit her.

'I beg your pardon,' he said, 'but you were bad-mannered. Who are you?'

'The lord's daughter,' she said sleepily. She let her hand fall back, and her cheek was pink from his blow. But he was glad to see he had not bruised her and none of his rings had cut her marble skin.

'Which lord?'

'Vaddix.'

'He's dead,' said Zulgaris.

'Yes. He was on the Spike Tower,' she answered, careless. She yawned, not covering her mouth – no need, it was flawless. He glimpsed the white, white teeth and rich strawberry of its interior. His erection hurt him, as it had sometimes done in boyhood when he had tried to abstain.

He would have liked to have her at once, but he would wait. She was worth a wait.

Her eyes were blue-violet now. Some trick of the light before.

'What's your name, little girl?'

She said, without pride or discretion, 'Vivia.'

Chapter Three

SHE THOUGHT HE WAS A villager.

For several moments, she thought that.

She was relaxed, still far away. She did not know she had slept through the winter, like a hibernating animal, in the chill cave of the bedchamber. But her body was somnolent and at ease.

Then, the first alarm – the man was dressed in steel, saffron, cloth-of-gold with stripes of black velvet. His face, like his garb, was not anything she had seen before. He was a lord, richer than her father. More immaculate. A foreigner. Dangerous, perhaps –

And she had drawn his blood. She had done it instinctively. What had he made of that?

Nothing much, it seemed.

At some other earlier time, his face might have fitted her dreams. But it no longer could. She had seen the ultimate face of all dreams, she had seen darkest day and deepest night personified. And that face – had been no face at all. She could not remember it, only a sort of mist crossed by the dark bars of brows and eyes and lips.

So, this one was not a marvel. He was a man. Her rescuer? It seemed so, for he was courteous, playful. She had heard other men speak to others this way – *Little girl*. She had never heard any *man* so polite to a woman.

He was some great prince. One of those softened by luxury. She had heard of them. Lords of other lands.

And she felt superior to him. Superior by virtue of her rough upbringing, the tough castle and evil father. By virtue of her femaleness too – for it seemed to her this had given her, extraordinarily, an advantage. And by reason of the thing which had happened to her, the unbelievable, dreamlike thing. She felt her own power. Her *survival*.

He had not hit her hard.

She had had his blood.

She said her name was Vivia, and sat up. (How he looked at her, as if she was a clever mechanism, a doll that moved.)

'There was a plague here,' he said.

'Yes,' she said. 'Everyone died but for me.'

'God protected you.'

She smiled. She did not circle or cross herself and this golden prince – his hair was like the face rays of Marius – frowned.

He said, 'What are you?'

'I told you,' she said.

'Address me properly,' he said. 'I am the Prince Zulgaris.'

'Prince,' she said. She combed her hair with her fingers and watched how he watched her. He fancied her, lusted after her, she could see. None of the men of her father's castle had wanted her, except for some far gone in sickness. Death, however, had loved her well.

She liked this human desire. Would it spell safety and *not* danger?

'What will you do with me?' she asked. 'Prince.'

'Your kindred are dead.' He added, 'You will need protection from my soldiers.'

She pointed her toes. Her shoes had lost most of their lustre in the cold. The gold sequins were dull.

'Thank you,' she said, 'prince.'

'Don't address me in that upland way either. Call me sir, or my lord.'

Vivia smiled. 'You're a mighty potentate. My woman told me stories of heroes like you.' She spoke childishly, coquettishly. It was instinct; in the same way she had bitten him.

Zulgaris responded, friendly. 'Your woman told you about me?'

'Oh yes. A golden prince.'

'Where is she?'

'Dogs ate her,' said Vivia, with distaste. She was growing bored. 'You'll take me with you,' she said.

'Shall I?'

'Or,' she said, coolly, 'will you leave me here? All alone in the empty castle.'

Zulgaris laughed softly. 'You're a minx, Vivia. You must forget this anthill if you come with me. And your father, who I would have killed if the plague hadn't done it. Or God. Possibly God himself struck down your father.'

'Whatever you like,' said Vivia.

He moved a step nearer, and she could see his lust, burning like three stars, at his groin and in his eyes. Would he rape her quickly and then want no more?

She huddled together and said, 'I'm afraid.'

He checked himself. He said, firm in his lies, 'You've no need to be afraid of me. I'm your protector now, Vivia.'

He had brought for her a thick red cloak, some fine wool lined with the fur of red wolves and trimmed by silver. This he wound her in. And so, wrapped up like a gift for him, she left her home.

More than that, she left her dream of the god.

As she was put into the little carriage, some other woman of the march displaced, Vivia knew a second's intense fear.

But then she recalled again what had already occurred. She had been told that she was now indestructible. Nothing could harm her.

And this prince was like, in turn, her toy. She could play with him. The first man she might manipulate. A fascinating game.

They rode away from the castle and she did not look back to see it. It trailed out of her life, a sound not a sight, the cries of the ravens.

Later she heard the river, and the wheels and hoofs and boots of the enormous army – never had she seen so many men – trampling down the stones and slush of the valleys.

But her long sleep had made her tired. She slept again.

Curled among the rugs and cushions of her borrowed carriage, which smelled of scent.

A sunset filled the space with chalky rouge, and then came night, and the whole creaking, thumping, grinding mass of the army slewed to a halt.

Vivia looked from the tiny window and beheld a new landscape.

She felt a glimmer of pleasure, and another second of fright.

Overhead the stars sparkled, and trees closed their heights. The army was setting up a smouldering tumult of fires.

No one came for a long time, and then it was a man in steel and gold, but not Zulgaris the prince. He gazed in at her, and then flicked forward another man who said she was to come out and go with him.

Vivia obeyed, and so walked through the noisy camp, past the vast gouts of cooking fires, where meat was broiling. Quite a few women were about attending to the cookery, or mending things. Inside a well-lighted tent, ten or so girls lay in abandoned attitudes, and two soldiers were already there, bouncing on white, half-clad bodies.

The knight rode behind Vivia and her steward.

It was needful, it kept the rest off, though they stared.

There was a small tent with a yellow flower painted on its side.

The steward said, 'You'll be all right here, lady. Someone will come with food.'

'And later on,' said the knight. But nothing more.

Vivia went into the tent. It was not large but nicely laid out, a bed of rugs and cushions, and curtains cordoning off a place with a little table and a chair. A lamp burned on a tall stand. It was of ornate iron, coal blue and orange, throwing odd flowers of colour about the tent's interior.

A woman came in. She did not look at Vivia, and was dressed like a servant. She put down a small copper bath and draped inside it a sheet of linen. Then a man came and poured hot water that steamed into the bath. He went out again at once. The woman went out, and another came and set a jug and a cup on the small table. She too vanished.

Vivia drank a little of the wine. It was very sweet and ripe, not like the coarse liquor of the castle. She sampled a little more.

She was however afraid to bathe.

Outside the tent, the maelstrom of the camp went on. Loud voices and shouted orders, the tramp of feet and detachments of horses riding by, so the mud splashed up and hit the yellow flower, and she saw the reflection of this inside.

Vivia lay down on the rug bed and closed her ears to the uproar.

It did not matter.

She was powerful now.

She slept again.

Zulgaris came with the food. The smell of savoury mutton and spiced bread woke her again, and she smelled too the aroma of his washed and perfumed body. She did not like it any more than she had liked the male stinks of her father and his men.

'Have you bathed?' he asked her at once. Vivia shook her head. He said, brusquely, 'Do so now, behind the curtain.'

Then, she sensed this continual and terrible masculine thing again, this power that was not like her power. She realized she had to obey him.

She did so. At least, since he was in the tent, and his bodyguard of men outside, no one would burst in on her.

There was a cake of soap – something she had heard of before, but never seen. Perversely she laved her body thoroughly, though the water was by now lukewarm. The blue and amber lamp had given heat, and the camp itself was quite hot from fires and breathing.

She found they had left her a dress. It was white, very smooth, and beaded with silver. She put it on and it did not fit her very well, rather too big, but the sash of blood red silk controlled it at her waist.

'Yes, now you're worthy of yourself,' he said. 'You must have cosmetics. There'll be women to tend you. A bed of silk.'

She had had those, dreaming. She looked at him in scorn, and he saw, and misinterpreted.

'Don't spurn what you've never known. You'll like these things, Vivia. You'll be mine. You must have the best.'

She picked at the bread and ate an apple off a silver plate.

She was not hungry, though a winter had passed.

What would it be like to take blood?

Did she yearn for it?

This urge was distant, cramped. It was not feasible. Although –

It seemed he would make love to her after the meal, and then there might be some chance. But no, he was too dangerous after all. How could she excuse herself? Ursabet had said, in transports of sexual joy, she had sometimes bitten –

He stared at her all through the repast.

He passed her pieces of what he ate and insisted that she sample them. He took the cut apple from her hand and devoured it.

They drank the wine.

'You know, Vivia,' he said, 'if you're to belong to me. You know what I must do?'

She stared. Why make this easier for him?

Zulgaris lowered his eyes, almost girlishly. It was, it seemed to her, her gesture.

'Can I believe,' he said, 'you were left a virgin in that dung-heap?'

Vivia lowered her gaze in turn. She did not know. What had gone on in her dream?

About five minutes after this, a man cleared his throat in the fire-dark outside the tent.

'Demed, Kazun, Tetchink. Come in.'

So Zulgaris said, startling her.

There they stood, his three knights. They wore silks now, as if already at home. Their swords remained about them however, habitual as penises.

'Thank you,' said Zulgaris, rising, 'for acting as my witnesses. These gentlemen,' he added to Vivia, casually, 'will safeguard your status.'

Only Kazun grinned. Demed looked stern, and Tetchink, who had lost his left eye, scowled.

Zulgaris drew Vivia up and behind the curtain, to the bed of rugs. She had realized before that the curtain was semi-transparent. And now Zulgaris lit with a tinder a second lamp, this one of clear yellow glass, beside the bed.

He went to her and slipped his hand into the loose neck of the white gown.

His hand came round her breast like a snake or spider.

'But – ' she said. 'They can *see*.'

'It's our custom,' he said. He breathed quickly. 'They *must* see. To know the compact's been sealed.'

Vivia stared in horror through the curtain, and as she did so, the tent again opened, and a thin eldritch woman slunk in behind the knights.

'Oh,' said her prince, 'my Witch. Yes. That does very well.'

Then he smothered her face in his. His tongue was enormous in her mouth. She felt herself choking, and fell back helpless on the rugs.

He pulled up her skirt at once. This was not what she remembered.

Immediately his hand went to her sex, and next his member was there. He pushed against her and she felt herself a locked room, and a ram was used on her.

He thrust without apology through and through, and she tore with a shrill scream.

Zulgaris clasped her. He reared above her, and he roared: 'She is a virgin!'

Then his length was inside her, sore and brutal and dominating. She could not resist, she let him do his worst. For some minutes it seemed he pushed and burned in her, and then he shuddered and dropped still on to her body.

Of course, the demon god of her dream had not pierced her. Of course, now she had been, as had always been her fate, deflowered.

As he pulled out of her she would not look, but she felt her blood run free.

And he whipped up the covering and displayed it at the curtain.

Vivia heard the old hag with the long black hair, say, 'A virgin indeed. You've properly broken *her*.'

Kazun laughed.

The other two men were nodding, and then they all went out, but for the witch creature, who hovered there, drifting up to the curtain, squinnying in.

Vivia caught the flash of her jewellery teeth before Zulgaris gestured the Witch away, and she too went from the tent.

Alone, after a short while, he took her again, now undoing her bodice, handling her breasts, at one point putting his phallus between her lips and telling her to lick him, but Vivia now turned her head away.

When he had had her twice more, she avoided him. 'It hurts.'

'It will. That's good, my pure little angel.'

'Leave me alone,' she dared to say.

But he was sated, and left her.

He slept silently, unafraid, at her side.

As the lamps bloomed into dusk and went out, Vivia leaned over him. But she did not want his blood. It was he, a human man, who had taken hers.

She lay in silence and her eyes seemed to grow so huge in the darkness that she had no head but *only* eyes.

How had she come to this? Power – she had none. She was his thing, like the whores in the other tents.

And they had seen.

She did not sleep any more.

TWO

Chapter One

ON THE MORNING THEY REACHED his city in the hills, Vivia had the horse dream again. She had had this dream several times during the journey. She could not decipher if it came from the cries of the plague-ridden castle, or from talk heard among the soldiers of Zulgaris' camps. Or had she put it together herself, deduced it?

She was climbing up the House Tower of her father's hold, and she knew that above lay the room with the dead horse in it. She did not want to see, but she must, and so she hoped only that it would soon be over.

Reaching the chamber door, she opened it, and there the bedroom lay, and the bridal bed with its lace and withered blackened roses.

The horse sprawled on the bed, and it was whole again. Not pale, but black and shining. And then she saw, as she had known she would, that it was not flesh which covered the dead horse, but dead flies attached thickly to its bones. It had a skin of flies, and they gleamed.

Black fly eyes looked out at her, and Vivia turned to run away, but the door was gone from the wall.

She woke, as always, alone in her tent, for he never stayed with her now, once he was finished.

She thought that she would never be free of Vaddix's castle, though she had left it far behind, a month of travelling.

Of Vaddix she was an orphan, but now this other one had her. She could not escape, could not even run away, for the ferocious soldiers surrounded her, who would rape, and perhaps kill her, without the protection of Zulgaris.

Ursabet had told her that dreams represented things, were omens and symbols. The dream of the god did not count in this way. *It* had been unique. But the dream of the horse must be the dream of Vivia's slavery.

The journey had been irksome. Though the carriage was cushioned, and though servants brought her food – she seldom ate it – and wine, which she sometimes drank, the constant rumbling motion enervated and angered her. Through the small window, clouds of mountains passed, and then other mountains, a river in spate into which she was afraid her vehicle would fall, meadows with flowers, lit by a thin bright sun. Between these views the soldiery and the knights came, and she would draw her curtain, not wanting them to grin in at her.

She was known, a woman Zulgaris had garnered. He had never done this before or so he had told her. She was supposed to be honoured. To bask in her luck.

Vivia no longer felt even fear. She was as helpless as when he had mounted and broken her before his men. She gave in because there was no other choice. She had never wasted her energy.

The dream of the vampire drew far away as the castle did not. It was precious, and she did not really believe it. What had happened was strange, but not as she thought.

She trusted no one. Not even herself.

Zulgaris, however, was real.

He came to her every evening. Not now to dine with her, only to lie on top of her, and later, to insist that she herself assume various positions – astride him, beside him, even once the infamous position of dog and bitch, which she had not refused (loathing it).

He no longer hurt her, or only by his squeezings. It was he who bit her flesh, not breaking the skin but leaving bruises. He was not rough, only thorough and passionate and selfish, in the way she expected of men. (Her first lover, after all, if he had even existed, was not a man.)

Once Zulgaris had even put his mouth to her vulva, and done something reminiscent of what the vampire had done, but Zulgaris had only one mouth, and besides, he did it only briefly, for his own enjoyment.

Though she had heard men boast of how hot they could make a woman, so she spasmed and shrieked with delight, and though Ursabet had boasted similarly of her own ability to come, Vivia expected no pleasure, got none.

When he had had her once or twice, Zulgaris would leave her, not exhausted now by prolonged congress, or not caring to lie at her side.

Vivia was always glad to see him go.

She took no pleasure even from his handsome crooked face, his strong firm body. She had known better.

They came down from the mountains and went by roads. Valleys, fields, villages. Now and then a high castle. All these Zulgaris, her lord and prince, had conquered, and his own men came out and welcomed him to feasts. Vivia was not invited to these. She sat in her tent and waited for him to arrive. He was never drunk.

One night he brought her a necklace of hammered gold with an emerald pendant, and hung it round her neck – her other jewels he had taken.

'This is my love token,' he said.

And then someone sang outside the tent, a love song. After which Zulgaris parted her legs and pushed straight into her, coming quickly with a long gasp. The giving of things, apparently, excited him.

The roads fell down to flatter lands. Hills rose, lavender in the twilight. The pitiless stars and the hard moon chequered the night sky, and sometimes she would see the moon through a veil above the roof of her tent.

Beyond grinning at her, no man offered her any insult. No one spoke to her, including the servants, apart from her master.

One night too he brought a leopard into her tent. It was female and hissed and snarled at Vivia.

'She's jealous,' he said, amused.

Vivia, despite the dream promise of indestructibility, was terrified.

'Make it go away.'

'Then I will.' And he sent the leopard, bristling and raging, out.

His Witch was like that too. Once this woman had had a division of soldiers go and dig something up from the land at the roadside. And the woman herself was up on her platform, which, for travelling, went on to a wagon drawn by four horses. The Witch stared down at Vivia's carriage. She made a sign, something malignant and swift.

Vivia wondered if some ill would befall her, but it did not, or – no new ill. She did not mention this incident to the prince.

The day before they reached his city, which he had told her of – she had barely listened – they moved through cultivated lands where the villages clustered one on another. From the houses men and women came out, and called, and praised the soldiers. Girls ran and hung flowers on their necks, and put primroses into the manes of horses.

Everyone was pleased.

Vivia sat like a stone.

That night he was brisk with her, telling her to lie on her face. He took her spread on her back, and her womb smarted at his actions.

She hated him. She understood this during those moments. Her *prince*.

When he was done, he stayed to drink wine, and told her tomorrow they would be at the city.

He spoke of it with an offhand pride.

'I have other places. This is my queen.'

She wondered then if he had a wife, but did not inquire. It did not matter, probably.

'I haven't tired of you,' he said. 'My little swan. Don't bother yourself. People will instruct you what you must do. You've never seen a city, have you?'

The fool. Of course she had not.

'No, my lord.'

'It will intrigue you. Those blue-green eyes of yours

will be round. And the comforts of the palace. You'll be astonished, Vivia.'

'Yes, my lord.'

He looked long at her. He said at last, 'You think I don't know your secret, pretty little girl. Don't ever make a mistake about me.'

What secret? Did he know – all her dream? For a moment her heart stopped. But then she dismissed this. She lowered her eyes, as she must always do, sick of him, not wanting to look.

He took her again, the ordinary way. She whined with affront, not meaning to. He took it for excitement. He kissed her and left her.

Why was his nose askew? He had tapped it once and said he had fallen from a wall. A few feet more, he might have cracked his neck.

She had the horse dream, and in the morning, when they moved, they got to the city.

It was called Starzion. Colossal walls enclosed it, with wide gateways filled by gates. His emblem was painted on them, a leopard and a flower – the same flower that had been painted on her tent.

Banners fluttered above on the blue windy sky. White and gold, with a stroke of black.

Inside were long streets, very wide, wide enough for all the soldiery, carriages, wagons, and machines of war on their grumbling sleds.

People lined the way, shouting and screaming. And a deluge of flowers fell over them.

Vivia sat in her carriage and saw the cheering red faces, flecked by a light spring rain.

They came into a huge square, and there was a church there – for Vivia had heard of churches. A facade of pillars and stonework like lace, and up above a great window with Marius in it, his head a blazing aureole of gold-work that caught and consumed the sun.

Across from the church was a building that must be the palace Zulgaris had spoken of.

It was like a towered cliff with blue roofs, raised above

a hundred steps, and Zulgaris, on his clever yellow horse, rode up these stairs, his knights following.

They went into the sand-coloured building and a vast door closed.

Vivia wondered if they would forget her, but soon enough the servant people came, and one knight to escort her, and she was taken to a side wall, over which gigantic trees towered into the air, dark green, solid like masonry.

They led her down an alleyway and so into the palace, which was to be her new prison.

It was like . . . the dream. The vampire dream. The illusion.

Was this more affective, or less, being actual?

She had three rooms. A room to sleep in, and a room to bathe in, and a room to sit in. All were very big. On the walls were panels of carefully painted wood, pictures of fruiting trees in green and soft red, and white birds. The bed had curtains of midnight velvet embroidered by golden stars, and the ceiling matched these, also blue and set with golden stars, and at the heart of every star, a radiant point that was a polished diamond.

Fleece carpeted the marble floors. The bath was marble, overlaid outside with silver. A silver spout brought water into it that was always hot from some arrangement of pipes, they said, in the walls.

The bathroom walls were inlaid with pictures of shells, and bizarre sea creatures, such as women with the tails of fish.

In the room for sitting was a fireplace, on each side of which stood a marble leopard. A fire ruminated on this hearth and had been sprinkled by perfume. There were tapestries, and a bowl of fruit that was not real but made from onyx and jade and scented woods.

They showed Vivia fabrics that were going to be fashioned into dresses for her, shoes and shifts. Yellow lace fine as a cobweb. Silk like green water. Gold sequins set with pearls.

A jeweller came to try upon her necklets, earrings,

bracelets, rings, tutting to himself when something did
not fit.

She did not ask where these treasures came from. They
told her – Zulgaris collected such items.

There were so many persons in her rooms. And the two
pretty girls who waited on her . . . not frogs or lizards,
this pair.

'Make them go out,' said Vivia.

And the pretty girls conducted the swarm of people
away.

'Are you hungry, lady?' asked the other pretty girl.

Vivia shook her head. She walked about the pale and
dark blue bed, and pondered if it was possible to sleep
on it. The day was quite young. He would not come for
a while. Perhaps even he would not come at all, now he
was here.

But that evening, as usual, when the unusual stained glass
light of her casements (unicorns, angels) was darkening,
he came to visit her.

Unusually too, he ate with her.

Vivia did not eat, she drank some wine.

'Tomorrow,' he said, 'we'll go hungry.'

'Why?'

'A fast,' he said, 'to celebrate to God my safe return. And
you must be part of it, because they know here, already,
that you belong to me.'

He had evidently not noticed, or did not care, how little
she ate. She pushed the dish of spiced beef away.

He said, complacently, 'Little Vivia. Did you like the
jewels and the silks?'

She looked at him. She would have to say Yes.

'Yes, my lord.'

'And you'll be safe here. With me.'

She simpered.

Zulgaris either did not note this, or thought it proper.

He finished his meat, and took a sliver of chicken with
floury pastes.

'But what a mystery you are,' he said, easily. She waited.
He said, 'To live a whole winter, as you must have done, in

that castle. Did you eat human flesh? Is that what sustained you? Do you want it now? I can have it supplied.'

Vivia pulled a face.

'No? What can it be you crave? What does she want, my darling girl?'

Vivia knew she must not say she wished him to leave her alone. That was not sensible. She said nothing, but raised her head, tilting her chin.

Zulgaris smiled. He ate the chicken and took a pastry from a gold platter.

'A little of this? No? Are you sulky, Vivia?'

'No, my lord.'

'Remember, I know you very well. And I am your ruler.'

'Yes, sir.'

'Good. I've never known a creature like you. So succulent, so lovely. But I'm too strong to be enamoured, Vivia. I think you know that too.'

Vivia lowered her eyes.

Zulgaris took another pastry. He peeled slices of green fruit into his wine.

'Try this.'

She sipped from his golden goblet. It was fragrant.

He said, 'You must never doubt me. You must be honest with me. What are you – a demon girl. I *know*, Vivia.' She blinked. He said, 'Mythology, and truth – all one.'

When he had ended his meal he stood up, and directed her to the bed. Here he undressed her like a maid, like Ursabet.

When she was naked, he mouthed and tongued all of her body, and she writhed, agitated from dreading him, and these amorphous intimations of a pleasure that could never be hers. Inevitably, having half roused her, he sought vengeance, putting his cock between her lips. She sucked him obediently, and presently gagged upon his swilling seed. He did not see.

How she hated him.

And for the first time, as never before, not even in the castle of plague, she wondered what would become of her, for how could she go on with this?

*   *   *

Zulgaris descended through the fortified palace of Starzion.

He descended only so far as a hidden room. To this he, and few others, knew the means of entry.

It was a type of alchemical room, all black, with a window of violet glass. On an ebony table lay a black glass bowl of ravens' feathers. And in a wormwood cup was a black wine which, on entering, Zulgaris drank.

A shape rose from a corner.

It was the Witch.

He studied her a moment, partly tickled at her physical appearance after the mellifluous beauty of that peculiar phantom girl he left above.

'Are you ready, Witch?'

'I am, my glory.'

He had laid the Witch once, in a ceremony of science, when orgasm had been needful. Her screams had rent the air. He did not forget, though he had not set a finger on her for years, and probably never would again.

She had not forgotten either.

She crouched to the floor of black and dead-blue tiles, and there she slit the throat of a drugged black dog she had brought in with her.

As the mess streamed, a crescent moon appeared at the violet glass, staring in. Her timing had never been less than canny.

'Now tell me,' he said.

'She is what you suspect,' said the Witch. She paused. She said, 'Destroy her.'

'No. It's too interesting.'

'You experiment upon everything,' said the Witch. 'Why not? But not this one.'

'But she's so beautiful,' he said, with knowing cruelty.

The old-girl-hag composed herself. She pointed up her owl's features at him.

'She'll have the blood in you.'

'Not mine. She knows me. I'm not to be played with.'

'Are you sure?'

'Oh yes,' he said, dismissively.

The Witch put her finger into the dog's blood and held it up. It glimmered blue.

'We must go down. I must safeguard you, my lord
prince.'

'No. It isn't necessary. But I allow you to work your
spells. Don't try to harm her. I'd know, I do know now.'

The Witch hung her head. Her girl's hair flared about
her, blacker than the dead dog.

Zulgaris left the chamber.

He knew the sacrifice of the dog was a stupidity, and
yet a *rightness* in the wall of the world to which everything
contributed. He allowed the crone her magics for she was
useful, his men feared and reverenced her, and enemies
ran away. But more than this. She was the age-old symbol.
The moon at its last. The word of woman. The mother he
had never known or wanted.

Chapter Two

VIVIA WOKE WITH DISMAY EVERY morning in Starzion.

On the fifth morning, as early sunlight dripped through the green, red and blue of the windows, the two women came with a new dress.

She had learned their names, Maura and Tisomin, and she watched them, their long smooth tails of brown plaits wound with silver sliding round their shoulders as they set the dress upright in a chair. It was white, and stiff with gold wire embroidery. A border with yellowish pearls and pink opals went down its front. Obviously, a dress of great ceremony.

'What is that for?'

'Today the prince will recognize you as his possession,' said Maura.

Vivia pulled a face they did not see. They were busy preparing the bath in the chamber of mermaids.

When she had been arrayed in the stiff white and gold dress, Vivia's hair was perfumed and combed out, and over her head was placed a golden cap of discs from which other discs fell and trailed down to her shoulders. Gold rings were put on her fingers.

It was less easy than usual to walk in the dress, and Maura and Tisomin paced along at either side of her.

They went down a narrow stair which she had never seen before, and this stair finally reached a door that gave on a garden.

The spring was full-blown and lush already in the

hills of Starzion. The garden had high walls up which small roses and long vines clambered. Fruit trees grew in trim blossoming avenues, and there were countless mulberry trees.

Two older women, dressed sumptuously in yellow, replaced Vivia's attendants, without a word. They were like jailors and conducted her along a paved path, by a white marble basin with water and small fish in it, and in at another door.

There followed some quantities of wide corridors, where men stood in the yellow livery of Zulgaris, swords at their sides and lances upright in their hands. The walls were covered by tapestries, paintings on wood. Occasionally a window, edged with coloured glass, would look out across the walls, roofs and trees of the palace.

They reached a double door inlaid by gold, which the guardsmen pushed open.

Inside was a dining room. It too was hung by curtains of yellow, and tapestries showing frolics, and the hunts of curious beasts, such as unicorns and two-headed cats.

Coming in from several doors, people in rich garments were assembling there, it seemed at least a hundred, and most turned to look at Vivia. Some muttered, and one woman laughed, but quickly fell silent.

Vivia was frightened. It did her no good to remember what she had been promised. Every moment, *that* dream seemed further off.

She felt childish and insecure.

The matrons took her to a place at one of the long tables, which were covered by yellow cloth massively embroidered and loaded with silver cutlery, knives and skewers, and a variety of cups, round goblets of gold, and silver vases, and other glasses of crystal.

Vivia sat where the women indicated she should, and stood behind her carved chair. In the other carved chairs the guests were sitting.

Then a loud voice spoke: 'The Prince Zulgaris.'

Absurdly everyone stood up again, in a flush of gems and crisping of fabrics. Vivia also stood. Her dress creaked.

Zulgaris entered. He wore black velvet edged with

yellow and gold. There was a flutter among the women. Vivia did not look at them.

Zulgaris did not speak. He took a chair with gold points at the long tables' head, sat.

Then the food began to come.

Vivia had never seen so much.

Great pies in the shapes of castles and towers, silver tubs of meat, salvers brimming with sliced delicacies. There was a peacock dressed again in its feathers, a weird nightmarish thing of cooked and misplaced glamour. The tail was spread and sequins flashed on the 'eyes'.

Cakes came, and gelatines. Wines were brought in slender jugs with curved snakes' necks set with beryls.

Vivia missed the normal arousal of the feasters, the signs of appetites anticipating. Were they so mannered, then, they did not show their need?

The food was laid all down the tables, piled before the men and women of Zulgaris' inner court.

Vivia saw his knights sitting close by him, Demed and Tetchink and Kazun, who had overseen his first assault on her. (She cursed them strengthlessly; they were men.)

Before Vivia now was a palace made of sugar, pastry and fruit, with gold leaf on its turrets. She stared at it.

All about, the other feasters sat and stared.

Zulgaris spoke. 'We give thanks to God for the gift of food, and for the gift of life. I, especially, thank Him.'

The men and women crossed themselves. Cowardly survivor, Vivia described the circle of Marius before her breast. And heard a woman say, 'Look at her upland ways!'

Not hungry, Vivia waited without much interest for the eating and drinking of this enormous breakfast to begin.

It did not begin.

The feasters sat rigidly in their chairs, while the fragrant meal smoked to coldness before them.

Not a morsel was taken up by anyone. Not a cup was filled.

Vivia heard gradually the stomachs grumbling and mewing round the table. A man belched softly behind his hand. Suddenly one of the women fainted and was borne out.

Hungry, they had assembled here for the torture of not eating. It was a strange fast, an act of supreme denial, to please a God who, Vivia had always known, always asked for ridiculous things.

Having teased this out, Vivia smiled inwardly. She had no wish to eat or drink. She was lucky.

Another one fainted, this time a young man. Zulgaris frowned disapprovingly. A woman retched once, quickly, into her scarf.

Vivia had now the desire to laugh.

Was this some hint of her power?

But Zulgaris, the torturer, sitting so stoically in his gold-rimmed chair, had not done it for her.

At last a clock chimed above them in the wall, a marble clock hung with gold and silver. Shaking a little, the company got up and turned its back on the fasting feast.

But the ceremony was not over.

They passed across the square, from palace to church, treading on a crimson velvet carpet that had been put down.

Inside the church was a glow-wormery of lights. It reminded Vivia of the lighted highway that she had glimpsed from space. The highway she had not, so far, seen in reality.

Boys sang, sounding like girls without souls.

The music ascended into a painted dome fogged with incense.

Other women fainted. It was hot, close, stifling in the church. More agonies for God and Marius Christ.

Vivia stood between her guarding matrons, and saw through the press of fine-clad swaying bodies. When a woman fainted it was like a tree cut down. Then Vivia could see a little better.

Into the church were brought the treasures of Zulgaris. An eagle of solid gold, with emerald eyes, sailed by; a book with covers of ivory inlaid by precious stones, amethyst and ruby.

Then there were other things. Through the press of bodies she was not sure . . .

Little gambolling deformed men with large bearded heads, and tall spindly beings, perhaps seven feet high. There were two men who were black as ebony, and another two, passing like ghosts, white as the ivory of the book, white hair and dead skin, and eyes like the rubies set in the book.

Vivia wondered if the incense was affecting her vision. She did not believe in magic here.

A fleshly eagle passed, claws on a rod.

But no, these were his possessions, for one of the matrons had begun, perhaps unable to resist, whispering to her.

'. . . His dwarfs and giants, black men and albinos. Do you see? And next are his animals, the best of them. The eagle, the leopard Talia, who has hunted men. And the cat with bear's fur. And the unicorn.'

Vivia craned after all. A unicorn – too late for her. (Unvirgin.) Was it? It looked – like a vast goat, with its single horn askew, but silky and white as snow.

Then the priests were speaking, and their voices, ringing round the dome, were lost to her, a jumble.

But now the people made way, and the matron who had talked edged Vivia forward. 'Go to the altar. He'll acknowledge you.'

It was like a marriage, but not one.

Vivia did as she had been told, and now the hundreds of eyes of the church, like the hundreds of candles, burned on her. Her cheeks flamed with a sort of rage. She looked unbelievably beautiful.

The tall fat priests, like mounds of white and gold and purple, raised their hands and blessed her. For Zulgaris said, 'She is mine.' And those three were there, Demed and Tetchink and Kazun. They swore upon the sun of Marius that Vivia had been taken by Zulgaris, and was chaste.

Zulgaris came and fastened a golden chain about Vivia's throat.

Something made her glance aside. She seemed to see,

duplicated like the candles and the eyes, all these chains
of his slaves, glinting, leering at her.

She put her hand to the chain. It was locked. There was
no way to be free.

The boys sang and another woman fainted. They were
moving from the altar at some hidden signal. She and the
albinos and the black men and the dwarfs and giants and
leopards.

Daylight hung blue beyond the door. It evidenced
nothing. Her matrons were by her again, and carried
her away, back over the carpet to the palace. Through
corridors to the garden. Up into the rooms of her prison.

He came in the evening.

'Poor Vivia, it was an ordeal for her, and no one had
explained.'

He had been drinking but was not drunk. He never was.
The fast then was over. But she had known. Tisomin had
brought her berries and cubes of melon and a jug of wine.

'Now I'm yours,' said Vivia.

'Now you're safe.'

Vivia wore a silk dress of riverine green that Maura had
put on her after another bath.

'Why do you want me?' she said.

'Why?' He laughed, fulsomely. He enjoyed it. He said,
'You're my gorgeous little angel, Vivia. And much more.'

'What more?'

'My demon girl.'

'Why,' she said, 'do you call me a demon?'

How could he know – the past? The dark?

'But I've made you wait,' he said. 'To see if you could.
And you can.'

She looked at the floor.

Never before had she been so afraid of him.

Zulgaris came to her and pushed her back against the
frescoed wall. Lifting her skirt, he took her. Obviously he
had wanted her since the morning, seeing her flaming and
glowing there in the holy church.

He squeezed her breasts and bit at her throat, just above
the awful chain.

'I don't tire of you,' he said. 'My perfect bitch of Hell and damnation and all non-existent subterranean things.'

He ended with a sigh.

She felt his seed run down her legs and as he left her, her skirt dropped exactly back into place.

'God exists,' said Zulgaris. 'The rest is foolishness. But we must pay court to it. Every lord needs some ritual about him. I'm glad that you marked yourself at the fast, but you must make the sign of the cross, not the circle. The cross reverences the suffering and sacrifice of Marius.'

'Yes, my lord,' said Vivia.

He was not enervated. He had adjusted his own clothing and now got hold of her hand. 'Did you like the garden that you saw?'

'Garden . . . Yes, my lord.'

'Now I'll give you a garden of your very own. Only those you want will come there.'

She thought, *he* would come there.

He led her from the rooms into an annexe, and through a door which she had never seen opened – he gave her the iron key.

Beyond was a courtyard, high up, perhaps on a roof, and wide to the sky. Above its walls were bars, and they had been gilded. She knew of course, here was her cage.

'Vivia may romp here,' he said, 'do as she wishes. Take what she wants. That fast today was nothing to you. But you've fasted nonetheless.'

She did not look at him.

The garden court had mulberry trees in painted pots and flowers in troughs. A marble tank stood in the centre with water and fish, like the other she had seen before. The ground was paved, and here and there were mosaics, a man with deer and hounds, a girl with lutar and maidens. Pillars ringed the walls round, below the gilded spikes of the bars. Ivy and vine had twined them. There were benches of marble, with bright cushions and transparent scarves draped there. Lamps burned low on the pillars overhead.

'Do you understand me?' he asked.

'No.'

'I think she does.'

'No.'

'What did she do when first she met me? Waking from her long sleep?'

'I don't remember,' said Vivia.

Zulgaris said, 'You're a wonderful find, my lovely girl. How did you survive in that castle of Hell? What evil spirit came to you there? Was it some outrage of your father's?'

Vivia said nothing. She looked at the pretty courtyard and heard the water bubble from the fountain that was shaped like a dove.

'You are,' he said, 'mine. And you may do what you want in your garden. Look, what's there?'

And Vivia saw a vague movement among the pots of mulberry trees.

This frightened her more, but in a moment a single female figure came out of the shadows.

She was young, very young, perhaps only eleven or twelve years of age. Silky hair hung down her back that was the shade of rust on a sword, shining as the sword before the rust. Dark eyes fixed on Vivia. Not on Zulgaris.

'Come here,' he said, and the girl approached. 'Now,' he said, 'what do you think of her?'

'Is she my servant?'

'More than your servant.'

Vivia waited, as she always did.

Zulgaris took the girl gently by the wrist and drew her near. She was dressed in white silk, with embroidered bands at neck and hem, and a girdle of red and silver twisted. Her hair was her best ornament, its excellent colour. She smelled of her hair, warm and new.

Zulgaris was drawing back the girl's sleeve.

'Look at this.'

There was some goldwork on the girl's arm. A bracelet? *No*. The skin – was *sewn* together by a golden thread.

'My physicians are very clever,' he said. 'I see to it that they are.'

Vivia gazed.

The girl's face repelled her, so blank and starless, as if she were half blind and did not mind it.

Zulgaris began to pick carefully at the golden threads.

Abruptly the flesh came undone.

A ribbon of scarlet, dark in the soft lamps that burned there.

'Now Vivia can do as she pleases.'

Vivia stared.

Blood ran from the wrist of the girl. Her vein had been cut, and then secured. Vivia shuddered.

'Drink it,' said Zulgaris. 'You can't hide anything from me.'

Vivia stood, prim, a stone again.

Zulgaris grasped her head, her skull through its mantle of jet black hair, and forced her down, down towards the welling seam.

She thought, *he* had told her she would come to this.

Her lips touched the blood. It was cool, not hot. Then hot, like fire. It – tingled.

Vivia's mouth opened. The blood ran inside.

From the satin wrist Vivia licked up the blood.

She licked and licked. It was quiet. It was like suckling at a breast . . .

Zulgaris drew her mildly back. Zulgaris snapped his fingers, and from the shadow now came a man in a long gown, who bent to the girl, lying at Vivia's feet, and sewed her arm together like the satin it was. Tailor not physician.

'And now,' Zulgaris said.

He put Vivia on her back along one of the benches, and the physician was gone. The girl – was gone.

In her mouth the velvet taste.

Zulgaris did not kiss her. He licked at her lower mouth and she knew again the former stirring, like leaves turning over.

When he mounted her Vivia arched her back.

She put her hands around him and caught his buttocks, forcing him through her, his tool deeper and deeper.

She had forgotten that he was Zulgaris and had hung a golden chain around her throat to make her his slave.

His sex ran through her caverns. Now he was not selfish. He forced her to acknowledge him.

Chambers of her body gave way.

Vivia screamed and was lost among a whirl of fires and night and silences.

'Good,' he said. 'My wicked little girl.'

She closed her eyes now, not to see him. But something yellow moved on the edge of her lid. She looked after all.

The terrible leopardess Talia was the last thing to emerge from the shadows of the garden.

Gilded as the bars and splashed with bits of their inner black, her eyes sizzled green. She wore jewellery, an anklet with a tinkling bell.

Vivia lay alone on the bench.

She sat up and pulled down her skirt, it would not help her now, and Talia, the leopard who had hunted men, snarled.

Vivia rose.

She felt light as stardrift on the earth.

She pointed at the leopard.

'*Down*. Down on your belly.'

The words came from somewhere in her heart, and Talia whined as Vivia had whined under another tirade of sex, and lowered herself.

Her spangled tail lashed the paving.

Vivia said, 'No.'

She went to the leopard and touched her on the brow. The tail stopped its whipping veering.

Talia's head drooped.

The growl in her throat, as Vivia scratched her forehead, was a harsh unwilling purr.

It was too bright. Too bright, the sun.

She told them to draw the draperies over the windows and only then would she get out of the bed.

The staining of the glass came between her and the light.

Vivia bathed slowly.

The two girls angered her and she slapped them, one after the other, and they wept.

Zulgaris had had her and she had – she had experienced the dreadful glory which only in the dream had she known before.

Did this mean the dream was true?

Yes. And she had drunk the blood of the young girl to prove it further.

Vivia did not want to dress.

She lay on the bed and willed Zulgaris to come back to her. She wanted his body. Now she would not be afraid. She would have his blood.

But Zulgaris did not come.

Bells rang tiresomely in the city of Starzion, and clocks chimed. Dogs barked. She heard the distant rumble of wheels.

How long this careful, searing day.

At noon the sun passed from her windows.

Vivia dressed herself. She drank a little wine and honey.

She made them show her all her dresses. She marvelled at the vivid colours. And the jewels the same.

What would she wear for him tonight?

To entice him.

The afternoon waned and she put on a blue gown that was like a sapphire, and not a single jewel beyond the chain that was locked at her throat.

Zulgaris did not come to her.

Then she took out the iron key.

She went, in the evening dusk, into the annexe, and unlocked the door of the courtyard where she might do as she wished. Girls, giants, dwarfs, eagles, leopards, were all one to her, now.

Chapter Three

TWO SOLDIERS HAD TAKEN HER from her village. She had been extremely afraid. They did not speak to her, had only bundled her on a pony, which she found difficult to ride.

They had been saying, in the village, that the Prince Zulgaris had come back from a great campaign in the mountains. Sometimes people were taken from the villages for Zulgaris to study. They never returned.

Gula knew she had been selected because of her hair. Her father had always said it would be her curse (her mother was long dead) and sometimes when he was drunk he would beat Gula, because her hair was red.

One of the soldiers, who had ridden in an hour after sunrise and were sitting by the well on their horses, had pointed at Gula's hair.

When they grabbed her, she dropped her pot of water. It broke.

Gula's father came shouldering through the gathering crowd, and the other soldier, who had not pointed, tossed him some silver.

'She's going to the prince's court. To serve a lady there.'

Gula's father stowed the silver. He bowed. She knew, he was glad to get rid of her.

She was nearly sick from fear at first, but then she felt only lost and hopeless. She was too unimportant for God to listen to. She had long since ceased to pray for any help.

They passed through the hills, and far off she saw the

glinting of vast waters, the sea she had heard spoken of. Away beyond lay the desert, she knew.

Gula became agoraphobic, and hid her face in her hand.

Then one of the soldiers did speak to her. He told her to look where the pony was going. If there were any accident, they would be held accountable.

Gula stared in terror ahead at the passing landscape. At last the walls of the city appeared above, with their watchtowers, banners, and the crowded roofs inside.

It was such an alien sight that suddenly everything seemed equally unknown – the smell of blossom trees along the slope, the rasp of grasshoppers in the grass.

Gula was conducted through byways and alleys of Starzion, and through a long tunnel of coordinating passages, that led at last into Zulgaris' citadel.

Here a woman took charge of her, and everything changed from frightening brutality to frightening luxury. There was a little room with windows that were closed by two panes, one of opaque white and the other of clear leaf-green glass. In the room were a white bed and a table with a mirror of pure glass, in which Gula saw for the first time, properly, her own worried reflection. And shied from it.

There were coloured tiles in the floor, washed by the green light, and a bathtub stood there which gushed warm water when a lever was depressed in its side.

Gula was told to bathe herself by the woman, who, while not laying a finger on her, stood by and watched, and now and then advised her that this place or that must be seen to.

Then Gula had to dry herself on a wide sheet, and after that the woman told her to select essences from the table with the mirror, and rub them into her body, under her arms, into the soles of her feet, between her small breasts.

Gula had been too fearful to be truly embarrassed, but the business with the essences made her blush.

The woman took no notice.

She, with firm rough strokes, rubbed scent into Gula's

unlucky red hair, and brushed it vigorously with a bone-backed brush.

Gula was dressed in a white gown.

She knew enough that she supposed she was to be led next to some man, who would rape her. But this did not happen. Instead a meal was brought to the door, and another girl, older than Gula and quite plainly dressed, laid it out on the table.

Gula was too nervous to eat, though the woman commanded her to do so. She managed some fruit and bread – she had never seen white bread before. Then the woman made Gula drink a little wine.

After this the woman went away, and a man came in.

This now was the moment of defilement.

Gula trembled and went white.

But the man, who was rather old, instead sat down on a chair and told Gula she was to serve a foreign princess that the Prince Zulgaris had taken during his battles in the mountains.

Because this was the story the soldiers had told, Gula did not believe it, but she saw at least she was not to be raped yet, or worse, given over to some experiment of the prince's. (Such things had been muttered over now and then in the village. The snatches Gula had caught had seemed very strange.)

She relaxed a little.

Then the old man explained that the door there led into a corridor, and so into a garden. Sometimes a chime would sound, and then Gula must go to the court. She would not necessarily be alone.

Gula did not ask why. She had not said anything.

Only when the old man inquired if she understood, did Gula meekly nod.

After the old man had gone, Gula sat alone.

She drank some more of the wine. She felt somewhat better. Was it more sensible to be optimistic? However, Gula's life had not fitted her for optimism.

At sunset (the white window pink, the green window brown) another old man entered in a long gown, and he examined her thoroughly, looking into her eyes and

nostrils, putting his hand over her breast – to feel the heart?
Then he told her she was to serve a beautiful lady, very
dear to the prince. And then he said she must be brave.

The servant girl had come in and lit a lamp, and by its
light, with a razor, the old man cut Gula's wrist.

Initially Gula did not comprehend what had happened.
Then she realized she would die now, and she slid on to
the floor. The physician picked her up.

The servant girl held Gula in a chair while the old man
sewed up Gula's wrist tightly. Soon the blood stopped.

Gula had not quite fainted.

The servant gave her more wine.

Perhaps an hour later, Gula heard a silvery chime.

The servant girl gestured impatiently at Gula.

Gula got up like an automaton, and walked through the
other door, down the corridor, and out into a cloud of
mulberry trees.

Soft lamps burned on pillars, and Gula looked across the
court. Gula saw a vision. It was two of the most beautiful
persons she had ever seen.

One was a man, like an angel out of the sun. He wore
gold and his hair was gold and his eyes. Beside him was
a woman dressed in something like green water. Her hair
was black as night. She was so pale, and her eyes were
like smoking jewels, green or blue or purple.

Gula went towards these beings more in fascination than
obedience. She was drawn. Now she really did believe in
magic.

Even when the man undid her wrist, Gula was not
properly frightened any more. Nor when the woman took
her wrist and kissed up the blood.

Gula floated away on the tide of the kisses.

When she woke up she was in the white bed. Her arm
hurt, and was very securely fastened, and also bandaged up.

Gula began to cry, not certain for what particular
reason.

Next day she woke to a sound of soft chattering, like birds
or squirrels.

Presently three girls came into the room.

They were Gula's age of eleven, or a little older. There was a similarity about them. They were pretty, pale skinned, with long shining hair, and one was blonde.

They stood looking at Gula.

The blonde said abruptly, 'What was it like?'

Gula said nothing.

One of the brunettes said, 'She's stunned. She can't speak.'

'Or she's stupid,' said the blonde.

Gula said, 'I don't know what you mean.'

'Look at her arm,' said the brunette.

They looked at Gula's arm.

The blonde said, 'When they took me from my house, they were uncouth men, and I didn't ask them anything. But I asked the old man. He said we're to serve a lady like the moon.'

'Yes,' said the second brunette who had not spoken before. 'She wanes, and we must give her our blood so she can be strong and bright again.'

'A bell in the floor chimes when she treads on it,' said the blonde. She was arrogant from former care. Someone had been kind and made much of her.

Another darker face looked round the door.

Gula realized she was a star among stars, for she had been the first.

She said, 'She drank my blood from my wrist.'

'What was it like?'

'Like my mother kissing me,' said Gula. She did not remember this, but she had often had to be inventive.

There were six of them, these young girls, including Gula. Only the blonde, Ingret, knew – and told them – that therefore, with their moon lady princess, they made up the magical number of seven. Zulgaris was an alchemist and would have taken care of such a thing.

The blonde was the daughter of a minor courtier. It had been explained to her that she was the natural leader of the virgins who served the Lady Vivia.

Gula, though, had been first, and Ingret was jealous

of Gula. She made Gula tell of her experience over and over, and then Ingret verbally clothed it with sorcerous trappings – the phase of the actual moon, the hour of night, the colours that everyone had worn.

All the six virgins were clad in white, but their embroideries were different. Gula's were red and silver, Ingret's lemon and gold, which of course associated her with the prince.

The other girls were humble, like Gula. They came from villages or low houses of the city. One, the swarthy-skinned Oria, had been born in a brothel and took care to conceal this. Her new bizarre life, as the slave of a vampire – Oria knew the word – was better than the sodden life of whoring for which she had been destined.

That evening, after sunset, when they had dined all together in a painted communal room at the centre of their apartments, they sat listening for the chime of the bell.

'This time I will go out,' said Ingret. 'The physician told me, when he examined me, that we must take turns, or we'll grow weak.'

Gula seemed weak and listless now. The other virgins observed her dubiously.

Oria said, 'I'll go too. She may need more than one.' Oria added cautiously, 'Ingret is very fine and may not be strong enough.'

Ingret frowned. She too knew that good breeding was connected to delicacy.

'Oria may accompany me,' she said.

The chime sounded at last – they had almost given it up.

All six virgins started. Gula felt a pang as Oria and Ingret passed from the chamber.

In the corridor Oria cannily remarked, 'How the princess will love your beauty, Ingret.' Ingret smiled. Oria said, 'You are more like the moon than she is. I've heard that she's dark, the vampire.'

'Don't use that word,' said Ingret. She looked unsure at last. 'Vivia is the moon, the queen of night.'

They stepped through among the mulberry trees and gazed across the court.

Their moon was sitting on a bench among the scarlet and

honey of the cushions. She wore blue tonight, a moon in the dusk.

But above the sky was dark and scored by stars.

No roof or pinnacle of the palace was visible beyond the bars of the court. They might have been hung high in space.

Chapter Four

 It was not the same girl that Vivia saw. Who were these? Presumably also hers, whatever else. Vivia beckoned, peremptorily.

Both girls came forward.

Their faces were not like the first one's face. These two were focused, and the darker girl looked cunning.

Vivia said, 'Hold out your hands.'

The two girls did so. Unlike the first girl also, no stitchery to undo. What then? She must bite them. Bite in the way Zulgaris bit her, but more deeply. Sharper. Was this possible?

The blonde girl had come up to Vivia. The girl bowed, her loose hair swinging all about her.

'I'm Ingret, lady.'

Vivia did not care who she was. She took up the right hand and turned it over. The smouldering vein ran all along the milk-white arm.

Vivia lowered her head and Ingret shuddered.

There was no resistance. As Vivia's teeth touched on the vein, it parted. It was not a bite but some sort of witchcraft. As if . . . as if Vivia now had power over matter.

The blood came. It was thick and sweet. Vivia drank, slowly, and Ingret began to croon. 'So lovely,' Ingret groaned.

After only a moment she slumped to the floor of the court.

Vivia looked at her, surprised. The girl had evidently had some kind of orgasm and swooned.

The second girl, the dark one said, 'I'm Oria, lady. I'm much stronger.'

'Come here then.'

Not knowing if she had had enough, or what constituted enough, Vivia took this one's wrist roughly and sank her teeth into it. Again the flesh gave way.

The blood was different, more sombre, like Oria's hue.

Oria said and did nothing, standing before Vivia, leaning a little into the bite, that was all.

Vivia raised her head. A single splash of red was on her pale mouth. She said, 'What do you feel?'

'Like my mother kissing me,' said Oria. When she smiled, her right eye closed more than her left, like a wink.

Vivia let her go.

'I've had enough.'

'There are three others,' said Oria, 'and the girl you had first, Gula. But they cut Gula's arm, didn't they?'

Vivia struck Oria across the face and the girl staggered back. She did not look affronted or upset. More as if the expected had happened.

Vivia said, 'What a lot you know.'

'We all know,' said Oria. She looked at the tooth marks in her wrist, little and perfect, like two tiny rubies. Already they were closing over. It *was* witchcraft.

'He's given you to me,' said Vivia. 'My slaves.'

'They told us you're the moon, lady.'

Vivia compressed her lips and licked off the drop of blood. Now she was pristine. No one could know what she had just been doing. And on the wrists of Oria and the unconscious Ingret, just two little marks like the stain of a flower, or as if a bracelet had pressed too hard.

Vivia got up.

She went to the fountain and looked in at the fish. She paced about. She plucked a rosy orange flower, and put it in the neck of her blue dress.

There were no leopards tonight in the bushes. Only the stars above.

Vivia left the court, and Oria bent over Ingret. Ingret stirred. 'Isn't she beautiful.'

'And cruel,' said Oria. She smiled again, secretively.

Zulgaris did not come that night. Vivia lay in her bed and thought of him with anger. How could she punish him? He was a man – invincible.

The blood moved strongly in her, and when she slept, she ran up the castle stair to the room of the dead horse, and when she burst the door in, the horse was galloping through the room, black as a coal.

She opened her eyes and saw a tall black shadow.

Was it the vampire? Had the vampire followed her?

But it was only the shadow of a chest thrown by the passing of the waxing moon upon a wall.

Vivia sat up in the bed, then left it and walked about the three rooms of the apartment. She felt too strong for sleep, too vital.

At a window she paused, looking through the coloured, moony panes, at the shape of roofs and towers below. Could she fly now? She did not dare to open the window and try. And yet –

Far off came the sound of music and laughter. Somewhere Zulgaris or his court made merry.

She did not know now if she was strong or strengthless. What were her powers?

She turned and took the flower she had picked from the table. She put its brilliant head into her mouth and licked at it. Could she make it live?

She laid it down beside a goblet and a dish.

She threw off the nightgown they had given her to wear and stood naked in the moonlight. She looked at her body in the mirrors of the room. She danced slowly, some old measure known in her father's castle.

In the morning Zulgaris came and breakfasted with her. She made up her mind that if he tried to take her sexually she would resist him (for she wanted him now). But Zulgaris behaved decorously, and they were waited on by servants.

Afterwards he led her down through the castle, and on to a long walk. Trees stood in pots, but there were guardsmen at intervals, who came to attention as they passed.

Below the walk were squares and gardens thick with cherry and walnut trees, whose blossom foamed pink and green in the spring breeze. In these lower courts Vivia saw again the creatures she had glimpsed in the church.

Three of the dwarfs were gambling on a squared board, shouting excitedly and using extraordinary oaths. Zulgaris pointed out to her their humped and contorted bodies, their large noble heads, their ancient features and huge noses.

The albino men were playing with a ball and bats under the cedar trees. They manoeuvred and pranced in silence, but for the slap of the wooden ball.

One of the black men only sat reading from a leather book.

'Where's the other?'

'He's sick today,' said Zulgaris, 'this climate doesn't suit him. My own physicians attend to him.'

Then they walked down a stairway and came into a round courtyard where magnolias grew mauve and peach-coloured, and here there were huge cages with silvered bars.

Zulgaris showed Vivia the white unicorn which was a type of goat, the cat with long reddish fur, the ostrich which rocked slowly from one end of the cage to the other and back again, majestic and bottom-heavy. There were monkeys playing more playfully than the albinos with bats and a soft ball of feathers. A big lizard with a skin like time crouched under a tamarisk.

Zulgaris fed fruit to an animal that was like a cat and a snake combined and had a bushy tail.

'You show me these things,' she said, 'to remind me I'm your possession too.'

'Do you need reminding, Vivia? Of course you belong to me. And I understand you very well.'

She looked at him in the sunlight, and thought of their bodies united in lust. She hated him far worse than when she had not wanted him.

They came into a long room where there were cases of

thick glass. In one of these sat a woman with the horns of a ram – but she was not alive – a statue or a mummy.

A thing floated in a greenish tank. Zulgaris tapped the side of this and long rays spread, and next an inky fluid, which clouded everything in the tank, obscuring the beast. A pale blue eye peered out at them.

Beyond this room was a tunnel which led down. This was barred by two iron gates and guarded by four men.

Above the tunnel rose a tower.

'Do you see the clock?' he asked.

She thought he was proud now as a spoilt child, like one of the magnified boys of her father's knights, strutting with a prized toy.

She looked at the clock set in the top of the sand-brown tower. The clock was white as snow and marked with many black numerals. On either side of it was a figure, one of gold and one of silver. A golden knight, a silver maiden. The hands of the clock were also of gold. They showed it was precisely noon.

'My tower of study,' he said. 'You must climb to the very top before you can descend to my private rooms. Would you like to go into that inner place?'

'Why should I?' she said.

He did not chide her for her rudeness, he seemed to guess and like its cause. He said, 'You will come there, Vivia. And one of your little girls. You must sample all of them and choose which one.'

Vivia said nothing. She suspected all at once that Zulgaris watched her in the court. Naturally, he would.

'Do you like my choice so far,' she said, 'lord prince?'

'You must do as you want. They're yours.' Again she said nothing. Zulgaris waited, then he said, 'Tonight, make your choice. At midnight someone will bring you to me. And you must bring your girl with you. Whichever one you want.'

'Haven't you a preference?' she asked. 'The blonde girl, perhaps.'

He said, 'No, I leave that to you.'

She thought maybe he would take the girl in front of her. They were nubile though so young.

She clenched her brow. Then smiled.

'Yes, my lord.'

Vivia walked in the afterglow into her courtyard, and the chime she had not heard had sounded under her foot.

As if they had been told, and perhaps they had, all six of her virgins manifested at once.

She looked at them.

One blonde, the swooning one, Ingret. And the dark crafty one, Oria. Three with brown hair of varying darkness, staring at her, their hands clasped, and one biting her nails. And Gula, the redhead.

There had been a knight of Vaddix's who had had red hair. But not like this.

It was more like, this hair, the red-orange flower Vivia had tried to give life, and which had withered overnight.

'I'll have all of you,' said Vivia.

She looked at them curiously. The youngest – Gula? – was five years her junior, probably. The others four or three years. Yet they were children. Yet . . . they were women in miniature. Each with her slender form and woken blossoms of breasts. The faces that verged upon knowledge. The closed look of virginity.

Had Vivia ever looked like this? She thought not. But perhaps she was wrong.

She went towards a flowering tree that stood close to the fountain. Its blooms were so pale they were almost without colour.

The girls trooped after her in their loose white garments. They smelled sweet, sweet as the tree, young and clean and perfumed. Their smell was not the raw male odour she craved now, Zulgaris and his scented sweat, the fire of his tool. No, they were like swans, or doves.

Vivia sat beneath the tree, on the ground, where cushions carelessly lay – to tempt her? The cushions too gave up an attar.

'Who'll be first?' said Vivia.

The girls flushed and jostled, hung back, tried to come forward. With the result that no one approached.

'I'll be angry with you,' said Vivia softly.

Ingret thrust forward.

'No,' said Vivia, and Ingret's face crumpled. She was not used to disfavour. 'You,' said Vivia, indicating a nut-brown girl. 'You first.'

The girl crept up and sat down at Vivia's feet.

'What's your name?'

'Zinel.'

'Give me your hand.'

The girl extended her arm mutely. She looked pleased and whitely scared.

Vivia bowed to the wrist and the blood came at a graze of her teeth, rapid and fiery, like wine.

Each girl *tasted* different. Ingret tasted *blonde*, and Oria smoky. The brown girl was like something richer yet oddly more thin.

Vivia took only a little, then she pushed the willing arm aside. The girl Zinel whimpered. 'Hush,' said Vivia. She beckoned the next one, the fairest of the brown girls. This one scampered to her, smiling. 'Why do you smile?' said Vivia. The girl's expression faded. She became serious. Vivia took her blood. Different again, cooler, more herbal. (Vivia had not bothered with her name.)

The third brown girl was timorous and cried. Vivia said, 'Stop that, or I'll slap you.'

The girl stopped. She said, 'I wanted to please you.'

'You'll please me by being quiet.'

This girl's blood was quite dull, sluggish and remote. She was the least interesting.

The last shimmer left the sky.

As she drank, Vivia saw from her eye's corner that Oria had begun to fondle the first girl, the thin one, Zinel. Perhaps Oria had meant to comfort Zinel.

Zinel twined her arms round Oria's neck. They lay back on the cushions and Zinel giggled.

Vivia left the dull girl, pushing her away.

'What are you doing?' Vivia said, to Oria.

Oria looked at her, and her right eye was closing in its wink. 'Consoling each other for losing you.'

Oria stroked Zinel's small curved breast. She half glanced at Vivia, checking to see what Vivia would do.

Ingret stood up.

'It's my turn with the princess.'

Vivia said, 'I've had enough.'

Ingret stamped her foot. Then seemed alarmed.

'Forgive me, lady, I didn't mean – '

Zinel moaned at Oria's touch, and the other two brown girls had begun on each other. They were kissing hungrily, like two lovers.

Vivia eyed them coldly. Had the scent of their own blood inflamed them? She said, 'You're sluts.'

Ingret reddened the length of her blonde face and neck. She kicked Oria in the side, but Oria took no notice. 'Make them stop, lady.'

Vivia beckoned Ingret to her and Ingret came quickly. Vivia had felt a sort of stirring, little more than a tickle of curiosity.

She put her hands on Ingret, feeling her slim narrow shape, contouring the two breasts as if she made them. Ingret shivered and shut her eyes. Vivia felt nothing.

She lifted Ingret's wrist and bit into it, perhaps unnecessarily hard. Ingret sank down, pressing her body into Vivia's body.

'I love you,' whispered Ingret.

Vivia received this accolade with utter scorn. She would make Ingret sorry. Vivia sucked more deeply, and Ingret's blood sprang sweet into her throat.

The brown and smoky girls, Zinel, Oria, the other two, were writhing now about the cushions, and blossoms, shaken apparently from the tree by the vibrations, fell among them. There was the scent of spiced oil – Oria had Zinel's breasts quite bare at last and was anointing them, rubbing her lips over oil and silky skin, nibbling the small nipples until they stood out in points. One of the other brown girls had her companion's wrist. She was sucking it, bloodlessly, nevertheless into a livid bruise, and the second girl meanwhile stroked at her own crotch softly, quickly.

More blossoms fell, and drifted on the spilled oil. The air was hot and aromatic.

Ingret had collapsed, but Vivia did not halt in her drink.

Gula had retreated to the shadows.

Chapter Five

❀ THE ROOM WAS RED, DRAPED in velvet, its few
pieces of furniture lacquered scarlet and gold. The
ceiling was a canopy of crimson damask. There
were two windows, one an oval of magenta glass on which
was inscribed a rampant lion in gold. The other window
was tiny. It looked out and down through a wall beneath
a ledge of bars. Into the lit court of Vivia the vampire.

Zulgaris watched the scene of Vivia's blood-drinking. He
had had this room coloured expressly. For blood and the
passions.

The little girls, all but Ingret and the russet one, Gula,
were toying with each other delightfully. Their brown and
white bodies intertwined, half naked, the skirts pulled up
and the bodices undone. The round flowers of white and
swarthy breasts with stars on them flickered under the
loving attention of little slim hands.

From above, the tree rained blossom. And Vivia sat
under the tree in her violet dress, milking the blonde
girl, who plainly was vastly aroused, part unconscious,
yet unable to keep still.

Vivia herself did not seem unduly involved. But it was
sometimes hard to tell with her, her face so lovely it was like
a mask, her fluent soft body so mature and yet so young –

Zulgaris had unlaced his loins and taken out his pole,
which he had begun to finger daintily.

As the girls writhed together on the cushions and their
animal little cries arose through the tree, he saw smooth
fingers active on the lightly shaven downy mounds of

pubes. And there the whore's daughter, the darker one, had her face just there, and he could make out the pink flutter of her tongue –

Zulgaris increased his motions. He rubbed vigorously, coaxing the firm head with his thumb.

The girl that Oria was licking had begun to come. Stifled gasping cries turned to wild insane shrieks. And this in its turn seemed to set off the other girl who worked on herself. Now the screams played in unison, a strange harmony.

Zulgaris felt himself engorge from the base of his spine to the tip of his penis. Flame ran down his back.

'Now.' He spoke hoarsely but distinctly.

And from before him, crushed into the space between his body and the window wall, the hag Witch raised a golden vase.

She pushed it up around Zulgaris' member and he jetted richly into this tube, his body bucking and his face squeezed in a grimace of pleasure.

Not a drop was lost. The Witch knew better than to fail him. The fluid was for use in his science. As he finished and stepped back, she plunged a golden stopper into the vessel.

When she had left the upper room, the Witch went down deep into the tower of Zulgaris, into a plain stone chamber where the phial of semen was to be stored.

Inside the shut door, she stood looking about. Countless potions, tinctures, unguents, oils and powders stood in containers, each marked with a symbol that only the prince, or she (sometimes) could decipher.

The Witch held the golden jar in her hand, then set it on a stone table, where lay an apple also carved and polished from stone.

The Witch remained looking at the phial.

She had some cause. It was not the same one in which she had collected the excretions of her master's excitement. Identical, however, this vase held the semen of a goat, which she had masturbated into it an hour before joining the prince in the scarlet room. By her own arts she could keep this fluid moist and render it sufficiently odourless.

She had never practised the deception of Zulgaris before.

It was true, he believed himself a mage. And was clever. Would he learn of the substitution? Would his experiment falter because of it?

The Witch did not think so. Chemical powers would also be at work, besides the force of Zulgaris' mind and her own, and the supernatural presence of the two other women.

The Witch spoke a word under her breath.

It was a foul word.

Long ago, Zulgaris had used her for his magics. Even aged, still he had used her, climbing upon her once with his golden body, serving her thirsty need with his hungry phallus.

She had come to him a traveller, skilful, but without temporal worth. This he gave her. He made her the attendant at his rites, the priestess of his armies, and protected her from the wrath of the church. Only one love-making.

But now he had found this other one.

This *young* one.

Cold as snow and hot as fire.

Vivia.

The Witch knew she must protect herself. *She* must take some power over Zulgaris. The essence of his manhood suited her well enough. Once she had had it in her body. But it would do, locked in the gold urn. She had her own clandestine chambers. And he, he trusted her, thinking she was only his.

Chapter Six

Now, **THEY BROUGHT HER A** silver dress.

Tisomin fastened Vivia into it. The neck was very low and a band of white lace showed, stitched with pearl. Her hair was put into a great silver net, fastened with buckles of opal.

At midnight she must go to his tower, and take a girl with her from the court of blood.

Vivia had exhausted Ingret. Servants had had to come – from somewhere – and carry Ingret to her bed. The others went, laughing self-consciously at their own antics.

Vivia called Gula from the shadows of the mulberry trees.

'He wants you for tonight.'

Gula looked terrified. Vivia did not take pity. After all, maybe Gula was wise to fear the worst.

In the silver gown, Vivia felt herself armoured against sex. No, he would not employ her.

The girl had been clothed in white again, a white robe bound with a sash of silver.

Soon after eleven had struck from the innumerable clocks of the palace and Starzion, a woman, muffled in black like an assassin, came to conduct them to Zulgaris' tower.

They threaded the stair, the lower garden, corridors. If they went the way he had taken her, Vivia did not know. Perhaps they passed among magnolias, and things rustled in cages. There was a long room, and perhaps the octopus peered from its tank.

When they came to the tunnel, the guardsmen there

stood to attention. Above, the huge clock was only a blur.

The woman unlocked the iron gates, but Vivia and Gula went in alone.

There was the scent of garden trees by night, but as they walked up through the tunnel this faded. Then began a smell of medicinal things, and of incenses, and of darkness.

It was dark in the tunnel, although bald torches burned in its walls at intervals.

They came up to a tall door made of some semi-transparent material, whitish, and as they stood there, the door opened wide.

No one was there, only a flight of steps going up and up, this time lit by lamps that hung on the walls in orbs of flame. The door closed behind them as they entered.

'I'm frightened,' said Gula.

'Why? He may only cut you up and eat you,' said Vivia, at her most callous.

She walked up the steps, holding her skirt from her feet with one hand. The child-girl came after her, breathing fast from terror and exertion.

It was a dreadful climb, up, up. Now and then came a brief landing, and in the walls were painted images from the Zodiac, but in grey and white and black, the crab, the virgin, the scales, the two kids of the Gemini.

Gula sobbed for breath.

Vivia found the climb did not weaken her, it only annoyed, troubled.

At last they arrived in a long hall. Here windows looked in all directions. (They must be directly behind the clock.)

Vivia walked to a window, and saw the nighttime Starzion stretched far, far below. Lamps shone in the city, and here and there a doorway or large window gaped with light. There was no moon.

Beyond the city the hills rolled down to some endless darkness that seemed, even by starlight, faintly to glow.

'What lies outside this city, do you know?'

Gula panted. She said, with difficulty, 'There is the sea. And a great desert.'

Vivia recalled, almost without concern, her glimpse of waters during her flight through the sky.

What was the limited view of this tower to that?

There was another door in the farther wall. It was black. It had already opened, mysteriously, inviting, like the other.

'Why don't you run away?' asked Vivia.

'Where would I go?'

Vivia nodded.

She went straight in the black door, Gula after her, and the door closed behind them.

Now they were confronted by a continuous mountain of steps falling down and down and down, as if into Hell.

Gula wept.

Vivia said, 'Shut your noise, you silly child.'

She set out down the steps in fury.

Presently poor Gula followed her, wincing and stumbling, with small cries.

Deep in the earth lay the workrooms of Zulgaris in his role of alchemist and magician. This was no tent on campaign, but a place built long ago within the confines of the palace, topped by a peculiar tower with a double flight of stairs. It was only possible to reach the subter of rooms by going to the head of the tower and then descending much deeper into the ground.

The outer room was white, hung with white velvet and laid with furniture lacquered white, or made of silver, A door inlaid by platinum blocked off the chamber beyond.

There were books in the white room bound in velum – white human skin. And vessels of silver gilt and alabaster. Jewels, amazing by their colour in the whiteness, poured out of chests of white wood.

It seemed to be a treasury, but what lay beyond the platinum-bound door was worth much more.

Vivia and her slave emerged eventually into the white room.

Here Zulgaris awaited them.

Like the jewels, he blinded by his golden colour, for he was dressed entirely in gold, and a golden circlet with a topaz bound the hair back off his forehead.

Gula stood gaping at his handsomeness, but Vivia flounced aside and would not look.

'You will tonight,' he said, 'take part in a great work. You need do nothing but be obedient to me. This then is the girl you chose, the redhead. Very good. Now I'll choose a jewel for each of you. You can keep these trophies.'

He went to a chest and pulled out a rope of garnets clasped in silver. This he hung round the startled neck of the girl. To Vivia he gave an emerald in the form of a beetle, pinning it to her gown above the left breast.

'Green for the love planet, Venestris,' said Zulgaris, 'and red for the sword planet.'

He surveyed them. He was in that moment clothed also in power. He laid one finger on his lips. 'You must not speak again, once you are in that place.'

Vivia said, 'Or what?'

'You'll die at my word, I'll kill you,' said Zulgaris gently. 'The same applies if you reveal to anyone what you see or do.'

He turned and spoke to the platinum door, which opened.

Beyond the door it was very dark. No lamps seemed alight there, and yet there was a kind of *sheen*, which once they went in, enabled them to find their way.

It was a huge area, and objects glittered and gleamed along its walls. Distantly a thing was, some ornament set far into the wall itself, and this was in the likeness of a man, but winged.

Between them and that shape a huge apparatus was set up. It seemed to hang from the ceiling – that was itself invisible. Enormous globes of glass, shaped like fruits – clusters of small ones like berries, larger vessels in the appearance of huge pears and apples – swung shining in the black air. They were suspended by chains of brass, silver and gold, and behind them turned slowly a skeletal clockwork of silver, incomprehensible.

On either side of the apparatus were grouped, again, the

images of the Zodiac, now in dim colours, archer and fish
and balance, lion and ram, others . . . and some additional
symbols also that were alien to Vivia and probably to Gula,
an old man carrying a sack, an angel, a toad with a knife
laid flat upon its head.

These visions also moved and swung like awesome dolls.
Feathers and garments seemed to flit.

Nearer stood a slab, an altar perhaps, of a stone that was
like a piece of fallen sky, so blue and glimmering, with hints
of stars and clouds caught in it.

The other side of the sky stone, they now saw, waited the
prince's Witch. She wore a black gown sewn with dark red
signs and the palms of her hands, which she held upright,
were silver.

Vivia noted the Witch with reluctant unease. She recalled
the platform, and the green flames.

Around the Witch's neck was a chain of diamonds that
spat white fire.

Zulgaris led Gula courteously to the foot of the sky stone
altar, and gestured that she must stand there. The Witch
was already at the altar's other end. What would go in
between?

Zulgaris had turned aside now to a curtained alcove. He
kneeled down, his power ripe about him, an aura that was
visible. He seemed to pray.

Cut into the wall above were the words: *While sleeping,
watch.* (Vivia could not read them.)

When Zulgaris rose, he had a knife brilliant in his
hand. With this he touched the hanging vessels of the
apparatus, and at his touch, each rang like a bell and on
a different note.

Then he moved about the altar in a triangulate motion,
to the Witch, to Gula, to Vivia. He touched each with
the tip of the knife. Vivia recoiled, but did not dare
to speak.

The air was dense with steams and scents and with
intention.

Then the magic began.

A dove flew straight up, right out of the altar, as if out
of the sky indeed. It was indigo in colour, and carried

in its beak four roses, one red, one white, one pink and one black.

As the dove lifted towards the invisible ceiling, these roses blended into two flowers of a blackish red, smoked and disintegrated.

The dove disappeared.

Zulgaris spoke a word.

The Witch said, 'The three women, who are the three phases of the moon, now unclothe themselves.'

Vivia was angry, but she did not remonstrate. It would do no good. She saw the Witch carelessly, almost disgustedly, divesting herself of her robe. And timid Gula, bashful, slipping out of hers.

Vivia stripped the silver dress with slight awkwardness, for Tisomin was not there to help. The beetle of emerald rang on the floor.

Now there was only the chain at her throat. And she was left in her shift, but the other two women were naked, even of their jewels. The crone raddled, skinny and hard as a wire, Gula soft, pathetic, pliant.

Zulgaris now crossed round the altar in the form of a square. He cut Vivia's shift open so it fell and left her as naked as the other two.

She bridled. They could steal glances at her, these underlings – then again they did not matter.

Zulgaris lifted Vivia and carried her to the altar and laid her there, flat on its surface, which was very warm.

He was stripping himself rapidly.

It was to be her, then . . .

Or was it to be her?

Naked, he stood there, glorious and stupid and golden. His manhood was alert and stood upright, and in the odd light his prick seemed powdered too by gold.

He went first to the Witch. He ran his hands over her body, put his finger in her mouth, and then evidently into her lower mouth. She allowed this, blank of face. To Gula Zulgaris went next. She hung before him helpless as one of the instruments of the giant apparatus. He made her touch his cock, and put his finger too into both her mouths.

Vivia saw tears run down Gula's face, silvery in the light.

Would he do these insulting things to *her*?

Zulgaris spoke another word, and the apparatus began to move rapidly up and down, and going round now in a circle. Bell notes came spontaneously from the vessels.

The light changed:

First of all, Vivia beheld above her two cages, hanging like the vessels. They too seemed to be of glass.

In one cage was a yellow cockerel with a vermilion comb. In the second cage brooded a white hen.

Then the light went to a thick turquoise green.

'Venestris,' said Zulgaris, 'rise over us, bringer of love.'

He touched Vivia again with the knife, above her heart.

In their cages the two chickens bustled with their feathers, and in the zodiacal figures there seemed to be a similar occasion.

The green light faded and was bloody red.

'Maxus, rise over us, bringer of conflict.'

He touched Vivia's genitals so weightlessly she did not feel it.

Now came blue.

'Hermis, rise over us, bringer of wisdom.'

Her head. The chickens were blue as sapphires. The hen squatted down.

Now grey, like rain.

'Satux, rise over us, bringer of time.' (Her belly.)

Purple. It soaked into Vivia's eyes like a drug.

'Vuls, rise over us, bringer of secrets.' (Her left hand.)

The purple dye seeped away.

Zulgaris was lowering himself on to her flesh. She would have shrieked with outrage, but did not risk it. After all, he had had her in front of witnesses before. In fact, neither of the other women, crescent moon and waning moon, looked.

Vivia felt his entry. She was ready, yet refused to enjoy him. Not in this way.

But he was slow, rising and falling on her. The light washed round them, a bizarre compendium of all the colours that had come from the five planets.

He rode her, not gazing at her body, but up into the air,

as the apparatus creaked and chimed and twinkled and tinkled.

And then an explosion of fire lit up in it, as if engendered by the rhythm of Zulgaris' groin.

The whole room lurched into life.

The high ceiling was still not visible, only a wreath of golden stars –

But on the wall beyond the rings of vessels – what thing was that with its wings and crossed arms?

Vivia started. The creature in the wall –

Her womb seemed suddenly to ignite, as the fire had done.

Suddenly she was torn towards spasms of ecstasy, unable to control herself. She uttered a thin high shriek, and heard – miles off – the vessels of the experiment clash in sympathy.

Vivia was borne upwards in the arms of her prince. Her dark prince. The vampire.

The ceiling of heaven was far away. She could see the stars, however, close as golden apples in a low-branched tree.

He had been in the wall of the alchemical chamber as in the wall of the cavern. Linked by screws and pins of gold. His teeth were diamond.

He flew with her so slowly, and yet again she felt herself dart effortless into orgasm, scream and fall back into another limbo of flight.

She saw the cockerel rising up and heard it crowing, and now the sun rose gold in the black sky, but a black lion swallowed the sun. And from the mouth of the lion rose instead a silver crescent moon, which grew to full, waned, and went out.

Two birds of fire fought in heaven. Then they burned, and from the burning they erupted and flew away.

Blood dropped in a snow towards the earth.

There were so many hourglasses, containing sparkling dust and black dust and dust like ground bone –

'The sun and the moon,' said a voice. It spoke of a marriage.

Vivia exalted and burst for the third time into bliss.

She would die. He would kill her.

She pleaded with him, but in silence. He had said she must not speak.

Fire, wind, a wave, a mountain, passed her.

She sank to earth, and blood lay in the rivers red as wine.

She saw the great lizard. It stood on the plain and now something dripped on it from the starry globes that sang overhead.

Vivia opened her eyes. She would not let him force her to come any more. She would resist it. She gritted her teeth and stared at his arched golden body.

Zulgaris bellowed a word.

And the room seemed to split.

Goldenness gushed through. It covered everything. For a moment Vivia too was made of gold, had been turned into it. She could not move. Even her eyes – eyelashes stiff as brushes –

And at the centre of her, the final spasm came and died, little more than a palpitation.

Over the shoulder of the prince (the yellow one) she saw the lizard on the floor in the black light which had replaced the gold.

But the lizard was still golden.

Every scale. It glowed and sparkled.

It was swallowing its tail.

It was swallowing itself.

It vanished into its own jaws, swam over, and was gone.

Vivia would not speak, but she pushed at him, the weight of him. She hurt as if at their first session.

And Zulgaris left her.

He was limp now, his vigour spent. He walked to the circle of hanging vessels. He stood looking at them.

The bottom of every one was filled with a liquid gold that blazed like fire.

Zulgaris laughed.

He said, '*Vivia.*'

Overhead the hen in her cage squawked comically. A golden egg dropped from her body.

The little girls were all over her.

Their little leeches of mouths, sucking softly. Silk tongues lapping.

At her breasts, her thighs.

Vivia lay in this bath of succulence. It was like the dream of her prince – her *first* prince. The wonderful mouths which had made love to her.

Something eased warmly into her secret part.

Vivia abandoned herself to pleasure.

She woke up before the ultimate moment had been achieved. She sat up, burning with a blush of rage that did not abate.

She was feverish.

She threw off the covers.

It was daylight, and the slovens who served her had not drawn the veils closed over the windows.

She shouted for them. No one came.

Ah. This was like that other time. The time of the plague. But such a thing was not conceivable here.

Vivia rose. She went to the windows and pulled across the slender silky cloth. The sun pooled on her skin and she burned white like fire. Nothing else. Not harmed.

Vivia stood remembering the night. She could not recall how she had come back here. But evidently she had.

And he, Zulgaris?

Her face changed, turned sluggish, nearly foolish.

Zulgaris was far greater than she had thought. He too, a master of illusion and sorcery – he had made her his thing. She had not only obeyed, she had been without recourse to any other means. His slave. *What had been set into the wall?* Vivia turned in fury. She went into the bathing chamber and the bath stood ready, steaming and scented, and by the side of it a silver goblet of wine.

Vivia drank thirstily. The thought of blood made her want more wine.

She bathed herself quickly and stepped out.

Zulgaris had come into the outer room and stood there looking at her.

She said, partly in fear, for she was very sore, 'Don't touch me.'

'Of course not,' he said. 'This isn't the time.'

How prim he was. She tried to feel scornful of him. But it was not easy. In any case, he was a man.

'There are oranges and peaches here for you to eat,' he said.

She wound herself in the sheet and went to eat the breakfast, not willing to dress herself in front of him.

He talked to her.

'The marriage of moon and sun,' he said, 'last night, we acted it, at the proper hour. It's the congress of Marius with his mother, the virgin moon. Sacred incest. It makes gold.'

'I saw,' she said.

'What did you see?'

'Birds of fire and a lion swallowing the sun.'

'Very good. You're a fine assistant, Vivia. Your unearthly quality makes you special.'

'The lizard vanished,' she said.

'Yet,' he said, 'it's in its cage, as usual. I've brought you a gift.' And he held out to her the small smooth egg of gold. This had fallen out of the body of the white hen. 'Take it,' he said.

Vivia took the egg. It was warm from his hand, and a flash of desire went through her body. It would be useless to attempt his seduction. For him, everything had its hour. Besides, he had used her up, she did not want to.

She put the egg on a table, it rolled a little then stopped. It shone in the occluded light of the windows.

'What do you know?' said Zulgaris. He leaned forward and caught her face in his hand. She stared at him now. 'An upland girl. Can you even read?'

'No,' she said proudly.

'There will have been no books in your castle, beyond perhaps a holy book in which you may have recognized a few chosen words – the marks for God and Marius. And can you count?'

'I can count to twenty,' said Vivia. She let him hold her face like a bird. She did not twist away.

'The clock on the tower of my rooms,' said Zulgaris, 'Describe it to me.'

Vivia was silent. Then she said, 'A gold knight and a silver girl.'

'The *numerals*, Vivia. Did you count them?'

'No.'

'There are twenty-four. One for every true hour.'

She drew back at last. She had not noticed the numerals on the clock. Did not care. A clock? What of the creature in the wall, the giant *bat*?

'Did you like,' she said, 'what the little sluts did?'

'How should I know?'

'You watch.'

'Do I?'

Vivia said, 'The blonde girl annoys me. She's a fool. And the dark one's sly.'

'You may lose the blonde one,' he said.

'I shan't be sorry.'

'You bled her out,' he said, 'she may die.'

Vivia was shocked, despite herself. She turned away. She had never killed, though sometimes imagined it, but that was always with a weapon.

Zulgaris said, 'No remorse, I see. Well, you must be faithful to yourself.'

He left her in her sheet before the dishes of fruit. What did he mean to convey? Only his displeasure?

Vivia supposed she should have pretended contrition, crossed herself, something.

Chapter Seven

DURING THE AFTERNOON INGRET DIED. She had not come to herself, and the extreme rites had been administered by two priests over her unconscious body.

The other girls kept to their chamber, save for Oria and Zinel, who played a board game in the communal room.

Once Ingret had stopped breathing, three old women came and washed her, combed her hair, and put her in a white shift. They were strong and lifted her into the plain wooden box themselves. A small wreath of myrtle was attached to its lid, to show Ingret had been a virgin. Then the lid was nailed in place by a carpenter.

By a side door and various yards, the coffin was taken out, and presently away in a cart, to the graveyard of Starzion.

Here, under the blossoms and the spring sun, Ingret was buried in a small slot of earth.

A solitary priest sprinkled water, oil and wine, and then the gap was closed with soil.

There were no mourners. No one had been told. Indeed, Ingret's family had no concern for her, once she was removed from them. Or they had given her up, since she went to the Prince Zulgaris.

The grave was in a quiet spot, under an apricot tree. All about the death garden stretched away, the markers of marble, wood and iron running to one of the city gates, and so into the hills. Between the graves stood cypress and oleander, and large bushes of rosemary to protect the dead.

About the apricot tree was a large plot of vacant ground. Ingret's, so far, was the only pit that had been dug here.

The myrtle had been tossed out on the mound.

A bird sang above the grave. Then it flew down and pecked wantonly at the myrtle wreath of Ingret's chastity.

On the first day of the next month, Zulgaris and his court and his knights rode about the city of Starzion. It was Zulgaris' habit to go forth in procession at intervals, partly to entertain the citizens, partly to display his earthly power. But also in a form of magical ritual, to go round the length of the city, like a hand around a clock, so renewing his claim to all of it.

At the front of the procession rode Zulgaris' guardsmen in their yellow and gold, and after these came an orchestra riding white donkeys and playing lutars, drums, pipes, harps and bells. Then there were girls throwing yellow roses, and after these the knights of lesser ranks, with white and yellow plumes and insignia of gold on their armour.

After the knights were drawn, by teams of white bullocks, a few machines of war, the favourite cannon in golden garlands, and perhaps a ballista that had done particularly well in some current fight, for Zulgaris constantly warred with other areas, keeping them in check, aiming ultimately to stretch his princedom, which already now encompassed the mountains, the sea shore, and the desert's nearer reaches, where he had built a fortressed town named Syr.

Behind the war machines, another orchestra, and then the prince on his gold horse, dressed in gold, with the golden circle binding back his golden hair. The sun itself.

After Zulgaris rode his companion knights, splendid, captained by Demed and Kazun. Then followed the court, riding, and dressed in every colour of the world, with its pet animals, large cream dogs, and monkeys, and cats on silver chains, and birds in gilt cages.

Behind Zulgaris' court were led some of his animals, the leopard Talia, in a collar of rubies, and other leopards hung with gems, horses and hawks and dogs, the eagle bound to the side of a chariot and now and then flaring its colossal wings in irritation, the goat-unicorn, and the lizard in a travelling cage.

At the back of the beasts walked the dwarfs and black men and albinos and giants, clothed in a fantastic way, with horned helmets or the masks of animals.

Vivia, Zulgaris' possession, rode behind these curios, on a white pony, side-saddle, in a snow white dress. She was veiled in blue against the sun from a little coronet of silver, and wore a silver half-mask over her eyes.

After her, on smaller ponies, rode her court of youth and beauty, the maidens Oria and Zinel, blonde Avra (who closely resembled Ingret, and was the daughter of a collecter of night-soil), Gula, Novia and Kisnen.

The maidens were also clothed in white, each with a particular colour embroidered on it. They kept very silent, being overawed and rather terrified.

The crowd named them as the girls of Vivia. And Vivia they named too, the name she had come to have, the *Night Queen*. For Vivia was Zulgaris' possession which was the moon.

Behind the vampire and her court came another orchestra, and then the guards of Zulgaris.

It was to the people of the city a satisfying procession, or a source of discomfort, for though he was feared by everyone, Zulgaris was not also loved by everyone.

None dared voice any dissent.

The streets of Starzion down which the procession traversed were wide and edged by poles where lamps hung against the dark. Broad-faced houses with gardens passed, civic buildings for the purposes of money and law went by, and well-decorated churches that had murals of Marius, angels, the delights of Paradise and horrors of Hell.

The sun was turning to the west before the procession had finished its progress, and as the light lowered and turned amber, torches were lit and the lamps on the poles began to be ignited.

The music sounded silly to Vivia, and the cheers and murmurs of the crowds who lined the streets and roofs startled her. She caught her own title and considered it.

Presumably they did not know what really she was. Or did they know, and only think her safely contained by the might of her master?

She grew weary, her back ached from her odd posture on the pony.

She was glad the dark was coming for she did not, now, like the sun, even though it did not seem to hurt her.

Her girls were so close she could smell their blood, but she did not want their blood.

She wished she had never been brought from the castle of death. She wished none of this had happened, and wanted to be a child again.

Strangely, strangely, Vivia, sixteen years of age, felt old. Worn and ancient from the taint of the dark one who had remade her.

If only it were possible to sleep and return in sleep to Ursabet, and the former world.

The night came and clad Starzion, Zulgaris' city, and the lights were garish and bright.

They came back to the palace and rode into a wide courtyard, that opened to receive them.

Cold and old and stiff, Vivia dismounted from her pony with difficulty, or thought that she did.

Her girls clustered about her.

Vivia turned from them icily, and went away with a servant to her prison with an emerald beetle and a golden egg.

THREE

Chapter One

THE MONTH PASSED. SUMMER FILLED Starzion, which grew very hot. Flowers were brought to Vivia's rooms every day by the servants. The whole city seemed to smell of roses, fruit, ordure, sweat, and baked stone.

The days were all the same. Vivia took to sleeping in the afternoons. Sometimes Zulgaris would dine with her, more often not. He came to her bed now only two or three times in every ten days. Had he tired of her after all? His ardour indicated he had not. Did he have other women? Vivia would not question. She doubted he would tell her the truth. And if he did, and it was so, what could she do?

She went to her courtyard and milked the young girls. Avra was stronger than Ingret and less demonstrative. Oria Vivia tended to avoid. But Oria and Zinel seemed happy together, the younger girl deferring and Oria superior and pluming herself. Vivia would take only one girl at a time. The scene of the orgy did not therefore repeat itself, at least, not in her presence.

Vivia had been bored in the castle of her father, and now she recognized a different and more intransigent boredom. There was no Ursabet to amuse her. No secret place to go. Her dreams had been usurped by unfulfilling reality.

She thought with care of the thing she had glimpsed in the wall of the subter room. The thing like the god who was a bat.

How could it be that Zulgaris had such an image? Its

dwelling had been the caverns far off. *She* had woken it. Was it possible it could also be here?

What did it mean to her?

A hot night came. Nightingales sang like clockworks in the palace gardens, and Vivia could not sleep alone in the blue bed.

She rose, and put on a robe of silk, and belted it close.

An idea came to her that, through some formless sorcery, she could cross all Zulgaris' palace, come to the tunnel below the clock-tower, enter, and somehow reach the subter rooms of his alchemical practices.

This was plainly absurd. However.

Should she attempt it, no one could harm her, even should she be accosted, for she wore about her throat the infallible symbol – the chain – of his ownership.

Could she recall the way?

It seemed to her she could.

She left the apartment, went down the stair, came to the garden. Was this door locked? Vivia would not try it. Instead something made her put her finger into the lock of the door. She was the key. The door opened.

The garden was hushed by night, even the nightingales fell mute at her arrival among them.

She crossed beneath the trees and dew dropped warm upon her face and hands. The smell of roses, ordure . . .

The second inner door gave without prompting.

Beyond stretched a corridor, wide, with mosaic floor. The night guards of Zulgaris stood at their intervals all down it.

What would they do?

Vivia glided into the corridor, a girl in a pale silk garment, her mass of black hair feathering behind her as she went.

Not one man moved. If any eyes followed her, she did not see.

Doubtless, if she was abroad, then she was meant to be. And women – were nothing to be feared in the general situation.

She turned this way, that, passing by closed doors of carven wood, by other passages hung over with curtains. Lamps burned, but here and there were dim stretches, and once a well of shadow, and in this place something brushed by Vivia, and suddenly she could see it clearly, and in that moment too she heard the tinkle of the bell. It was the leopardess Talia, patrolling the corridors.

But Talia paid Vivia no attention beyond a brief, perhaps subservient, flinch of her tail.

Moonlight fell through windows on the floor.

It seemed to Vivia that now she could see as a cat does, as the leopard had. But before she had thought of this, she had not been able to, which was curious.

She tried her theory, looking askance down the darker lanes and byways, seeing nothing. And then setting herself to see, and *seeing*, in a sort of dusky lens, every facet, even to the glimmer of carving on a door or chair, even to vague figures that seemed now and then to linger behind long curtains, embracing humans, or supernatural things set loose by nightfall and emptiness.

At last she found her way out again, and passed along Zulgaris' walkways above the courts of his creatures.

The moon blazed now, and turned the leaves of the trees to hot ice. No one was abroad here, but for the sentries, who might have been statues.

She went down among the magnolias, into the place of cages, and the animals did stir at her passing. The snowy goat-unicorn turned its head, and the bear-cat growled in its throat.

Vivia breathed into the air, willing everything to silence. And silence fell.

The lizard was in its cage. It had taken on the hue of night, a dull soft black.

At the door to the room of cases and mummies, she touched the lock, and the door opened. This could only be magic, for Zulgaris would undoubtedly keep all this area secure.

Suppose someone were to apprehend her now? She would say she had been walking in her sleep. It seemed so simple.

The octopus banged against its tank. In the bubble of green glass its blue eye floated. Vivia raised one hand,

and a cloud of ink shot from the beast, blackening the water.

She came out and saw the tunnel and the four men guarding the iron gates.

Vivia descended.

She stood between the men and their faces were like stone. Could they perhaps not see her? Had she been granted, against human things, a cloak of invisibility?

Vivia said, 'I'm on the prince's business.'

She touched the huge lock of the gates, and one of them swung slowly wide.

A seed bloomed in Vivia's mind.

It was not herself who had managed this. It was her first prince, the dark god, her vampire lord. Truly he was in the subter, and had called to her.

She felt afraid, gratified.

She went in and up the tunnel to the tower.

There was a difference, for under the cascade of steps which led down, the white room had not remained. It had gone away, actually gone, and instead there was a wall, and below that a drop of thirty feet or more, into some abyss.

This smelled of old death. Perhaps someone had fallen in there long ago.

Vivia touched the wall. It was moving. On a pivot, the whole piece was rotating, and soon enough another room came into view.

In the dark Vivia beheld nevertheless it was a room of palest rose, curtained and adorned like the other white one, with books, scrolls, boxes of jewels that shone like green and red blood through the night.

Vivia stepped into this room, fearless and sure now.

She approached the other door, which was faced with gold.

There came, as she touched it, a flash of fire or lightning, the rush of a wind.

As these faded she saw that the door had a guardian, a silvery two-headed hound with jaws that dripped bloody flame.

Vivia screamed. Then she controlled herself. An illusion – it would not hurt her.

She spat into its dual faces, and the hound went out like a candle.

The door opened and she stepped through.

There was a sentence cut into the wall. She could not read it. It said: *Do not deny resurrection to the dead.*

A corridor ran away with doors at either side. In the nearest was a grille.

Vivia went towards it, hesitantly. And abruptly a head appeared there. It was the head of a donkey. It did not bray. It spoke.

'Look what was done to me!'

Vivia did not reply, and the head went up as the creature climbed on some piece of furniture to display more of itself at the grille. It had a man's body.

'I was burnt. He put this on to me. I didn't know till they showed me.'

A smell of awful rottenness came through the grille.

How could it speak?

Vivia walked away and the creature sank from view.

In another door was a window shaped like a star. Through this Vivia saw a woman lying on a pallet. She was naked, and her lower part was a worm, a huge worm, that twisted over and over on the straw.

Vivia wondered if she were only dreaming.

In the next room, that had bars across it, two men had been joined together. They sat sadly in the darkness and would not look at her. They had four legs but only two arms, between them.

Vivia took the turn of the corridor and there was a huge door made of ebony, apparently, carved all over by figures of demons and other winged things.

Vivia went to the door, and it gave, without her even touching it.

Now, she was in the subter, though not in the room where Zulgaris had 'married' her.

Darkness, luminous to *her*. She saw a huge skull, white as an almond. Inside was wedged a glorious honeycomb, and bees, small and almost black, buzzed to and fro, in and out of the eye sockets. Two hands of gold held the skull and seemed to be trying to crush it. On the wall behind was a lionskin.

Elsewhere, a balance of silver rested on the point of a steel sword. The sword was wreathed by white poppies.

Another door barred the way. Above were carved the words – meaningless to Vivia – *Know yourself*.

Vivia pushed the door, and was in the subter room.

It was gigantic, and now the apparatus of the experiment did not fill it up, it seemed to stretch for a mile. Indeed, hills seemed faintly discernable at its extremities, hills just rinsed by the moon. But the moon was not there. Unless it was Vivia herself.

She passed by sundry things. A deformed apple tree with fruits of silver. A temple built to an odd triangular design, transparent, within which lay a knife. A fish that was partly real, or seemed to be, but it had a head of brass. Either a real fish changing to metal, or a metal fish coming alive . . .

The hourglasses were ranged across the room. Every so often one of them would upend itself with a clank, and the sand run the other way. This seemed to happen at random, but probably did not. They were taller than Vivia, the intruder.

One was full of diamond dust which glittered. In another it was the dust of bones, with tiny fragments still whole. Another held powdered ebony, or soot. A fourth had something in it like pink smoke.

An hourglass reversed itself. Vivia saw that, behind the sand inside the crystal, there crouched a tiger. Then it was gone.

There were symbols cut into the walls, or into the distant hills – foreign, unreadable even if Vivia had been a scholar.

Things ticked and twanged, and from miles off a music seemed to come and go.

The smell of the chamber was sweet and open, like a country hill at evening.

The figures of the Zodiac stood still. She saw them all, and the other more unorthodox images, old women, girls, cats with double tails, snakes that swallowed towers.

Vivia moved on, and found the wall was there, despite the illusion. Beyond it, or deep inside it, the hills were or seemed to be. Nearer there was granite.

And in the granite – the being *was*.

. . . Elements of limbs and arms and wings. At their apex a masked, helmed face.

A huge bat, with the face of a man. Or even – of a woman.

She remembered, and cold waves of heat moved up her body. The sound of wings. The exquisite warmth which drew on her. Ascending into Heaven.

And then the face she could not, even now, remember at all. So pale. The dark bars of the eyes and brows. The mouth. The *mouth*. And then the red in the eyes and on the mouth.

Her prince.

Vivia had been kneeling for a long while.

Nothing had happened.

She looked up again, and now she saw it, clearly, the god in the wall of Zulgaris' subter.

It was not the same.

No. The face had become a golden mask of the sun – incredibly, the sun mask that was shown on the face of Marius Christ. But through the mask, *below* the mask, something glinted. Eyes, lips –

There were golden joints to the skeletal being. Could it be they held it together? At the elongated elbows, at the wrong-pointing knees, the sockets of the thighs – golden joints and pins and screws. Yes, she had seen them when she lay under Zulgaris on the blue altar that was like the sky, and now no longer there –

The hands too were golden-pinned. And in the interstices of the wings, golden *chains*, fine as cobweb.

Vivia became aware of a table between herself and the god. It was a table of brass, and on it lay a single silver counter, octagonal in shape. And a cup of glass, unfilled.

Vivia stared at these things in turn.

She rose, went to the table, took the counter. She held it up and saw, beyond it, as if through a spyglass, an opening in the wall that matched the counter's shape.

Vivia went quickly and pressed the counter into the wall. Then stepped back in fear.

A whirring, clacking noise came from the being.

Slowly, as if painfully, it stretched itself, the joints and bones and wings.

And then the right hand went out, out and out, for the arm of it was prodigiously long. Out and out, and then folded back. And the bone fan of the gold-pinned hand went to the golden sun-mask.

It drew the mask off its face.

And so she saw again, as she had already thought that she had, the vizor of skull. And in the skull, no eyes, but long, long dripping teeth of sheer-cut diamond.

Its left arm was moving now, out and out, folded back and down.

It reached for the glass goblet on the table of brass, so delicately.

The glass was raised up, to the vanished lips. It rested between the diamond fangs. Tilted. The residue of something ran out, *red*, and stained the cracked stone-bone of the jaw.

Blood? Did Zulgaris feed it blood? But it was – a toy.

Only that.

For now the glass was set back on the table and the arm folded home.

And the whirring slowed.

And the counter fell out of the slot, straight back beside the empty goblet.

Vivia let out a terrible cry. It was like the shriek of her orgasm in this very place, but pain now, worse than pain.

He had brought it to this. A god. So powerful was Zulgaris. So blind and idiotic and banal and foul and *wise*.

Vivia bowed together. A dull hurt was in her belly. She saw the golden mask had been put back upon the subtle fiendish face of bones, and now the whirring stopped entirely.

'My prince,' she said, 'my lord.' She wept.

Her dream had broken.

She had no choice now but to vacate this spot, to retrace her steps to her rooms – and could she recall the way? It seemed to her finally she was confused and could not.

And if Zulgaris should find out –

She dragged herself from the chamber, and there she was in the white room. A lily lay upon the chest of jewels.

Vivia fled.

No one detained her. Nothing seemed to notice.

Chapter Two

DAYS WENT BY, SEETHED IN summer heat. Vivia grew sullen. She did not want to leave the bed, but lay there, white as an icon, on the blue surface.

Tisomin and Maura tried to tempt her. Fruits and flowers, iced wine. (The ice cut from deep wells.) Board games, and views from the windows – which showed, actually, only roofs.

Vivia did not, even in the warm evenings, go to the courtyard of virgins.

Zulgaris did not visit her.

On the fourth afternoon a man was shown into her apartment.

From his long white gown and insignia, Vivia knew him for a physician.

She hurried the clothes of the bed around her.

'Draw these curtains back,' said the physician. He said, to Vivia, 'The sun is off the windows, and you should have air.'

'It stinks,' said Vivia.

'Nevertheless, it's good for you.' The physician approached the bed. 'I must examine you.'

'No.'

'If you won't comply, my assistants must come in and hold you.'

Vivia cursed, an oath of her castle.

The physician was not shocked. He smiled. 'I won't hurt you,' he said, blandly.

But he did.

He pawed her body with fat hot hands, and at length told her she must lie back, as if he meant to join with her in the sexual act.

To her horror he probed her inner reaches. She screamed in outrage, and Tisomin (traitress) held her firmly.

The physician washed his hands in a bowl of scented water Maura brought.

He smiled again.

'Good news, lady. You're pregnant.'

Vivia stared at the man, speechless in utter disbelief.

When Zulgaris came, it was at sunset, the sky stained and flaming.

Tisomin, who had held Vivia, she had sent away, her face red from slaps. Maura hurried out.

'Poor Vivia,' said Zulgaris. 'Are you very frightened? You'll have the best of care. And I'm glad. I like the notion that you're carrying my child.'

'The fool made a mistake.'

'He's no fool and he hasn't made any mistake. You're in your second month. You conceived beneath me on the blue altar. Can you imagine how perfect and exact that is? The child of alchemy. The offspring of the sun and the moon.'

He was dressed in regal black embroidered by flowers.

She hated him worse than ever before. Although Ursabet had told her of pregnancy, she had never properly menstruated. Often she had missed several months. He was lying.

Yet – why should he?

'I don't want a child.'

'It won't trouble you. Nurses will rear it. Anyway, you may change your mind. Though I don't see you, Vivia, as a mother.'

He advanced towards her.

Vivia said, as she had said to the physician, 'No.'

'The damage is done,' said Zulgaris. 'It can't be occasioned twice.'

He took her quite carefully. She had no pleasure. She hurt still from the roughness of the physician. She loathed her own body. Did not believe any of it.

They dined in silence. A roast and vegetables and bread and pastries, all of which he sampled. She took nothing.

'I don't worry about you,' he said, 'I know you find your sustenance elsewhere.'

He was insultingly beautiful, with his crooked nose and long looped mouth. The gold flowers glittered.

He did not know she had entered his subter, bested his demons, seen the clockwork creature in the wall.

But then, had she dreamed that too?

At midnight (clocks struck) Vivia crossed the annexe and unlocked the door of her courtyard.

The lamps burned as always. The mulberry trees were thick and darkly green.

A girl came from the shadows. Gula.

Vivia said, 'Fetch the others. All of you.'

Gula vanished at once, obedient slave.

Very quickly the girls came out, in their modest white nightwear. Gula and Avra, Zinel and Oria, Novia, Kisnen.

'Stand in a line, there, by the fountain.'

They did so.

Vivia scowled. She showed them the knife she had kept from the languid dinner table.

Zinel, Novia, Kisnen looked scared. Avra looked only vague. Oria . . . pleased. Gula merely accepting, subservient.

Vivia went to each of them and slit their little nightgowns staight down. Each fell off, revealing the budding nudity of the six girls.

Vivia surveyed them. She dealt as she had been dealt with.

She went to the flowering tree, which now was only massed by thick black-green.

'Come here.'

They came slow as deer approaching an uncertain pool. Oria was pretending. Oria was not truly afraid.

'You first,' Vivia said to Oria.

Oria came near.

Vivia seized her wrist. She slashed with her teeth, which suddenly seemed long and sharp as the fangs of a leopard.

A great gout of blood poured from Oria's wrist. Vivia drank.

Then she pushed Oria back, knowing the wound would not close swiftly as usually it did.

Oria was staring –

(Vivia thought of her irregular menses and how she had seldom bled. Like a fortress of white stone, holding in its vital fluids.)

'Now you,' said Vivia to Zinel. Zinel made a funny little noise. She came forward reluctantly, and Vivia seized her.

Again the slash of leopard teeth. Zinel bled copiously. Vivia drank.

Her lips and chin were red, and blood had splashed on her bodice and into her lap. As if . . .

Zinel ran crying to Oria, who, clutching her own arm, did not comfort her.

Kisnen Vivia summoned next, then Avra, then Novia. Then the girls stood in a blood line. Pools of blood spread on the paved ground.

Vivia's eyes glittered. They looked black, vicious and unhuman above her scarlet lower face.

Vivia said, 'Why are you crying? Don't you want to please me any more?'

Oria said, 'The blood won't stop.'

'Yes,' said Vivia.

And – the blood stopped.

The five girls were looking down at their arms, where the little needle marks of tiny teeth were now all that showed. Yet their bodies were splashed, like Vivia's, from the deluge.

Novia laughed nervously. Kisnen swayed but did not fall.

Vivia was not appeased. She called Gula.

Gula approached her with the old blind look. It was this one Vivia had not formed an opinion on. She was perhaps more fearful than the others, more slavish. However, she had a peculiar dignity.

Her hair appeared the colour of blood in the hot disturbed lamplight. The lamp flames jerked and flickered. Was a storm coming?

Vivia seemed to hear the low rumble of thunder across the hills beyond Starzion. But sounds were sometimes deceptive here. Carts drove through the streets by night, dogs barked at the moon, bells endlessly smote and rang.

More blood was necessary. It was a hunger, but not like the need of food, which Vivia, anyway, had never properly known. It was more a thirst – yet not a thirst either.

Vivia saw in Gula's eyes the abject and accepting fear of death.

In her rage, Vivia bent and tore her wrist wide open, a horrible wound worse than the others. Vivia sucked and guzzled, making evil bestial sounds. The other girls panicked and ran away, even sly Oria.

Gula did not cry. She looked lost.

Vivia held her across her lap and the red stains spread and spread.

Satiation came suddenly.

Vivia pushed the girl away, and Gula fell full length on the paving. Blood spilled from her wrist, then stopped. The mark was still terrible. She would be scarred for life.

Thunder came now, and a blare of lightning that turned the court as white as snow.

Vivia went sluggishly to the fountain and washed her face and hands, and the fish sprang to taste the eddies of blood.

Gula lay in the garden courtyard for a long while after Vivia had gone away, her rich gown swishing like a snake.

All Gula's short life she had known no love. Even her allegory of Vivia's first assault on her was typical: she had never felt a mother's kiss, but assumed it would be violent, like a bite.

Gula was not self-pitying. She had no pity for herself at all. Perhaps she thought that she deserved all the ruthless cruelty she had sustained.

It was just that she ached from over-use. Her mutilated arm was a cipher for her whole body, her mind, and her soul.

Finally she crawled from the place, managed to get up, and walked to her small chamber. In no area within did a lamp burn. All the girls lay in terror in the dark, afraid to move, as if by moving they would draw down some worse fate.

Gula too lay down in the dark.

She did not cry, as some of the others, stifled, did.

To cry would imply she had, in some corner of her brain, believed there was an option of kindness, which she had somehow missed.

The dark ticked away, now and then censured by rolls of thunder and a green flash through the window of green glass.

Long before the storm ended or the sun rose, something in Gula's body had made the decision that she too would die.

Chapter Three

THE WITCH CAME TO VIVIA like a jackal.

'I expected you'd send for me,' she said, this woman, not truly old and maybe never really young, standing there skinny and hard, with the gems of her teeth and the serpent in her right ear gleaming.

Vivia crouched in her chair.

'What do you want?'

'No, no,' said the Witch, 'what do *you* want?'

'Go away,' said Vivia. And then, 'Does *he* know you're here?'

'No, *he* doesn't know. He'd be in a fuss if he knew. He'd think we were up to something, you and I.'

Vivia remembered the hag standing at the altar as Zulgaris fucked *her*. The hag had been a presence only, the old moon.

Mysteriously, or not so strangely, perhaps, the two attendants had disappeared. The Witch had entered without preamble.

Vivia, still slovenly and lethargic, watched the Witch with newly dilated eyes.

'Let me tell you then,' said the Witch, 'what you want. To be rid of your bellyful. Or am I wrong? Do you want to carry Zulgaris' bastard, and get a hurt crooked back, and veins all blue in your white legs? To vomit and go short of breath? To lie about sick all summer and then spend days and nights heaving it forth, screaming in agony, like some cow in a field? Eh? Is that what you want? And do you

think he'll like you when you're all blown up and ruined,
lost your figure and half your hair and teeth? Well?'

Vivia recollected the women of the villages and the
castle, big with child. It was a fact they sometimes had to
have their teeth pulled – the baby had taken their strength.
And many were never the same after.

Vivia did not believe in the baby. The baby was nonsense.

And the Witch was her enemy.

'What's it to you?' said Vivia.

'I like you,' said the Witch. 'You make him good-natured,
and then things go nicely. Once you're all fat and distem-
pered he'll go off you properly. Then there'll be trouble.'

Vivia did not believe her. Full of blood, Vivia felt strong.
It might not do any harm to see what plan the Witch
offered. Ursabet had been canny in such things and would
have helped.

'Tell me what you mean,' said Vivia.

'I can mix you something. You'll puke, but you'll get rid
of the problem. He'll think you miscarried and be gentle
with you. You're his little treasure. And he'll want to try
again. But for sometime after my dose you won't have to
bother yourself about that.'

'If I told him what you'd said to me – '

'Then I'd tell him that you called me. And that you
listened.'

Vivia frowned. 'Suppose I don't want your muck?'

'Please yourself. Once you get fat and ugly you'll be
sorry, and it'll be too late then.'

'I'm not carrying.'

'Aren't you? Don't you feel it already, like a lump of lead
in your guts?'

Vivia blinked. She curled her hands around the arms of
the chair.

'I'll accept your potion then. I may not take it.'

'No, you may not. Don't wait too long to decide. Ten
or fifteen more days and I can't help you. See, I've done
it up already. In this little vial. It will taste nice, like
honey.'

'It'll make me sick.'

'You'll spew, but that would happen anyway from the child. No one will be surprised.'

'What else will happen?' asked Vivia. She did not relish her own discomfort and had seldom been ill.

'Oh, you'll feel you've a cart wheel in your belly going round. Then the blood will come and that will be that. Your own mistress again.'

'What payment?'

'Give me something if you like, to make it binding. I don't ask. I'm serving him in the long run, though he'd never see it.'

Vivia went to the table of precious fruits, hovered, thought otherwise. She passed on into the bedchamber and lifted the lid of the jewel box. Out came the necklace he had given her long ago, hammered gold with a pendant of emerald.

The Witch quivered when she saw it.

'Too fine. His love gift. He'll miss it.'

'Then I'll say I think Tisomin stole it and sold it. She's a bitch and it serves her right.'

The Witch smiled her awesome teeth. Another one was turning black and would soon be dug out for another jewel.

She weighed the necklace in her hand. Then set the vial of honey abortion on the table.

They told the servants who attended to them that Gula was not well. Which the servants could see for themselves. A physician did come, in the afternoon, but he did not stay very long, nor prescribe very much. They were expendable. Like Ingret, the most they could hope for was a burial in the rites of the church.

Avra went to see Gula. Avra was the oldest, thirteen years, and felt she was meant to do this. She stared abstractedly at Gula's white sunken face, an old-young child's, and went away.

Oria and Zinel did not come at all.

Later Kisnen and Novia crept in.

'Look,' said Novia, 'how carefully they've bound your arm. You'll get better.'

'I shan't get better,' said Gula.

They sat and looked at each other.

Kisnen said, 'She was wicked. She was like – a fiend.'

'She's a vampire,' said Novia. 'We were only lucky until now.'

'What'll happen next time?'

'She may even be gentle. Something had angered her.'

Kisnen snivelled, but in the presence of death her weak tears seemed superfluous.

Gula sighed.

She would be replaced by another girl, possibly another redhead, as Ingret the blonde had been superseded.

Novia said, 'My uncle told me a charm against vampires.'

'What is it?'

'It wouldn't work here. There are different kinds. And *Vivia* is a woman, too.'

Kisnen spread her hands.

'I know a story about vampires.'

Even Gula looked at her.

'What is it?' Novia asked eventually.

'There were travellers,' said Kisnen in an important, breathless little voice. 'They'd journeyed for months across the desert. The snow lay everywhere and they were without hope.' (Again Gula sighed.) 'Then they came on a great town. The gates were open, and the travellers went inside.'

'What, no soldiers, no sentries?' asked Novia.

'None. And inside on the street no one was. All the big houses were empty, and in the marketplace, the snow lay unmarked. But there was a well, and they broke the ice and drew water. It was the first pure water they'd had for a long while. They decided to remain in the town and people it themselves.'

Novia shook her head wisely.

Kisnen said, 'All over the town they found amazing statues. Very lifelike, standing by the buildings and in the gardens, and sometimes even in the halls of the houses.'

'Ah yes,' said Novia.

Gula, even in her extremity, looked frightened.

'The first night fell, and the people slept in the town, in the houses. It was very cold, and they kept to their fires. In the morning many were dead, white as stone, with the blood drained from them.'

'Yes, yes,' said Novia.

'But then,' said Kisnen, 'when they went to bury them, they found a great granary that was full of grain. They were pleased, and quickly buried their dead, and set about bread-making. All day they ate the hot bread. But then night fell again.'

Kisnen paused.

Gula closed her eyes.

Novia said, 'More deaths?'

'Many, many more. By sunrise half the travellers were now dead. And all the same, all drained of blood.'

'What did they do?' asked Novia.

'They held a council. Some were for leaving, and some were for staying. Then a young man stood up. He said he and a chosen few others would watch all night and see what happened.'

The three girls waited in silence.

Kisnen said, 'That third night, the man sat up with his friends, and they kept to the shadows of a great hall, while the others lay near the fire and slept. Presently a terrible blue cold settled on everything like a frost. The young man said to his fellows, *Can you feel your own hands?* And they could not. He said, *Can any of you move?* And they could not, nor could he. And then even speech froze on their lips.'

Novia clasped her hands.

Kisnen said, 'Then into the hall came three of the statues, walking as if made of flesh and bone. They went straight to the sleeping people and feasted on them, biting them with their stone teeth in the throat and wrist, drawing off their blood. Not until the sky turned grey did the horrible dinner end and the statues leave the room.'

'How many died?'

'A hundred souls,' said Kisnen.

'And the young man?'

'When the sun came, he and his fellows found they

could move, and they roused the living and told them what they had seen. And when they went to look closely at the statues, they saw that every one of their mouths was stained with red.'

Novia crossed herself, then added a circle for good measure.

Gula did not do anything.

Kisnen said, 'The last of the people fled the town, leaving their dead unburied, for the dead bodies felt to their touch as if they were *turning into stone*.'

Novia gave a soft shriek.

She said quickly, 'I know a story, too.'

'Yes?' said Kisnen, her duty done.

'An old woman and an old man lived in a hovel in the country,' said Novia. 'They had only a few chickens and a cherry tree to feed them, and they lived poorly. Then the winter came.'

Novia looked round the room; although hot with sun and full of summer odours – sweat, flowers, dust – a shadow sloped there. This day was going too.

'Evening fell,' said Novia. 'And as the sky turned black, the cottage grew dark despite the fire, and something knocked on the window, and then on the door.'

Kisnen shuddered.

Gula opened her eyes.

Novia said, 'The old woman and the old man never had any visitors, they knew it was nothing good. *Keep very still*, they said, *and it will go away*. But the knocking came again. Then it stopped. *Light the lamp*, said the old man, *the room is growing dark*. So they lit the lamp, and sat to their mean supper.'

Kisnen said, 'Then the knocking came again.'

'Yes, so it did. And much louder. On the window and the door and on the roof. And something said, *Let me in, I'm hungry. Go away*, replied the old woman in terror. *We've little enough and can spare nothing*. But the thing only knocked on the walls. Round and round the house it went, and all this time they saw nothing, only the black window full of winter night.'

'What did they do?' asked Gula softly.

'What could they do? There was no one to help. They put the last log on the fire and put the last oil in the lamp. And they prayed. But God was busy.'

'Hush,' said Kisnen, 'don't blaspheme.'

'I'm only telling you the story. The night wore on, and finally the awful knocking stopped. The old man and woman were so weary they got into their bed. *Do you think the oil in the lamp will last, and the log on the fire?* But the fire burned down, and the lamp burned down. They couldn't help it, though, their eyelids drooped and they fell asleep.'

Kisnen now circled herself. Then crossed herself.

Novia said, 'In the last hour of black night, the very darkest of all, the old woman opened her eyes. She said, *Is that you, husband, rustling about?* But her husband slept at her side. The fire had burnt out, all but one ember, and the lamp was dead. Then the last ember winked and was gone. The room was black, and in the blackness something moved. It dropped on the old woman soft as a blanket and before she could cry out, it had her throat and drank her blood. When she was empty it took the old man too.'

'What was it?' breathed Kisnen.

'It was the night itself,' said Novia. 'The night was the vampire, and once it could get in, it had them both.'

They looked at Gula.

She seemed very ill, but she said, 'I only know what they said in my village.'

'What was that?'

'That once all the babies died, and it was because a young girl had died in childbirth, after a vampire's bite. And she came up from the grave. She walked down the village street by night, and slid in under the doors, and drank the blood of living babies till they perished. No one could find her grave, so no one could stop her, which they'd have done by putting a knife through her heart, cutting off her head, and burning her. But they knew when she was coming, because the mirrors cracked and the milk turned in the breast, and every sharp thing became blunt and every blunt thing sharp.'

'But how did it end?' asked Novia.

'When all the babies were dead,' said Gula feebly, 'she was able to rest.'

'That's a terrible tale,' said Kisnen. 'Is it true?'

'They said it was.'

The room was now rather dark, though not so dark as the cottage in the story. Last dim drifts of golden shadow hung from the white window, but the green window was blue.

'Gula must sleep,' said Novia.

Gula said, 'When I sleep I shan't wake up.'

Both girls glanced at her.

Kisnen said, 'Are you afraid?'

'No, I'm tired. Perhaps it will be better. The priest always said it would.'

'But your sins,' said Novia.

'What sins?' asked Gula, in her innocence.

Outside the room, Kisnen said, 'We'll all end up the same way. Vivia will kill us all.'

'No,' said Novia, 'only the weak ones.'

'*We've* sinned,' said Kisnen. Their hands intertwined, then fell apart.

'There'll be time to make amends,' said Novia.

Vivia studied the vial the Witch had given her.

She did not know whether to drink the draught or not.

The Witch was not her friend, but what she had said was plausible, and after all, if Vivia were to become powerful, as she might, through her assistance on her back at Zulgaris' spells, then the Witch might need her.

The Witch would not dare to harm Vivia, for Zulgaris would know and punish the woman.

Here, Vivia was wrong. The Witch did choose to harm Vivia. The Witch had listened to gossip, and the same rumours which informed her of Vivia's pregnancy also told her how Tisomin and Maura were out of favour. (Vivia herself had confirmed this.) If anything bad befell Vivia, these two might easily be blamed.

Besides, the Witch had now a small wax image formed in the shape of Zulgaris. It had his crooked nose and clown's mouth, and hair made of gold thread. In its construction had been mixed Zulgaris' semen. This would give her some hold over him, some means surely to influence him.

The Witch had therefore gambled. She meant very definitely to hurt Vivia, to kill her if feasible. To this end, the essence in the vial was entirely poisonous.

Vivia, ignorant, considered it.

The day ebbed, and Maura lit the lamps.

By lamplight, once the girl had gone, Vivia considered the vial some more.

After all, possibly Vivia had not conceived, in which case nothing would happen, except perhaps her menses would appear.

Alternatively she did not want to bear a child. It was unthinkable. She had never thought that such a thing could happen to her, even if she had been saddled with a husband by her father, Vaddix. Ursabet would have assisted Vivia to remain barren.

They brought Vivia food, and she picked at it. After her glut of blood she wanted nothing any more. She felt very strong, invulnerable.

Now was the time to take the medicine.

She delayed.

In the night, Gula woke. She had been dreaming an angel was carrying her up to Heaven. All her misery was over. It was a lovely dream.

When she woke, she became sure that nothing so good would happen to her. Her death would not be easy.

Already she felt feverish and aching, and horrible pains lanced through her head and belly.

She leaned from the bed and was sick on the floor.

Then she lay longing for water and it had all been drunk, and no one would bring her any more.

The room was dark, and she thought of the story of the old man and woman and the vampire night. She thought of the vampire statues. But Gula was not afraid, now. She believed the tale of her village, and even that did not distress her. Such things happened.

Gula thought of Vivia. Vivia was so beautiful, so perfect.

Gula wished that she might have had Vivia to herself, and
that Vivia had been kind to her, at least sometimes.

The angel in the dream had resembled Vivia, black hair
and green eyes and velvet wings.

If only Vivia would come now.

But Vivia had no thought for Gula.

Gula did not matter.

Dry as a leaf, Gula lapsed back into sleep. Now devils
waited for her. There was no reason given for her torments.
She had deserved them simply by existing.

Midnight chimed, and Vivia, waking from a leaden doze,
counted the strokes.

Then she got up from the bed.

A lamp still burned in its pink crystal in the outer room,
and by its filtered light Vivia went to the table with the box
of jewels.

The golden collar was gone, and this would be blamed
on Tisomin, who had held her for the poking physician.
Instead, topmost, the emerald beetle gleamed up at her.

Beside it, the Witch's vial.

Vivia took the vial, uncorked it, and swallowed the liquid
at a gulp.

It tasted, it was true, slightly of honey, but mostly of
black and bitter roots, pale flowers, and crushed insects.

Vivia gagged at once.

Then she stood, naked and pearl, waiting for an immedi-
ate assault.

But gradually the nausea dissipated.

She felt quite normal now. Even a little soothed and
placated, as if the herbal had done her good.

She returned to the bed, and pulled the cover up to her
breast, and lay there with her hands folded over herself.
Perhaps it would do nothing at all, the Witch's drink. Vivia
shut her long-lashed eyes contemptuously and allowed
sleep to woo her.

Chapter Four

NEVER IN THE CHAPEL IN the village, or in the instruction of the priest, had Gula seen or heard of such an angel as this one.

It was made of stone, grey and dank, and mosses grew on it, even in the petals of its wings. As it moved the fabric of it groaned and *ground*.

However, it guided her through the subterranean tunnel, which seemed to pass beneath a river or the sea, for the walls of it were wet, ran with water.

Gula was so thirsty.

She wondered if she might stop and lick at the walls. But somehow she knew the angel did not allow this.

Now and then it turned its stiff neck and looked at her from stony eyes.

Gula followed.

She felt lonely, but she was used to that.

They reached a wall of rock.

The angel touched the rock with one finger, and a thin new stream ran out. It was very red.

Was it wine?

The angel beckoned Gula.

Would she be permitted to drink now?

As she came closer, Gula realized the running liquid was blood. But she was so desperate at last she did not mind, actually wanted it –

But then the angel signalled her to stop.

In frustration, Gula wept a little.

The rock was opening. It was a round hole, and it gave on sheer blackness.

The night was in there, night without stars or moon. Night of nothingness and silence.

Gula stood looking at it. The angel beckoned her once more, showed her she must go in.

And Gula, who had never had a say in anything, even the death of her body, went forward because she must, and into the hole of night.

She had never known such pain – was it hers? Yes, she must be bleeding now, and it hurt in the way Ursabet had said it would, although never until now had it done so.

Vivia pushed up from sleep.

Instantly her eyes flew open and a fearsome boiling occurred in her belly. The room spun and she leaned from the bed and vomited on the coloured floor.

The sickness was long and ghastly, and as it eased, still the roiling thunderous pain in her belly did not.

Vivia surged up and through the underwater quality of the swaying room, saw Maura standing transfixed.

Maura said, frightened, 'Is it the baby? Oh lady – '

Vivia remembered.

She had swallowed the Witch's brew to be rid of the baby.

At the simple memory of the brew, she threw up again, more violently than before.

There was blood in the mess, even she could see.

Vivia whined with affront and fear.

She fell back on the writhing bed and waited for her plunging womb to give up its invader.

'Shall I fetch a physician, lady?'

Vivia screamed as her entire belly seemed to twist – like a *wheel* the Witch had said, but this was more as if a whole carriage was racing through her vitals.

'No – what does he know about – anything – '

'Oh, lady,' cried Maura again.

Vivia kicked and leapt in tumult.

Something was quite amiss. She understood. After all, she had been poisoned.

The priests sprinkled holy water on Gula's corpse, and

said over the questions and responses of her absolution.

They swung the censer and anointed her forehead with a cross of sweet-smelling oil.

The girl was very clean, she had been laid out already by the three old women, her hair combed.

The priests finished their office, and stood looking at each other over her clean white cadaver. Nearby the coffin rested with its myrtle.

'The second one to die in her service,' said the fatter priest.

'Yes. And so young.'

'It's very strange. Do you know what they call her in the streets?'

'The woman Vivia – no.'

'The succuba.'

'Would the prince – '

'The prince is intrigued by all things curious. Remember the hag he keeps to work maledictions on his enemies.'

'But that,' said the thinner one, who was not very thin, 'is in the practice of the war-like prince's work for God.'

'The woman Vivia, however, may be in the nature of one of his experiments. He is an alchemist and treads a slender line between the light and the dark.'

The thinner priest held up his hand.

'He's our good and generous lord.'

'Just so. Doubtless the girl was sickly, like the other one.'

When they had gone, the carpenter came, and the old women put Gula in the box, and it was nailed down.

By back ways it went out into the city, and into the small covered cart. Towards the graveyard of Starzion.

Vivia was barely aware. She knew that men had come and pulled at her, and pushed at her belly. Then others bathed her with cold cloths but she burned. They held bowls for her to vomit into and took the reeking matter away.

Late in the day, Zulgaris came, a tall golden figure.

Now she hated him the worst of all. She would never be able to hate him more than at this moment. But then – she would not survive to hate him.

He held her hand.

'Oh, my Vivia, my beautiful girl – what have they done to you?'

Maura and Tisomin had vanished away. They were locked in unpleasant places, for they had been poisoning their mistress. Jealousy . . .

Vivia screamed feebly.

She tried to see if blood came yet between her legs, but it did not.

Zulgaris was gone and a physician was feeding her some gruel.

She vomited all over him and partly rejoiced, in her agony.

The quiet plot in the graveyard that lay about the apricot tree was touched by the descending evening sun.

The priest had performed his rite above the slot of earth in which had settled Gula's coffin.

He spoke calmly of how Marius Christ had lain in the earth behind the stone a few hours only, before rising glorious to his disciples, radiant as the sun. There was no death. All would rise.

When he had gone, they closed the hole with soil, and threw the myrtle of Gula's virginity on the mound.

A nightingale sang and it was very peaceful. The whole graveyard stretched as if asleep.

The last light faded in smooth warm veils, and the evening star came up.

A hunting fox trotted between the tombs, reached the two graves under the apricot. It snuffed at Ingret's place, dug for a moment, not very vigorously, then left it.

At Gula's fresh grave it stayed, looking at the ground with black fierce eyes. Then it turned to stone. For half a minute it was struck there, as if frozen. Then it bolted away, down the avenues of death, into the cedar trees that ran towards the hill gate.

Vivia was floating on a river of night. Stars sparkled below her, and further below still, huddled her pain.

She thought that she had surmounted death, or was she

only dying? It seemed to her a black door lay before her, distant as yet, but drawing closer.

But she could not die. No. She was young. She was Vivia.

And – what he had said to her.

'Dance with me,' he said.

Black in the bed as the womb of a panther, and so she was the panther's child.

But the panther lay over her. Had made exquisite love to her. Darkness. The prince of night. The king. And she the Night's Queen.

'Why won't you stay with me?'

'In a way I shall.'

She said, 'People will try to destroy me.'

He said, 'Nothing can kill you, Vivia. Nothing. Can fire kill fire?'

'I don't understand.'

He was a column of darkness, and she another. She stood upright and her death flowed out of her like the blood which had not come.

Had she invented these words for him to say? Then at some level she must know –

There was no pain. The stars still glinted below, but that black door had vanished.

Nothing but the wonder of the healing night.

She was the moon. The moon waned and waxed again. Soon she would rise radiant before them all.

She slept the sleep of renewal.

In the coffin under the mound of earth, what woke was not quite Gula. Perhaps Gula had gone, or perhaps Gula still slept inside the fibres of this new creature.

The new creature was strong, however, and had purpose.

It was eager.

It reached up, and with nails grown in a few hours to intractable talons, it clawed away the dry wood of the coffin lid.

Earth fell in on it. It did not mind.

Was it at all Gula, that which sat up through the mound

and caught upon its head, upon red hair full of splinters of wood, the myrtle crown of virginity?

The face was Gula's face, framed by her hair. Her young body. But in the mouth, the teeth of a *cat*, the canines now extraordinarily long and sharp.

This rose from Gula's grave, and stood, still upon the ground, beneath the apricot tree.

The nightingale had closed her music.

Only the star – Venestris, planet of love – shone high up in the east.

Gula, or what now was left of Gula, looked about.

She had been so obedient, this little girl. She did everything that she was told. And they had told her that those bitten by a vampire might become a vampire. And that these then went about in the dark.

Gula – who else? Gula's remnant – watched the horizons of the city in their rising stars of lamps.

Then she picked her way, on bare white feet, through the avenues of the graveyard.

She went, not towards the hills, but towards that sea, that maze of life, Starzion the city.

Gula did not know cities, but what Gula now was did not bother. The new Gula wanted those living things.

It took her a long while to traverse the ways of the graveyard.

She came at last into a narrow humble street, half dark with meagre lamps.

Gula walked down the street.

And in the houses, the mirrors cracked, and *dripped*. A woman feeding a child gave a cry as the child turned its head, wailing. Her milk was sour. A dull axe left outside turned bright. The knife of the husband was furred by a rust like red hair . . .

Bells and chimes sounded the hour.

Gula went on. She passed a tavern and the song faltered. She passed a church and the solemn choirboys began to giggle.

By the fountain in the public street – the water was rotten and slushed in muddy gusts, stinking.

A dead tree uncurled some thin clear buds –

Gula came to a house at the corner of a square. Its upper lights were out. A young girl was sleeping there. The family below ate and drank, as Gula glided up an outer stair.

How to get in. A lattice on the window against thieves.

But the vampire had gone in under the door.

Gula pressed herself to the lattice and she passed through. (The lattice crumbled.)

In the room, a neat bed, and the girl slumbering. Her hair was black as a raven and Gula had smelled it.

Vivia . . .

If only Vivia had been kind . . .

Gula went to the bed in her pale grave clothes, the white myrtle, plant of Venestris (love) upon her head. She breathed on the sleeping girl, who slept more deeply, more deliciously.

Why had they put her to bed – she had been betrothed that day and was excitable.

Gula did not know or care.

She lay down beside the raven-haired girl and stroked her, her full breasts and curved stomach, the girdle of waist and black silk of her loins. Gula slipped her hand across the girl's vagina, but, clawed, did no more.

Gula bit into the neck of the sleeping girl (who dreamed that her bridegroom did all this to her). Bit deep.

Gula, the vampire, drank the blood.

At last, at last, her raging thirst was quenched.

Chapter Five

BUT WAS SHE BETTER? SHE thought so. The milk they gave her was white and cool. She lapped it up. Swallowed it. It filled her stomach with peace.

Vivia lay and looked at the coloured panes in the windows, at the painted trees on the walls.

She had no pain. She was precise and whole again.

Zulgaris came.

He stood looking at her, and she lay looking up at *him*. She knew her beauty through his eyes.

'Thank God,' he said.

'God,' said Vivia.

'You lived. What strength you have. But in the church they prayed for you. I saw to it they did.'

Vivia laughed.

Zulgaris – frowned, as usual.

He said, 'Tell me your dreams.'

'I didn't dream anything.'

'I think that you did.'

'It was confused,' she said. She lied, 'I called for you, but you weren't there.'

'I was often here. You didn't know me.'

He too had lied.

Vivia was pleased. Her hatred of him had reached a peak and faded. She felt lenient.

'Tisomin,' she said, to test him.

'The two women were strangled,' he said. 'And buried without the rites of the church.'

'Thank you,' said Vivia meekly.

He did not know then, who had worked on her. But the one who had done so – what must she be thinking?

(For Tisomin and Maura – stupid sluts – Vivia had no concern.)

Zulgaris had had roses put into the vases. He touched her forehead quietly with one finger.

'You haven't lost your loveliness.'

Vivia smiled with closed pale lips, narrowing her eyes like a cat.

Two new girls waited on Vivia. They were physically similar to Tisomin and Maura, with long brown tails of plaits. Vivia did not bother with their names.

After a day or so (during which the curtains were pulled back only at evening) Vivia, watching the sunset on the floor, decided she would go to the courtyard of girls.

She did not especially want their blood. She had an urge to count them.

The iron key seemed unwilling in the lock.

Then the door gave, the courtyard lay before her. As always. The lamps softly alight. Twilight in the upper sky. Deep green in the trees from the lamps' luminescence, and shadow from the dark.

The fountain played.

Vivia stepped forward.

And a girl came out from the mulberry trees.

Vivia looked at her.

'Who are you?'

'I'm Denka, lady.'

'Where is Gula?'

'I don't know, lady.'

There was a whisper in the court. It said, *She died. She died.*

Denka was about eleven years old. Her skin was white and her hair a reddish shade. Not red like Gula's hair.

'Do you know what will happen?' Vivia said.

'They told me – you'd take my blood.'

Vivia made a flicking gesture with her hand and the new Gula came to her. *Denka.* Gula, like Ingret, was dead. Like Tisomin and Maura too.

Vivia took the porcelain wrist carefully.

She bit with caution. Took only a little of the perfumed weird stuff. She had missed it. Did not want it. *Wanted* it.

She pushed Denka back and the girl was docile.

'Fetch me one of the others.'

'Have I displeased you?'

'Don't be a fool.'

Denka scuttled away. She had none of Gula's languid, timid grace.

Presently Oria – it would be Oria – came out.

'Where's Gula?'

'She's dead,' said Oria. She added, fawningly, 'She wasn't strong.'

'Aren't you afraid?' asked Vivia.

Her eyes burned in the lamplight, but Oria only said, 'I'm very well, lady. Do you want me?'

'No. Go away.'

At the first lightening of the dawn sky, when the cocks crowed from the outskirts and the inns of Starzion, the vampire would skulk to her tomb.

She traversed streets swiftly, sometimes unseen, or taken, if she was, for a prostitute whose night trade was now done.

The way through the graveyard was easy.

As the beginning pink rays dropped through the apricot tree, Gula struggled beneath the soil, back into her vacant box.

She lay and listened, and a high whistling in her ears lulled her asleep.

She slept all day under her bank of earth.

If any saw disturbance in the mound, they took it for the work of birds or foxes, who often desecrated such graves. In winter wolves might come.

Day failed, flared, went out. Night returned.

When the last red had gone from the sky, Gula heaved her slight progress up again.

The continual labour did not irk her.

It was her destiny.

In what was left of her brain, she had a sense of rightness.

She did not know that she searched for Vivia among the black-haired girls of Starzion. Only knew that what she did was what she must do.

And Gula searched.

Along the slim back lanes, across the wide squares. She turned to lighted windows and later, to dark ones.

Gula's thirst was no longer physical. It was their sweetness she desired. To place her lips on the warm white throat or wrist, to pierce with her cat's teeth and feel the wine trickle into her. Like honey. Like love.

It was as if they loved her. For they gave her something. And they did not mind. Oh no. They murmured and stretched in their sleep, inviting her. Sometimes a white hand holding her head to the wound. Sometimes a spasm of pleasure, which, if she had had any true memory left, Gula would have recalled from the court of blood.

In the morning these courtesans of Gula's innocent awful lust were found.

Sick half to death.

On their bodies these marks. Like two bright little rubies; as if a brooch or bracelet had been pressed too close.

As they sickened further, they spoke of dead sisters or sisters they had never had. Or of their bridegrooms, or young men they fancied. And the parents raged. But that did no good. The young men had witnesses. The sisters were dead.

The black-haired girls became very ill. *Gravely* ill.

Physicians came like white crows to the houses.

They prescribed herbal tonics, medicinal baths, tinctures for the little punctures that perhaps, poking in at a lattice, some night-flying bird had caused.

Birds and cats were killed.

Men stood on guard at the doors to sleeping chambers. But to no avail.

Gula, when she came, repeating her visit, stole in like mist. She was only corporeal in certain ways. She believed she could slip under doors – did so.

Hearing their girls sighing and moaning and groaning, hefty fathers ran in with sharpened knives – that had grown blunt.

No one was there but the girl, her breasts laid bare, her nightgown rucked up, her naked feet – and on the ankle, perhaps, two small rubies, glittering –

Word spread.

Something came among them.

They called on the priests to watch all night. And where the priests were induced (by money) to do it, Gula did not attend.

In her loosened pebble of memory, she knew the vampire must fear the cross, the sun, the circle, the holy vestment. Fear holy water and singing, if nearby.

Even so, those girls once bitten did not recover. They paled down to wax. They were like pretty, smooth old women, seated in their beds and chairs. They ached. Their feet were cold. They dreamed. They folded the wings of their youth – and died.

Gula did not know that she caused death, even in absence, death. Gula knew nothing, save what she was and what she must do.

She continued her work, diligently.

Vivia sent word to Zulgaris' Witch very simply. She said, to one of her new attending girls, 'Fetch her here.'

And, before the day was out, there the Witch was.

They were alone. The drapes still covered the too-bright windows, and the Witch came like a shadow now.

She stood looking at Vivia.

The Witch was dressed in a gown with gold on it, and she had on all her bracelets. Had she tried to impress, or was this some ballust of her power? Either way –

'Are you frightened now?' said Vivia.

'*I?*'

'You. What you tried to do to me. But you didn't succeed. I'm too strong.'

'I did nothing. It was what you wanted.'

'You sold it to me. Persuaded me. But you see, I haven't told *him*.'

'*He* wouldn't believe you.'

Vivia said, 'He'd believe most things I said.'

The Witch considered this.

'The drug was too vigorous. I was unwise. What do you expect?'

'You know you can't hurt me,' said Vivia. 'Here I *am*.'

'There you are. Of course I'd never try to hurt you.'

'Better never try,' said Vivia. She paused. Then said, 'Why do you love Zulgaris so?'

'He's the prince.'

'You love him as a man but he doesn't want you. You'd like to magic yourself young again.'

'Like you,' flashed the Witch. And so gave herself away.

Vivia said, 'If you insist on being my enemy, I can have you killed.'

'I doubt that.'

'Well, but it might be unpleasant.'

The Witch scowled. Her decaying tooth ached. Her joints were stiff. The summer heat did not always agree with her. And there Vivia was. Stuffed full of vitality and blooming.

The Witch said, 'And . . . the child?'

Vivia hesitated now. Her face was like a mask. 'They tell me, I still have it.'

'Are you glad?'

'No.'

'I daren't try to spare you a second time.'

'No.'

'But I can help you. Unguents so it doesn't spoil your skin and hair. Rinses for the mouth and lower lips. I can keep you pleasing for him.'

'Don't trouble,' said Vivia. 'I know now, I can be anything I want.'

'Try to be free,' said the Witch.

Vivia said, slyly, 'Perhaps I don't wish to be.'

She went into the other room, opened the jewel box, and took out the emerald beetle.

She gave this to the Witch.

'What are you bribing me for?'

'We'll be safer as friends.'

'We are not.'

Vivia said, 'Let's pretend.'

In her voice was, unbeknownst to her, a faint whimper

of childhood. She did not want to war with this woman who, in such a perverse way, reminded her of her nurse, her mother – Ursabet.

The Witch listened. She thought Vivia would destroy her if she could, but so far could not. It was better to be friends, against the man if need be.

'Spit on your hand,' said the Witch.

Vivia did so.

The Witch spat upon hers.

They rubbed their palms together.

'Water sisters,' said the Witch. 'There are other ways. This will do. I won't do anything against you.'

The Witch stared at the floor.

Vivia said, 'Make a magic for me.'

The Witch shrugged, and crouching down, she formed a circle of pallid fire on the tiles.

'There's your child – look!'

Vivia did, and saw a golden man child strutting, about two months old.

Vivia did not believe in this, for she did not, even now, credit her pregnancy. But she thanked the Witch. For she had bent the Witch. She had tamed her. A little.

Chapter Six

 A STONE-MASON STOOD IN HIS doorway, looking down the street. The porter stood beside him anxiously.

They were watching a funeral pass. A black-haired girl had died, a rich man's daughter. Her death chariot was draped in black and pulled by black horses limned with silver. A man walked before, beating a drum, slowly.

The stone-mason crossed himself, then went in.

He went up to the chamber where his young wife lay, propped up on pillows embroidered by golden spangles.

Beside the gold and red, how deadly pale she looked.

'You seem better today, my love,' he said. They had only been married a year.

'Oh yes. Much better.'

Her black hair poured round her. He could see her breasts shining through her nightgown.

Even in her sickness, guiltily he still desired her.

The mason's wife smiled. 'Come into bed with me.'

'No, it isn't right.'

'Yes. I'm so much better today. And – look how my heart beats.'

She caught his hand and put it on her heart and the breast between.

The stone-mason came up rigid as a stone.

He got into the bed, and they laughed and felt each other over. Her mouth tasted bitter from the physician's stuff, but he did not mind it. Soon he was deeply bedded in

her. She came in moments, gripping his back, fell down,
and then pleaded for more.

He had never known her so eager. As she climaxed a
second time, he noted, even in his frenzy, a dark patch,
not hair, beneath her left arm.

'What's that mark?'

'Oh, I've bruised myself. It's sore.'

'Poor girl,' he said.

The other marks, on her wrist, had almost faded.

She would soon be well.

The plague began in little ways. A woman who fainted,
another who turned dizzy. Some had been the victims of
a bite, and some not. Men too sweated and rubbed their
heads, blaming the summer sun.

The heat was truly unbearable. The sun seemed to
glare through a magnifying glass, beating down on them
without pity.

By afternoon, many were sick. As yet the news had not
spread.

Physicians came and went among the houses of the
better-off. By sunfall three physicians had taken to their
beds.

A few persons were very desirous of sex, but not all. It
was perhaps the same plague, yet it had changed. Some
were only lethargic.

The black boils came out slowly, in the armpit, behind
the knee, in the groin.

As you passed down a street of the poor quarter, you
might hear the sound of retching in three or four houses.
Soon the smell began. It was thick and dirty, hanging over
the city, clapped to it by the lid of dark blue evening sky
after the sun had gone:

In the night, men and women raved. They left their beds
and ran into the thoroughfares.

A group of drunks met a woman in a white shift, and
took her one after the other against a wall. She shrieked
with joy, and clamped them to her body, then ran off,
leaving her black flower of death among them.

A watchman saw another of these women, a young girl

with long red hair, but she passed silently, and no one accosted her. She seemed on a mission that was perhaps sacred.

He himself did not detain her.

He glimpsed her passing in at the doorway of a small poor house, and thought they had opened the way for her. (But Gula, of course, had passed right under the door.)

When morning came the crowing of the cocks was brazen and harsh and hot as fire. The sun came up like a ball of molten whiteness.

Already there had been deaths, and carts started to go about Starzion.

By noon, the sun at its most horrible, the cry of plague was going up and down. They looked for help, possibly from Zulgaris. None came.

In the afternoon they began to set up braziers on the streets, burning aromatics to ward off the sickness. These, with their medicinal smell, only added to the encroaching bad flavour of the city. The smoke clouded up and gradually, as in the most threatening passages of holy scripture, the white sun turned red as blood.

By the fourth day of the plague, strange portents were spoken of. Red frogs had been seen leaping out of a well. In another place water drawn from a stream had turned red and salt.

Nearer the centre of the city, clocks struck the wrong time. Birds flew round and round a particular tower or roof, refusing to settle.

Rats set on and devoured a child.

Close to the fine streets that surrounded the palace, a wheel fell from the air and killed six persons.

The priests preached, behind walls of fumigatory incense, on the sins of the people of Starzion which had caused such a punishment.

But another rumour came now, ran and swelled into a low cry.

Night creatures preyed on the city. It was these shapes of terror which had brought the plague. The name was given:

Vampires. Whose fault? Why, who harboured strangeness? He had not helped them, their golden prince.

The cry was low, still. It rumbled through the alleys and touched the borders of the fine streets.

What did the prince keep in his menagerie? A unicorn, a bear-cat, dwarfs and giants, black men and white. And one other thing. The girl who was like the moon. What had been said of her? That she waxed and waned. Something must feed her.

Like a tide, the choked noises washed as far as the gates of Zulgaris' palace, on the twentieth day, when the city stank and the sky was black and the sun only a crimson hole. Every hour the bells tolled, wagons and carts, chariots and carriages bore away the dead.

Zulgaris appeared before his palace, on his golden horse. He spoke calmly to the citizens who had gathered there. He told them that his own physicians, skilled in remedies against the plague, would go about Starzion. He told them to pray and not to be afraid.

A procession of priests went through the city, clustered by gold and silver, the white-clad boys swinging the incense, and before this procession had completed its circuit, some had fallen from it.

But Zulgaris' physicians were known by their bird-beaks, which made them look so comical and so macabre together, the beaks of special herbs which protected them.

There had been many hundred deaths.

Zulgaris, shut in his glowing palace, where ice came from deep wells and cool fountains played, Zulgaris had not helped them. His physicians did only what the other physicians had done, and charged more. Whole families perished.

Now there were reports by night. Women with unbound hair and clad in grave-clothes, drifting through the streets. Women who vanished in under doors.

The victims were girls with black hair. And they in turn might be infected, made into vampires, that came back poisonously to bite and spread plague.

They went in the black morning. The light was so poor from

the smoke of the plague fires – and from other fires, for so many had died now, that in open places the poor would burn their dead. Forced to carry lamps and torches, three hundred and more people, flooding down the evil streets, and so to the biggest burning pit of all, that lay against the graveyard.

Here the men worked like devils, seen fitfully through clouds of black stinking smoke and the shift of flames. The night-soil carriers, the beggars, earning coin by doing this act of arson on the dead.

Beyond the pit, the graveyard, all its trees and monuments wreathed now in the smoke, lost in a grim dusk.

They passaged into the avenues, and there the crowd stopped, waiting, as the white horse was led reluctantly forward.

It did not like the spot, that was plain. Already it tossed its head, its neck was garlanded with myrtle. It was a virgin mare, and on its back, sobbing, sat a girl with long, long black hair, that fell over the horse's sides, just clothing her body, for she was naked. A virgin too.

They must go about the graveyard, the unhappy horse and the weeping, frightened girl, passing over the graves. And where the horse stumbled – *there*. There the vampire was.

It was the old way, the pagan way, to which they had resorted in desperation. No one else would help.

Even so, they crossed themselves, and as the crying girl and the horse started out, there were some prayers.

The horse moved slowly, her groom walking about six feet behind, not too close, for he did not want to be.

The girl, her feet dangling, tried to stop her tears, for fear *something else* would hear her.

Over the first low grave the mare went.

Not faltering.

The people pressed after with their float of lamps.

In the rougher parts of the graveyard there were quantities of fresh graves and few markers. Buried in haste –

The horse must pass over all.

Now and then the groom must touch her rump or side with his stick, guide her to a mound she had missed.

They ascended, bit by bit, up into the better areas.

Round bold houses of marble now the horse must go. Horse and girl shone whiter than the smoky tombs.

The crowd coughed and stifled itself in anxiety.

A man fell, and a woman bent over him. 'He's only tired. Been up with his brother three nights –' But they were shunned. An island of space was left around them as the crowd crawled on.

Round the columns of rich graves, over the stones of brass, black with smoke, not bright.

Threading through the cypress trees and by the bushes of rosemary that perhaps had protected the dead too well.

A woman in the crowd began to sing a hymn. A few joined her, but it had a pagan eerie sound in the black mist. The hymn was left off.

Did God see? Was God angry?

Was the punishment of the plague for them, or to warn Zulgaris of his vainglory and alchemical wickedness?

The mare and the girl strayed round and up, up into a plot beneath an apricot tree, which strangely, even as the graveyard was filled, had been left almost empty.

The horse faltered.

She moved a little aside, danced, and the groom beat her lightly on the flank and darted back.

Then, stepping over a mound, the horse *stumbled*. Stumbled and came to a halt, stock-still.

Terrified, the girl craned to see who would help her.

They were directly poised upon the grave.

And then –

And then the mound itself gave way. The soil caved in as if much eroded. The horse slipped in to her hocks, wriggled and shook herself, neighing with distress.

But up out of the collapsed grave came a pure white worm. It had five heads with crowns of steel.

The craning virgin girl, turning wildly – her long hair swung into the pit and the white worm seized it, seized a great hank, and pulled.

Screaming, in a flurry, the horse kicking, a flare of black hair, the girl was hauled off and down, and fell into the gap in the earth.

The horse shook herself and jumped, bursting from the grave. She ran away along the avenues neighing, and no one ran to catch her.

They stood in a wonder of horror, staring in at the seething of the earth.

Then the braver ones rushed forward.

A vampire had no true power by day. (Although the day was so dark.)

They reached and scrabbled and they too took hair. They pulled up their shrieking virgin from the pit and threw her aside, and then they had the other one, the *thing* –

Yes, it was what they had been told of. It had the form of a young girl, and long red hair. Its skin was succulent and firm, no signs of decay.

It moved only feebly now in their grip. Yet it did move. It was not dead. Not properly.

They flung it down and one man struck a lance straight through the body, through the breast and heart.

The vampire mewed and writhed and blood gushed from the wound. Fresh, stolen blood, so very brilliant in the dullness.

Gula had barely time to turn up her head. An axe crashed upon her neck, severing her skull from her body.

It was as she had been instructed. For the second time, obediently, thoroughly and completely, Gula died.

They pushed the pieces of the body back in the grave, and a wood-man came and cast in kindling. Fire was struck.

The bonfire burned merrily.

Then they turned to the adjacent mounds.

There was only one, but this they uprooted with picks and spades and with their bare hands.

The lamps burned all about the rise. The apricot tree, catching a spark, flamed up and burned too, like a beacon.

'It's not enough,' said a man at the front of the crowd, a man who had hung back until now. 'All those that were bitten – '

'Any,' said another, 'who fall sick – '

'Look for the marks!'

The yell was taken up.

They turned upon each other.

'You were scratching – was it a bite?'

'What's this? A flea, you say.'

The crowd fought together and knives were drawn.
Women screamed.

A man came behind the petrified virgin girl who had
ridden on the white mare. She had been touched by the
vampire. He strangled her quickly, then decapitated her
and thrust her on the blaze.

Zulgaris listened to the news from the city in an ornate
room with frescoes of hunting and dance.

'It disgusts me,' he murmured, 'these antics of lower
man.'

Later he went to Vivia.

She sat in a carved chair, her feet in bright slippers on a
blue footstool. Beautiful Vivia. His prize. He wanted her at
once, but desisted.

'You must do something for me,' he said. Vivia looked at
him. What else did she do? Zulgaris said, 'At midday they'll
bring you to a room. Were you taught the fundamentals of
religion? I think you were. You have only to answer the
priests, and there'll be someone to whisper to you if you
don't know.'

Vivia said, 'Why?'

What a child she was.

'Have you heard of the sickness in the city?'

'No. Perhaps.'

'They think,' said Zulgaris, 'you're a vampire.'

Vivia stared. She said, 'But – '

'We must show them that you're a true daughter of the
faith. No vampire can endure sunlight, can touch the cross
or sunburst. No vampire can speak the name of Marius
Christ.'

'Marius,' said Vivia, 'Christ.'

'Exactly.'

Vivia played with her golden bracelet.

'The sunlight's too fierce for me. I don't like it.'

'You must put up with it.'

'Can't you then,' she said, 'do what you want?'

He looked astonished. 'No one would stand against me,' he said, 'but I prefer harmony.'

'What shall I wear?' she said flirtatiously.

'White.'

When he left her, Vivia considered. Was she in danger? What sickness was in the city? She had heard some vague idea of it from one of the waiting girls, but not attended.

Now when they came, she asked them.

'There's plague, lady.'

Vivia shrank. She told herself she was safe inside the golden walls of her prison.

At midday Vivia stood in a glittering room accented with gold and crystal. Despite the smokes of the city, here the sun splashed from a million points, and filled her with a sour panic. She did not show it, stood like marble in her white gown.

In the chamber were the heads of certain powerful families of Starzion, courtiers, soldiers and knights. (Demed, Kazun, Tetchink.)

Zulgaris sat in a great chair. He looked utterly just, composed, benign and tolerant.

The priests filed in, stiff and clanking with golden breast-plates and silver censers.

The whisperer, a tall woman, told Vivia to walk out into the centre of the patterned floor.

The woman followed her, a pace or two behind.

There they halted.

Vivia, so lovely and so small in that high rich room. It was like a holy painting, some saintly virgin on trial.

A priest in a golden mitre spoke sonorously to the spectators. He mentioned God and the strength of God's church. Then he bowed to Zulgaris.

The priest turned to Vivia.

'Are you the woman called Vivia?'

'Yes.' Vivia sounded haughty. She was a little afraid.

The sun showered on her. She felt transparent. But no burn appeared on her skin, she did not shrivel into ashes.

'Do you know the name of the Christ?'

'I do.'

'Then speak it.'

Vivia spoke it. 'Marius Christ.'

'Have you any reason to fear that name?'

'No.'

'Who is He, Marius our Lord?'

'The redeemer.'

'How did He redeem us?'

'He died for our sins.'

'How did He die?'

'He hung on a cross and was pierced by a lance.'

'Did he then die?'

'For a few hours. Then He rose from the dead.'

Vivia rolled off these facts quite confidently. As a child she had been forced to master them. Even Ursabet had tested her.

Now, however, the priest said, 'And do you, Vivia, hope for redemption through the sacrifice of Marius?'

Vivia lied: 'Yes.'

Something was moving. It was a huge icon, a cross of ivory and silver with, nailed to it by diamond-headed nails, the sunburst of Christ.

This effigy was brought forward.

The woman whisperer hissed, 'Kneel down.'

Vivia knelt.

The cross drifted forward and its shadow fell over Vivia, blotting out the animosity of the noonday sun. She was grateful.

'Repeat the words of the penitent,' said the priest.

Vivia did not know them.

The whisperer said softly, 'I gaze in wonder . . .'

'I gaze in wonder.'

'On the symbol of everlasting life . . .'

'On the symbol of everlasting life.'

'Through which even I may ascend to God.'

'Through which even I may ascend to God.'

The cross was lowered, tilted. It leaned over Vivia's kneeling form, and for a second then, as it seemed to balance in the air, Vivia saw the possibility that it was ominous.

At the centre of the golden sun was a huge pearl. The eye of Christ.

They had lowered it now so that it was directly before her face.

'Kiss the image,' said the priest.

Vivia raised her face. Would she die now after all? Was there a God and would He strike her? She had killed Ingret and Gula. She had lain with Death – or the Devil.

Vivia kissed the pearl, which was cool and smooth.

Nothing happened.

They lifted the huge thing away from her.

The whisperer put her hand under Vivia's elbow and Vivia got up.

'She is innocent,' said the priest, 'in the sight of God.'

There was a muttering around the chamber.

Vivia saw grim shallow faces framed by glorious collars and headgear. Ringed hands that twitched maybe for her throat.

They had not been convinced.

But here was Zulgaris' page, handing her a golden rose.

Vivia took the rose, and then the woman led her from the room.

Zulgaris raised his goblet and toasted the knights who dined with him, the men of the Second Rank, Kazun, Tarusp, Urt, Kriva, and Demed, the First Knight.

These dinners were held generally at time of festival. But even so, the food had been brought to the table, roasted like burnt honey and with a crown of olive.

The men wore silks and were garlanded with roses. Zulgaris also had a garland of violets and yellow iris.

They did not sit, but half lay now on the couches. The wine had flowed and flowed on.

'This trouble in the city,' said Zulgaris, 'I must bring it to an end.'

Demed said, 'They're filthy, sir. They're running from house to house, bands of them, killing young girls.'

'The stink of the fires comes even into the palace courts,' said Tarusp.

'They throw live children on to them,' – Urt.

Kriva said, 'They're afraid. They speak against the prince.'

Zulgaris shook his head. 'They have sunk to the levels of the lowest animals.' His face was tragic. The five knights looked at it now with uneasy attention. 'Haven't I given them a city to rival the capitols of ancient times? Haven't I given them conquest and peace?'

The knights banged the table.

They had never seen Zulgaris drunk before. Or was it drunkenness? They had always known, since the days of his childhood, not to fall out with him. Starzion had dared.

'I've no time for these complaints – these threats – yes, they have deemed it necessary to threaten.'

'The fools,' said Demed.

'Well,' said Zulgaris. 'I'll dismantle my rooms of alchemy. That much I will do.'

The knights gaped.

'Even the great tower,' said Zulgaris. He smiled. They had never seen him look crafty before, either.

Or had they seen it and taken it for something else?

Zulgaris said, 'I mean to leave Starzion. You, my captains, my household, will go with me.'

'A battle?' asked Urt.

'No, I'm not going to war. I'll visit Syr. I've never seen it, though it's mine.'

The knights exchanged short glances.

Demed said, 'Who will be in charge of Starzion, sir?'

'We shall see. Starzion. First I'll make it a gift.' Zulgaris rose from the table. 'There was an old pagan custom to avert plague. A feast of flesh. Combat and banqueting. A spectacle. For the people.'

'Knights,' said Kriva, 'fought to the death.'

Kazun said, 'But that's not what you intend.'

'In the old days,' said Zulgaris, 'the populace ate the dead knights, to ensure protection against illness.'

Tarusp laughed. Then fell silent.

There was a great silence.

'Demed,' said Zulgaris, 'as my First Knight, you'll fight. And Kazun. All of you.'

'If you command it, my lord.'

'I ask it.'

They bowed to him. Their faces now were grim, like the faces of the household dignitaries who had watched Vivia kiss the sun.

But they did not argue with him.

At thirteen, when he had fallen from a wall and broken his nose, Zulgaris had had his tutor put to death – a slow death by whipping – for saying that he had been careless. They were his champions. They must obey even his request.

Chapter Seven

AT THE EDGES OF THE huge square before the palace, long tables had been set. They had white cloths on them, and were laid with great silver plates of food. Mounds of bread, rice, and meat, cakes and fruits, nothing especially decorative, but still largesse and colourful. And he had lavished silver on them, the people of his city Starzion.

Wine, too, for there it was, ruby red and yellow as piss, in round silver bowls and quaking silver jugs. Glass goblets – the finest – stood about for all to help themselves.

It was the sky feast, the feast of flesh, laid out for the old gods to see. And the old gods would say, Behold, an offering. And the plague would end. So they had once said.

The city, despite the pretty tables, was a shambles of plague.

Smokes rose from every side, columns of wavering blackness into the leaden sky. The sun was white today, burning savagely through. It was very hot, and airless. The stench of smoke, and worse . . . right up to the square before the place it had come.

On the far side of the square stood the massive church, its facade of pillars, and Marius in his window, his face a golden sun.

In the middle of the open space, the ground had been marked off. A wide square inside the square, and fenced areas led on to it.

Here the fighters would come to their combat, a clash of

arms to show the gods, like the feast, that flesh was only flesh. A primal sacrifice, the death of men, ancient as the sacrifice of Marius Himself.

The crowds had gathered at dawn, long ago. The rims of the square were packed now by people, and others had clambered up on the walls of adjacent buildings – the householders knew better than to push them off.

This was the day of the people. Zulgaris was wooing them.

In their mansions, his wealthier and more aristocratic citizens had closeted themselves, refusing to join in. Only here and there, some rich man who thought he could not catch plague and had the common touch, idling among the people, some lady in a carriage, half frightened at the nearness of the mob, yet glad enough to watch the spectacle to come, the great fight.

Zulgaris' shining knights. The very best.

Zulgaris himself appeared above, and for a few moments, as the crowd quietened, they heard the thump and judder of picks striking at the inner buildings of the palace. He had told them, his subter rooms would be dismantled, and for six days his soldiers had been at the work, chopping down the great tower, which fell in a rush, dissecting the inner rooms.

Things had been borne up. The vast clock with its statues and twenty-four numerals, had been carried down on ropes. There was word of priceless books, jewels that changed their shade, clockwork beasts that talked, a clock-work knight.

Zulgaris had gathered up his animals too, although this the people did not know. He had gathered up and packed away many things.

They were grateful to him. They shouted to him now. Surely he would protect them against the plague. The golden prince.

They forgot they had reviled him. Called him a wanton and a sorcerer, a harbourer of vampires. Doubted him.

Half the city that could still walk, was still healthy, seemed to have thronged this place.

Zulgaris raised his hand, and heard the last notes of his

final treasures being uprooted from the centre of the palace. Nothing was to be left, and in another hour, nothing would be. Elsewhere the carts stood ready, and from their stable had come the twenty camels on their broad hard feet.

The rest were prepared.

And for his messengers, his *assistants*, they were ready too.

Zulgaris spoke to the crowd, and wished it joy of its feast of flesh.

They cheered him until they were hoarse. He smiled sardonically at their fickleness.

Demed stood in his armour by the large stallion they had led out for him.

He tingled with rage and with a kind of fear that had nothing to do with nervousness at the fight.

He had been matched with Tarusp, and would beat him. Then, he must kill Tarusp. Tarusp knew this, and with a white face, had gone to confess his sins and receive the final rites while living.

After this combat, Kazun and Tetchink were to meet. The outcome was less sure.

And after them, Kriva and Urt, and Urt would undoubtedly win. But Kriva had spent the night drinking and whoring, determined to exact the most from his last few hours on earth.

Never had Zulgaris asked this of his knights. Death in battle did not count. It was chance, or the hand of God.

But to match them like this in a contest to the death. Friends and comrades, the Companions of Zulgaris. Never had he been sane, their prince, since he took that girl –

Demed fondled the neck of the stallion, between the flanges of armour. It was uneasy, trampling up sparks from its hoofs in the yard where they waited.

Then the trumpet sounded.

Demed dropped to one knee to God, crossed himself.

'May I be forgiven – '

He mounted with slight aid from the groom and manipulated the horse out of the low gate, along the tunnel, and into the fenced area of the square.

*　　*　　*

The sun burned over Zulgaris' palace, and at last the crack
of the picks upon the inner rooms had fallen still. The work
must be complete.

Demed turned his head, and saw Tarusp, clad in gorgeous coral red, riding out bravely to meet him, along the
fencing at the other side.

The crowd roared for both of them, next stuffing the
holes of its corporate face with roast duck and handfuls
of rice.

This scum – yes, they deserved their fate. The wrath of
God was on them. How many times had they shouted
for Tarusp and for Demed, as the two men rode out on
Zulgaris' endless wars, cheered them as they returned, and
hung the garlands on their necks.

Tarusp saluted him across the space. His pale face was
wry, before he pulled the vizor down.

Demed saluted in turn. 'Forgive me, brother.'

He stuck in the spurs and dug the horse riotously
forward, half out of control, and almost lost his balance for a moment, before ingrained skill caught him
back.

They met with a crash. Spear smote on shield, both
rocked from the impact and stayed whole.

The crowd – jeered. It *jeered*.

God punish them.

Their punishment was coming.

Demed wheeled the horse, and Tarusp wheeled, and
the eddies of smoke which penetrated quite thinly here,
swirled like a dancer's veils.

They spun and careered round and came at each other
again. This time Tarusp was dislodged.

He fell with a stunning thunder on to the square, and
as Demed swung heavily to follow him, he saw the
Marius in the church window look on with His serene
face of fire.

Demed lifted his sword and cut purposely to Tarusp's
left, then vaulted to the right and brought the blade in
under Tarusp's upraised arm, where the gap was.

The sword scraped on rivets and Tarusp groaned as it bit
into the flesh.

That was where the boils came. A plague blow.

He meant to be quick, Demed. He would not linger, not for the stinking crowd, or for Zulgaris, maybe watching from some window up above. Or for that girl, that beautiful little bitch of a girl who was a witch or monster, or some other unclean thing –

Tarusp's swipe almost had him. Demed cursed. He said, 'Well done, brother.'

Tarusp laughed. 'Not good enough.'

'No, not quite.'

Demed leaned forward and sliced Tarusp's left hand clean off above the wrist, where the gauntlet ended.

Blood gouted, royal red, the colour the foul sun was turning.

Tarusp did not cry out.

He dropped to his knees and his head sank forward.

Demed slashed the links of the helmet with his sword and pulled it free, exposing the long strong neck and dark young hair.

'I'll see you in Paradise, brother.'

'Or in Hell. God bless you, Demed.'

Demed's sword whirled and Tarusp's head sprung down on to the ground, its face amused, and lips parted as if for a kiss.

Demed stepped away.

The crowd was howling.

This was what the old gods demanded.

Demed had expected guardsmen at once, to carry Tarusp's body off the square. But there was a delay.

And suddenly groups of them, of the people of Starzion, were running forward.

Demed thought he would see then wrench off Tarusp's armour and devour him, and the sword in his hand was hot as flame, to cut around him.

But instead they were only dipping scarves and rags into the blood, to carry off for souvenirs. And one man dipped in some bread, but he did not eat it.

Kazun killed Tetchink after a longer fight. The square rang with their blows, and in the end both were staggering, but the mail in Tetchink's armour had been damaged in the chest region, and at last Kazun drove in his sword.

Tetchink died swearing. His loss of an eye had made him vulnerable after all.

Kazun strode from the square leaving the people to do as they liked.

The last couple, Kriva and Urt, were as quick as Demed and Tarusp had been. Kriva was ill from drink and made a poor show.

The crowd sneered and reviled him and refused to take any of his blood.

After the battle, the servants came and sprinkled the square with sand.

The crowd milled and argued, unsatisfied now the display was over.

A curious silence held the palace, from which, they had been told, clowns and acrobats would come to entertain them.

The smoke had grown very thick.

They coughed and grumbled.

Seizing more wine and food from the tables they ate and drank.

Some now were for going home.

The tailor who pushed his way from the square was quickly conscious, as he came into the narrower streets, and the noise of the crowd faded, of some uproar elsewhere in the city.

It was a sort of groaning sometimes cut by thin wild shrieks.

The plague had made a similar noise, but not quite.

In all the smoke-dark houses clustering by the road, no one was alert or alive or even present, and so this street gave no evidence of what went on.

But moving out of it, the tailor found a press of people, hurrying forward.

The smoke was very thick here, and it was difficult to see much, but sick were there on litters, and the tailor shrunk aside.

'The gate,' a man said, 'get to the gate.'

'What's after you?' inquired the tailor, intrigued despite himself.

'Don't you know, you fool?'

'Know what? I know you shouldn't carry those filthy sick about the streets.'

'Get out of the way. Run if you want to save yourself.'

They went on, going down a side alley.

The tailor looked up. Something made him do so.

The sky between the smokes was very red. Almost like a sunset. Had so much time elapsed?

He thought not.

And then he heard the other sound, distant and yet distinct. The crackle of a burning brazier. And it came to him that if it was far enough he could not see it, he should not be able to hear it, either.

The fire had begun – here and there. Somehow.

In barns of the outskirts where grain was stored. In cellars under the street. In a pie-shop. In a tavern where the drunken owner, sozzled, burned to death.

In twenty or more places. Fifty or more.

The slender yellow tongues picked up about the thoroughfares.

There was so much fire, the burning pits of the dead, the flames of precautionary aromatics, it could have spread from anywhere.

It pushed towards a centre – the palace of the prince.

Yellow heated to scarlet.

The black smoke turned to a rare, proud purple.

Soon the streets were full of the flying shrieking ones. The sick, too weak to move, dragged on litters, or left to fry.

From almost every house in those poorer quarters, screaming and praying.

Like the lost souls shown in Hell, roasting . . .

It advanced swiftly on the square of the feast of flesh.

No acrobats had come to entertain, no clowns to jolly.

The crowd milled, examining its bloody trophies, drinking from the fine glasses, a quantity of which by now were smashed.

A man at the square's edge, looking back into the wide streets, saw the fire coming. Did not know what it was.

It was like a storm, a *red* storm. It poured over the sky that had only been dark and onerous. Thunders sounded, and spurts of lightning, which were simply the hungry mouths of the fire biting up some new inflammable thing.

The man turned sluggishly to a neighbour.

'Look – '

They stared together now.

As they did so, a miracle occurred.

A spark from the fire lodged in the first man's hair. He smouldered and he did not feel it, for everywhere was now so hot and the sun like a gong –

Until, and at once, his hair burst into fire.

He turned shrieking to confront the square of the feast, and hundreds saw him.

It was a man, and his head was a sun of flame. (His screams had been scorched out.)

It was Marius.

It was the Christ.

And in terror not love they bolted, stampeded, ran against walls, were trodden on and crushed, and behind everything, reeling in on them, the blood red sky.

Chapter Eight

❧ ALL THOSE DAYS, SHE HAD listened to the mallets and picks, pulling down his inner place.

Like the collapse of a phallus, that tower. (What of the creature in the wall?) They had told her what all this meant.

Vivia heard, astonished.

Had Zulgaris gone mad?

He did not come to her, and if he had, she was not sure she could have judged his mind, for they all seemed touched by craziness, the servants, the two girls who tended her.

Then they began to pack up her gowns, in boxes of cedarwood, and next her jewels, her shoes, certain ornaments from the rooms.

They were to travel elsewhere.

She heard, having questioned the girls, that there was to be a fight in the square. A combat. To appease the people.

Vivia was not interested by this.

She had journeyed before. But this now seemed odd.

She wished he would come and tell her what had happened.

'Where is he going to?'

'To his town in the desert,' said the girls. 'To Syr.'

Vivia did not care about this either.

She was faintly angry. She was heavy.

Was that the child?

She did not experience nausea, or sleeplessness. Only

irritability and the strange low spirits which now assailed her.

Nothing seemed promising. Of course, it never had, but never before had she felt this inertia, this antipathy.

Intimations of old age reached her once more.

The bat wing of death was still stretched across her body, invisible, yet real.

Vivia fretted.

But a day came when the girls dressed her for travelling. Her box of jewellery was put into her own hands, and then they descended into the lower garden.

The sounds of picks had stopped.

Vivia thought of her court of girls, and did not trouble. She did not want their blood. Wanted nothing.

In a courtyard she was ushered ceremoniously into a carriage.

'You must stay quiet, lady. Don't look out. It will take a little while. Someone will come.'

Her two girls were plainly frightened.

Then the door was shut – the window had been irreparably shuttered, or so it seemed.

Nothing was on view.

They started.

Vivia wept, and stopped herself. She was losing nothing. Nothing mattered.

The carriage rumbled over uneven ground, and now there was a noise beyond the rattle of the vehicles, the trotting of horses, a great mysterious grinding sound. Shouts came and screeches – but far away.

Vivia smelled the smoke and stench of the city worse than ever. She wound her veil about her face and presently fell asleep.

When she woke, the carriage had halted.

It was very quiet, as if she were alone in a wilderness, and in rage or alarm, she hammered on the window shutter with her fist.

Someone ran and opened her door.

'Where have we come to?' Vivia asked.

'We're in the hills, lady. They're looking at the city.'

Vivia said, not grasping this, 'Then so shall I.'

The court of Zulgaris was on the slope. Carriages were everywhere, and horses stamped, unnerved, scenting the air.

Below, soldiers, his army, as she had seen before.

And beyond, the layers of the hills, and far down, something bright like a jewel.

The sky was mulberry red and streaked by tails of violet cloud.

Was this a sunset?

The wind brought the odour of meat and perfume, a ripe delicious smell, but over that the char of other things, burnt wood and crisping stone. The summer aroma forced beyond itself. A furnace.

'What is it?'

'Starzion's burning, lady.'

Vivia stared.

And Starzion burned.

How many miles away it was, on a sea of flame. She could not hear the wails and screams. The wasted prayers.

Starzion with its bells and chimes, its towers and gardens and churches. Starzion with its people.

'Some spark from the burial pits,' said one of her stupid girls.

And Vivia stared.

And Starzion *burned*.

BOOK THREE

The Powers of Littleness

ONE

Chapter One

DOWN THROUGH THE HILLS IT came, the procession of men and beasts and things.

Along tracks that ran by villages, and here the people came out and stared.

Where was he going now, their prince, with his standards of leopard and lily, yellow, gold and white and black? Where? To fight with whom?

Some had seen the red sky at his back.

What had happened? Was it the great city? Had the prince in turn been routed?

They got no answers, the few that dared to ask the stragglers of the march, they were pushed aside. One burly villager who insisted was shot by a crossbow bolt through the throat.

Down then through forests of chestnut and lime, cedar, ilex, groves of acacia. Willows curved beside the streams. Fountains fell from above and coiled into long rivers. Juniper trees and eucalyptus clung among the rocks. There were orange trees, the fruit like green and golden balls. A fertile fragrant land.

Cows roamed in meadows and goats grazed the high pastures. Herders gazed at what went by.

The land grew more dry, and pine trees rose up in dark arrow-heads.

The villages were more infrequent.

The terrain levelled, and the hills ran away on the right hand, and leftwards was a plain, coloured in ribbons by summer flowers, yellow and crimson, pink and blue.

There was a road. Along it stood torch-poles, and as the dusk began to come and the noise of crickets in the grass of the plain vied with the noise of Zulgaris' retreat, a band of men rode on ahead and lit the torches.

Vivia saw, her window now unshuttered, that they went by night along a road lit both sides by flaming brands.

Perhaps she had come to the place she had seen in her dream of flight.

Bemused, she did not think much of it. It had looked more effective from the air.

Zulgaris had come to her only once.

The procession-retreat-march had halted in a valley, and Vivia was drinking, quite reluctantly, some warm goat's milk which one of the women had brought her in a silver bowl.

'That will do you good,' said Zulgaris.

He looked the same as ever. Handsome, set.

Vivia said, 'Where are we going?'

'Haven't they told you? To Syr, in the desert.'

She did not ask about Starzion. She had heard and seen evidence of what happened to villagers who did so.

She said, 'How long will the journey be?'

'Not long. You must take care. The child.'

'Oh,' she said.

Her stomach was almost as flat as it had ever been. She had no symptoms any more. In a handful of days they had gone away, and hourly she expected to bleed, to be free of the (imaginary) burden.

Zulgaris took her up on to a hill and showed her something vague in the distance. The sea.

They would come to the sea, and pause there.

There was a great hunting lodge where they might rest.

Was he running away? Surely he must be. But that would be normal, so perhaps he was not.

Also in the distance, from the hill top, Vivia saw the fleet of grey camels, loaded with enormous packs, and drawing long sleds.

'They're carrying my tower,' he said.

It was in pieces, blocks of masonry, the massive clock,

and also, it would seem, all the inner items, the chests of gems, the alchemical books, stones and bones. The vessels. Even – could it be – the bat-god creature from the wall? She did not ask, for possibly she was not meant to know.

No one had told her, and yet in a way she guessed. How soldiers had gone in and cut the throats of Zulgaris' experiments, the half and half things that moaned and mourned in those secret chambers. Then the soldiers had been killed by others. Very few had seen the hidden mechanisms and toys. Zulgaris would safeguard himself immaculately.

But she – had seen. Oh yes.

It was not discussed, even among the rank and file, the burning of the city. It was referred to solely as an act of God.

The camels shuffled in their ropes, and from where she stood, she faintly heard their burping grunts.

The assemblage was strange, and never stranger than when it was moving. This Vivia did not ever properly see.

The villagers and herders had seen it. Some circled themselves or drew the cross.

The soldiers and their pack animals, the rolling ships of carts and carriages, the cages of Zulgaris' beasts. And the camels hauling lumps of stone, and there, wrapped in fleeces, the mound of the clock. And there a silver arm. And there the golden cupola that had topped the tower.

How bizarre these visions, sailing by, sailing down to the plain that led towards the sea.

Belly-high the horses now in a sea of flowers, and by day the bees gathering all around them, and flies enraging the horses and the men.

They had left the road of torches. They were like wild travellers with their only course the water ahead.

Vivia dreamed of the bedchamber, and when she had opened its door, the horse was there, standing by the bed.

It was jet black now, and it shone from grooming.

She knew she was to marry Zulgaris, and quickly they came and drew her down the stairs, the black horse following carefully, its hoofs scraping on the stone steps.

Outside the castle was a long white road. So white she thought fresh snow had fallen on it.

The carriage too was white as snow, and decked with white and silver ribbons.

Vivia wore a blood red dress.

She got into the carriage, and Zulgaris was there, not smiling, but waiting.

He too wore white.

The black horse walked behind the carriage, which moved very slowly, pulled by three grey camels.

The sides of the road were lined by people clothed in black. Their faces were black with soot, and torch-poles also lined the way, smoking without fire.

There was no noise.

The people in black watched the white carriage, and Vivia burning in it like a flame, and the black horse of plague walked behind.

Once she had been married to Zulgaris, she would have to have the child.

But perhaps the child would come out dark, like the sooty people, and die.

Vivia opened her eyes in the darkness of the carriage where she had been sleeping.

She put her hands on her stomach. There was no doubt, it was not the same. It was hard and slightly rounded. Something was in there.

What had the dream meant? Ursabet would have had some suggestion. But then Ursabet would have rid her of the child.

They reached the sea.

It was an unsettled day, wind blowing over the plain, which had turned by now to grass and rough wild grains.

Trees loomed, and the land gave way, fell into a pit, and there was a vast water, an abysm of it, the colour of blue steel. It rushed in, lashed itself, turned back. Laces of foam spilled along the stony shore, and bruised white around the rocks.

Vivia thought it a peculiar river. It did not surprise her.

The hunting lodge was a vast building of towers and courtyards, haunted by odd servants who, neglected for a decade, had done as they wanted, and now stared in wonder and terror at the arriving master and his horde.

By sundown a fire roared in the great hearth of the hall. It was cold by the sea, the season again changing ahead of itself, autumnal already, though Zulgaris had informed her a current ran through the water, which made it always warm.

Vivia slept in a small wooden room, carved with wooden icons. The sea hissed. The bed was damp, and full of hot stones which turned chilly. Smoke from a brazier irritated her eyes. She dreamed of Starzion burning, and hissing people danced happily in the flames.

When she woke, she felt her stomach again. Was it rounded and more full? Her garments still fitted her.

In the morning, from a narrow window, she saw seals playing along the shore, and did not know what they were.

Her women brought her food and drink.

One asked Vivia decorously, almost shyly, if she wanted to see any of the little girls.

Vivia had not thought her court had been brought with them. She had not missed their blood. Did not want it. 'No.' But curiosity made her add, 'Where are they? Where have they been?'

'In a room nearby. And they travel in the carriage behind your own, in case . . .'

Vivia had believed they had been abandoned to the fire. She had not minded. (Oria burnt to a cinder.)

Although she did not want their blood, she said, 'Go and fetch me Zinel.'

The maid did as she was bid, and ten minutes later, the brown little girl, Oria's particular friend, stood squirming on the floor in the room of wood.

'Here I am,' she said.

The women had gone, and Vivia took up the fruit knife and toyed with it, to frighten Zinel. Which it did.

'How is Oria?'

'Oria's well.'

'What did she think of the fire?'

'We were all very scared, lady. We thought –' Zinel flirted, 'you might have been harmed.'

'But I wasn't. And neither were you. Who started the fire, I wonder. What does Oria say?'

'Oria says,' Zinel broke off and looked uneasy. 'Oria says wicked soldiers of the prince's started it, but the prince had them killed.'

'Give me your wrist,' said Vivia.

Zinel did so, cowering and pleased.

Vivia bit to hurt her, and took only a mouthful. It tasted thin and bitter, Zinel's blood today. She pushed the girl away from her.

Zinel snivelled. 'You're very cruel, lady.'

'Yes. Get out.'

That night Vivia was summoned to dine in the hall with Zulgaris and his own court of chattering, zealous priests, knights and nobles.

There was a spurious festive air, and toasts were called for, and Zulgaris was copiously blessed.

Demed had a long face, however. He did not smile. And Kazun smiled too much until his face seemed to crack and grow slack, and then he too stopped smiling.

Zulgaris was as usual. He said that at Syr they would lead a simple life, amusing themselves with military tests, hunting in the desert, books and music. It was as if everything, including the burning of Starzion, were an exercise. Probably, it was.

Vivia was not singled out for special notice, yet the eyes of the court were often on her. She felt their animosity, jealousy and mistrust. She must find a way to avoid such gatherings.

Tetchink was not at the feast. She asked her woman later what had happened to him, this one-eyed third witness to her earlier humiliation.

When Vivia heard he had died she was not sorry.

Chapter Two

THE LAND ROSE AGAIN AS they left the sea.

The water drew away in a dull blue line.

In the uplands, summer was over, autumn was over, and a young winter began. Mountains appeared in transparent far off shapes. The cold wind blew.

The soldiers of Zulgaris the prince trudged over the miles, through the new bleak landscape.

Behind them came the packhorses and the carts, and behind these the camels who pulled the pieces of stone and the huge clock, dragging time with them, and the hidden things from the secret rooms, of which the soldiers were generally superstitious.

'It's cold,' they said, unnecessarily.

'It was warm enough in Starzion.'

'Quiet.'

'Rather be there, would you?'

'Shut your row.'

'Fried.'

They did not discuss the beginning of the fire, but many crossed themselves when it was mentioned. Several had lost people in the conflagration, women they had had on the side, bastard children, old grannies.

When Zulgaris told them they must march, they had had no choice. No space to go and look.

One man sang a sad song as he marched, about the girl he had loved and lost. Presently he was beaten and left off.

The soldiers who guarded the rear of the march, where

the camels were, seldom spoke. They kept wide of the
ported items.

The men who drove the camels were blank faced.

The sun shone without heat or colour in a pale blue
sky. Sometimes one of the animals in the cages called or
growled. A hawk circled the upper air from time to time,
watching them.

They made a camp by the shore of a lake of sand. It drifted
in ripples to the play of the wind. The sun set over it in
rosy lines.

In the darkness, the constellation of the Maiden burned
above the camp.

Vivia sat in her tent, warming herself. Thick furs had
been spread on the chair and put by for her to draw on.
Fleeces and furs covered the pallet. Two braziers flamed.
Outside, the earth crunched with white frost, and on the
sand-lake the starlight glittered like knives.

She had not seen Zulgaris for days, and then only
glimpsed him, riding among the carriages on his yellow horse.

The journey was irksome, more tiresome than the first
she had come on with him, up into the hills.

An atmosphere of depression had covered the march or
retreat, to which Vivia was not impervious.

The woman – there now seemed to be only one –
brought her wine, hot bread and meat. Vivia ate some
of the bread.

'Where are my girls?'

'Just over the rise, lady.'

'Go and tell Oria to come here in an hour's time.'

Vivia, alone, brooded. She had wanted to send for
Zulgaris' Witch. Surely the Witch would know something
– of where they went, something of interest. Vivia had
gained a slight power over the Witch, but not enough
to be much use. Oria would be a better bet. Somehow,
infallibly, her slyness would have learned things.

Then again, what did it matter? Here Vivia was, going to
some unwished for place, away from some other unliked
region, her belly hard and round.

When the hour was up by the little hourglass, Vivia heard light steps crackling through the frost. Oria was not challenged by any of the scattered guards. Like the woman who waited on her, they knew she belonged to Vivia.

Oria entered the tent.

She wore a travelling dress and a thick fur. Obviously, these girls had been cared for.

Oria bowed. 'Yes, lady?'

Vivia glared at Oria.

'Sit on that cushion.'

'Thank you, lady.' The fur slipped from Oria's gown. She rubbed her hands. 'The tent's so warm. One could go naked in it!'

Vivia said, 'You're impertinent.'

'I'm sorry, lady.' Oria was not sorry. She looked pleased at being singled out. As always, sly.

'Who started the fire in the city?' said Vivia.

'Wicked men.'

'Who?'

'Who knows?' said Oria. She added piously, 'Unless it was the judgement of God. They were very bad. They doubted the prince.'

Vivia had her answer. She said, 'What do you know about Syr?'

'It's a big prosperous town. The prince will delight in it.'

Vivia was not really fascinated by any of this. She said, 'How do you entertain yourselves, the six of you?'

'We tell stories. We play games. Sometimes . . . we dance.'

'How do you know to dance?'

'My – mother taught me – dances.'

Vivia considered. Oria's beginnings were obviously dubious. A faint curiosity stirred in her, and Oria, her invisible antennae quivering, ventured, 'Shall I show you one, lady?'

'No.'

Oria said, 'There was a story in the city. In Starzion. Ingret and Gula rose from the dead. They became *devils*. They roamed the streets by night, and drank the blood of young women. This is what spread the plague. The citizens had to kill them again.'

Vivia said, 'A silly tale.'

She thought that the plague was however due to herself in another fashion. Had she brought it there clinging in her hair and on her skin? They were protected in the palace and so did not succumb. But she had ridden through Starzion on the white pony.

Oria got up. She said, 'The dance goes like this.'

Arrogant little beast, she wanted her own way.

Vivia shrugged.

And Oria allowed now her dress to slip off from her shoulder.

Demed, Kazun, Urt, sat drinking in a yellow tent in the finer area of the encampment. They were not so near to the great pavilion of the prince.

Outside the camels grumbled at their pickets, their thick wool cloaking them from the cold. By the sea they had been fed daily on fish, and now reeked of it. The fish stink mingled with the cold glassy air and the aromatics in the brazier.

'He's in good spirits,' said Kazun.

'Yes. Looking forward to his entry into Syr. The man in charge will shit himself. A few days' warning from a messenger, and then Zulgaris in person.'

'The fort will be makeshift. Not up to the standard of Starzion.'

'He'll like that. Rough it. Flex his muscles in knightly exercise. Play with that girl of his.'

They sat and looked at each other.

'What is she?' said Urt. 'The witch woman is bad enough, but they're used to her. She's been lucky for them. The men mutter about the other one.'

'His whore,' said Kazun.

'No,' said Demed. 'Remember he values her like the animals and the freaks. She drinks blood. It's common knowledge.'

'A vampire full of the prince's child,' said Kazun. '*That's* not lucky.'

'We'll see how our luck will go.'

'The soldiers complain,' said Urt. 'The men in my command are restless and dirty-mouthed. They don't speak directly of any of it. Not even the fire.'

Demed said, 'Many of them lost someone.'

'Zulgaris lost his city,' said Urt.

'And we,' said Demed, 'even before that. We lost our comrades.'

'Kriva,' said Kazun, 'Tetchink.'

'And Tarusp,' said Demed.

Urt said, 'It wouldn't have hurt, a show, a bit of blood. Some wound the rabble could see.'

'But not enough,' said Kazun, 'to kill.'

'Our brothers,' said Demed, 'He made us do it.'

They sat in silence.

Outside the camels snorted with obscene laughter. A thin pinkish moon was coming up above the strokes of the distant mountains.

'They hate the stuff from his tower,' said Kazun finally. 'It frightens them.'

'It frightens me,' said Demed. 'God knows what blasphemies he's committed in that place.'

'You hear stories,' said Urt.

'We've *seen* – '

'A man with a horse's body.'

'A woman with a snake's head.'

'He had them put to death. A mercy.'

'But the stones are thick with it.'

The wind blew.

'Even that clock,' said Kazun, 'unnatural. Twenty-four places. Damned.'

Oria had done a dance she said was called *The Hare*, leaping and spinning, and her dress had come undone, and now she took it off and danced softly in her shift.

This dance was called *Candle to Bed*. Oria slipped and dipped about the tent, her bare feet – she had taken off her boots – slithering on the rugs.

Through the thin shift her body was quite visible. The dark mass at her groin and the tawny points of her nipples. Her hair swung. She murmured snatches of tunes or auto-encouragement.

Vivia watched her. She had an urge now to grab Oria and bite her and drink the blood. But the urge was not very strong.

Oria wanted to seduce Vivia. This was apparent. Vivia thought Oria a fool, but not such a fool as the others. Oria was motivated by self-interest.

Oria skipped, her shift flipped up, and showed her nude almost to the navel.

Vivia was faintly annoyed now.

The tale of Ingret and Gula fluttered in her mind. They had risen from death, vampires as she was.

Strange thought. Had she herself died in the castle of her father? What was she, then?

Urt refilled the cups; they had long since sent the servant boy away.

'What should we do? Something, surely. Our honour,' said Kazun, 'in the muck.'

'The men talk nonsense. They tell stories of rebellions and great men struck down.'

Demed said, 'That's too simple. Take care.'

'Yes,' said Kazun. 'He may guess.'

'He guesses nothing,' said Urt. 'He thinks he has the right to do everything as he wishes, and he's done it, and we obeyed him. Even to – even to the fire.'

'I wonder when,' said Kazun, 'I'll start to hear those shrieks in my dreams.'

'Like a child with a sand-castle that displeases him,' said Demed, 'kicked flat.'

Outside, beyond the humped slopes of the camels, the soldiers at their thin fires.

How cold that night on the high plain.

How cold the coming desert.

Zulgaris in his golden tent, and that white candy of a girl, that vampire-thing, cosseted in her nest.

'It should be sudden,' said Urt.

'No, it should be wise,' said Kazun.

Demed said, 'No hand raised against him. We swore an

oath. Zulgaris must remain.'

'But – '

'In life,' said Demed.

They sighed. Kazun threw a coal into the brazier and at its sizzling they lifted their heads.

Somewhere the leopards snarled in their fur-wrapped cages. Farther still, some creature barked on the plain.

A long journey. They had come a long way.

Oria poised.

'I can show you a dance now, lady. It's a naughty dance. May I take off my shift, princess? I'm so hot.'

'If you must.'

Oria drew the shift off over her head and her dark hair frayed up in a cloud.

For a moment she looked beautiful, and Vivia was oddly sad. Her youth, lost for ever, danced before her.

Had her own mother taught her any dances before Vaddix murdered her? No, she had taught Vivia nothing.

Oria moved slowly, swaying. She had not said what the dance was called, but now she smoothed her hands over her body, along the budded breasts and down the high curved girlish belly. (Vivia felt a stone inside her.)

Oria smiled, secretively, some memory perhaps? Had she danced this dance before and been recompensed?

But Vivia hardly saw her now, saw her through a veil of amorphous feeling, gloomy and dark and still.

Finally Oria drifted to her, and laid herself down, naked and yielding, across Vivia's knees.

Vivia looked at Oria.

A bizarre tenderness filled Vivia. She felt deeply contrite. And something made her lean down to kiss, sadly, Oria's dark plum of a mouth.

But before their lips touched, the sensation peeled off. The sadness and tenderness left Vivia in a gush, like the blood which had not come.

She passed over the lips and sank her teeth in Oria's throat.

Oria squealed, and Vivia held her by the neck, half choking her, drinking in vast gulps the spurting redness.

As she did so, Vivia thought that now Oria would die. And when Vivia let her go, Oria dropped to the floor, limp and unconscious.

From her throat the blood went on, and swiftly formed a ruby pool on the rugs. She snored.

Oria's swarthy face was pale yellow.

It was all her own fault.

Vivia slept that night with Oria lying nearby. (Ursabet.) Later the woman walked in, stood like a statue, came alert and went out. Then a man arrived and wrapped Oria up and took her away.

Oria was buried in the sandy barrenness of the high plain, by three men who dug a grave, grim-faced. She had no rites, except a quick muttering from a small grey priest, a man who belonged to the soldiers. He thought she was a prostitute who had died during the night.

After Zulgaris' processional march had gone away up the ascending land, in the blank morning, the grave was left to itself.

Would Oria lie still all day, and, at nightfall, come up to wander the bleak and scarcely populated place?

Oria was not Gula. Oria did not feel obliged to come back and suck the blood of others. Oria was not obedient and easily led. Even in death, canny. More sensible than when alive.

Oria did not rise.

And overhead the hawks gathered, or the crows, for the grave was not very deep. And presently the foxes would come, and a wild cat strayed from the hills below.

The rumble of the march took a long time to fade from the wide bowl of the air. Not till it had passed did the first crow come down.

Chapter Three

 VIVIA, A DAY AFTER, WOKE to terrible pain. She knew what it was, the blood was coming at last. But when she looked, the bed and her body were pristine.

The woman bent over her. 'What is it, lady?'

Vivia could only moan. Who would help her now? Then the pain sank. She gripped the woman's hand. 'Fetch me his Witch.'

The Witch came wrapped in black furs, with bone ornaments in her hair.

'Do you trust me now?' she asked.

'No.' In the vice of the pain once more Vivia knew, from Ursabet's cranky dialogues, what was happening. 'But you won't betray *him* a second time.'

The Witch allowed herself a smile.

'Oh, no.'

'I'm miscarrying.'

'Let me see.'

The Witch came and examined Vivia, thoroughly and without roughness. 'It doesn't seem,' she said.

'Give me something for the pain,' Vivia demanded, past caring for further plots.

The Witch directed the woman, in Vivia's sight, to prepare a cordial and mix it with wine.

This Vivia drank and slid into a pain-laced feverish sleep.

They had camped again on the high plain. The camels were recalcitrant and needed rest.

Tonight they would move on, travelling by moonlight.

Vivia dreaded the motion of her carriage. When would the agony end? What would happen?

The Witch was there again, instructing two men on how they should carry Vivia to the carriage.

Vivia screamed in rage and pain, to no avail.

As soon as they had set her in the carriage and gone away, a rush of hot fluid burst out between her legs.

Vivia, only partly aware, dug her nails into the Witch's potion-hardened hand.

'Don't claw me. I'll help you.'

'Is it the blood? When will I be rid of it?'

'Soon enough. But it's what I thought. Not blood, but water. You're giving birth.'

Vivia knew that she had not carried the child long enough.

'No,' said the Witch in answer to her incoherent gasps. 'Not nearly long enough. But then, from the feel of it, it's an unusual child.'

'Does he know?' Vivia wished Zulgaris could be made to suffer as she now did.

'Someone has told him. He knows that I'm with you. He sent a midwife, but I sent her off. Believe me, lady, you haven't got much to push out. You think you hurt, but it should be worse.'

'Worse!'

The carriage began to move, and Vivia found oddly the motion eased rather than exacerbated her pain.

The Witch said, 'Do you never crap or piss?'

Vivia turned her head at this crudeness. The Witch laughed. 'I'm your physician. Better answer.'

'Sometimes.'

'Are you human?' asked the Witch. 'Marius Christ knows what you are. His curse on us all.'

She spat and made a sign, not cross or circle.

Vivia writhed and a horrible movement began in her belly.

Soon after the Witch laid her out on the seat of the carriage, and massaged Vivia's slightly rounded stomach.

Then she peered between Vivia's legs.

She grinned, showing her new jewel.

'We must have witnesses to this. They'll have to stop again at the crevasse. I'll send for them then.'

Vivia's body heaved to be rid of the obstacle that now began to emerge from her womb.

She lost track of everything, and even when the carriage halted once more, and men rode up and down outside, Vivia did not know it.

Then they were carrying her again, and she had been returned to her tent, or to some tent that was darker, and smelled of incenses and attars.

A man stood swathed in black, and from the haze of her delirium, Vivia thought *he* had come back to her, and she held out her arms. But she glimpsed his little eyes, and they were human. Some servant in Zulgaris' service. There was a woman too, fat and silent.

The Witch pulled back Vivia's soaked skirts and pressed cruelly on her belly.

Vivia shrieked.

And out of her body slowly slipped a smooth black oval thing, about the size of her own right hand.

This the Witch seized.

She held it up. The Witch *laughed*.

The other two stayed silent.

Through a film, Vivia saw what had come from her. It was an egg, black as coal.

She stared at it in wonder, and asked herself if Ursabet had lied. Were the births of women like those of birds? Surely not. She had heard infants crying in the straw, seen them streaked with blood and matter from their mothers' wombs.

'Go and tell him,' said the Witch to the man who wore black. 'Tell no one else.'

The man went out.

The fat woman came and stripped Vivia and bathed her. All the while the Witch stood there with the coal black egg. She held it like a trophy of some victory.

Vivia said, 'It isn't a child.'

'Yes. We shall see what it is.'

Vivia knew a searing hopeless loss.

She closed her eyes, and when she opened them, only the fat woman sat by her.

'Where is she?' said Vivia.

'She's gone to him.'

The Witch had taken the black egg, hidden in some shawl or veil, taken it to Zulgaris.

'Better sleep, lady,' said the fat woman. 'At dawn we must go on.'

Vivia knew only she would not die. Tears ran down her face into her hair. She was too weak to stop them.

It was leaden now, with a mysterious sheen. Slender silver veins had appeared in its surface.

The egg rested in a cradle of shavings above the glowing brazier.

Zulgaris gazed at it.

He had sent the male witness away. The man had no tongue, which even the Witch did not know. He had described the event with difficulty, drawing images.

The Witch had brought the egg.

Her, he had not sent away.

He might need her aid. Was he not sure what this marvel would do?

She had said only one thing, 'Be aware now. She's a demon.'

Zulgaris had laughed.

His seed, generally unfruitful in the wombs of women, had formed this thing. It was not only Vivia's.

He did not see it as a punishment, but as a strange reward.

At first light they would go on, over the treacherous bridge between the plain and the plateau of the desert. The egg would certainly have matured before then. Already it had changed so much.

The heat shone around it.

He recalled a sentence from his books. 'You must make an enemy of the stone and overcome the stone to attain your desire.'

'Look,' breathed the Witch. 'Do you see?'

Zulgaris looked more closely. A tiny crack was running up the side of the egg. And then another.

'What safeguards are there?' she said.

'Enough. But it can't harm me.'

The Witch drew back, and from some area of her garments she took out a small pouch of powder.

'Put that away. Do as I tell you.'

She obeyed him.

Twenty or more little cracks on the eggshell now. Fissured, a spiderweb.

Zulgaris touched the egg. It was only warm. He picked off a piece of the magical shell. It should be ground down, and he would swallow it, like the gods of old.

The entire shell shattered suddenly outwards, bits flying off into the shavings and into the fire, where they crackled.

Zulgaris stalked forward to regard his child.

The dawn came like sour red wine, and showed the fearful gradient, the huge, iceless crevasse that fell down into the earth. The natural bridge that passed among the cliffs of rock, over to the wild plateau where the sand began, white and cold as a sea of frost.

They did not want to cross. The men were wary and the animals fractious.

Nevertheless, the crossing was begun.

Men lurched forward. The carriages jounced. Everything passed at a walk, to go faster was not wise.

The cold heat of redness left the sky a sere white-blue.

The cliffs towered, full of flints and debris. The old bones of things long since vanished from the world. As men would vanish one day. And all who safely crossed would vanish.

The pack beasts were reluctant and the caged beasts howled and defecated. The leopards crouched to the floor of their enclosures and gave off an acid stink of fear and anger.

A soldier stumbled. His comrade pulled him up and away from the edge. The soldier who had fallen wept. 'My mother,' he said, 'she died in the fire – '

Behind the carriages, the packhorses and the army, the camels with their slithering load.

Even by day, there was a scum of frost on the ledges.

A sluicing noise. A shout.

Three camels slewing as the weight behind them slipped, sloughed to the abyss –

The drovers ran, slashing the ropes. The camels sprang forward.

One man skidded from the rock and dropped into the depths below. He did not cry out.

The great clock, the clock of twenty-four numerals – a round creature on the lip of the descent. The statue of the knight went over first, silent as the man. By a fluke, the maiden stayed sidelong on the track. But the clock-face was tottering, rotating, trying to decide.

It spun out of its fleeces and dived over, plunged down.

The soldiers grouped, shouting and swearing.

They watched it go.

The flinty sides of the crevasse speared at it. Petrified trees cut at its face.

It fell behind the falling man – the knight had already struck with a tolling clang – overtaking the human body in a curiosity of gravity.

And as it flashed home upon a beak of rock, so he crashed against it.

Up through his chest, through his grey robe, exploded the bent hand of the clock, the hand which had told the hours.

The man's mouth was a silent hole. His robe turned crimson, and the red moved over the clock-face.

In the upheaval, something else.

From behind them.

The soldiers turned. They saw that five camels had collided, missing the edge of the Hell-dip, floundering. And up from their midst, something flourished.

It *stood* upright.

It was a wall, or piece of a wall. But there in it, as the wraps coursed off like black water –

The sun caught silver, iron, gold, *diamond* –

The soldiers bayed, most of them in terror.

It was the icon of Zulgaris' hidden chambers. A thing like a skeleton, yet with skeletal wings outspread. Its face was a sun mask, dislodged.

It gestured to them, its arm sweeping out, roving inward. Its fingers – bones – touched its mouth. From which two diamond fangs depended.

Some of the men had gone to their knees.

What was it?

A general wailing and growling and calling roiled along the deadly slope.

As he rode along the lines of men, Demed reflected on their innocence.

He spoke to them easily, calmly. The hubbub died, and they listened to him.

He told them there was nothing to be afraid of. They had marched well and were brave and honourable. They liked that, for they had been acting in an undisciplined and cowardly way. Demed reassured them.

'The prince is in your hands,' said Demed.

These words, dropped so neatly into the speech of reassurance, went quite deep. He saw them thinking about them, and rode on, complimenting and calming.

The soldiers began to cheer Demed.

He had bothered to come and see to them. Where was Zulgaris? They did not ask, but he saw the cloud behind their faces.

The curious object from Zulgaris' tower was muffled up again, but they gave it a wide berth, letting the camels and drovers see to it.

Demed knew they would begin to discuss this as they had not discussed the fire. And then they would talk of the fire, and the retreat from Starzion, too. There had been too much for them, now.

In their cages, as he went by, the animals shivered and snapped. Amidst the cages was the huge tank with the sea beast in it. The soldiers were afraid of this also, and the fear was mutual, its water continually smoked by ink.

Demed was satisfied.

All around the hostile faces which warmed at his approach, and faded thoughtfully as he rode away.

The men of his own command were immoveably loyal to him. He had always seen to their comforts and rights. And Kazun and Urt could say the same. The lesser knights too were swayed by what their superiors did and said. There had already been some dialogues. Nothing decisive.

Demed rode back along the lines of men.

He spoke to some by name, and they turned to their companions as he left them. 'See, he knows me. Knows my worth.'

But Zulgaris had not troubled.

She lay in the carriage, between sleep and waking and death. So it seemed. She hurt. She longed for the rumbling and rattling of the vehicle to end.

She thought that if she had been only a girl she would be dead by now. But then, an ordinary woman would not have brought forth what Vivia had.

The black and silvery egg . . .

She dreamed of it. She dreamed it broke and a black crow flew out, a raven, an eagle.

It had not been hers. It was his fault. His sorceries and vanities.

How long since she had seen her prince?

He had the horrible thing. What had he done with it? He and his Witch.

When they stopped, which seemed often to happen, the woman brought Vivia things, sliced fruit and wine, herbal drinks, fresh blankets and furs. The carriage had been cleansed and was scented.

Vivia slept on and on. Woke and woke.

She cried sometimes, not knowing for what, as she was bounced blindly over the awful terrain.

The evening came in through the veiled window, dark blue with knife points of stars.

It was the constellation of the Maiden, which once Ursabet (forgotten) had told her of. A girl chained to a rock, sacrificed to a monster. Freed.

At last, the carriage stopped and stayed still.

Vivia lay, whining with relief.

Presently a man came to the carriage, and Vivia's woman walked deferentially behind him.

'You're to come to the prince.'

'No,' Vivia said.

Neither paid any attention.

She was stood up by her woman, in the carriage, swathed in furs, and drawn out into the dread of the freezing star-frosted night.

She walked on sand now, felt it through her boots. And looking up, she saw, against the indigo sky and silver lights, fine snow falling.

Her woman supported her and the man walked before.

She did not assemble much of what went by, the tents, the fires, peculiar beasts, the soldiers, who seemed very quiet.

Zulgaris' yellow tent. She entered its obvious magnificence with an indifferent irritation. And with fear.

Gold tassels cascaded. Braziers smoked perfume. And through a succession of inner curtains the man conducted Vivia, and left her in a small hot space, hung with yellow silk, and with a lamp of red and green.

The prince came in and stood looking at her, as the other man went away. Zulgaris was alone with her.

'How are you?' he asked.

'Quite ill. The rolling of the carriage makes me worse.'

'I'm sorry. Not far to go now. A few miles, and a few days. Have you seen the desert?'

'Yes.'

'It doesn't impress you. But then, why should it. What a marvel you are yourself, Vivia. Don't you want to know?'

'What?' she said. She understood quite well.

'The thing to which you gave birth.' He did not speak with wrath or revulsion, only with a mild pleasure. He was pleased. What else?

'They took it away,' she said.

'Well, you could hardly nurse it. But you haven't any milk, have you?'

Vivia, who would have hated her body to have produced

nourishment for a child, averted her face. She found the conversation, as she had known she would, distasteful.

'I don't know what happened,' she said. 'Your Witch was there.'

'Yes. And she brought me the fruit of your womb. Our offspring. Would you care to see it?'

'No,' said Vivia immediately.

'Are you so frightened? It's a wonder. You must. I want you to.'

'Then I must.'

'Good.'

He lifted aside a curtain, and there was another magnificent area, full of furniture and lamps and hangings and the smoke of the braziers and their scents. Empty of any people.

Vivia advanced through into this place, and Zulgaris followed her.

He took her arm lightly and led her to a table. A broad silver bowl lay there. Only that.

'Look.'

In the bold light of ten lamps it was easy to see inside the bowl.

Easy.

A tiny dark shape filled the bottom, lying like a fruit indeed. A fruit of stone.

It was a small gargoyle, some ornament –

A dark smooth grey, of long and slender form, without genitals or any normal marks. Legs and arms and strange clawed hands and feet. The face a mask, with flat stone eyes. Behind it, two half-closed stony wings, on which it lay.

Who had carved it? What artisan? It was some mockery from his sorcerer's tower.

And then it moved.

Only a very little.

The flicker of a wing, a twitch of its stone arm.

The head turned slightly, as if it tried, in its obduracy and the unloving hardness of the silver bowl, to be comfortable.

It lived.

Zulgaris said, merciless, amused, 'The egg cracked and this was there. Your infant, my pretty little mother.'

Vivia did not speak. She did not draw away.

Her fear only crystallized and turned her cold. *This* had been inside her body –

And yet, now that she saw.

Oh, it was not his. Not the child of Zulgaris. For it resembled another.

'What do you say?' he said.

Vivia answered, 'What will you do with it?'

'Keep it, of course. Watch it. I've tried to feed it, but it will take nothing, not even water.'

'Have you tried,' she said, 'blood?'

'The preference of its mother? No, not yet. Perhaps I shall, or could that make it dangerous? It must be kept docile until Syr. Then I can tempt it.'

'It's horrible,' she said, but mostly because, perhaps, he expected this.

Now she was not horrified. Stunned, almost angry.

Somehow *he* had given her this child, the first prince of her dream. How could it be anyone but *he*? For it was like him, like his image in the cave. Like also that thing Zulgaris had, but apparently Zulgaris did not see this, or if he did, gave it to other associations.

The creature moved again. Did its stone eyes look at her? Could it see? Had it any senses, of smell or taste or feeling?

Vivia had a strange urge to touch it, but it was like the child's foolish desire to finger flame.

'Poor girl,' said Zulgaris. He was patronizing, and blind as the stone. 'Will she be afraid now to join with me in congress?'

'Yes.'

'But we must. When the proper time has passed. What your womb has made me – '

Vivia laughed softly.

She thought she would never have a child by Zulgaris now, probably not possibly by any man.

What the vampire had done to her had taken away that

chance, and she was glad, confident. It had been worth the
hardship.

The stone child had stopped moving.

Sudden tears burned behind her eyes. She was sorry for
it and hoped it would soon die – or cease to exist, for surely
it could not properly be said to *live*.

'My Vivia,' said Zulgaris tenderly. He took her from the
place and made her drink wine with him. 'You must be
better guarded. And you shall have a beautiful room in
Syr. They'll make it for you. And a garden. Everything
you want.'

Vivia wondered, in silence, what she wanted.

Chapter Four

THE SAND STRETCHED IN ALL directions to the veiled cones of the mountains. The sky was between blue and grey, the sun a white blot. The cold wind pressed like a steel sheet against the camp, which now looked small and insignificant.

On the grey sand had formed patches of snow and ice. Fires burned palely, like droppings from the acid sun.

Something moved, not as the men sluggishly moved. This huge tall thing strode forward. It was powerful, and those in its way hurried aside.

It was a knight. A knight taller even than Kazun.

The black armour of the knight gleamed. At the side of the knight hung a heavy sword with an iron hilt set with one star-like jewel.

The vizor was down, the face obscured.

The soldiers fell back, pointed.

'What is it? It isn't a man.'

'Where's it going?'

They turned, and saw that the unhuman knight strode towards the little flowered tent of the cursed girl, the girl who drank blood.

Had Zulgaris finally sent an executioner?

They followed the knight warily.

The black knight came to the tent of the vampire girl, and swung about. It took up its position before the tent, and stood, right hand – not a hand – across its body on the hilt of the sword.

A soldier spat into a slate of snow.

Others muttered.

Not to finish her then, to guard her from them.

When Vivia stirred, she was shown the knight. The man who had last night conducted her to and from the pavilion of the prince, displayed the great black engine that was not a man, standing there at the entrance.

'It's a clockwork, lady. An automaton. The Prince Zulgaris has employed it in mock combats. It's very strong. Your champion.'

Vivia was of course afraid of the clockwork knight.

She cowered in her tent until it was time to pack up and leave, and then she sidled past and hastened to her carriage. The black knight swung behind the carriage. It would stride after. And after the knight came the carriage with the virgin girls. (Now there were only five of them. The magic number of seven had been spoilt.)

As they journeyed on, Vivia thought occasionally of the knight behind the carriage. She mistrusted it utterly.

Mostly she forgot, and gazed mesmerized at the dreary landscape, the sands and white stares of snow. The mountains looked distant as the moon. The world now was also like the moon.

Vivia's thoughts went back to her father's castle, the lush fields and foliaged trees, the river.

She recalled her childhood and Ursabet's stories.

Would it be at all possible that, in Syr, she could escape from Zulgaris?

Doubtless not.

Perhaps he would tire of her, when she did not produce for him a succession of macabre stone babies.

Now it seemed to her she had not borne that awful thing at all. It had not happened, and certainly not to her. She contented herself with that.

Zulgaris, that morning, had had a dish of the powdered stone from the shattered shell of the egg brought to him. And measuring out a dose, he put it into wine.

He did not pause. He drank the draught.

Almost at once he became aware of a tingling of energy

and strength. He felt renewed, and more powerful than ever.

He laughed, as they set out, and rode on his yellow horse.

He went up and down the lines of men with a company of knights, and spoke cheeringly to them all.

But the soldiers were downcast and unkempt. Their captains had not kept them up to the mark. Then Zulgaris ordered punishments. Men were taken aside and lashed two or three times. Rations of food were curtailed.

Satisfied, Zulgaris rode back along the wandering column. He observed the camels that were the colour of the sand, stepping haughtily on the snow.

The pieces of the alchemical buildings dragged forward.

He had been enraged at the loss of the clock.

Men had been flogged for that and left lying.

Later Zulgaris returned to his carriage and read esoteric books. He drank wine. His brain hummed and felt galvanized, as if lightning moved lightly in his arteries. There was a box by his elbow, padded like a cradle, and something lay in it.

He wished fervently he might lie with Vivia, but not enough time had elapsed since the birth, and he was not a barbarian. There were no other women worthy of sex.

He mentioned to Demed, who rode at the window, the lax condition of the men.

Demed excused it. The desert made them strange, hollow. Demed commended his master on Zulgaris' strong, stern reprisals. That would wake them up.

The Witch rode on her platform on the wagon, pulled by four horses.

Swathed in her furs, she did not mind the cold. She had a hood of leopardskin Zulgaris had given her years ago.

She twisted something in her hands, unseen by the straggling marchers below.

It was the wax doll made to resemble the prince, and mixed up in it was Zulgaris' semen.

The Witch toyed with the doll, sometimes touching its loins, tickling, and remembering.

He was lost to her now. Perhaps it was even her fault. Some sort of new madness had come over him, after she had made the effigy.

He had burned Starzion, his prize, and now his soldiers were muttering, and soon it would be time to go away.

He travelled with the grotesque thing, the stone baby, in a box.

The Witch had only seen that baby once.

How beautiful the egg had been, coming glistening from the velvet interior of that girl. And then the shell cracked and the nasty imp was inside it.

Stone, made of stone.

The Witch hated the stone baby. Even more perhaps than Vivia, certainly as much as she hated Zulgaris.

She stared at the desert pityingly. It did not match her withered coldness.

Gently she slipped the pin into the wax head of the effigy. It would not pain him. It was worse. Let it do all its work. Why should he be happy when she was not and never could be again?

Chapter Five

NIGHT DESCENDED FROM A GREEN sky.

The march lay again becalmed.

Zulgaris' camp made its several noises. Hammers and cauldrons, fires that spat, the horses and the huffing camels, the caged beasts. The sullen sea-murmur of human voices.

'They dine better than we do – offal and crusts. It's roast lamb for them and pickled fish.'

They spoke of Zulgaris' playthings, the albino men, black men, dwarfs.

'Even the animals eat better.'

'He cares for *them*.'

'And that white whore with the machinery to guard her – '

'Well, he fucks her.'

'They say she pushed something out. A deformed child.'

'What about that other thing?'

They sat in silence, ringing their thin red fires.

'The thing in the stone with the gold face of the Christ. It beckoned to us. I saw it. So did you.'

'It's the skeleton of a saint, a precious icon. It had wings.'

'What does it mean to us?'

In small groups, caught in the telepathy of anger and unease, all across the camp, men rose and ambled towards that spot, hedged among the camels.

The soldiers who guarded the place argued with them. But they were of one mind. The drovers got up and went away.

The camels stood high as stones in the starlight.

They uncovered from its ropes and fleeces the piece of wall, and there it lay before them, the icon of the saint. All bones, its golden mask tilted from the under-face. In the same starlight, the long teeth glinted, flashed. What did they portend?

'Lift off the mask.'

One brave one wrenched it away.

They saw the eyeless face of the emaciated saint, a skull with teeth.

'No holy thing. It's the *Devil*.'

'We've been carrying the Devil with us!'

They backed away from it, and it lay there on its spine and wings. Still now. They recalled how it had gestured to them, calling them to the Pit.

'Get the priests.'

'They're his. They won't help us.'

The crowd of men, more than three hundred of them, milling on the sand.

Someone rode towards them – two knights, human, in the gold-tipped armour of Starzion which was no more.

Demed and Kazun.

The soldiers grouped around the knights, and stopped their horses.

In a tide of bodies, Demed and Kazun sat there.

'He's kept a monstrous devil – the Evil One himself – '

'Zulgaris has betrayed us.'

Demed waited a long while for quiet, and at his side Kazun waited too.

Silence fell again, and in the silence one man said, 'He burned the city.'

'Yes,' said Demed, 'so we have learned.'

Silence again. And then a single guttural voice: 'He should pay for it.'

After that they were shouting. They were valorous and fierce and hot and eager in the freezing night to which the traitor had brought them.

They would riot now, anyway.

Demed took their head like the mane of a bolting horse.

'Are you all in agreement?'

'Yes!' they howled.

'Then we will represent you to him.'

It turned, the mob, one live sinuous thing, and as it ploughed back across the camp, the others rose to join it. Even the women came, with ladles in their hands.

The tide washed in over the sand, up to the boundary of Zulgaris' golden tent.

Here the sentries came to meet them, and Demed waved them away. 'His army wishes to talk to him. Dare you say no?'

Zulgaris came out eventually, summoned by the continuous shouting of his name.

He looked surprised, no more than that.

'What's this?' he said, as if something ordinary had occurred.

And the army boiled and thundered, five hundred men and more brought out of the city, and at their backs now the drovers and the servants, the men who tended the beasts. Shouting, yelling. The night droned like the vaulted roof it seemed to be, and from their place the camels roared like dragons.

'Demed,' said Zulgaris.

And in the press he saw then his other knights, of the second and third and fourth ranks, and then the knights of the lesser company, and they had been yowling like the rest.

'Sir,' said Demed, 'we have a complaint against you.'

'Don't be a fool,' said Zulgaris.

'Nor you, sir,' said Kazun. 'You must listen.'

'What? To a bloody rabble? Are these the men who followed me from Starzion? A pack of little mangey yammering dogs.'

They growled then, like dogs.

Demed said, 'Give over your command to us, Zulgaris. I can't answer for your life otherwise.'

'My *life*?'

'Kill him!' squalled a man in the crowd. And then the other cries burst up. How he had fired the city, how he had roasted their children and women alive. How he had abandoned half his forces there. How he had led the rest of them here into the waste. And he practised infamous sorcery and had made them party to his worship of the Devil, damning their souls.

When the tumult died, after several minutes, it was Demed who spoke again.

'Seize him. He's no longer your prince. He's betrayed you.'

And they shouted *Demed! Demed!*

They rushed forward and ten of them grasped Zulgaris, felled him as he attempted to resist, half stripped him, beat him, kicked him as he lay on the earth.

'Enough,' said Demed.

And they left off.

They stood back, and Zulgaris was crawling on the sand, his face bloody, his twisted nose bloody, blood in his bright hair, one eye closed up.

They looked at what they had done, and a vague terror settled on them. He was surely no longer anything.

Demed said, 'He's special. Once our prince. He must not be harmed.'

And, having harmed him, they drew off, and Zulgaris got up like a bowed and broken beggar, hardly able to stand. A soldier steadied him, and paced away.

Zulgaris said, through his blood, 'I'll make you – '

'No,' said Kazun, 'your time's over, my lord. We won't kill you. We'll give you to this desert you like so much. Let that care for you.'

Demed said, in his musical far-reaching voice, the voice that had said farewell to Tarusp, 'In the clothes you have on, with a bottle of water. That's how you'll go. They'll drive you out. You leave your goods to us, in recompense.'

The soldiers howled again. The women laughed.

'And your things we'll keep to amuse *us*,' said Kazun.

And Urt said, 'The beasts shall be *our* pets. But not that bitch of yours, that vampire woman.'

The soldiers whispered.

Demed said, 'Her we can burn.'

The soldiers now laughed, thinking of the cheerful bonfire.

Urt added quickly, 'The little girls are all right. They're toothsome. We'll keep those. They had no choice. The priests can make sure of them. They're virgins.'

Zulgaris had fallen down again.

One final soldier kicked him in the head.

Vivia woke from her deep sleep because the woman was shaking her.

Vivia shouted in outrage.

'Lady – lady – '

The woman was terrified, and presently she ran out again, and through the opening in the tent, Vivia heard the curious new noise of the camp. Roars and yells and rushings to and fro, the faint shrieks of the five little girls not far off, the notes of the beasts whose cages were being crowded, the cough of leopards paraded on leash.

Vivia got up and pulled on a woollen robe. She belted it tight, and in that moment a grinning soldier came straight into the tent.

'Cold, girlie? We'll make you nice and warm.'

Then darkness filled in at his back.

The man was seized, upended, and flung down.

The black knight from the doorway stood over him, and the soldier, who had thought this demon shut off, gibbered with fear.

The sword rose and fell and the man's head rolled across the tent to Vivia's feet, its mouth still open to ask her another witty question.

Vivia, dumbfounded, waited in suspense.

No one else came in, although the fearful noise surged all about her now.

Then the tent fell, was pulled down around her.

Only the fighting machine Zulgaris had sent remained upright, and as she crouched on the ground, it stood over her, the black sword raised high.

Soldiers were trying to pull her out.

The black sword smote and men screamed as their hands and arms dropped free on the ground in washes of blood.

The disturbance lasted mindlessly for some minutes.

Then came a firm clear voice.

'Vivia, come out. No one will hurt you.'

It was one of his knights, one of the men who had watched her sexual defloration.

But the sides of the tumbled tent heaved, and Vivia crawled compulsively out of it.

Her champion strode after her.

She emerged into a glare of torches. The soldiers stood to an immeasurable distance, she could not see beyond them. But there was Demed on his horse.

Men lay bleeding on the sand.

Vivia got up.

The champion had raised its sword high.

'Don't touch her,' said Demed. 'That thing will guard her. It's a mechanism of the tower.'

Men spat and called names, against the knight, and against the girl.

Vivia slunk back against the metal man, which was preferable at last.

Kazun sat his horse to the left. He now spoke to her.

'Zulgaris is done for. You're ours, Vivia, to do with what we want.'

'Burn her,' the men shouted, 'burn the abomination, the bitch.'

Demed beckoned and a way was made through the men. Other men pushed forwards, carrying thick looped ropes. They had crewed the machines of war, and knew their work.

They cast, and the ropes came in.

One caught Vivia about the shoulders, scorching her breasts and arms, tearing her to her knees.

Others ascended over the black knight.

Now all the soldiers were pulling, bellowing and even laughing.

The mechanism of the knight toppled with a flailing crash. It lay spasming, its legs going like those of a gigantic black armoured beetle.

It was powerless now, and Vivia was theirs.

Chapter Six

SURELY SHE WOULD DIE NOW, after all. Yet she could not die. Plague and childbirth had not killed her. Poison had not. Yet – *fire* –

They had built the pyre cheerfully – had some of them seen to Starzion with such glee?

They laughed and joked as they built it.

Vivia, held in her rope, was silent, and cool. She felt afraid – but indifferent, a curious combination. There was nothing she could do. She despised them all.

Somewhere Zulgaris lay, also roped up, not conscious. She had been shown him.

And the leopards of which he had been so proud, walked on leash beside the knights and captains, growling and purring at titbits. She would have switched her allegiance as diligently, if permitted. Men were powerful, must always be placated, or run from.

When the pyre was finished to their satisfaction, men came and dragged Vivia towards it. Her woollen gown trailed over the sand and snow, and she watched it curiously, for some reason. It *interested* her.

They pulled her up against a hard straight post, tied her there securely. They were very decorous, being careful where they put their hands. Of course, she was sorcerous. They put on to her face a tin mask – the mask of a felon. She saw now only through the eye-holes.

She wondered where the Witch was, and if this woman would come to see, to gloat. But there was, in the thick rings of men, no sign of the Witch, though a few women were scattered there, even the whores from the pleasure pallets, with cheap bright things glittering in their hair.

And the knight of metal, her champion, lay writhing on the ground out of sight, just behind the nearer tents.

Vivia stood, roped and bound, waiting for the fire.

She wondered if she should pray.

A priest was standing at the pyre's foot, offering her a cross and a sunburst.

Vivia turned her head.

God, if He did exist, was a fool. And yet, too clever to listen to her.

She thought of her vampire prince. How he had told her she could not die. Now was the moment for him to come, and sweep her away on coal-black wings.

The dim sky was clear. At some point the sun had strengthlessly risen, making everything visible, yet only dully so. Torches still burned viciously. In a way, it was still night.

Then the torch came and touched the foot of the mound of kindling where Vivia was tied.

She felt a flare of terror. It filled her with heat before the flames could do so.

Oh, it was not possible she could survive this. No, no. Her flesh would crisp and fray away, her bones would splinter. Shrieking she would perish in agony before these oafs.

The soldiers were cheering, making new jokes. Toasting her death in wine and beer. She saw them through the smoke of the fire and the smoulder of her fear.

Then the first rush of the fire hit her. It was like a vast slap – so hot, so *cold*, a wash more like water than flame. Vivia screamed, and her hair flew up like a blown cloth.

The fire curled, came round her, covered her. Vivia was on fire. She squalled with fright. Walls of flame rose before her eyes, and hid everything but death and the melting mask of tin.

Then the flames sank, and she stood there naked. The fire had burnt off her robe, melted the tin mask. But Vivia – was not touched. Not a hair of her head. Intact. Pristine.

She stood in the fire, which raged about her now and

temporarily hid her from the crowd of soldiers. She saw what the fire did. It plucked the cords off her body and devoured them. It ate the wood, so now the floor of sticks and staves on which she stood gave way a little.

But Vivia the fire did not harm. (Can fire kill fire?)

As the smoke began to fold away, the soldiers after all saw Vivia, standing up in the pyre. The ropes which had bound her had gone; she was whiter than the snow, fumed over by the tide of her own black hair.

And the fire – *played in her. Through her.* It was like lightning in a cloud.

This they saw, and dug each other in the ribs and said, *Look, she's burning now.* But she was not and soon they began to realize this.

Vivia the vampire, the abomination, was not alight. Was not harmed.

Even, she had begun to *finger* the flames – idly, like a child. (She was as amazed as they were.)

The soldiers started to wail. To point and push at each other now, to exhort God. Their toy had failed.

Some ran forward and threw in torches, into the pyre, and the torches blazed and wood crackled, and Vivia, standing, dropped several inches down to the level of the sand, and stood there.

Presently it occurred to her that her ropes were gone. But she was nude, and only the fire shielded her.

Then something else happened.

The flames, which crossed and recrossed her body, began to weave a sheath about her.

They clothed her slowly in a dull red dress. The dress was shapeless, and it glinted. Bits of fire were still alive in it. As it settled it darkened, and the fires went out of it with the brightness. Energy – had remade itself, to suit her.

Vivia stepped off the pyre, which still burned at her back, like wings of flame.

The tin mask partly adhered to her face, like a new mask of gleaming sequins, and down her throat it had run, mingling with the melting of Zulgaris' golden chain, to form a necklace, and in her hair it sparkled like crawling silver ants.

The soldiers at the front were pressing back, yelling and cursing. Those behind turned to run away.

A demon – and they had not subdued it.

It walked towards them.

Vivia was cool as ice now, direct from the fire.

A priest stood before her, waving at her a cross and sun-burst, the same priest who had wanted to see her burn.

Vivia struck him aside. A priest was not a man, Vaddix had always denied it.

As he fell away, Vivia laughed.

She felt young and strong. She felt happy. Triumphant.

So small and slender, and a woman, yet she was more strong than all of them.

She saw behind the tents, the metallic knight, still flailing and kicking in its ropes.

She was stronger than that, too.

Scornfully, she indicated the knight.

And two or three soldiers, staring at her in terror, ran to the automaton and cut it free. Then they pelted away.

All the camp was running from Vivia.

She stood in a wide space now, and the fallen knight had got up, righted itself, and knowing her by some alchemical means, strode over to her.

It took up its stance at her back, sword partly raised. It would defend her, even though there was no need.

And what now?

Vivia stood at a loss.

It came to her slowly. Zulgaris lay somewhere nearby, she had seen him. She must also free Zulgaris.

This was not affection or romance, not kindness or altruism. It was merely that she was used to him. In Vivia's world of the moment, he ruled. And his fall did not lessen him, though it had destroyed him. Ruined, yet he made sense to her. Like a blasted pylon in the desert; still recognizable.

However, some of the soldiers were coming back. They were running and stumbling, and in their midst was the real knight, Demed.

Demed looked at Vivia. His face was unreadable. Prob-ably he thought they had made a mistake in her burning, and for this reason she had survived. But the soldiers were shouting of a miracle, or of a demon, and Demed waited some while for them to grow silent, and then he spoke.

'Then the woman must be driven into the desert with the man.'

The aptness of this statement, which had a sort of God-like, scriptural ring, calmed the soldiers. They began to shout his words.

Vivia realized that Zulgaris would be given to her to take away.

She knew this at once, and how it must be done.

Her garment was nearly black now, and most of the tin drops had sloughed from her face and throat and hair. She looked only beautiful, but not as if anything prodigious had happened to or through her.

Someone came, carrying Zulgaris like a bundle of clothes.

This man threw Zulgaris at Vivia's bare feet.

Vivia regarded her prince in silence. She felt a strange sensation.

Then she turned to the metal knight.

'Pick up your master.'

Would it understand?

Apparently it did. Rudimentary language and orders had been allotted to its grasp.

It leaned down and pulled Zulgaris up, across its body. His head lolled (golden) over its sword arm.

'Go into the desert, Vivia,' said Demed. 'Go far off. And God have mercy on you.'

Vivia smiled. The soldiers leaned away. She did not need God.

So she walked, clad in fire-made black, her black hair streaming, over the grey desert with its scales of white snow. And behind her walked the black champion, carrying the gold package of the defeated prince, Zulgaris.

Black and gold on the pastel of the wilderness, they left the upheaval of the camp behind, its tents and smokes and the one towering smoke of the great bonfire that had not worked.

A wind was rising, and whipped the sand up stinging and brittle. The sun was invisible. Things had changed.

Talia the leopardess had been courteous with the soldiers, who fawned on and petted her. The men who generally had charge of her had gone away, but even so, much was made of her, there was no occasion for her anger.

In a necklet of sapphires and her anklet and bell, she walked up and down the lines of murmuring men, allowing them to feed her slivers of meat and little pastries, the things she had been used to.

If she missed Zulgaris, she did not demonstrate this.

Nevertheless, the feverish quality of the soldiers did not cause her serenity. She was cautious and not utterly at ease. They seemed to want her approval.

Dangerous, Talia lashed her tail, once, twice, and went round the cordon of anxious men again.

The smell of fire added to her disquiet.

Finally most of the men left her, and Talia was there, untethered, her leash held in the hand of a man who, slightly drunk, had preferred her company to the sight of a burning witch.

Talia sat on the icy sand. She licked her shoulder, as if savouring the black poppies of her markings.

When the man fell asleep, Talia saw a movement out beyond the camp.

She was used to hunting. She turned to this with fresh interest.

A large white hare was feeding on something, something dropped during the blandishments of the soldiers.

Talia rose like pale honey, and the leash slipped from lax male fingers.

She did not like the odour of the camp. It smelled iron with lusts and fears.

Besides, the journey had been foul, the bumping and toiling, the encagement, the abyss under the bridge, to which Talia had responded with a pool of golden urine.

Beyond the camp, the desert was crisp and cold and dry, and smelled of old forgotten things that, amalgamated, were a collective of freedom.

Talia sprang for the hare.

Which, quick as the wind, raced away from her, its huge hind legs kicking up a rind of ice.

They ran for perhaps a mile, and then Talia's jaws closed on the body of the flying thing.

She made short work of it. A snap, an evisceration. Her carnal feeding in the waste of ice made a deep red rose.

When she was done, the bones lay perfect, and the leopardess put down her nose to inhale from them the last of their charm.

As she did this, a wind came, rucking the sand before it, violent and without premonition.

Talia had come to a rocky place, a chasm in the desert, but this meant nothing and offered no shelter.

Instead, instinctively, the cat crouched down, and put her face into what was left of the body of the hare.

As the sands blew over her, the pocket of air beneath the corpse sustained her. She lowered her flanks and hackles, lids and ears, and prepared to wait out the storm.

She had put over herself the guise of an old woman of the camp – in extremity, she was not proud. She shuffled through their lines, cackling, with her bundle, like any old crone of the cook fires, who had made their hashes once and now sought to gather goodies by reason of their uprising.

No one challenged her. A few of them, who were drunk, laughed at her. One threw a clod of snow – nothing sharp, it was soft malice. She was one of their own.

She was contemptuous of them, always had been. These men. These soldiers. Zulgaris' playthings on his board of war. And she too had made them work at her bidding.

Not any more.

The Witch went carefully, not hurrying. She left the camp as if for some natural urge, then made off over the frost-salted dunes.

Soon his camp was far behind.

She laughed to herself then, bitterly. She had been his

downfall. Through her jealous arts, she had turned his brain. So he fell. And that girl – they would kill *her*. Burn her probably, as a witch.

The Witch went out into the waste. In her bag were all her most vital potions and amulets, she had left nothing but rubbish – to confuse. And, too, she carried the wax dummy she had made of her former master. It still had the pin straight through its head.

But she had something else.

She had gone to his tent, in the aftermath, after they had called him forth and thrashed him (she had watched this) and there she found, before the rest of them came to root and ravish, the box. The box with the imp in it, Vivia's fearsome child-thing.

And this also the Witch took up.

She did not scruple to touch it, and indeed it did not move in her grasp. She stuffed it in the bag. She *wanted* it. It was like desire. A *need*.

There were prints in the sand. A big cat had come this way. But the Witch was not afraid. She was powerful, and to her a cat was nothing.

The desert also did not daunt her.

All her life had been forms of hardship, or going without. Even gaining the gems in her teeth had cost her pain. She did not complain. She suffered what she must and struck back where she was able.

The ground rose a little, and then dipped down. The Witch knew she was not so far from the town of Syr. Conceivably, by means of divination, she could reach it. But then again, the mob of soldiers might also head for that place. Some ramshackle village of the desert might assist her more.

She did not bother herself. Her most urgent mission was before her.

After about half an hour, she came on the bowl of a natural arena, an area of stone with sandy floor but harsh walls of granite and pumice. Peculiar rocks lay round it, like crouching animals.

She looked at this with satisfaction.

She drew off the shabby eldritch cape she had worn to

avoid the soldiers, and stood in her bronzy hard skin above the rocky shelves, flexing herself.

The wind had been blowing up, now tossing her hair like the mane of a young girl. Somewhere a storm was raging in the desert.

The Witch opened her bag.

She took out the wax of Zulgaris.

She laid it on the sand, and gazed at it, then toed it with her left foot.

Then she drew out the other thing.

The stone baby – the imp.

It lay like nothing in her grip. No movement and no sound. No sign it lived.

Yet it did.

She had seen that it did.

The Witch felt it over without dismay or care. She poked at the sexless juncture between its legs, and prodded at the wings.

No response. Nothing.

Its face was a gargoyle face from some church. No motion and no sense, and in the blind eyes, no light.

The Witch spat on its breast. And hurled it away, against the downslope of the pumice walls of the arena.

She saw it shatter. It broke in several bits, and these shot away and lay at angles presently on the sandy floor of the drop.

The Witch did discern a movement then, a sort of wriggling of the pieces. But this might be a trick of the eyes.

The wind growled.

The Witch looked up, and saw the sandstorm coming, and at once she hurled herself flat and smothered her face in the folds of the robe of disguise.

But the storm passed over her. It was nothing. It had come before and this was only some outriding essence of its power. A little thing.

However, after a few minutes, when the Witch emerged from her cover, she saw the whole region oddly altered. The sand had been swept up freshly over the arena floor, and all the bits of the creature she had cast there had

vanished. All around lay fine fragments, perhaps of the
shells which, mystically, littered the waste.

A rock nearby had become different.

It had a face, like that of a cat pressed down to the
ground.

And even as she watched, a cake of sand fell off, and
there two rocky eyeshapes were, and the curious carving
of two ears, sharp whiskers. It was like a leopard's mask
made in stone. The eyes opened then. They were liquid,
bright and green.

The Witch stood astounded.

And more sand flaked off and there the whiskers stood,
and then the face appeared, yellow and spotted, the face
of the leopardess Talia.

The Witch knew her next moment by her necklace, and
called to her placatingly.

The Witch did not really fear Talia, and was not quick
enough to speak her spells, which in any case would not
have worked.

From the uncovered rose of the hare's blood, the cat leapt
out, hungry still, and directly at the thin scrawny neck of
Zulgaris' Witch.

They fell with a flat thud on the rock's edge, and the
Witch screeched some charm, but Talia, who did not care,
tore out the Witch's throat.

Blood showered, its wonderful red of no moment to the
beast, who, in another instant, lowered her mouth to feed
on vitals.

All around lay scattered the paraphernalia of the Witch's
art. All the marks of her survival, now of no use. All were
spangled red.

A red vein too slipped across the dummy of the prince,
and sank in there slowly.

The storm and its following wind had moved away.

The noises of feeding had stopped.

In the sand at the rock's base, something moved. And
then another thing.

A small rat, which had come from its burrow in the
rockside, turned its quivering attention to these areas. It

dug busily, then like lightning it sprang back, sat upright a second, before darting away.

On the sand lay a bit of broken stone, nearly black. It was in the shape of a tiny arm.

The arm spasmed. It wriggled. Blindly.

And nearby, other sections also moved, under the sand.

Smashed, the gargoyle baby had not lost its life, or whatever animated it – perhaps its soul.

Something motivated it now, sightless and stiff, to attempt a rejoining. Each severed part was labouring, on the surface or deeply buried in the sand, to reach the other segments.

This horrible struggle continued ceaselessly, and without respite.

Day passed over that place, a bleak day of the frozen desert.

Once more a rat came and pawed at the sand, jumped back startled and ran away.

The stone creature was not good to eat.

As evening fell and the cold sun sank, and bluish shadows creased the cracks of the snow, the broken demon child struggled on, the worms of its arm and wing shuddering at the rock's base, and elsewhere the ghastly movements in the deeper sand.

Had the pieces come any nearer to each other? Was it possible? Could they wriggle on like this, mindlessly, for ever, in this worst type of living death? What instinct possessed them?

Above, where Talia had fed, the blood and remains faded to black and white as the dark began to come. The uncompassionate stars rose in the black air.

Chapter Seven

FROM HER THROAT, THE SMEARS of the melted gold chain Zulgaris had bound her with, and of the tin dross from the mask, gradually flaked and fell. Vivia was aware of this, as she walked, the last memento of the fire.

They had not been able to burn her. Fire did not kill fire.

Behind her, the automaton stalked, carrying Zulgaris the prince – prince no more – across its body.

Where were they going?

Vivia did not care.

She exalted, and lifted her head to the blowing wind, and when the wind died, to the bare sky.

She was not afraid of the waste of sand and snow, the cold rafts of which felt hot to her unshod feet. She need fear nothing. Not now.

Then, at a rise in the terrain, she paused, and looked around her, lording it over the desert.

Was she hungry? She had been promised, animals would feed her blood. It seemed she would be able to call one up, out of the waste. It would lie at her feet and offer her its throat.

Behind her, Zulgaris groaned.

He had done this from time to time. He lived, but had lost everything. She had saved him.

Vivia turned. The automaton was some way behind, and moving very awkwardly now. Its long strides had shortened and it lifted its legs in a peculiar ungainly fashion, jolting the burden it bore.

Sand had got into its joints. It was only a stupid doll.

Vivia called imperiously, 'Here, come here.'

The black knight advanced, and when it finally reached her, she saw that Zulgaris had regained awareness, rolling his head, attempting to get some control over his beaten body in the knight's grip.

'Vivia – ' he said.

'Yes.' She considered. She said, 'I'm all that's left to you. They tried to burn me and your chain melted.'

Zulgaris groaned again.

He struck the knight.

'Put me down on the ground.'

The knight did not obey.

Vivia laughed. 'It only listens to me. Didn't you make it like that? I wonder why it's happened, then. Put him down,' she added to the knight.

It did as she said, but its movements were now so cranky, Zulgaris hit the earth solidly and rolled a few feet. He cried out.

Vivia watched.

As if she had asked him, he said, 'My ribs are cracked. Fuck them to Hell. Damn them.'

'They wouldn't kill you,' she said.

'No, they remembered I'm the anointed of God. But this – '

Vivia said, 'You've nothing left.'

'In Syr,' he said. He coughed and held his side. He tried to sit up, and partially succeeded. 'I must get to Syr.'

'Who'll know you?' she said.

He took no notice. He rubbed at his battered face, and blood dropped from his nose. One eye was swollen shut, the other bloodshot and desperate.

'They'll come to my aid at Syr. I'll punish that rabble. That rabble.'

He ranted for a while, and Vivia stood on the ridge, gazing away at the formless lines of the desert, like a still sea, on which the sun was now setting in a pale amber silence.

Without his chambers of sorcery, his books and artifacts, he was powerless. He was helpless. As the lizard, swallowing itself into nothing.

Two or three hawks or carrion birds flew over.

Zulgaris said urgently, '*Vivia.*'

'What is it?'

'You must help me now.'

She said nothing, glanced at him without pity. He had always in some form been her enemy.

(Behind him, the knight was like a pillar of darkness, like a black beast up on its hind legs.)

'Do as I say, Vivia. Remember, I've been good to you. And you're mine. That was why they spared you.' Plainly he had not heard what she told him of the fire. 'You can help me now,' he said. 'I'm weak. I'll need strength to get to the town.'

Vivia waited.

Zulgaris said, 'Your blood's magical, Vivia. Let me drink your blood. That will save me. Perhaps . . . give me immortality, who knows?'

Vivia had recoiled. Not at the idea of his drinking from her as she had only done from others, as only the vampire had done from her, but at the knowledge he would want to cut her skin to come at the blood.

'No,' she said.

'Yes, Vivia. I must. I must have it. If you want to save me.' In scorn she stared at him. He misread, with his one eye (Tetchink), her expression. 'Don't be afraid. I'll live if you let me have the blood.'

The black automaton made a sound. It was a sort of grunt, some aspect of its metal settling. The night was coming and a deep ray of cold penetrated the atmosphere.

Vivia shivered. But the cold could not hurt her either.

If Zulgaris took her blood, would he become like her – 'magical'? She did not want this to happen, and did not believe it would. Hers had been a fabulous communion. And only Gula and Ingret, who had been in love with her, had dared to rise from death.

Zulgaris kept on and on, ordering her to do what he wanted.

She could leave him, walk away across the waste. She was unique. She was invulnerable.

But she did not want to leave Zulgaris. No, she liked his weakness, his dependence. Men had dominated her. Now she could, slender and small, exert her power over him. He was at her mercy.

Very well then, he could have her blood. She would make her flesh part for him, and close after, just as she had made the flesh of the little girls do.

She went to Zulgaris and held her wrist in front of him. He seized it eagerly, putting his cracked and bruised lips to her skin.

She felt her vein open to him. It was a strange sensation. But as he sucked at her life fluid, she felt only strong. She ruled him. And when she had had enough, she closed herself against him, as never before had she been able to close her body against Zulgaris.

'We'll be safe in Syr,' he said. 'You shall have everything I promised you. You'll be safe with me.'

She laughed again, noiselessly.

Under the shadow of the black knight, there in the tireless wilderness, Zulgaris sank back and slept, and she sat, stars in her hair, laughing on and on inside herself.

When the dawn broke, Vivia watched it. It seemed fresh and new to her; she had never properly studied the dawn before. Lines of warm colour barred the east, then died, and only the grey-blue hollow of the sky was there. What symbolism did this have? The glory of sunrise that so quickly faded to normality.

Zulgaris woke and sat up.

He stared around him. His handsome face looked noble in its injuries, and then at another angle, funny.

'My Vivia,' he said. 'I'll give you another golden necklace.'

He meant the chain.

Vivia knew that he would not. Zulgaris' reign was ended, but she did not tell him so now.

'Your blood has done me good,' he said. 'I can walk today. Syr lies that way, so I think, judging by the position of the sun.' He rose. 'You may tell your guard to move,' he added indulgently.

Vivia glanced at the black knight.

She doubted it would go any further. Its joints, clogged by sand, showed now quick hints of rust.

But she beckoned it and said, 'Come on.'

The knight made a grating noise. It could not do anything.

Zulgaris stepped around it. He touched and tapped various points of its carapace, and spoke a couple of words. But to no effect.

'It was a toy,' he said. 'You don't need it now. I'm here.'

They left the knight standing jet black on the dunes, casting a straight black shadow.

Zulgaris made no mention of what had occurred now. He spoke of Syr, his town in the desert. He seemed to think he need only arrive there to be welcomed and feted.

Zulgaris walked unsteadily but spoke vigorously.

He told Vivia that the centre of Syr, its opulent houses and palaces, were built into a maze. No one could find their way there who had not lived there a long while, or who did not have some plan to the area.

A governor kept order in the town. Zulgaris would make himself known to this governor. They would resume a life of luxury. All malcontents would be punished.

It came to Vivia that Zulgaris was quite mad.

They walked over the sand, and the sun moved also, diagonally. Snow crunched under their feet. Neither did Zulgaris seem to feel the cold, although his clothes were ragged from the onslaught of the soldiers.

Vivia went before Zulgaris. He did not direct her. Presumably she travelled in the right direction, or what he believed to be so.

Vivia felt careless.

At noon they sheltered from the sudden brightness of the sun beneath a tall stand of rocks.

Here Zulgaris once more asked – demanded – blood. Vivia gave him her wrist and let him drink. It hurt her this time, and soon she pulled away.

'It strengthens me,' he mumbled.

But there was a grey tinge, like that of the waste, to his

countenance. On his neck was a strange red mark, like a band. It had grown more vivid as the day went by. She took it for another bruise.

When the dark began to come, Zulgaris said they would stop. He said they must make a fire tonight, and produced from the wreck of his rich garments – which now looked like the poverty-stricken rags of some gaudy hawker – a tinder, and lit flame to a few small dry twigs they had gathered, as they went, from random rare bushes.

The fire burned and the day went out. Soon the fire went out.

'We must try to sleep.'

He reached for Vivia and fondled her breast, but soon he sank back.

Sleeping now he snored, in a thick stupid way. She moved off from him, and sitting up on the dunes, she saw a cat-like creature pass perhaps a quarter mile off, trotting in shadow form over the dark sand.

In the morning Zulgaris raved. He shouted against the soldiers and his officers, the knights. He swore terrible retribution against them – the cutting off of noses and genitals.

His bruised eye had begun to open and it was blood-red.

Later he crawled to Vivia and rocked her in his arms. He told her she should have gardens of peach trees and peacocks and fountains. There was a fountain in Syr fed by a stream that ran both hot and cold.

There was treasure at Syr stored in hidden vaults.

Vivia listened idly. She stroked his hair.

In her scorn, she had grown half fond of him.

He slept lying against her, and when she grew tired of this she eased him on to the sand.

She prowled the dunes.

She looked where the moon rose, round and cold and white, and willed some animal to come to her. But nothing came, until, hours after, a little rat-like thing approached.

Vivia felt scornful pity for this. To feed from it would be to kill it. She paid it no attention and presently it went away. Perhaps its advent was a coincidence.

She dreamed she drank blood from the neck of a wolf –
as she had done, maybe, below her father's castle.

When she woke Zulgaris was beside her, pawing at her
body, mouthing her wrist.

She pushed him away.

And he obeyed her.

When she got up to walk on, Zulgaris was flaccid. He
stumbled often. He had begun to mutter to himself.

Days passed, and nights, in the waste.

Zulgaris grew less and less lucid and Vivia, so it seemed
to her, more so. She did not mind if they did not reach
the town. The waste was strange and avid, but nothing
threatened her. And still she felt her glowing power.

Zulgaris she kept at bay.

He was healing, but there was a scar above his lip, and
on his neck the red band constantly changed shape and did
not vanish.

Sometimes he fell down, and then she would wait for
him, standing there, offering no assistance.

He talked on and on about Syr. He said there were
statues sculpted like the figures of the Zodiac. It was a
lush oasis. Many streams and wells fed the great ponds
and fountains.

Vivia was not especially intrigued.

Possibly five days after they had left the camp, a sort of
tufted dog came to their sleeping place, and Vivia crooned
to it. The dog lay down in her lap and she had its blood, or
some of it.

The blood had a tangy curious taste. She could never
have mistaken it for anything human.

Afterwards it ran away, and she wondered if she had
only dreamed it. She did not feel any different for the
sample of blood. Although Zulgaris kept telling her that
her blood had saved him, and that now he might live for
ever as she would.

Would she? Vivia scorned this too. She was young. Life
had always seemed endless.

Finally, she let him drink again, from her left wrist. He
gulped greedily and soon she shut him out.

Then he lay on the sand, moaning to himself like a man in a sexual dream.

He said her name over and over.

When the morning began to come, Vivia saw an object out across the dunes and the snow patches. There were trees, towers, roofs shining. It could be nothing but the town. And she felt a depression of her spirits.

TWO

Chapter One

He did not know it – his blood was turning to dust.

That was what the ichor of Vivia had done for him.

It was his own fault, asking for it, not thinking.

Or, thinking he was omnipotent: the debacle with the soldiers had taught Zulgaris nothing.

Then again, there was a pin through his head – and on his neck the changing blood-mark of the Witch's gore, spilt on the wax image, which now lay lost in the sand.

As they approached a gate of the town of Syr, Zulgaris looked at it, puzzled.

It was not, the town, how he had had it planned and built. Inwardly he could make out the towers and garden-tops, the cupolas of green bronze and gold. But other towns had accumulated about the inner, perfect town, like rubbish. And successive walls had been built to contain them.

The sun hurt his eyes, and he walked behind Vivia, although he had not meant to.

The guards – there were two – in the gateway, turned playful, crossing their lances.

'What do you want?' one asked.

'To enter,' said Zulgaris, 'I – '

'No riff-raff,' said the guard.

'Send for the governor,' said Zulgaris. He tried to remember the man's name, and when he could not, a surge of awful weakness almost brought him to his knees.

Vivia said, 'We want to come in.'

'What for?' said the guard. 'Don't you like the desert?'

The other guard said, 'The town's full of layabouts, rogues. It can do without two more.'

'Wait a minute,' said the first guard. He looked at Vivia. 'What's your trade, girl?'

Vivia said nothing.

The other one laughed. 'You can see. She's young and pretty. What else.'

'And he's your owner, is he?' asked the guard, indicating Zulgaris, who stood leaning a little, gasping. 'Don't think much of him. You need a protector, little girl.'

Vivia understood they had taken her for a whore. She was not astonished or affronted. She said, 'Let us in, then.' Although she did not want the town, they were here now, and must proceed.

The first guard took hold of the neck of her garment (which the fire had made her) and peeked inside.

'Very nice. Very attractive. What'll you give me, to come in?'

Vivia stood there.

The guard said. 'I'll be your first customer. How's that? And for payment, that's your entry to Syr. His too, if you like.'

Zulgaris tried to speak, and the other guard left the gate and clouted him. Zulgaris did fall now. His body was becoming accustomed to blows and had learnt the correct responses.

The first guard pulled Vivia through the gate and into a corner of the wall. Behind them, an open place was full of people and noise, but no one seemed to pay any heed. The guard yanked up Vivia's skirt and squeezed her centre in his hand. Then he injected himself into her swiftly.

She felt the force of him but she was no longer a virgin to experience pain or shock. She knew she would never again conceive.

Indifferent, she let him heave against her and when he growled for her mouth, she let him kiss her. He came quickly, bucking into her body, and next instant his seed ran hot down her legs.

He withdrew. 'Yes,' he said. 'You should make a fortune.
All right, pass on.'

Vivia stood in the open space, while people jolted around
her, until Zulgaris came.

'What – did he do – '

'What men do.'

She was superior. Nothing had hurt her. It had been
easy. So was she a whore now? She supposed that she
was.

It was suggested to her by some atom of her mind that
once (in her father's castle) she would have resisted such
treatment to the point, perhaps, of wounding. But now.
What did it matter? She was above it all, as if floating over
her body in the air.

Zulgaris was shaking.

'My Vivia – '

'It doesn't bother me. He let you in. That was what you
wanted.'

In despair now, Zulgaris gazed around him.

Probably he had realized at last how hopeless was
his case.

Vivia looked at him. He himself had raped her, over
and over. That he was a prince had presumably made
this acceptable. But all men were princes, vilely elevated
by their masculinity. Even so, simple to deal with if you
did not resist.

Vivia was hungry. She wanted fruit and bread and a cup
of wine.

She led Zulgaris like a sheep towards a brown building
that offered such things. Doubtless Zulgaris had some
trinkets still about him that could be used to purchase
food and drink?

They entered the building and sat down in a corner. The
room was full of men, most dressed for travelling, and from
a yard came the cacophony of donkeys, camels, and other
beasts.

A boy came and sloshed down a jug of liquor.

Vivia said, 'Bring fruit.'

The boy glanced at her. 'There's dates and apples. What
money have you got?'

Vivia indicated Zulgaris, but he only stared. 'Do as she tells you, wretch. I am the Prince Zulgaris.'

The boy crowed and ran off. Presently a burly man came to the table. 'Out you. Get out. No maniacs in my house.'

They were put back on the street, the drink untasted, to the pealing bray of donkeys.

For hours they wandered the byways of the lower town. If the inner region of Syr was a maze, then so was this.

Zulgaris did not recognize it. He might have been transported to Hell.

Open sewers yawned, reeking, with filth and dead animals awash there. From alleys leprous beggars issued out. Women of no beauty, covered in warts and ripe with dirt, stood in crannies of the walls, and plucked Zulgaris' sleeve, whispering, 'I can be yours,' before letting go in disgust.

On broader streets streams of pack-beasts passed them, and they were almost trampled more than once. In narrow thoroughfares, men with diseased faces slipped by.

There were hovels built into the sides of bigger dwellings, and near a public well (where a guard stood, charging money from those who wanted water), a street opened that ran down against one of the inner walls of the town. Here were warrens like rat holes, constructed of rubble.

Finding themselves here, Zulgaris began to rock himself, and Vivia came close to striking him.

By chance or fate, they arrived at a hole which was empty, that had no stink of occupancy, and into this Vivia pulled her prince.

He did as she insisted and soon crouched against the wall.

He was praying now, long complex elegant prayers of Starzion.

It was all left to her, as she had known it would be.

Vivia was still exalted, she did not mind the stench nor its intimacy. She did not trouble at her apparent vulnerability on this river of debris. No, she was for ever above all this, and might drown herself in it without consequence.

Never had she known such freedom.

She abandoned Zulgaris without a word, and went out into the thread of street, and so into the broader ways.

Here she stationed herself like the women she had seen, and after a while a man passed leading two horses. His clothes were fair enough and he was quite clean. Vivia plucked at his sleeve.

'For dates and apples and wine, I can be yours,' Vivia said.

The man looked at her. 'Come with me.'

He took her to another tavern, but made her wait outside. He told her to keep to the shadows, or others would be after her. Quite quickly he brought her five dates and an apple, and a leather bottle of wine which they shared. In a grassy plot – the grass was yellow – behind the inn, while the horses mildly grazed, he lifted her skirt and kissed her mound, before entering her quite gently. He climaxed with a shiver, and pressed on her a silver coin.

This, with much amusement, she took back to her prince in the hovel by the wall.

Chapter Two

WINTER PASSED SLOWLY IN SYR.

Some mornings fine snow had fallen in the streets that turned grey as the day wore on. Tall palm trees were edged by frost like lace, and geraniums and peonies hung black and bitten from the shelves of narrow barred windows.

From a flight of steps that led to a large and ornamental well, situated strangely in the poor quarter, it was possible to see down into the heart of the town, to the complex interior that Zulgaris had said was constructed as a maze.

The towers stood tall, gold and green and blue topped, and cedars rose above high walls.

Zulgaris still spoke of Syr's centre. He said that tomorrow he would be stronger, and then he would seek the governor. But each tomorrow came and Zulgaris had not improved and again spoke of tomorrow.

He rambled of other things. His childhood, his father dead, brought up by tutors and philosophers, more clever than they. At twelve, a tyrant – or a master. Zulgaris spoke of his accomplishments, and his wars, against this area and that. Other men were barbarians. He spoke of his knights and their betrayal.

Vivia scarcely listened. She brought food for Zulgaris to eat, although he did not have much appetite, and wasted away. In a month his firm skin hung on his bones and a streak of white had appeared in his yellow hair. He did not look handsome now, but cadaverous and foolish, the twisted features and large eyes at odds with this tragic laxity.

He slept a good deal.

Vivia was out by day, whoring in Syr. She found it very easy, and actually laughable. Now and then, when a man was attractive – she chose the better ones, although quite often a foul one chose her (she never repulsed) – and took care over her, she experienced pleasure. Once an orgasm shook her and she was loath to let the man go, looking for him afterwards about the streets and shabby markets, but he had gone away.

Syr was always full of travellers. They made on for other cities whose names, when mentioned, meant nothing to her. Caravans passed through the desert and Syr was a well-known watering place.

Vivia, not finding the man again who had brought her to fulfilment, soon forgot him. She had learned how to do as much for herself, with her fingers, alone in the hovel by night, as Zulgaris slept nearby, snoring and grumbling in his sick sleep.

To the hovel she had brought certain comforts. Pallets of straw that was not verminous, a broken table, and a piece of coloured glass, bright deep red, which by a thong she hung over the open doorway. In the morning the sun passed through it and lit blood-stains on their skins.

The red mark on Zulgaris' throat went up into his face, then journeyed out of sight on to his body. One day she saw it had gone down on to his left hand. What it was Vivia had no idea, and it did not exercise her thoughts.

She did not think very much at all.

She went about the dirty, squabbling, smelly lower town, conscious of her grace and – paramount – of her enormous hidden power. For the first time in her life she knew utter confidence. Nothing could hurt her – at least not in any major way. She might do anything – and need do *nothing*.

But she enjoyed her job as a prostitute. It gave her something to pass the time, and she need not stay in the hovel with Zulgaris and grow bored. She roamed everywhere about the circle of the outer town, finding

endless new sights and witnessing new scenes – women
fighting at a well, a thief being mutilated before a crowd,
herds of sheep with bells, and the great ram which led them
with painted horns and mask.

In return for her freedoms, she received food and money,
drinks of wine.

She never took blood from her customers. For the most
part she did not fancy it, and felt besides no pressing need.
In addition, although she was so safe in her unique form,
invulnerable and untrammelled, she did not mean to start
a hue and cry on her heels.

She liked to come back to Zulgaris, also. He was an
anchor in her life. To see him so belittled, so helpless,
to feed him when he was too weak to lift the food to his
mouth, to help him to the refuse pit which all the street
used as an easement, these things tickled Vivia.

When he spoke of his greatness and great works, though
she hardly heard, it was a lullaby.

He was making a sort of confession, and she was the
uncaring priest.

It seemed all this would go on indefinately.

Vivia woke, and the crimson shard cast rubies into her
eyes.

She sat up, and taking the wooden gourd of wine from
beside the bed – the gift of her last transaction – she
drank.

The hovel was silent, although outside the usual morning noise went on.

Zulgaris was missing from his pallet of straw.

Vivia rose and pulled her robe about her, belting it as
always with a piece of cord.

Day by day his brain had seemed to function less, and
his limbs were not much better. She had foreseen a time
when he would shit himself before she could aid him to
the midden.

Where then had he gone?

Vivia went out and stood in her doorway, and a ruffian
who had had her several times (and was very courteous
in sex) greeted her cheerfully. He always paid her as

best he could, a string of onions, the piece of crimson glass.

'Have you seen my owner?' Vivia asked.

'Old yellow-knob? No.'

Vivia looked about. The hovel-dwellers had emerged as they always did hastily into the cold sunlight. Women were scouring the heads of their children for nits, and a man had been knocked senseless near the wall – a common vision.

Vivia left her position and went up the street.

She emerged in the place where the public well was guarded by the man in leather with the knife.

There Zulgaris was, arguing.

Zulgaris was saying that he had rights to the well. He was the prince.

An interested group stood about, encouraging him and cackling.

Vivia went up to the guard, and handed him money.

'Let him have some water.'

'All right, since you've paid.'

'No, no,' said Zulgaris. His voice was that of an angry old man. 'It must be given. This dog shall suffer – '

'Shut your face, you,' said the guard, 'fuck yourself.'

He patted Vivia's flank, he too had had her, and she had got free water for two days. 'Take the nuisance away.'

Vivia led Zulgaris back to their hole, and pushed him down on to the pallet.

'Here, eat this cheese.'

'I don't – I can't – bring me Demed.'

Vivia raised her eyebrows. 'He betrayed you.'

'Demed? Demed's loyal and wise. He knows who I am.'

Vivia put the cheese down by the pallet on a dry palm leaf.

'Here's some wine.'

'The liquor of Maxus,' said Zulgaris. 'Red for misfortune. Look at his eye hanging in the doorway.'

Perhaps she should not leave him, but she had got word of some festivity in the central town that might spill over. She would make money today.

She left him.

* * *

The lower town was as it always was, and yet there was a surge towards the inner walls of the central part of Syr. A procession of some sort was apparently to take place.

Vivia went with the tide of people.

She was pushed through an opening in one wall, and across another muddle of streets, and so, wedged against a cart drawn by oxen, through another wall of pale stone.

The gateway was arched and lined by blue, and guardsmen stood laughing, not exacting any fee.

Within the second wall, Vivia saw, above and about those who had thrust in with her, a portion of the inner pocket of Syr.

Tall buildings rose, and a long broad street ran down, paved in black and white squares.

Over this girls were going, clad in flimsy dresses that must chill them on the winter day, and casting branches of palm on the roadway.

She had come in time to behold the procession.

Vivia stood still in the press, and looked between the shoulders of those in front of her.

Presently a group of musicians came, banging drums and sounding silver trumpets.

After these strode ranks of soldiers with banners.

Vivia recognized at once the insignia of Zulgaris.

With a surreal fascination she watched, as the army of her prince – whom she had left mumbling in the hole of the hovel – strutted along the gracious street, their boots and the hoofs of their horses cracking the branches of palm.

The banners were the leopard and lily, and after them came the true leopards, with collars of jewels, walking on leash. And then the albino men went by, and the black men, and the dwarfs. The tank passed with the octopus, spouting black ink. And after this all the other animals, the eagle and the unicorn included.

Finally, the cheering of the crowd increased to a stupendous volume.

A man was riding by on a golden horse. He too was clad in gold, but his hair was not golden.

Vivia knew his face.

It was the knight Demed, and on his neck and fingers flashed a hundred gems.

Vivia said softly to the man beside her, 'Who is that?'

'Demed, the prince.'

'Is that his name?'

'There was another one,' said the man, idly. 'They've been waiting in the desert, making terms with the governor. Who cares? It's a great show.' After Demed trod camels decked in gold, drawing nothing. 'What do you charge?'

Vivia glanced at the man, who was poor. She was not kind but never risked abuse.

'A cup of wine.'

'I'll take you to a tavern when this is over. I've got cash for the holiday. You can have two cups, and the inns here are good.'

The inn was little and modest, in a side street. But after the wine, the man took Vivia to a room, and laid her on a pallet. He had her three times, jolly from the excitement of the procession.

When he slept, Vivia went down a back stair and so came out into the core of Syr.

The procession route, when she returned to it, was covered by trampled palms, the defecations of the beasts, and a few dropped favours the crowd had not picked up.

Bells rang from towers, and somewhere a clock was chiming. Vivia counted fourteen strokes.

She walked through the byways of inner Syr.

If it was a maze, it did not seem to be, yet even so she was soon lost. People ran about, and outside the taverns men stood drinking the health of Demed and his army, who were now in the fortress of Syr.

Vivia considered if she would tell Zulgaris what she had seen. It was doubtful he would understand.

She found herself in a street of rich houses, and paused to look at them. Here the large cedars were that foamed over walls, and in the street's centre a fountain played. It had figures of stone, a scorpion with a man fastened to its back, who had the head of a bull, and a woman holding in one hand the sun and in the other the moon.

Vivia went to the fountain, and climbing its steps, dipped her fingers in the bowl. But the water was only very cold.

Someone called.

'You, you, girl.'

Vivia turned, ever obliging and remote.

A fat man stood in one of the ornate doorways. He beckoned her.

Vivia went to him.

'What's your business here?'

'I came to see the procession.'

'Are you a woman of the streets?'

Vivia smiled.

The man said, 'You must come in. My master saw you from the window.'

Vivia, interested, entered the mansion.

Inside was a large hall, with a broad hearth where a fire burned. Brocaded curtains closed off other exits and entrances, and a flight of stone steps went up, by which grew a mulberry tree in a pot.

Another fat man was on the steps, and he beamed at Vivia.

'Why, what a find she is.' He came down in a jouncing and ungainly way, and stood close to her. 'Are you a whore?' Vivia smiled again. 'Well, I have employment for you. Tonight you will entertain my guests. Can you take on two or three men?'

Vivia said, 'Yes.'

'You'll address me as sir.'

'Yes, sir.'

This second fat man, who wore silk and furs, smiled in his turn. 'You shall have a pretty gown. You may keep it. Tonight you'll feast. I shall reward you afterwards as I see fit. What a beauty you are. You look like a lady.'

'Oh, no,' said Vivia, sensibly.

Insipid women who disapproved, bathed Vivia in a copper bath, and then gave her essences to rub into her skin. All this was familiar. Eventually they brought her a purple dress, half transparent, and in her hair were woven violets and little chains of gilt not gold.

After these attentions Vivia was left alone in a room of many cushions. From a latticed window she watched the sun dip and begin to sink, thick yellow as the banners of Zulgaris who was now Demed.

From this night she might earn a quantity of money. She wanted this from a sort of empathy – for among the other women, dreams of such an event, that was, being picked by some rich man for his feast, represented value beyond belief.

The lamps in the house were lit, and a man came and conducted Vivia down to a lower room. It had very realistic paintings on the walls of lions and doves, fruit trees and flowers. The padded chairs stood about tables that already sagged with food.

Vivia was to recline on a couch of silk, and might eat what she wished.

A gauzy curtain was let down between Vivia and the rest of the room, but it was transparent and she might be seen quite clearly through it. (She thought again of Zulgaris and how he had had her behind just such a curtain. This had mattered greatly then. But no more.)

The fat man's guests arrived. Two were fat as he was, and one much fatter, and one very thin, yet without the look Zulgaris had acquired; a healthy thinness.

They were crowned with blooms of paper by the servants, and then perfumes were sprinkled, and the fat man who had invited them spoke a grace.

After that they ate, and somewhere music was played, and occasionally one of the guests got up and came to the gauzy curtain and looked in at Vivia, and leered. But they did no more than that.

Vivia also ate a little of the feast. A small boy brought her morsels on a silver dish. She drank the wine, which was yellow, again like the banners of her ruined prince.

The fat and thin men toasted Demed, and as the evening wore on, toasted him more vociferously. The former regime had been corrupt. There had been one who was evil, who had practised evil. Now honour was restored.

Syr would be mighty and wealthy. Otherwise, they spoke of incomprehensible business and the food.

At last the fat man who had invited Vivia came up to the curtain.

'Come out, my pretty. Show the gentlemen what you are.'

Vivia came out. She stood on the patterned floor, and, unerringly, let slip her gown, as she had seen Oria do, off her shoulder and off her breast.

'I'm first,' said the fattest man.

'My dear Karp,' said the host, 'you are my guest.'

Vivia understood she would be taken on the couch before the rest of the dinner party.

She let the fattest man grip her arm and guide her there, and when he gestured, she undid the girdle of her gown and let it fall entirely.

The other men applauded.

'So white!'

'Such a lovely bosom.'

They watched impatiently as the fat one mounted her, rubbing at her breasts and licking her nipples. His penis was very small and his bulk made it hard for him to get into her. Vivia wrapped him with her legs, and heaving and huffing, he came in a few moments.

After this guest, the other fat ones took her. One was more skilful and stroked her secret parts until a wisp of pleasure stirred in her. But he too was very quick.

Their scented sweat had scattered her, and crushed on the bed was a tiny cake that had fallen from the silver platter.

The thin man did not want her.

They mocked him and one said a boy should have been provided.

Then to prove his efficacy, he too came and fucked Vivia, but his eyes were screwed tight, and she suspected that he did not climax.

Vivia lay on her couch as the guests were torch-lit away into the tranquil night of central Syr.

Then the host returned.

'Now you will joy my bed, sweetheart. Come along.'

She followed him up the stair and into a bedroom, where he was fussed over by two male servants.

He drank a crystal glass of wine, and offered none to Vivia.

'You're a lovely thing,' he said. 'I might keep you. You pleased my friends. But are you ready to please me?'

Vivia waited.

The fat man waddled round the bed, which was hung with velvet and had copper medallions depending from it.

'Lie on your face.'

Vivia did so. She recalled this uncomfortable method from congress with Zulgaris.

But then the fat man put all his weight upon her back, and began to fumble at her anus.

Vivia became aware that he would enter her there. Never before had this happened. She did not like it.

She forced her way from under him.

'What?' he asked, red and aghast on the bed. Awash with wine and food he found it difficult to rise and accost her. 'You won't? But you must. I've bought you. You'll do as I say.'

'No,' said Vivia. 'Take me the proper way.'

'What nonsense is this? I decide. Lie down, you cunt.'

Vivia stood, naked, in the midst of the chamber, and the fat man floundered and got upright.

'I'll call my man and you'll have twenty lashes. See what that will do for your creamy skin.'

Vivia grasped that she was in an awkward predicament. Never before had a customer insisted on some means she would not entertain. And now the door was locked – she had seen him lock it and stow the key – and four walls held her in with him. Could the lash wound her? Perhaps after all –

He lunged to his feet now, magenta in the face and wallowing. His member loomed from a set of gonads like pink chicken skin. His fists were very big, and he had besides seized his belt, which had a buckle of gold and steel.

'Do as I say, you slut. Lie down, or by Marius I'll flay you myself.'

Vivia turned, and the wall pressed against her. There was no escape save *through* the wall.

Vivia was suspended between reality and truth.

For a second she wavered, knowing what was possible and what was not.

But then she recalled the fire, *recalled* it, and pushing her hand into the wall, she slipped after it, straight through the painting and the marble and the brick.

She slipped through and out the other side and *floated* down the distance to a yard, where trees grew in jugs.

Behind her in the house she heard the strangled outcry of the fat host as he underwent a seizure of the heart.

Vivia did not mind.

She pressed through the second wall, that of the yard, and emerged into the street.

It had been like nothing, like a change of temperature only, not even like pushing through mud. The fabric of the building had parted, twice, without trouble.

On the street, in the maze of Syr, she remembered she was naked.

Would the air form a dress for her as the fire had done? (That garment now left lying in the fat man's house.) But suddenly the purple dress, the whore's dress, if slightly less vaporous, was on her again, magicked out of nothingness, or remade, delivered from the night.

Clad in this she passed like a violet ghost along the thoroughfares of Syr, passed tall buildings, saw the fortress in the crook of a wall, where Demed lay tonight. And so came to a gate, and went through, quite ordinarily, and unchallenged – evidently a prostitute on her business – and so got back into the familiar squalor of the lower town.

She walked in a dream, and laughter was in her again.

She had been paid nothing for her services beyond her meal. But oh, she had been repaid.

She could walk through walls.

What could she not do?

Chapter Three

DREAMILY VIVIA RETURNED TO THE hovel against the wall. She could smell the perfumes of her own body and the violets in her hair (a shame she could not keep them alive; one lapse in her powers). Once or twice a man had stopped her, but tonight she had not acquiesced. She told them she had been summoned to a particular house, and they let her go.

It was late. In the street of holes, furtive noises went on and a few lights burned muddy red.

Vivia went into the place she shared with Zulgaris. He lay in the dark, sleeping on his pallet.

Vivia sat down on hers. Soon, like a tired child, she too drifted asleep.

But dawn was not far off. A couple of hours after, cocks crew in Syr and the rummaging sounds of the hovels grew louder.

Vivia sat up again and glanced at Zulgaris.

What would he say when he saw her dress?

Would he, befuddled, question her about the centre of the town, and what she had seen?

Zulgaris did not move, and in a little while she went to him and pushed him quietly. No response.

She began to smell an odour. He had soiled himself, which had never before happened.

Vivia stepped back. The prince was dead.

She went out into the street, and one of the men who had had her was passing. He asked her what the matter was.

She said, 'He's died.'

'Well, he was very sick. I've seen it before. The blood turns to water.'

But Zulgaris' blood had turned to dust.

The man fetched another one and they took the body out of the hovel. They carried it up to the midden and left it there. And next birds came to feed, as they did on the excrement. This was the usual practice of the slums of Syr. They did not bother with the graveyard.

Vivia sat inside the hole of room, and the red drop of light from the doorway stained her hands.

She felt depressed. Despite everything, her anchor was gone. First Vaddix. Now this one. Now she was alone.

Of Zulgaris' power which had been crushed, she did not think. Nor of the fact that conceivably her blood had worked the trick.

Vivia mislaid but did not forget what she herself had accomplished. She could walk through a wall, but the sorcerer prince of Starzion had only been able to die.

She did not mourn, but she sat in a lethargy of thought, wondering what she would do now.

At least, the body had been removed from her chamber.

A man came scratching at the doorway.

'He's gone?'

'Yes,' said Vivia.

'We could do it here, then.'

Vivia did not object.

They lay in a corner, not on her pallet or on Zulgaris' empty bed of straw.

Did his ghost watch?

Vivia half believed it did, for the straw rustled, but probably there were vermin now in it.

When the man had finished he gave Vivia a loaf.

In the days which followed, other men came to visit her in the hovel, and sometimes when she went out after custom, coming back, two or three were hanging about there.

She turned no one away now.

Up on the midden, vultures fed on the redundant

remains of Zulgaris, their ragged wings flapping on the hard pale sky.

At the town's centre Demed was the lord, for she heard a little talk of him, how brave a knight he was, and how worthy to be a prince.

There was some ceremony one afternoon, and although Vivia did not go to see, she heard the bells ringing from the heart of Syr.

To her, the central part of the town represented the night she had walked through two walls and floated to the earth.

She did not try to do this again, and yet she remained convinced that she had done it.

Matter was her slave.

However, she went on with her trade, and was by now known in the quarter as the Purple Whore. For her dress.

Vivia was now quite comfortable. She did not really miss Zulgaris, for he had never properly been there. She felt contempt for his bones lying on the midden, he who had been so mighty now vanished without trace.

Sometimes a curious yearning, which she had experienced in early adolescence, swept over her, and she would sit in her doorway, with her chin in her hand.

Her beauty was remarked on every side, though some found her too slender. There had never been so gorgeous a prostitute.

The women hated her mostly, but did not much show it for fear of the men.

She never went hungry or thirsty. She had no craving for blood. Though once a dog came to her hovel, and she fed the dog and then fed on it, to see. There was no difficulty in doing this, and the dog ran off afterwards, apparently unscathed, the mark on its throat fading.

The dull days of winter suited Vivia, and in the summer she would keep more to the hovel.

She did not plan. She felt settled and complacent.

Chapter Four

THE WINTER ENDED AND SPRING moved rapidly over the town. Peach and cherry trees exuded a deluge of blossom. Even the rancid corners of the lower area were brightened by vines and flowers.

Vivia put on a dark dress she had bought from a dealer in rags, and drew a veil over her head. She avoided the sun, but it shone in through the door hole and blazed in the ruby shard. Did she really mind it?

One morning she walked by a narrow greenish canal, and let a man have her against the stonework, with the sun streaming upon them and on her naked breasts. The experience did not mar her.

Why should she dread the sun? Fire could not hurt her.

She took to walking in the sun, but after several days, a feeling of colossal sadness weighed her down. Then she retreated to the dark end of the hovel and wept. She did not chide herself now for weeping. But she blamed the sun for her melancholy, and began to avoid it again, even tending to go out preferentially by night.

Usually the dark was furtively restless, full of night people about their work, cutthroats and other harlots, collectors of dubious rubbish, thieves. A little world of febrile villainy.

One night a robber who had her gifted her a silver pendant. Vivia sagely bartered it the next day for food and water.

She would return to the hovel in the hours before dawn,

and sleep, often dozing on through the morning and the early afternoon.

She came to herself fully at sunfall.

In her dealings she kept strictly to the lower town.

Vivia flew over the desert. Her veil spread like a wing and it was this, she thought, that bore her up.

The moon was round and bone white and the sky luminous as a basin of clear water.

Below the desert curved and purled, and in its midst the town lay. Seen from the air, Syr had a peculiar shape, as though begun mathematically, but then spoilt by its accretions of outworks.

Smokes rose from the slums, and inwards, the paved and chequered roads stretched in and out of ornate bridges and arches.

Vivia flew low above the town. The air was cool and sweet, and pleasant smells rose from central Syr, aromatics and confectionaries, and the fragrance of night gardens already touched by summer.

She came down light as a dark feather beside a statue of a lion, and in the wall of a nearby house, a window with a complicated lattice was alight.

Vivia knew that she dreamed.

She floated up weightlessly to the window, and pressed her moonlit face to the lattice.

A young girl lay on the bed, gauzy curtains undrawn, a lamp burning low on a stand.

She was a redhead, the girl, like Gula – as, of course, in the dream logically she would be.

Vivia swam through the lattice, watching mildly as its curlicues passed through her flesh, or her flesh through them, and out the other side.

She was possessed of a craving for blood, and it was this which had brought her here. The girl was young and vital, white-skinned, and beautifully clean.

Vivia stooped to her wrist, which opened in the familiar little red wounds. And Vivia sucked up her nourishment.

The girl whispered in her sleep. The covers slipped from the pearly breast and the lamp guttered and went out.

Vivia returned through the window without a backward glance.

She flew silently over the sleeping couth heart of Syr, and back across the hushed rat-rustling outer environ.

Beside the high fountain on the steps she dropped down, unseen, for she was a dreamer, and drank from the water in the bowl. A filament of red uncurled from her lips.

She walked to her hovel in the wall, and did not wake until noon.

It seemed to her that she had had this dream before, yet now she recalled it vividly.

Her head-veil lay across the pallet, full still of the smell of the moon and the gardens of inner Syr.

There were men talking on the street, under the fretted shadow of the magnolia tree, a thing of porcelain in a rut of vileness.

'A sickness in the good part of the town. Young girls wasting away.'

'Do you remember the yellow-head – that girl's owner? He died of something like that.'

'The Purple Whore? Probably she poisoned him. He couldn't keep up with her doings.'

Vivia was walking along the street. She heard with preternatural acuity what they said.

A sickness . . . young girls of the inner town.

Her dream –

Vivia moved by the men, and one propositioned her. She went with him to a piece of rough ground, and there he had her.

She felt no urge to take his blood.

Had she taken blood elsewhere?

The dream had been like sleepwalking. Had she then *flown* in her sleep?

Why not? She was capable of anything.

The redhead sleeping and the soft white breast, the warm red blood which tasted of cinnamon.

'Better not go into the centre of the town,' said her customer, doing up his drawers. 'There's a sickness there.'

Vivia looked at him and said nothing.

She went back to the hovel – this had been an unusual day-time excursion. Now she would stay awake and wait for the night to come. Then, she would see . . .

Night came.

Vivia left her doorway, and walked along the thread of street to a dark place, where an open drain was. At this spot many of her customers had had her.

She could not be seen.

Vivia willed herself up into the air.

She rose several inches off the ground at once, then dropped back, releasing her momentum.

Was it true then? She had flown, and drunk from the veins of girls in the central part of Syr.

Again she lifted, up, up. The hovels were now beneath her and two men came skulking out, and one glanced up and glimpsed her. 'Look – a strange crow – ' But the other paid no attention, and the first plainly did not know what he had seen.

Vivia sailed over the midden, and into the deep blue sky. It seemed she could fly up and touch the glitter of the stars, but Zulgaris had lessoned her long ago, they were very far off.

The town lay small and smudged with murky gleams, and beyond, as in her dream – which had been reality – the desert stretched smouldering in moonlight.

To feed then was her quest. How long had she flown in this way, and drunk blood from the clean bodies in the clean beds?

She did not really fly. She floated, upright, as if standing in the air. She passed over the town like a moving figure on a gigantic invisible clock.

Vivia flew above the inner town. She hovered above the fortress. There was a noise from there and golden lights. Demed, the new prince, feasting his war-like captains. She was not bothered with Demed. If she could have come at him she might have killed him, but only because he was the enemy, not from any notion of revenge. She no longer missed Zulgaris, if she ever had.

Many houses beyond the fort were in darkness. Who lay

sick and had she caused it? Was she always the harbinger
of plague?

But there was no nuance of illness on the walks and
gardens.

She came to a high window and peered in. An old man
lay in a rich bed sleeping uneasily. Vivia flew away. Only
maidens tempted her, maidens and young women who
slept alone. Men, though she used them and gave them
all, still repulsed Vivia. Only the vampire prince had she
reverenced. But he was not a man.

She was seized with sudden gladness at the memory
of Zulgaris' death, and laughed aloud. And in a nearby
building they took this musical sound in the air for the
curious cry of some animal that had got into the town, a
wild animal of the desert.

She flew for perhaps two hours, untired, and then came
down into a garden of peach trees. Here among the
blossom Vivia admired her reflection in a tank of water.
She played her hand among the silver fish. She let one
pass right through her palm. Yet, when she wished to be
solid, she was firm, and they butted against her. Blossom
caught in her hair. She was real and not real. She could be
what she wanted.

A sudden idea came to her in the garden that she might
leave the town and walk away. The desert would feed her
if she required it. She might find some other populated
conglomeration.

But then, why trouble? Syr was small, but occupied her.
She did not want anything more.

She went up over the wall like a smoke, and getting out
on to the street, she saw a low building with windows that
made slits of light. A dull murmuring came from it.

Vivia paused, and as she did so, a band of soldiers swung
into the street.

There were nine or ten of them, rough armoured bodies
and the ready swords she remembered.

Instinctively Vivia drew back into a porch, but they had
seen her.

The soldiers washed down on her.

They were the men of Starzion, the men who had

followed Zulgaris, and overthrown Zulgaris, and now cleaved to Demed. Did they know her? No, for she was a being of the night, no demon, a young girl in a part transparent dress.

'Here, pretty, you come with us.'

They had forgotten the unburnt witch-abomination in their new antics at Syr.

They did not want her name.

She was drawn with them to the low building, and next they edged her in through a door guarded by a surly porter.

The lamps were dim and down some flights of stairs they all went, the soldiers loud and merry, and so came to a door which perhaps lay under the ground.

This was opened after they had knocked and called out the word *tiger* three or four times.

Other soldiers were inside and the light was even darker. Wine cups moved, and Vivia had a cup pressed to her lips. The vintage was gloomy and coarse like the area and company.

'Who's she?'

'We'll take her to the altar. Have her there. To honour it.'

'And she'll scream like the last one.'

'So much the better.'

They were pulling her through the crowd of men, three in particular manhandling her, forcing her, and she let them. Men were all around, stinking of their maleness, sweat and night.

She passed into a sort of cave, and everywhere were hanging up shields and swords and knives and lances, trophies offered as if in a hall or chapel.

And then she saw where there was light after all. It blazed across a wall of broken bricks, and caught there in sparkling lines and brilliant snags – something was in the wall, and it had been hung with rosettes of silver and gold, with strings of pearls, and trinkets less fine, but which even so burned.

Vivia halted.

'She sees it now. Don't be scared, girlie. It's the Devil

himself. Lord of your profession. Arch pimp. You don't
like God now, do you? Or Marius – the fool. No. This is
your prince. Isn't he grand?'

It was the bat-god from Zulgaris' alchemical wall.
Stretched there, with jewels on its bones and the struts
of its wings, the sun-mask rested now *behind* its head, a
ring of golden fire.

'Brought in secret to Syr,' said another of the men thickly.
'Even holy Demed doesn't know.'

'It's kept us safe,' said one.

'Worshipful evil.'

'Hell himself.'

They stopped in self-induced reverence.

Vivia gazed, and saw in that moment how ludicrous it
was, the vampire thing in the wall. Its diamond teeth shone
and before it stood an altar, a table draped in red cloth, with
a bowl of old blood on it which smelled.

'I'll take her now,' said the most pushy of the men. He
led Vivia to the altar and politely moved the blood bowl
away. He held the wine to her lips again, and Vivia turned
her head. 'Drink it, you cow. You'll need it. It's turn and
turn again. Twenty men or more will have you. All who
fancy it. It's good for *him* to see how we respect him.'

He shoved her back on the altar, and her head was
slammed down on the hard table.

He tore her bodice so her breasts were bare, and from the
cavern, so full of drunken moody men, rose cheering and
the sharp odour of hot sex.

Vivia watched the vampire.

How could she have mistaken it for anything miracu-
lous? Here it was, presiding over these rapes and dirty
fornications.

The men pressed nearer. She recalled how they had
meant to burn her alive.

The foremost attacker had taken out his cock, and she
saw it nodding at her like an obscene snake.

She knew a revulsion for everything she had done, for
every man who had had her.

And for the bat-beast she knew hatred. It was not her
prince but some travesty.

And the soldier forced his penis into her body. *Vivia sank away*.

She sank straight down, through the table and the cloth, through the very floor.

She heard the soldiers shouting, as they had shouted when she eluded them the last time.

But she was in darkness now, she was in the very earth.

Above her, the vista of riot and lamps closed over and was gone.

Deep in the sand and stone that lay beneath the town, Vivia knew a moment's horror. But then she passed on, and matter gave way before her so easily that when suddenly she came on a runnel of fresh water, she trod through it for a minute, not realizing that now her path was already open.

Then she rose again. Up through the solid foundations of the streets.

Her head was in the moonlight, and then her body.

Nearby the water plashed. She stood beside a fountain in the shape of a great snake, and there below, some streets away, she saw a low building with slits of windows, and a noise came from there –

Vivia raised her arms and rinsed them in the moon. And beheld a man standing alone below the platform of the fountain.

He spoke softly. 'A trick of the eyes – you seemed to come up out of the paving itself – '

Vivia laughed. She crossed her arms over her breasts.

His voice was young. It said, 'You shouldn't be here, girl. Not so near to that inn. It's notorious. The soldiers have taken it over. Better come with me.'

'Oh, no,' said Vivia.

'I won't hurt you. I don't want anything. But I'd like to see you safe.'

Vivia leaned on the fountain and traced the water with one finger, her bosom shielded by the other arm.

'Go away.'

'Don't be stupid,' said the young man. He came abruptly

and gracefully and quickly up on to the platform, and seized Vivia's wrist.

As he dragged her towards him, the moonlight caught each of their faces, and described each to the other.

'By the Christ,' he said softly. 'Who are you?'

But Vivia did not answer.

Tears sprang suddenly from her eyes, which in the dark were blackly violet.

'Don't cry. I said, I won't harm you. But what are you doing here? Where do you belong?'

His voice was full of wonder. He was young, only four or five years her senior, and she was so beautiful it was like pain, sheer agony, under the starlight and the moon, beside the quivering mercury of the water.

But to Vivia he was more than all that.

For, pale and dark, he had the face she had not seen in the soldiers' hall, the face she had never fully comprehended. Yet now here it was, firm and sculpted in flesh and bone, and set with eyes far blacker than any night.

The face of her maker, the vampire, her true prince.

BOOK FOUR

The Hag

ONE

Chapter One

 Up fifteen stairs a thin door opened in the side of the wall. Beyond lay the studio of the artist Ruslem.

He lived above a wine shop, in this one square room. In the corner lay a broad low couch, slung with covers of every colour and type. A bronze ewer and a metal basin stood nearby, and a table with a lamp of pale brown glass. Clothes and a few books lay on the floor – poor books bound in rough cloth.

The rest of the chamber was his workplace. Wooden panels rested against the walls, and stretched canvases, some already painted over. On a frame under the one barred window was a canvas, with a picture of girls dancing on a lawn. (It seemed to Vivia she had seen this before. She had – or a version of it, on the wall of the fat man's bedroom, although not the wall she had passed through.)

The work was beautiful, fluid and very lifelike. Drops of dew hung from flowers like the purest glass. Every petal, every lash of every eye, was delineated.

Elsewhere in the room were small figures and heads made of clay, and one in a dull smoky marble.

Ruslem was popular and kept busy. Although far from rich, he did not especially want for anything, and had in fact been coming from a dinner party in the core of Syr, eager to get back to his labours. Finding Vivia he had been distracted.

Now she stood still as he went about and lit the many lamps and candles.

Both were in a state of wonder. He only at her beauty,

which to the artist and the man equally were irresistible. But she was mesmerized. Although she knew that this was not the being who had taken her beneath the dark castle, yet the resemblance was, to her mind, awesome.

The human quickness of him startled her therefore. But only added to her amazement.

'Tell me your name,' he said, looking at her as no one had ever looked at her.

'Vivia.'

'What a name. Like velvet. Do you know how beautiful you are?'

She did, but now felt it wholly for the very first time.

She lowered her eyes, overwhelmed by him and by herself.

'Where do you come from?'

'A city.'

'How did you come here?'

'With the army.'

'My God. Are you someone's wife?'

'I'm a whore,' said Vivia, with a faint satisfaction.

Ruslem frowned. 'I can save you from that at least. Model for me. I'll pay you whatever you were given.'

Vivia smiled secretively.

The young man, handsome as a god – beautiful in a way that put out Zulgaris or any man like him in one breath, like a weak fire – walked round Vivia.

She had uncrossed her arms and her breasts were bare.

'I must paint you like that. But in a black gown. Black for the whiteness of your skin, bringing out all the tints in both.'

Vivia did not mind his talk, although she did not truly understand it. He spoke now of preparations of paint. Canvas he had ready which he would use.

His voice was musical.

Vivia sighed.

'Are you hungry?' he asked her.

She was not, but said yes, sensing he wished to put food into her mouth as a means of staking possession.

He went to a cupboard and took out bread and cheese, and a black bottle of wine from the shop below.

These things he set on a table, and they ate together and drank the bitter wine.

'You must sleep in the bed. I won't bother you. You'll have had enough of men.'

Vivia gazed at him. She said nothing.

Despite what he had promised, he watched her take off her dress with burning black eyes. And when he had offered it, she washed herself with water from the ewer and basin.

She lay down in his bed and pulled the covers over her. They smelled of paint, as did the whole room, and faintly of his young and healthy body. She snuggled into them.

Ruslem paced the floor. He said, 'I shan't sleep tonight. I must draw you at once, from memory, or as you sleep. Will you mind that?'

Vivia said that she would not.

She was lethargic and comfortable, but neither did she sleep. She watched him move about the room and take the painting from the frame and put a scroll of paper there, fastening it with pegs.

Vivia tingled. She thought of how she had been ridden by Zulgaris as the planets flamed their dyes above the sky altar. How she had come in ecstasy. Would this man pleasure her?

She longed to touch him. See him without clothes.

And deep within her, another stirring. She wished to sip at his blood.

For he was the god, and the god had given her a bloody rose. The juices of young girls were nothing to this urging, nor the blood of Zulgaris that she had never wanted, except perhaps out of rage.

Tingling yet calm, after all she did sleep, and woke in the hour before dawn.

He lay beside her, decorously separate, his head on a pillow, fully clothed. Both his vows, of leaving the bed, of staying awake, negated.

Vivia leaned on one elbow, and watched him.

He slept in silence.

His beauty was more marvellous than she had remembered on waking, his black hair spread across the pillow.

His shirt was open at the neck, and there, in the column of his throat, the pulse worked evenly.

Vivia leaned closer, and inhaled the summery scent of his body, and his hair.

Lightly she kissed his mouth.

His eyes opened.

'What is it?'

Vivia slid her arms about his ribcage.

He said thickly, 'There's no need – '

Then he had seized her and pulled her on to his body.

He kissed her deeply, entering her mouth. His was fresh and clean and dimly flavoured by the wine they had drunk. His mouth was like a vortex to her, and she was quickly lost in it, falling down through some inner swirling space.

He turned her and plucked the covers off her nakedness.

He kissed and tongued her breasts, going over and over them, murmuring.

Vivia writhed with delight. She tried to undo his shirt and he, laughing, undid the garment, and threw it off.

She revelled in the hard whiteness of his body, the two jewels of his breast, the line of bones under the skin, which in the failing lamplight was mysteriously visible. As he eased out of his nether clothes, she beheld his phallus upright and bold, neither repulsive nor laughable, but smooth and glowing like a lance, and with a star of moisture glittering on its tip.

Vivia, with a wild hunger, drew this weapon into her mouth, the act Zulgaris had demanded and which she had loathed.

Now she sucked on the man with lust, and heard his groans of pleasure, which made her in turn shiver with joy.

He disengaged himself suddenly, and travelling down her body, put his own lips to her lower mouth. His tongue entered her here like a liquid feather, tickling and teasing her body in a way that was unbearably delicious.

This the god had done to her, and reminiscent of the god, his fingers, like other soft hot tongues, were on her breasts.

She felt Ruslem over every inch of her. Even where he did not touch her, there still she felt him, flickering and caressing, like the wings of moths.

Vivia's body arched upwards in an uncontrollable spasm, but before this overwhelmed her, he had moved again and entered her slowly and thoroughly, so that she felt him to the base of her spine.

She climaxed in his arms as he stared down at her. She cried and screamed and the room echoed and she seemed to fall again through space, but he fell with her, sobbing in orgasm on her breast.

Vivia lay like death.

She looked up into the ceiling of the studio, where shadows hung like curtains.

In the barred window soft rose had flushed.

Vivia knew a wounding sadness.

She clutched her lover to her, but already he had sunk back into sleep, locked within her body.

Aftershocks still rippled through her loins.

Vivia folded Ruslem in her arms and held him as closely to her as flesh and blood are able to hold anything.

Chapter Two

✦ FOR SIX DAYS THEY SCARCELY left that room.
   Ruslem went out only to visit the wine shop and
   buy liquor and food, or to fetch water from the well.
Vivia he would not let go out. He said he was afraid
someone would snatch her up.

They made love furiously and gently, savagely and
serenely, day and night. The moods of sex were always
changing. He rode above her, she galloped upon him. He
took her as others had, against the walls, on the floor.

Sometimes he spoke poetry to her that came, he said,
from books he had read, but which must – somehow –
have been written to her. Women with midnight hair, sea
green eyes, and lake blue eyes, lips like flowers, breasts like
oblivion and the groin the centre of worlds.

He drew, with long sticks of charred wood, Vivia's image
over and over, cursing and saying he could not grasp her
beauty. She was elusive.

He asked her questions of her origin, and she did not
lie, except in one matter – the second fount of her life, the
vampire. Or what she had become.

She did not, ironically, tell Ruslem any of that.

But of the rest of it, her father and the plague, Zulgaris
and his alchemy, she spoke freely.

She was not sure that Ruslem believed her. He would
look indulgent when she spoke, sometimes puzzled.
Sometimes he laughed. Or frowned.

Vivia experienced much that was new.

When their bodies ground together, striking fire, she

forgot everything, but at other times she was growing strangely afraid.

She did not understand what this fear was, until one day when Ruslem, who had gone to the inn for wine, did not return for an hour.

When he re-entered the room, Vivia flew to him and clung to him.

He had met friends in the street and idled to talk with them. He had told them he had found a goddess, but not invited them to see.

He was surprised but not displeased by Vivia's anxiety.

Vivia, in wonder, realized that she was now fearful of losing him.

She liked them to be closeted in the room.

Outside there were dangers. Other females even might draw him away. For she had never had any proof that a man could stay faithful with one woman.

On the seventh day, Ruslem told her he must go to see one of his patrons, a rich man in Syr, whose name he said was Karp.

Vivia recalled the one named Karp from the fat man's feast.

She begged Ruslem not to go.

Ruslem insisted that he must.

She could tell that, again, he was not angered by her pleading, that he thought it natural and took her possessiveness as his due.

Ruslem was human.

He was gone all day, dining at Karp's fine house.

Vivia fretted.

Her fear grew into a rage – unlike the rages she had felt at Zulgaris, and yet in some ways similar.

Ruslem had power over her.

She knew that when he came back to her, she would melt into his arms and body, murmuring with lust and need.

But she recalled that she was a sorceress, who could burn and not burn, pass through walls, fly. A sorceress who drank blood.

* * *

Ruslem returned in the dark with a lamp, and Vivia sat quietly on the one stool in the studio.

'Here I am, you see. Quite drunk, but otherwise sound. He wants me to paint another scene for him on a bathhouse wall. Well, I'll do it. A few naked nymphs and the old boy will be satisfied.'

He approached her.

Vivia was silent.

'See, I brought you sweets in a napkin. Try this one, it's made from strawberries.'

Vivia ate the sweet, and as its lush taste rolled across her tongue, she felt a ferocious hunger, of which before there had been only vague intimations.

'How much,' she said, 'do you value me?'

'More than I can ever say. Words are useless against your value.'

'What would you do to please me?'

'Almost anything.'

'Almost . . .'

'Anything, then. Anything in the world.'

'When I tell you things about me, you don't believe them.'

'Vivia – but you colour what you say.'

'No. And I have something to tell you which I never spoke of.'

'What?'

Vivia took Ruslem's hand and stood up.

'I was corrupted,' said Vivia, primly.

'I know. But I've changed you.'

'No. I don't mean that I was a whore. I was taught to do something.'

Ruslem put his arms about her and kissed her hair. 'Black as darkness,' he said.

'My heart too,' said Vivia dramatically. This amused her. She said, 'Give me your wrist.'

'My wrist? Very well. Are you going to bite me for leaving you all day?'

Vivia said, 'Yes.'

Indeed, it was true. Her rage at him had driven her to take what ultimately she desired of him. Her lust was momentous, in that second, not for the ecstasy of his body, but to fill her mouth with his blood. To *swallow* him. To *have* him.

In the lamplight a shade of unease did cross over his eyes.

His smile was gone.

He pulled back his cuff and gave her his left wrist.

Vivia bowed her head slowly.

For a moment she thought after all she could not do it, but then the two bright marks appeared against her lips, and she felt the waters of his life welling over into her mouth.

He tasted like fire. Like wine and fire. Her teeth closed on his wrist and made fresh wounds. The glory of him washed down into her body.

He said, softly, 'What are you doing to me?'

Vivia did not answer.

She drank.

Only when she felt him stagger, a slight rocking motion, did she realize, and lifting her head, she let his wrist close over.

Five red wounds were on it, sealing to darkness.

Ruslem held these out before him.

He sank down on the stool. He said nothing.

Vivia put her hand on his shoulder.

She felt a combination of victory and great fright.

'I drank your blood. I'm a vampire.'

'So you have, so you are.'

She assisted him to the bed, where he dropped, and became instantly asleep or unconscious.

In the morning the marks would be gone.

Would he remember?

Ruslem was strong, and woke only with a heavy head from the wine of Karp's cellar.

But he did remember.

He made love to Vivia, and as the crucial moments pressed in upon her, she found her mouth at his throat, and he jerked his head away.

This sexual union ended without culmination for either.

Ruslem sat on the couch, looking at her.

Vivia was not sure if she had been about to drink from him again, from the throat . . . She had killed Oria by doing this, but then Oria had not mattered to her. Ruslem – was everything.

'A vampire,' Ruslem said.

'I was famished for your blood.'

'Because you love me?' he asked.

Vivia checked. Was it this, the root of all her turmoil? She had never loved anyone or thing. Did not know how to recognize her emotion.

But, 'Yes,' she said, to placate him.

'Do you want to kill me then?'

'I shan't kill you – ' she cried. 'Zulgaris gave me a court of little girls, and they served me with blood.'

'Are you supernatural?' he asked. His face was hollow and very still, the eyes like pools of his blackest paint. 'I think you are. That first night – you came up out of the ground . . .'

'Oh yes,' she said, 'I can do that.'

She turned and pointed at the table, and the table moved, jumped a space, and everything on it rattled. She was entertained by this. She got up and ran to one of the canvases by the wall, and showed him, and then she made one of the figures in the painting move from left to right and back again.

Ruslem watched. Then he lay down flat on the bed.

Vivia stole to him.

'Do you hate me now?' A raw pain ached in the centre of her, almost physical.

'I'm – afraid of you, Vivia.'

'No,' she said. 'I'm only Vivia. I'm yours.'

He said, as she lay beside him stroking his hair, 'A demoness from the night, here in my room.'

'I love you,' said Vivia, having learnt the words. She began to cry. She wanted him to see her tears.

'What can I do,' he said. 'I'm your slave.'

And turning back to her, he began to make love to her again, violently, as if he must subdue her.

*   *   *

Vivia abstained three days from the blood of Ruslem, and a deep gnawing commenced in her body, like an insatiable hunger.

She ate continuously, meat and cheese and bread from the wine shop, fruit and sweets that he bought for her. She drank wine until her head span. She came to him constantly for love.

Finally, in the night, she woke, and she had fastened on him. She gulped from his left wrist (the right, the right hand of the painter, must not be touched). She thought he did not know, that he slept. When she forced herself to leave him, she saw he lay watching her, with half-unfocused eyes.

'My Vivia,' he said.

She said, 'I can fly. I can fly over the air and the night. I'll go. I'll take the blood of others.'

And she rose straight up off the bed, and up through the ceiling and out into the night.

She was mad with terrors.

As she circled there over the night of Syr, Ruslem ran out on to the steps below.

When she drifted eastward, towards the moon, he tried to run after her.

She saw him dart through the maze of streets of the inner town, over the chequered paving and beneath the arches.

Then she had outdistanced him, moving without the hindrance of side turnings and buildings, through the sky.

She swirled in at a window and took the silky arm of a young girl, little more than a child.

But then she let the arm go in disgust.

She did not want it.

She wanted only the blood of her lover.

Was this what the vampire had felt when he drained her? Had *he* loved her then?

But she had become like him.

Vivia returned to the studio, and Ruslem had not yet reached it.

He came in near dawn, dishevelled, and seeing her he began to cry.

He wept like a child and she held him close to her.

They slept coiled together, and in the day when they woke, they did not speak of any of it.

That day, he told Vivia again that she must model for him.

He had purchased a black gown and a black veil, and in this he dressed her (carefully, like Ursabet) but leaving bare her exquisite breasts and arms.

Into her right hand he put a lutar with a carved and gilded frame. He told her to hold this loosely.

He began to work upon the canvas before the barred window.

His handsome face looked thin and desolate, and never had he appeared more wonderful to her, or filled her with such greed. At the same time she knew a grey despair.

This look, even more than her fabulous beauty, Ruslem began to catch upon the skin of the canvas.

He worked tirelessly and made her stand all day, motionless.

She waited in a dream of darkness, and he drew her dream out upon the painting.

On her arm, and in her ears, about her waist, he had put cheap gilded ornaments that he would paint as rich ripe gold.

Her feet were bare.

Sometimes tears ran down her face.

He did not paint her tears.

He was callous now. Slaves do not pity their masters.

For many days, and through the nights, Ruslem worked on this painting of Vivia.

When finally he left off, he would lead her to the table, and offer her food she was too tired to eat, and wine.

When they lay down, he would offer her his wrist. Vivia did not take his blood again until the fifth night, then she could have drained him, and only by steel of will did she coerce herself into leaving him alone. He was by then unconscious. And she watched over him through the dark.

In the morning, when she woke, she found that he was up and about, feverish and pale, and on the wall of the studio he had roughly, but effectively and realistically, painted a door. Closed.

Before it, also painted, stood a pot, and painted vines curled round it.

'Your exit, my lady,' said Ruslem.

And as if in a trance, she went to it and passed through the painted door in the wall.

Outside she floated to the stair, unseen, and stood there sobbing.

After an hour, a man came by and asked her price, and Vivia fled back up the stair to the artist in the studio.

He made her dress again in the black robe, its bodice pulled out over the fake golden girdle.

All day he painted, and as the sun was reddening late in the summer window, he threw down the brush.

'It's done. My masterpiece.'

'May I see?'

She had avoided it until now.

'Yes, you must. Come and look at yourself.'

Vivia came, in her despair and fear, and looked.

The flesh of the girl in the painting was pale and warm, her breasts tipped by dull garnets. Her hair was almost hidden. Her eyes were blacker than his own.

Her face brooded. Not only had he caught her misery, but her avidity.

Vivia stared, astonished.

Was this herself?

Behind her he had put – not land – but the sea, grey and louring, with a crack of yellow light upon the water.

Ominous birds flew over, perhaps caricatures of Vivia herself, flying through the air.

'What do you think?' he said.

'It's beautiful.'

'And so are you.'

'And horrible.'

'Ah.'

He pushed her against the wall, and had her without foreplay or sweetness.

Even so she trembled in his grasp. And he cried out. He turned his head so his throat was against her lips.

She took her reward in frenzy – and in carefulness.
Stopping almost as soon as she had begun.

But Ruslem staggered back.

'You bitch – you fearful bloody bitch.'

Vivia slowly took off the garments of the painting. She
pulled on the plain gown he had bought her and belted it
with the sash.

'I'll go away.'

Ruslem dropped to his knees.

'Don't leave me.'

He crawled to her, abject, then rose and held her in
his arms.

She had never known such loveliness or such agony.

Chapter Three

THE FORTRESS WAS CRUDE. IT was not like Starzion. Demed told himself that he preferred its honesty.

He stalked its corridors and chambers. The governor had made everything over to him. Demed lived like a prince, but a prince in exile. (Zulgaris would have lived like this.)

Demed had sent men back to the city, to see what could be done. Zulgaris' name was blackened.

In the ascendant.

He sat now in the audience room of the fort, Kazun at his right hand. Urt adjacent.

Servants stood ready with cooled wines.

The man, a wealthy man of the central town, bowed low.

'As I say, prince, it's a great worry to us. The streets aren't safe to walk.'

'And they hold these revels every night?'

'And by day, also, sir. The worship of an obscene thing has been attested. It's been seen – various women – taken there for sport – And now they've set up an altar to a female demon. They've said that she came from the desert, a witch they couldn't burn. And she visited them and vanished from their midst. Stupid stories, but they're like children. *Dangerous* children.'

'My soldiers. They shall be punished.'

The rich man was gratified.

When he had bowed his way out, the new lords of Syr conferred.

'They have that piece of wall with the thing in it.'

'It frightened them before.'

'And now they reverence it as the Devil.'

'They must be rounded up and made an example of.'

It would be quite easy. Discipline had grown lax at Syr, but most of the troops were insanely loyal to Demed and the other knights. They would make the force to set on others.

A tavern was their venue.

Easy.

Urt said, 'And do you credit the idea that she – that slut, Vivia – that she lives?'

'The desert will have finished her,' said Demed. 'It finished Zulgaris. They're buried somewhere in the dunes, the sand blows over them.' (There had been rumours of a strange sickness in the town, but the soldiers and their blasphemy were blamed for this.)

Kazun said, 'Soldiers are fools. They should be driven out, too. Don't leave them in the town. Scourge them and cut off their noses and send them into the bloody desert.'

Demed nodded slowly his ungolden head. He was always careful to agree with his knights. He had come to watch, too, his own back.

That night Vivia woke.

Something was scratching on the bars of the window, some stray night bird . . .

Then she heard the shouting several streets distant.

She rose and left her lover sleeping his exhausted sleep.

From the window she saw a slanted column of red smoke going up into the dark sky. Something was burning in Syr –

She watched in fear, but the fire did not spread, and presently lessened. The shouting continued, and she heard an angry clashing, like sheets of metal.

At last, when the sky began to widen with the hint of dawn, Vivia returned to bed.

She lay there, pressed to Ruslem's back, her lips against his spine.

And heard the curious scratching again, now the shouts were dying down.

What could it be? An owl or raven of the desert for some reason drawn to this window – a crust of bread lay on the table, perhaps it scented food.

Vivia turned slowly.

Against the pallid aura of the coming day, she saw a mass of darkness pushing at the window bars. It was not large, yet too big to find a way in.

This frightened her all over again.

She got up and ran at the window, flapping a cloth she had pulled from the bed.

The creature veered and moved away.

Its shape was odd, batlike yet heavy.

Then it had gone, and the sky was pink and wholesome, only a streamer of smoke across it.

Vivia went back a second time to the bed.

Ruslem had half woken and turned against her.

'Take my blood.'

'No,' she said.

'You take it when I sleep. You drug me with your eyes, and feed on me.'

'No, no,' said Vivia.

'Take my blood and then – ' he pressed his arm to her mouth. Vivia moved her head.

But again he brought his flesh to her mouth, pressing her head into his arm.

'I have beautiful dreams when you do it.'

Vivia drank, and Ruslem lay only half aware on the pillows. She saw the dreams pass through his eyes like – smoke.

He told her at noon, after he had gone slowly down to the wine shop for bread and meat, that the soldiers who worshipped the Devil were being scourged and mutilated, and would be driven out of Syr.

He did not seem interested in this, or in anything.

He did not go to look at the painting on its frame.

Vivia had stood long before it.

She could not see herself in the smouldering visage of the girl, though her body she recognized.

She was so young. And yet – and yet it was as if this

were a painting of her youth and now she had grown old.

She had felt this pressure of age before.

Ruslem lay on the bed.

She fed him grapes and morsels of bread. He would not take much.

When he slept, she walked about the room. Sleeping, he had left her again.

She lay down beside him, trying to sleep too, but sleep would not come.

Besides, he was restless. He turned and flung out his arms, he spoke in his sleep, to friends and adversaries, to his patrons, to some priest, and, once or twice, to her.

The day hung low above the town. It was burnished and tarnished together, the light falling in tapers on the furnishings and floor, changing the ewer into gold. She saw this, she thought, with an artist's eye, having learnt from him.

Near sunfall, he woke.

'I want to take you to the wine shop,' he said. 'Show you to them.'

Vivia flinched. 'Why?'

'Your beauty. They don't believe me.'

He was white and strained, and a cold sweat stood out on his forehead.

Vivia did not argue with him. She got up and washed herself, and put on the plain dress.

Ruslem slung on his clothes. Sometimes he lost his balance, holding to the table or a wall.

Fear was now black within her. She fell towards a bottomless abyss.

The wine shop was low and grimy, with vegetables hanging from the ceiling, and bottles standing by the hearth.

They sat at a wooden table, and gradually acquaintances of the artist gathered round them. At Vivia they gaped, and as the drink flowed, began to toast her health.

Ruslem was boisterous, laughing and telling jokes. He boasted of Vivia, and again, as the wine went round, began to say that she could make the figures in his paintings move, walk through solid walls, and cause the table to dance.

The friends of Ruslem called for a demonstration, and Vivia, now all fear, felt fear also of them. As she sat petrified, Ruslem said, 'She shows this magic only to me.'

'Not the only magic she shows you, I think,' said one.

The others agreed.

They sang a song in praise of feminine charms, and Vivia stared at them like a child surrounded by mad people.

Very late, under the sparkling stars, he led her home up the stair to the studio, himself stumbling with drink and weakness. The friends cheered below in the inn court.

Alone, he tried to make love to her.

His body would not now obey him.

He indicated his flaccid member, so glorious when aloft, damning it.

He slept more soundly and more silently.

And in the dark she heard again a scratching at the window.

Was it death?

Had death pursued her here?

Vivia thought of the girls who had died, Ingret and Gula and Oria. Now she regretted them.

She lay rigid and cold, not looking to see what was at the window, until at last the noises stopped, and only the bell of night was there over all things.

Chapter Four

FIVE DAYS AND NIGHTS NOW passed, and Vivia did not drink the blood of Ruslem.

It made no difference.

Every morning he was weaker, and every dusk weaker than he had been that morning.

At first he could not use the latrine and must employ a pot, cursing with shame. Then his bodily functions seemed to fail. He neither ate nor defecated, drank nor urinated. He no longer sweated. He complained that his mouth was dry, but could not swallow any water. She moistened his lips with a cloth.

She had killed him. He died before her and she was as helpless as he.

She did not dare to feed him with her blood, for that was what had finished Zulgaris, she knew. Medicines she did not know how to get, although on the sixth day, muffling herself in the black veil, she went down to the wine shop and said that Ruslem was sick. They told her of a physician, but she could not find the street. Men she asked the way of propositioned her and called her a bitch when she refused. Women would not speak to her.

Besides, her soul knew a physician would not do any good.

On the seventh day Ruslem had great trouble in breathing, and she propped him high on the pillows.

He sat holding her hand, and gasped at last, 'Well, you've killed me.'

She would not deny it. Her eyes burned with her fear and tears could not get through them.

'I want you to live,' she said.

'But it was your nature to destroy me. Never mind. I've painted my best work through you. I'll be remembered.'

After this, he breathed more easily, and slept.

Vivia watched him through the night.

The thing came scratching at the window as it generally did. At last she went to see.

In the smored rays of the brown lamp, she made out a human, almost childlike shape, hard, stony and shining. Its wings were those of a bat.

Vivia spat through the bars, 'Leave me alone! Go back to Hell where you came from.'

She believed that she had dreamed it when the creature went away.

As the dawn came, Ruslem woke and asked her for wine. He managed to drink some and a spurious colour filled his wasted face.

'What will become of me?' he inquired softly.

In that moment, Vivia recalled. Ingret and Gula had loved her, and she had been told that they *returned* after death. Ruslem loved her more than the two girls had done, with the mature love of a grown man.

She said, unfaltering, 'You'll come back to me, and be with me for ever.'

As she spoke it, the pain and fear lifted from her heart, and she was as light as down.

'Is it true?' he said.

'Yes. You'll be like me.'

'A demon.'

'No. My only love.'

'Vivia,' he said. He closed his eyes.

Sand running from a glass, that was his life slipping from his body.

He lingered through the day, and Vivia watched him, almost impatient to see the end, that the beginning might commence instead. Yet too her pity ached in her, far less awful than her terror had been, yet prevalent and raw.

If only he need not pass through death at all.

But death came, and near sunset she understood that he had ceased his shallow breathing. His heart did not beat.

She stood a long while gazing at him.

It was a repetition of her days, that dead bodies lay with her in her room. But now she need only wait.

How long? How long would he linger in the twilight before he forged back to her?

She could not recollect Gula's term of death, if she had ever known it. Or Ingret's – for someone had said Ingret rose too from the grave.

Starzion had killed them. But no one should harm Ruslem. He would be her companion. Together they would slide by under the earth like snakes, or sail the moonlit skies like eagles –

Vivia clasped her hands.

She leaned and kissed his dry burnt lips.

An hour later the most terrible thing in the world happened.

There was a heavy knocking on the chamber door, and after a few moments it was thrust open.

In swarmed some of those friends Vivia had seen at the inn.

'Look at him, the lazy wretch, lying in bed at the hour of drinking.'

'No, he's sick, like they said.'

The men came, and examining Ruslem, found he was dead.

Then they looked at Vivia.

'Poor girl, she's crazy with grief.'

One gave her wine, which she drank automatically. Another went for a priest, and soon hurried back with an elderly man in a priestly robe, who mumbled the rites of the church over Ruslem's body.

All through the night, people came and went. Two old women stripped Ruslem and washed his body, muttering lasciviously in an undertone.

The friends perched in the room, which they had also crowded with wine bottles. They were soon drunk and maudlin, wandering about and choosing for themselves which of his pictures they would take.

The biggest work, which was the painting of Vivia, they left alone. One of them explained that the rich man Karp would undoubtedly claim this, against money he had given Ruslem a month or more ago.

If anything scratched at the window, it was not heard.

Dawn arrived, and with it a rough wooden coffin, into which Ruslem's body was lifted, and the lid nailed down.

Vivia could do nothing. As with his death, she was powerless to intervene. She could not tell them they must not bury the artist, that he would rise.

However, she knew the coffin, and any earth they piled upon him, would not prevent his emergence. Gula was not half so strong as Ruslem, and she had apparently found such things no hindrance. Vivia herself would not.

She walked behind the coffin, which had been loaded on a cart.

They went by chequered roads towards a gate which led into the desert, and here the graveyard was, presided over by marble statues of angels and huge crosses edged by gold. The tombs were of the best and worst, and the near worst ones were of clay, like beehives, and the very worst mere mounds of sand.

To such a grave Ruslem was conducted.

His friends drank and swore and wept, and the priest intoned antique words, while a little boy swung a censer.

The coffin slid down, and for an instant a cold anchor pulled Vivia's heart after it.

But she paid no heed. She had no doubts.

The loose earth and abundant sand were piled on to the grave, and stones laid there to keep out predators.

It was over.

Two of the men had tried to befriend Vivia, because they fancied her very much, but she remained aloof, and they respected her mourning.

She wondered when they would leave her alone.

Back in the wine shop, they made her eat a little food,

and plied her with wine. She was irritable, longing to
escape.

When finally she left them, and climbed up to the studio,
Karp was there, the other fat man she remembered from
the fat man's dinner.

Karp, who had had Vivia, did not recall her.

He stood with his servants, who were appropriating
many of the pictures from the studio. The large canvas
of Vivia Karp was rubbing his hands over, admiring the
bare breasts. Quite plainly he would take the picture and
use it for his private masturbation. Yet its living model he
gave little attention. He had one of the servants throw her
some silver as he left.

At midnight, when the roistering in the wine shop had
stopped, Vivia drifted up into the sky.

And now she revelled in what she did. For he too would
come to this.

He would be with her.

She would no longer be – alone.

The sky was full of clouds which moved fast, like a great
herd of migrating beasts.

Under their canopy she sailed, and reached the graveyard of Syr.

She came down unerringly on his grave.

It was a stark place by night, and off across the desert
something howled as if in grief.

Vivia sank on to the mound of stones and sand. She sat
there, and folded her veil, which he had given her, about
herself.

The night smelled of night. And of dusts and fumes of
the town, drink and sweets and flowers.

Faintly Vivia heard the music of some celebration. Someone had said . . . the soldiers who worshipped the Devil
had been driven out, and there was to be a festival.

None of this was her concern.

She looked about her.

The yard was full of quiet graves, houses of the dead who
would not rouse.

Nearby a group of clay tombs rose.

One of the friends of Ruslem had told her, as if trying
to interest and cheer, that these graves were mere tunnels,
packed in by clay.

Vivia gazed at them in the light of the setting moon.

How long would she have to wait?

Not long. Surely not long.

He had loved her. Her presence would draw him back,
like a plant into the daylight or the dark. She had looked
into his eyes.

Day came. It blew hot as fire on her cheek. She sat up. She
had been sleeping on his grave.

There was no disturbance.

Ruslem had not woken in the night.

Vivia looked about her again.

It was a dreary vista, and at its little distance, how silly
and unimportant the town, with its caps of blue and gold
and its muddle of slums.

She lowered her head for her veil had slipped.

She waited.

All through that day she waited, and an awful old
remembered boredom came to her.

The wind flowed like a heated tide over the sand, and
sand heaped up against the grave.

Mirages moved out in the desert.

She saw carriages, and a black horse galloping.

Flies buzzed.

The angels blazed white.

When the sun sank at last, a soft breeze filtered across
the dunes.

Vivia rose, and drifted about the tombs. She looked at
them in the diminishing light, pitiless. She did not care
what had become of any of them. Only one man mattered.

That night drunkards charged out of the town and roved
between the graves.

Finding Vivia, one man tried to have her, requiring
her price.

She would not let him. Not wanting to use her sorcery,
she fought him with all her physical might. And in the end,
dead drunk, he went away.

She stroked the earth and called his name, 'Ruslem, Ruslem . . .'

The stars moved over the sky and the sky turned pallid and sunrise came.

Vivia sat bowed now.

She felt bent and old, dry as a bone. Shrivelled.

She longed for blood, but only his blood would have succoured her.

Vivia recalled her mother. Her mother had loved her.

Sunk in reverie, she saw another funeral come out upon the sands.

A burial of pomp, with women strewing black paper flowers. Incense rose in towers and turned the sky purple.

She would see ten more funerals, the high and the low, as she waited in that place.

Time . . . It was endless, like yarn that had been drawn through iron, like gossamer through needles. Seasons passed. But they were not seasons, only hours.

She waited for a hundred years. They were perhaps twelve days.

Every minute her spirit warped a little more.

Every night, she flew beneath the moon.

She searched for him upon the face of the earth. But the sum of the earth was only Syr. She saw none like him. Her love.

The wind blew and the sand rustled.

How many candles had burned down? How many lives? Ten funerals she saw. But others festered on the rubbish tips, devoured by birds.

Vivia sat above the grave of her lover.

Once some women passed, and one walked back to her. 'Come away, poor girl. You mustn't mourn. It's God's will. To sit here is a sin.'

Vivia pushed her hand off.

The stones shifted under her as the sand shifted.

She peered down, and there he lay, invisible, under the ground.

Perhaps twelve days, twelve days and nights. The moon coming and going and the sun, like a peculiar machine, an alchemical machine. She did not know the formula.

Vivia waited, waited. Waited.

She felt so old. Her skin was withered by the sun, her hair burnt grey. Her eyes had dimmed. She was limp and stiff together, like a doll badly made.

(So beautiful she was as she sat there, her hair like ink, her skin like flowers, that those who entered the graveyard marvelled at her.)

A night came. It was the thirteenth night. Perhaps.

Vivia stirred.

She wanted to drink water. Not blood. No blood ever again.

She stared at the grave beneath her.

Ruslem had not risen.

She lay down on the grave and pressed her body into the stones, and passed through them, and the sand and thin soil, straight into the grave of her lover.

She came against the wooden box, which the sand had preserved, dry and hard.

Vivia moved through the box, and in the tiny space, she hung above his body.

The intensity of the box – had rotted him. He was rotten. His green flesh crawled upon his bones. Maggots fed on him.

She saw – she saw his heart, dull magenta like a ruined flower. His heart was eaten. His white skull leered through the luxuriance of his hair. His teeth showed between his lips.

He had no eyes.

Vivia lay there in the dark, seeing Ruslem by means of the lamp of her vision. Seeing truly. He was dead. Rotten and dead.

This could not come up into the world. If it did – no. No, this would not rise.

Vivia *rose*.

Up into the dry air of the graveyard.

She stood on the grave of her lover who was dead and putrid and lost to her for ever.

She held her veil about her face, shielding herself from the bold eye of the moon. She did not shed a single tear.

It was not possible. In the past she had prevented herself and punished herself if she wept.

But no tears could compass this. It would take an ocean, and the sea was far away. And, in the picture, which Karp rubbed himself over, the sea was only paint.

TWO

Chapter One

VIVIA WENT BACK TO THE studio.

It had been despoiled.

All the paintings were gone, the clay and marble heads also. More. The wine shop, for some debts, had removed the ewer and basin, lamps and candles, the covers of the bed. Even the poor books someone had had. And the black gown.

Vivia sat on the bare couch in the barren room, and gazed about her at the scene of her first and only love.

After a while, she noticed something peculiar.

The window bars had buckled. As if something had found its way in. Her gaze dropped to the floor beneath, and there, in some spilled paint, were tiny paw prints, two by two, each with a little crack across them. But this did not intrigue her. Nothing could.

She felt a boredom now that could never be relieved, a boredom compounded of grief, regret and loneliness.

She could fly through the air but she did not care about this. She was invulnerable – did not care. She could have what she wanted. It would be simple for her to find another handsome young man and seduce him. She did not care. Did not want. She wanted and cared for only one thing. That was gone and would not, despite the cruel, lying stories, come back.

When the morning broke, Vivia absently heard the noises of the town. They were loud today. Probably the festival to celebrate Syr's expulsion of the dangerous soldiers was beginning.

It was.

Soon revellers, already drunk, passed by under the window.

The heat came early. And the sun shone very bright.

She did not like the sun. But she must go out into it. She did not want to stay here.

As she was getting up, one of the friends of Ruslem, the second who had fancied her, ran up the fifteen steps and knocked, opening the door.

'Poor Vivia. Will you come with me?'

'No,' said Vivia.

'I can look after you. It's the festival today.'

'No,' said Vivia again. And, reluctantly, 'Thank you for your kindness.'

He lingered. He said, 'If you should change your mind, come to the white house by the dolphin well.'

Vivia said that she would. He left unwillingly, and when she was sure that he had gone, she too went down the stairs.

She had with her, tied into her sash, the silver Karp had thrown her. She did not know why she had brought it with her, but almost at once she found a use for it.

A man approached her, drunk and laughing, and asked her price. Vivia shook her head and handed him a silver coin. Astonished, the fellow let her go.

The streets about Ruslem's studio were of the poorer type that existed in central Syr, and on this day they had been infiltrated by the lower town.

Women in ragged gowns went by singing, their heads crowned with fresh roses.

All the celebrants had roses, it seemed, from the highest to the lowest. Children carried them, women and men had put them in their hair or pinned them to their clothes. They were the blatant symbol of summer, pink and carmine and creamy white. Their perfume mingled with the odour of unwashed flesh.

Vivia passed by, unthinking, the inn where the soldiers had worshipped the bat devil in the wall. It had been gutted by fire, and now people were scrambling there and a priest stood intoning a blessing.

Vivia reached a gate, and went out of inner Syr, into the rowdy madness of the lower town.

Why she did so she did not guess. She could not be free of her pain. It walked with her, leaning on her heavily. Yet she must move. Must descend. Instinctively, she sought for something, not aware of what.

The riot of the lower town –

Every man and woman of the world seemed to her to be there, a multitude that pressed willingly one on another, making itself familiar.

Men grabbed and fondled Vivia as she went by, but they did so with every girl and even with mature women that had grey in their hair.

This was a great celebration. Evil had been driven away. A new beginning. Rebirth.

The irony was lost on Vivia. It did not occur to her. And yet she hated the laughing, jibing, joyful crowds. Everywhere this insane happiness, and she at its core, a bitter seed.

Many in the crowd wore masks, some uncouth and some complex and gilded. The suns of Marius were there, and moons, and the heads of unicorns and dogs. In all were laughing, smiling teeth. These flashed at Vivia. They made her dizzy.

She walked on. A gilded ox breathed beer in her face, and two large hands cupped and squeezed her breasts. 'Come with me, girl.' She gave him a silver coin, and like the other one, startled – probably reckoning himself lucky – he let go.

On another street the crowd adhered to the tumbling walls, as a procession went by. Threadbare priests carrying their yellow candles, and in the midst a wooden statue of Marius Christ, garlanded by roses.

The irreligious crowd applauded.

Women began to kiss the feet of the statue and the hems of the patched priestly robes.

Food was sold at every corner. Cauldrons of spicy meat that might be dog or cat, hot bread, and sticky strangely coloured sweets.

Wine booths and sellers of beer abounded.

A woman sold squashy peaches coated with a glue of sugar, and these the children dashed away with.

Vivia arrived in a square between brown buildings. The windows were crammed by lookers-on, and on the ground, a puppet show was taking place.

Brought to a standstill by the crowd, Vivia stood watching too.

On the raised stage of planks, figures with large heads, mounted on sticks, danced and wove, while unseen manipulators shouted in imitation of the dolls' voices.

The Devil was there. Yes, it was the Devil who had come to Syr. Somehow they had made him. He was thin and black, with claws, and the open-work wings of a bat. His face was a black skull with long teeth of glass. His eyes were red. But there was one salient difference. He had a long, long nose.

This curious mockery jiggled up and down, lording it over Syr, all the souls of which, he said, would be carried to Hell by demons.

The demons came. They were of many sorts, fanged and horned, but one was brought to prominence, and this was a woman with long black snakes of hair. She wore a mauve dress, and her bulbous breasts were bare, the nipples large, like bloated lips.

She too had a long nose.

The purpose of these noses – for all the demons had them – was quickly made plain.

A band of knights in tin armour and golden spangles bounced on to the stage.

They took the Devil and his demons by the neck, and with their swords, pulled by strings, chopped off their noses.

Noses scattered into the crowd, which screamed and fought for them.

'Now drive them out into the desert,' said the foremost knight, who wore the most gold . . . Demed?

The demons, the noseless woman in mauve among them, were driven across the stage.

'Ah,' cried the knights, 'smell the sweet roses.'

They sighed and called and tapped their own noses, which were intact.

The crowd took up the cry.

They raved over what they could detect, because they had not lost the organs of smell.

Then a gigantic wooden beast, perhaps a dragon, crawled up on the stage. It opened enormous jaws and snapped, and one by one the demons, and the Devil, fell into these and were swallowed. The Vivia doll went last and vanished without protest.

Vivia blinked.

A man beside her, not knowing her, as none of them did, for a demon, nuzzled her neck. '*You* smell good. I'll give you a meal if you'll do it.'

Before Vivia could reply, another man had seized her breasts from behind and was fumbling them. To her surprising surprise, she felt another hand thrust between her legs.

Vivia did not struggle. It would in any case have been impossible, the crowd was like a wall.

She let them do what they wished. Neither could they have her, there was no room.

Presently all three, losing interest, for another instalment of the demon play was in progress, let her go.

Vivia slipped forward through the crowd.

She came among women.

The puppets were showing the knights riding out now to battle. A war machine of paper and wood was drawn across the stage. Banners waved, the lily and the leopard. The head of the Devil, somehow disgorged from the dragon, was borne on a pike.

A fat woman turned and kissed Vivia on the lips, her fat tongue gliding into Vivia's mouth.

Vivia pushed her away.

She edged sideways, and was abruptly in an alley by a seller of sweets.

To her amazement, Vivia felt tears cool on her face.

The children ran shrieking through the lower streets of Syr. They pulled at their noses and sniffed things. *They* could smell. In turn they stank.

Vivia wandered now. Where was she going?

How many men had stopped her, tried to fuck her. She had given them money, and all had left her alone.

Vivia.

What was she? The one beautiful human thing left in that town?

But then – not human.

The dragon had swallowed her image.

In the endless thick of the crowd, there was a wagon, and a woman screamed there. Again Vivia was forced, by the amount of people, to pause and watch.

The woman lay in the wagon, her legs spread wide, her belly a mountain.

Other women bent over her.

She strained and howled.

Her face was a mask that was made all of flowers, and it too had smiling teeth. Behind the smile, her agony.

She was giving birth.

At the festival of life, *new* life.

Vivia stared. She remembered.

Suddenly she saw the shock of the blood-red head appear, pushed from the heaving vagina. And then the women had it out.

The screaming stopped.

In a welter of blood, the new-born was disengaged, lifted up, roughly wiped, and passed around.

The mask faces kissed the fragile body. The teeth of the masks were pinkened by the mother's blood.

'Look, look – a boy! See this tassel?' A woman vaunted the baby, which had begun, like a whistle, to cry. 'I'll meet you in thirteen years, my duck.'

Vivia saw the baby, and the mother lying like a sodden cushion, still holding out her arms, given wine.

Milk spilled from her breasts.

Vivia shuddered.

Her birthing had not been like this.

Was it death she had brought out?

All at once, there in the press, her nostrils clogged with the reek of roses and hot blood, it came to her.

In her father's castle, surrounded by death, she had longed for life.

And now, in the midst of life, she longed for death.

Death and darkness. Silence. Leaden sleep with no awakening.

It was not possible. She could not die.

A man kissed Vivia. His crown of roses was askew and a trickle of blood – some thorn? – ran down his cheek.

'How much?'

She had no silver left.

'I have a disease,' she said, 'plague. I'll die soon.'

The man recoiled.

She thought, was it conceivable? Could she die despite her powers, her invulnerability?

Now she seemed to pass through them easily. Why? Oh, yes, the crowd itself was moving.

The body of people rambled around Syr, drinking and laughing.

It came at last to a lower gate which, like a gate of the central town, led out into the graveyard.

The heat of the day had gone. The sky was milky blue, and the sun an amber eye, in the west. Clouds like camels stood above the orb.

They roved between the graves, the people of Syr, laying their roses there, on marble and sand alike.

From the throng broke a figure.

It was a corpse, a corpse of rags, and its face a skull – but the skull was a mask.

It cavorted, jumping over graves.

The people clapped and sang.

Then the corpse fell down. It writhed. Out of the coverings and the mask broke a young man, whole and beautiful, clad only in a loin-cloth.

The crowd bawled.

Life – life from death.

He danced over the graves.

Had not Marius the Christ promised that those who believed in Him should rise like Him from death?

Vivia wept silently, and the crowd surged away from her, after the lovely, half-naked young man.

At last, standing alone, she covered her face with her hands.

A million tears she had never shed poured from her.

Until she was dry as a gourd.

She stood lax then, her hands at her sides.

The crowd was far off.

The sun was setting like a red, red rose.

So she came to the tombs of clay, which were now in deep blue shadow.

A moon was rising, slender, in the east. It seemed to give no light.

There was one tomb. Its entrance had been broken in. She could not think why. It was no place to rob.

Inside she glimpsed the dark tunnel. A few scattered and clean bones.

Vivia thought of the vampire beneath the stone of the castle.

It had slept. *Slept*.

Was sleep, too, credible for her?

She cleared the entrance of thin weeds and sand. She crawled into the lightless funnel of the grave.

There was no smell. Nothing but earth.

She lay on her back carefully.

Far off, she heard the voices of the crowd dying away, and the light that filled the tomb's end was now limpidly grey. Soon it would be night.

She might, by her will, pull the tomb in around herself. Who would disturb her then?

She lay, trying to rest.

But she felt no intimation of sleep. Grief was like a white hot spike that pierced her, end to end.

Although she did not understand now for whom she grieved. Was it for herself, or for the man she had known . . . his name seemed alien and strange . . . Ruslem.

Night fell, and all the crowd, superstitiously, had fled. The graveyard of Syr lay calm and quiet on the brink of the desert.

No doubt this town would fail. (Demed would die.) It would be abandoned and the desert would claim it.

All covered by sand then, this place. Hidden. Buried.

Vivia lay insomniac. She knew only pain. She was frozen with pain like age, and heard wild dogs yowl across the distances.

Chapter Two

It had struggled to regain itself, and by its own psychic strength had done so. This battle had been terrible, worse than the smashing of its limbs upon the stone.

Rejoined, it had achieved the power of flight, its heavy stiff wings ungainly in the torrents of the air.

It sought her. By instinct – it was little else.

A mother. It had had one. She had been taken from it.

Yet – it knew her. Knew the aroma of her body and hair, knew the sensation of her flesh. It had grown inside her in its covering of granite. How could it not?

Finding her, still it had not met with her. And then – then she chased it away.

It mourned. Its miniature sorrow was vast as a sea of tears.

Even so, it did not believe in her rejection.

It was her child.

At length it came in by night on the graveyard, which, to it, was only another more abject town. It sailed down among the graves and found the tombs of clay.

It could scent her. Of all the roses, she was the best.

Vivia heard the rustling at the tomb's mouth.

She thought it was a rat.

And then something chill and heavy, a stone which moved, crawled into her arms.

It lay on her, deadly and solid. Her impulse was to thrust it off.

She knew. It was the demon-child which she had birthed in an egg. It had haunted her.

But as she lay there, too tired to dislodge it, she felt how it curled into her body, and laid its stony awful head upon her breast. It did not need her milk. It needed something more terrible – her love.

Slowly she raised her hand, and laid it on the thing's back, between the wings.

It shivered and curled further in upon her flesh.

How cold it was – and yet, already, its contact with her had warmed it.

Its heaviness was just, like an answer to her weeping. A stigma made absolute – and so, palatable.

Vivia encircled the creature with her arms and held it, experimentally.

It began softly to make a babyish purring noise.

It was happy. She had made it glad.

It would sleep against her through the coming endless breadth of night.

For the very first time her tension lessened. A drowsiness filled her. She had found a sort of peace.

'Sleep, baby,' she murmured, as she had heard the women of the castle do, 'sleep, my love.'

And in her mind, which now was darkening, she heard the words she must speak for Ruslem:

In my sleep hereafter, your memory.

The tomb fell in and sank together.

Only the faint moon shone.